PASSING FANCIES

PASSING FANCIES

A JULIA KYDD NOVEL

MARLOWE BENN

LAKE UNION
PUBLISHING

Published by Lake Union Publishing, Seattle

www.apub.com

Amazon, the Amazon logo, and Lake Union Publishing are trademarks of Amazon.com, Inc., or its affiliates.

ISBN-13: 9781542044646 (hardcover)
ISBN-10: 1542044642 (hardcover)

ISBN-13: 9781542007139 (paperback)
ISBN-10: 1542007135 (paperback)

Cover design by David Drummond

Printed in the United States of America

First edition

PASSING FANCIES

CHAPTER 1

Paul Duveen was the whitest man Julia had ever seen. Stepping into his apartment on West Fifty-Fifth Street, she had no problem spotting him in the crowd. Ivory hair crested high above his doughy face, and eager teeth burst forth as he regaled an audience with some amusing or perhaps scabrous tale. Presiding over one of his infamous Thursday-evening salons, he wore an alabaster dressing gown and bleached pigskin house slippers. Apart from deep-set brown eyes, everything about him was incandescent. The man glowed.

Unseen hands bore away her Egyptian shawl as Julia lifted a martini from a passing tray. She raised it to salute her host across the room. Duveen—Pablo to his friends—returned the greeting through a fog of smoke. Perhaps he remembered last week's invitation, perhaps not. His slurred shout made no distinction.

Julia sipped her drink—delicious, real gin—and gazed about the apartment. There was something daring and defiant going on here, a snub to all the parties in Manhattan and around the world lumbering along in the old, dead ways of before the war. All things boring and dreary had been swept away; even the walls were the color of tangerines. From across the room a bronze bust scowled beneath the coils of an abandoned silver boa. Above it hung an immense angular painting depicting shards of at least one, possibly two crimson nudes. Tipsy jazz hiccuped from a grand piano in the corner. The musician curled like a smitten lover over the keys, paying no attention whatsoever to the two women swaying to a private beat behind him. Everywhere, conversations bubbled and swirled.

Most remarkably, the party was mixed. A dozen or more Negroes mingled amid the throng of whites. The rumors were true, then. Julia had never been to a party where Negroes did more than disperse canapés and cocktails or sweeten the din with half-heard melodies. She could almost feel the rumble of polite society creaking asunder, of modernity muscling apart the old walls built to separate those fiercely regulated realms of *us* and *them*. Here and there, at the bolder edges of Manhattan society, those walls were cracking. People of all shades were squaring their shoulders and dancing through the breach. Not many, and not always safely, but each time, another brick wobbled.

The other guests looked pleased and even proud to be there. Julia felt a twinge of pride herself. She'd found her way to the still-rough edge of the growing century. After five years of living abroad in London, this was why she had returned to New York. This was where she wanted to belong. Here she hoped to make her mark.

She threaded her way through a quartet of noisy men expounding earnestly on Freud toward a massive glass-fronted bookcase. Even from across the room she'd recognized a gilded red spine that beckoned for a closer look. Like most modern young people, Julia indulged a number of minor vices. Hers included an impertinent curiosity about other people's books. It might not be judged as indelicate as exploring others' closets and cabinets, but it ought to be, because it was just as revealing.

She was right. It was a copy of the recent Bodley Head quarto edition of Oscar Wilde's *Salome*. That Duveen owned this edition, which reproduced Aubrey Beardsley's famously decadent illustrations, told her more about him than hours of polite conversation. It confirmed Duveen was one of those men who ventured well beyond the borders of social respectability. Julia knew the type (even shared its impulses from time to time) and also knew that what most repelled could most intrigue.

"Your frock is divine." A low voice dripped like warm honey over her shoulder.

Startled, Julia steadied her grip on the *Salome* and turned to see a woman gazing down at her. About her age, she guessed: old enough to vote but not yet thirty. At least six feet tall, the stranger shimmered in a sea-green evening sheath. A matching turban framed her pale, symmetrical face. Long prisms of crystal beads hung from her ears. Beneath tapered brows her charcoaled hazel eyes, like the curve of her neatly painted lips, never wavered in their calm overture. Two realizations, and their dissonance, struck Julia with equal force: the woman was beautiful, and her gaze was guileless. By the age of three any female understood that such beauty was a powerful tool, to be wielded for profit and advantage. Yet Julia saw neither calculation nor naivete in this face, and her interest quickened.

"Not *quite* Vionnet?" the stranger asked, dipping her glance to Julia's dress. "But divine all the same."

Julia covered her second surprise with a smile. The pedigree of a woman's wardrobe was as undiscussed as her age or weight. A year ago she might have rebuffed the inquiry, but tonight—if races could mingle at posh midtown parties, if a woman could travel about the city alone at night—it seemed absurd to demur over a less-than-couture frock. Not French, no.

Another of Julia's vices was an occasional indulgence in exceptionally fine things. She enjoyed, as one of the family solicitors had put it, a lifetime of money. For a brief but agonized time last fall, it had nearly been otherwise, and she no longer took lightly her good fortune or the independence it gave her. Both subjects were still tender ones.

Fine clothing eased many pains. Tonight's dress was a year old but a new favorite: rich yellow silk, embroidered with a thousand tiny pearls across a sheer bodice that rose almost to her throat. She seldom wore dresses with much décolletage, as, on her, low necklines had little to say. In back the dress dived eloquently toward her waist, and the skirt's narrow drapery fell to just above her calves. With it she wore stockings clocked in the French fashion, caring not a jot that few Americans had yet embraced the style.

"Made in Mayfair," she confided, flinging yet more discretion out the window like a prewar corset. "More or less."

Julia's smile deepened as she qualified her frock's provenance. She was sworn to secrecy but couldn't wait to share the compliment with Christophine. Technically her maid and housekeeper, Christophine was infinitely more dear than that, less a lifelong employee than something between a sister and an aunt. And she was a blur of talent with needle and thread; she'd modified this very dress just yesterday to pass an idle afternoon. She'd adjusted the neckline, tapered the hem, and added a thin undulating trail of satin down one hip, which caught the light when Julia moved. The effect was subtle and surprising, and she adored it. How glorious that this stranger had noticed. Who was she?

The turbaned woman said her name so quietly that Julia had to watch her lips to catch the words: Eva Pruitt. They spoke of fashion lightly, as one did, plumbing each other's interests and tastes. Talk soon spiraled into cries of "Yes!" about the latest marvels out of Paris and Milan. Julia began to itch with curiosity. Was this regal beauty simply another avid patron or something more? She finally had to ask: Was she a model or perhaps even a designer herself? To her surprise Eva Pruitt said she adored fine clothes and indulged when she could, but no, she had no connection to the fashion world. She was a writer.

Julia blinked. She took pride in her ability to spot writers in a crowd. They were usually as obvious as artists. She had seen at once that this party was full of writers, as Pablo had promised. It was only left to learn which carousing fellow might be the young Fitzgerald, and if indeed that was Dreiser slumped in the velvet armchair, lost in Scotch and all that melancholy. Was the remarkable Miss Millay about, perhaps in another room? But Eva Pruitt's placid beauty had fooled Julia. She was nothing like the woman writers Julia knew in London, who were either fashionably unkempt in trousers and their lovers' bowlers or unfashionably so—dowdy in indifferent hats and ancient frocks.

"You too?" Eva asked. She gazed at the *Salome* Julia cradled against her waist. Curiosity swam in her eyes. "One of yours?"

Julia could almost hear the great Wilde's mirth at this confusion, but not, unfortunately, the witticism that would follow. She fumbled for some fraction of the cleverness the moment deserved, until she saw the gleam in Eva's eyes. They shone droll and mysterious, as if she had laid a tarot card on the table and it was Julia's turn to interpret it. Perhaps there was no confusion, only a riddle. Some kind of merry enigma beckoned from Eva's sphinxlike smile.

Julia felt her calves tense for balance, as if she'd been buffeted by a sudden thrilling gust. Had she found, so quickly, her first author? Or rather, had this extraordinary woman found her?

Like most restless females prowling most parties' smoky rooms, Julia was on the hunt. Her quarry, however, was not men but writers, preferably poets. She was a printer, proprietor of a small press devoted to finely printed limited editions. Few in New York knew of her private Capriole Press, but that would soon change. Once she was settled, she would announce herself with a suitable splash.

Julia wavered. She might be hunting for prospective authors, but writers were forever hunting for publishers. It was a subtle game. Tempted as she was to declare herself, she needed to know more about Eva Pruitt, and any other writers she might yet discover tonight, before showing her hand. Better to hold her cards close for a little while longer.

Julia shook her head. No, not a writer. "But I know someone who fancies a go at detective stories." She intended to feign a glance about, as if Willard Wright, the sole (thus far) author she knew in New York, lurked somewhere amid the room's stew of chatter, but found she could not drag her eyes from the flawless face watching her in return.

"Everyone's a writer these days," Eva said. "Pablo collects us." She eyed Julia as if she were the more exotic creature. (She was not.)

Julia asked what kinds of things she wrote.

Eva smiled. In a soft, conspiratorial lilt, she said she'd recently completed her first novel. Like every other writer in the room, Eva said, she was hoping to catch a publisher's eye. Pablo had been sweet about it; he'd promised to put in a good word for her with his friend Arthur Goldsmith. *That* Arthur Goldsmith, her gaze confirmed. The eminent publisher. She lifted her hand to show two crossed fingers.

Julia mirrored the crossed fingers and dropped her voice to an equally private register. She asked Eva what her book was about.

Shifting her gaze to the open door of the bookcase between them, Eva began to describe her novel in slow, thoughtful spurts. It was drawn, she said, from her experiences working at Carlotta's—a cabaret, she explained when she realized Julia did not recognize the name. With each languid sentence, an entrancing voice emerged. Deep, fluid, and unhurried, it bore the scar of a long-escaped accent, something southern. Its music expanded to enfold the two women and shield them from the room's commotion. They edged closer and closer, until they were touching, arm to arm, turning a wall of bare shoulders to the party. Once or twice someone brushed the back of Julia's dress, and indistinct voices rose and fell nearby, but she ignored them, mesmerized by the remarkable woman so close she could smell the faint lemon scent of her flawless skin. She could count the seven diamonds that anchored each of Eva Pruitt's earrings.

Julia followed little of the melodic drawl. A small effervescence tickled her pulse. She'd met few strangers of interest since returning to New York last month. Here was a woman who intrigued her, not only a writer but a woman apparently blessed with that rarest of combinations: natural elegance, sensuous beauty, and artistic talent.

At the prospect of such an acquaintance, Julia's spirits began to stretch, her muscles to hum. She felt a shift in her bones, a turning forward toward the new and unknown, toward what mattered. She had work to do yet that evening—she'd come to explore the literary landscape—but to make a new friend too would be a jolly sweet bonus.

A squeal turned their heads. A small man stood on a nearby chair, bouncing on flexed knees as he chanted a poem in a sunlit Jamaican accent. Black curls frothed about his ears, and rouge blazed on his cheeks and lips. His feet were enormous, clad without socks in dusty Cuban sandals. He reminded Julia of the more entertaining bohemians who occasionally held court at the London gallery she'd once known well. With a second squeal Duveen folded the fellow into a one-armed bear hug. He set him on the floor and two-stepped with him off toward the piano, his martini trailing gin across the carpet.

Before Julia could ask Eva more about her novel, a black sleeve, taut and swift as an arrow, thrust abruptly into view between them. Two Negro men in evening clothes joined them. Eva went quiet. She introduced them as Jerome Crockett and Logan Lanier. Poets, she said. Fine poets both. "Very fine."

Lanier, who looked no older than a schoolboy with smooth, plump cheeks, shook Julia's hand with polite church manners. His friend, however, fixed her with a wary eye. Crockett was as tall as Eva, but alert posture and a crisp white collar propelled his chin an inch above hers. Close-cut hair covered his head like sculpted black lather. From his lapel smirked a small gold pin bearing three Greek letters: Phi Beta Kappa. A scholar, then. When he dipped his head in mute greeting, Julia stole a peek at his shoes: the room's lights sparkled back at her in their impeccable shine. She'd half expected to see spats. Had a silver-tipped cane been checked at the door?

Lanier demurred at Eva's praise. He confessed he was as yet only a humble student of poetry. "Jerome is the true talent in the room," he said of his older and more somber friend. "Have you heard what they say, Miss Kydd? That one of his poems is like a semester at Yale?"

"No more than a week," Crockett said. "Even at NYU."

Lanier clutched his heart in mock injury.

"Jerome won the Gardiner Prize last month," Eva said.

Crockett's mouth trembled on the brink of a smile before regaining its gravitas.

"Miss Kydd has a friend who writes detective stories," Eva told the men. "You know, puzzlers. Like Conan Doyle."

Crockett's jaw twitched.

"You know. Sherlock Holmes." Eva's face bloomed in a wide smile. "You *know*!" She straightened his tie with an affectionate cluck and, her profile gleaming like a bright cameo against his dark cheek, kissed him warmly on the mouth.

He breathed something into her ear, slid an arm around her waist, and solemnly asked Julia to excuse them. Eva brushed Julia's hand and murmured something as they moved away, but Julia was too stunned to catch her words. Watching the couple recede into the party, she felt another jolt of shock travel her spine.

Were Eva Pruitt and Jerome Crockett lovers?

A white woman and a Negro man?

As she watched Crockett's dark thumb idly circle the nub of Eva's hip, Julia's shock changed to fear. Were they mad? To share a dance floor or mingle over martinis was bold enough, but open intimacy? This was America. Negroes were swung from trees for less.

CHAPTER 2

"Are you a book fancier, Miss Kydd?" Logan Lanier asked. He nodded to the *Salome* still pressed into the folds of Julia's skirt.

Julia reshelved the book and latched the case's door. In truth she was a keen lover of books, though as with many bibliophiles, her enthusiasm exceeded a simple pleasure in reading. The clandestine childhood hours she'd spent in her father's library—his collections of Aldines, printed Horae, the daunting Baskervilles, the anvil-like Kelmscotts, with pages as ornate as Persian rugs—had kindled in her a passion for the textures, colors, and heft of books' bodies, a love quite unrelated to their contents.

Not waiting for an answer, Lanier's round face bobbed above his prim white collar. He said he longed to own books, beautiful ones, as much as to write them. Especially modern poetry firsts, when he could afford them. Did she know of Cuala? Julia didn't much care for the rustic design nostalgia of the Cuala Press—a small handcraft operation run by Yeats's sisters in Ireland—but yes, she said, she knew it. As a young bookbinding student at Camberwell, she'd once made a portfolio to house a friend's collection of Cuala broadsides.

Another fellow materialized out of the party. He greeted Lanier and turned to Julia. "I know you," he said. "The girl with the new press! Julia, right? We met at a Colophon chili-and-poker night. Russell Coates brought you. I thought you went back to London." He extended a hand and introduced himself as Austen Hurd. "Just Austen. No *mister* for me."

Julia had recognized him even before he'd mentioned their meeting eight months ago. She'd been a guest at an informal gathering of younger Colophon Club members. It had been a rare evening of pleasure during those stressful weeks. Hurd worked for Boni & Liveright, one of the most important literary publishers of the day. Liveright was the lucky bastard (Hurd's words) who'd scooped the field in 1922 by gaining the American rights to publish Tom Eliot's *Waste Land*. She'd heard a ringing earful about it at that party, the first stop in a long and splendid evening in the company of another bibliophile, an evening that had helped persuade her to return to the city of her birth. Much of her time in New York last fall remained a painful and unsettling memory, but that evening and that friend—now living in Santa Fe, alas—still glowed with the promise of the city's new fascination.

Lanier's eyes sparked at the words *new press*. Among a small circle of local book collectors, including Austen Hurd, word of Julia's Capriole Press had leaked across the Atlantic, which gratified her enormously. A year ago her small edition (fifty-five copies on handmade Barcham Green paper) of Virginia Woolf's *Wednesday*, an ethereal prose poem (or possibly only a four-page sentence), had stirred interest among London's small but growing population of wealthy gentlemen ravenous for rare and beautiful books. Add a touch of the refined risqué—a lithesome nude line engraving by Eric Gill—and they'd gone into raptures. New York bred an equally avaricious specimen of bibliophile, the most elite (that was, wealthy and male) of whom congregated at the eminent Grolier Club. Julia's Capriole Press would never pander to Grolier tastes, of course, but it was a glorious thing to have such devotees, and she longed to feel that pleasure again. Another minor vice.

She stuck to her resolve not to declare herself as a publisher quite yet. "Capriole's on hiatus, I'm afraid," she said. "At present I'm merely a collector." The writerly shine in Lanier's eyes dimmed at this news.

Calling herself a more garden-variety bibliophile may have deflected one man's eager attention, but it inflamed the other's. Austen demanded to know more about her collecting interests. His face was an appealing one: short waves of dark hair coaxed away from his forehead, eyes watchful as a playful dog's, and skin the color of weak tea. His smile was askew—the right corner of his lower lip sagged, and only one cheek puckered—but it curled his whole face. When she mentioned a fondness for modern fine printing, he concurred with volcanic enthusiasm.

Lanier edged away as the conversation galloped off through talk of the great private presses, of Kelmscott, Ashendene, Doves, and Vale. It swooped around the Roycrofters studio of poor American Elbert Hubbard—lost on the *Lusitania*, his work now so painfully out of fashion. It flitted out to the brash Californian printers mining typographic gold in San Francisco and dallied over the prettily voluptuous new French editions with pochoir illustrations, of which Austen knew little but begged to hear more.

"I'm sailing to England soon," he said, his voice furred with a slight lisp. "First time, if you can believe it. I'm going to meet Francis Meynell—do you know him?" Julia knew of Meynell and his Nonesuch Press in London but had not personally met the man. Before she could say as much, Austen's grin blazed, alight with shoptalk. "Or how about Gibbings, that fellow who's taken up Golden Cockerel? Gorgeous wood engravings. His Brantôme knocked my socks off."

"Robert Gibbings, yes. He's planning a *Samson and Delilah* next. And"—Julia paused, teasing his open-mouthed anticipation—"they say Eric Gill may join him."

"In Berkshire?" Austen's collar had escaped from his lapel, warping the knot of his tie.

The simple question, asked with his disproportionately excited lisp and crooked grin, made Julia laugh. To her astonishment, she couldn't stop. Rocking her forehead in her palm, she laughed all the more helplessly when he echoed her with his own steady chug.

"I'm sorry," she choked, wiping tears from her cheeks. "It's just that look on your face."

He offered her his handkerchief. "It's my most devastating effect." He leaned forward. *"There was a young printer named Julia—"*

He paused. *"—but don't let her elegance fool ya.*

". . . She dabbed at her eye, afraid she might cry—"

Another pause. Then a rush: *". . . at the sight of a gent so peculiah."*

Julia doubled over in fresh laughter, catching her frock's shoulder strap just as, mercifully, Duveen's voice boomed above the party's commotion.

"Everyone! Lovelies!" Duveen stood near the piano, waving his arms. The sleeves of his dressing gown billowed like nautical flags. The room quieted. Julia and Austen recovered their dignity, more or less, and moved to join Lanier at the front of the crowd.

"I promised a surprise, and you shall have it," Duveen shouted as two maids passed through with trays of champagne glasses. "Time to announce the next Goldsmith great!"

He glanced about, greeting late arrivals with a wave of his left pinkie. Hope and anxiety jostled on every expression. Suspense grew as he affected hesitation, dithering with fluttery hands. The drama was more cruel than entertaining, and a few brusque voices called out for him to stop farting around.

Duveen laughed, spun, and lifted the back hem of his dressing gown in rude reply. "That's for you hyenas." He cued a trill of piano keys to quell the answering barks and howls. "All right, all right, settle down.

"To the century's next great literary sensation." His outstretched glass sailed wide as his voice sailed high. "To the next great New Negro voice!"

The crowd seconded his toast, champagne sloshing, but uncertainty shadowed most faces. Who? Which of them was to be lifted into eminence by the coveted Goldsmith imprint? *Negro* narrowed the field considerably. Standing beside Julia, Logan Lanier had stiffened, alert and unbreathing, all modest charm forgotten. Across the room, Jerome Crockett's face was a study in dignity, eyes downcast. To hide his gleaming hope?

"To *Harlem Angel*!" Duveen shouted. "To our very own Eva Pruitt—as brilliant as she is luscious!" He pulled Eva to his side and mimed an ecstatic slurp of her shoulder.

The crowd gave a boisterous cheer.

New Negro voice? Harlem angel?

A second shock joined the first as Julia tardily raised her glass. Eva Pruitt was colored?

∽

Lanier emptied his champagne in a single gulp. "To Eva," he muttered. "Poor fool."

Even Austen was speechless at this sour dismissal of his friend's triumph.

"I'm sorry," Lanier said quickly. "I wish her well, of course. It's just that she may be in over her head."

At Julia's confusion he went on. "Don't you know? Eva's been stoking rumors about that book for months. Pablo's been mad to get it for Goldsmith."

"Pablo wants Arthur to champion Negro writers," Austen said. "You heard him. He says it's the coming thing. Horace—Liveright, my boss—wanted Eva's book too, though I can't see why."

"Why do you say that?" Julia protested. "It must be very good if both Liveright and Goldsmith are keen for it."

"It may be terrific. I only meant we never saw more than a few pages. She floated a teaser, is all. Pablo claims he's seen the whole thing, but I'm not sure I believe him. Everyone else got only a couple of chapters. She's playing coy, whipping up interest and plenty of drama, but it's a dangerous game."

"Dangerous?" The only threat Julia could see was to Eva's exquisite dress, being tugged and pawed in the clamor of so many trying to congratulate her at once.

Lanier took a drink from a passing tray. "She won't say much, except that her book packs a wallop—dirty doings revealed, sleazy scandals, that sort of thing. Everyone assumes it's about her life singing at Carlotta's."

"She's a singer too?" Julia exclaimed.

"Didn't you know? This year's sensation."

"I hear she's hidden the manuscript," said Austen.

"Hidden?" Julia wondered at this further hint of melodrama. "That seems drastic." In her experience novel manuscripts were hardly fare for cloaks and daggers. More often the sight of one emerging from a writer's satchel cleared a crowd, reminding editors of overdue appointments and publishers of vanishing budgets.

"No one knows where it is," Lanier explained. "Let alone what's in it. But it must be juicy if she's afraid Leonard Timson, her boss at Carlotta's, might get ugly about it. That's why Pablo's making such a silly whoop. It will be a bonanza for Goldsmith, if it's as lurid and"—he pronounced the next word carefully—"*colorful* as she hints. A true July-jam race novel. I'm just afraid our Miss Pruitt may have lit a fuse with this one. She'd better hope it blows up in someone else's lap."

Through the smoky sheen of the hot room, Julia considered Eva's turbaned head rising above the mist of embraces and kisses. What would such a lovely creature know of lurid scandals? Even more mysterious was the notion that Eva Pruitt could produce anything incendiary. No, Julia decided. Disappointment blurred Lanier's judgment. And Hurd clearly relished gossip.

Across the room, a new fellow had settled at the piano and was teasing out syncopated tunes that made shoulders jump and dip in countertime. Only Jerome Crockett seemed impervious, still displaying no reaction to Eva's startling triumph. With a stony countenance he deposited his untouched champagne behind a massive vase of calla lilies and pushed his way toward the hall, away from the throng squeezing forward to celebrate Eva's success. He answered every greeting with a terse nod.

"Mr. Crockett seems to share your misgivings, Mr. Lanier," Julia said.

Lanier considered his friend. "Jerome? He's just curdled they went for Eva's jazzy tootles over his string quartet. Can't say I blame him. Goldsmith should have taken his collection of poems. It's the best thing I've read all year, though difficult, heady stuff. If his name was Crockettovich or O'Crockett, something obscure and European, Goldsmith would be panting for it, but from a straight-arrow American college man, no. Much less a colored one. I tried to tell him to throw in some sonnets full of jigs and shines and rent parties, but he couldn't take the joke. He's been touchier than ever."

"Maybe Eva's good fortune will console him," Julia said.

Lanier gave a small shrug. It seemed the kindest note on which to end their speculation. Julia excused herself before Austen could ensnare her with another rambunctious conversation. She had work to do.

Over the next two hours she met a succession of poets, actors, and novelists; a clarinetist; a sculptor; a playwright; and a pair of self-pronounced skunks too sozzled to be amusing. She penciled two or three names beneath Eva's onto her mind's list of possible candidates for a Capriole production, pending a closer look at their work, and noted others whose vanity or boorish grievances she'd take pains to avoid. She never got close enough to Eva to congratulate her, as the merry knot of well-wishers surrounding her remained stubbornly dense. When it finally loosened, Julia saw with a pang of disappointment that Eva was gone, likely slipped away for further rounds of private celebration. There was nothing more for Julia to do than declare her evening a success and commence the search for her shawl.

She found it amid a jumble of guests' wraps in Duveen's library (which she wished she'd discovered earlier) at the end of the apartment's long central hallway. A ginger tortoiseshell cat with languid gold eyes guarded the array, nominally, from her repose on the desk's blotting pad. Julia stroked its chin, coaxing a low purr from the regal creature. On leaving, distracted by the new Bremer Presse *Iliad* lying on the sofa atop its mailing wrappers—Duveen followed the German fine presses as well?—she collided with Austen Hurd.

"I'm such an ox," he apologized as she adjusted her frock. "I no sooner meet a daffodil than I damn near squash her." Julia rather liked this compliment—referring, she presumed, to the hue of her dress—as it was every bit as clumsy as his pursuit of her. In a rush he added, "I can't rest without hearing more about that new *Delilah*. Come with me to a party tomorrow night?"

Julia was not one to feign or inflate a social schedule. The past months of financial uncertainty and a difficult transatlantic move had brought her to the brink of exhaustion and ill temper, but she was ready now. She'd finally ventured forth on her own into her new city, and the party had rekindled her social energies. She felt refreshed, restless to entangle herself again. Soon, if possible. Even if New York was not yet firmly under her feet, London was at last behind her. Her years there had been glorious but also shadowed—with memories of poor Gerald, her doomed first love, and the other false starts and disappointments by which she now hoped to steer more happily forward.

Before she could reply, Austen hurried on with needless enticements. Horace was always throwing parties, he said. Tuesdays and Fridays, at least. This week was to welcome a new author in from the provinces—Nebraska, he thought. Pablo and Arthur Goldsmith would certainly be there, taking a victory lap as Eva Pruitt's new publisher. "You'll like Goldsmith, Julia. He loves books more than women. Maybe O'Neill will come, maybe little Vincent Millay, leading poor Bunny Wilson on his lovesick tether. You never know who—"

Thwack! A sharp slap of palm on flesh sounded from the hallway.

The door to the opposite bedroom was ajar. Eva Pruitt, shoulders heaving, stood nose to nose with Jerome Crockett. Both held their hands away from their bodies, clenching in and out of fists. Julia's first instinct was to defend her. To a proud man like Crockett whose lover had outshone him, and in such a public way, Eva's success would scald. Julia drew breath to protest, but Austen shushed into her ear.

He was right. It was impossible to know who had struck whom.

Eva grabbed her lover's wrist. Crockett jerked free with a force that squeezed a soft *ooof* from her lungs. She seized it again and pulled him to her side, spinning them both toward the door.

Austen drew Julia back into the library's shadows.

"Leave them be," he whispered as the couple moved down the hall to rejoin the party, arms curved stiffly around each other's waists. "Some lives are complicated. Especially writers'."

CHAPTER 3

More from habit than hope, Julia glanced down the broad hall of Philip's apartment. He was likely out, but occasionally light beneath the library doors announced a rare evening at home. It had been two days since she'd seen him. For most of her childhood he'd been little more than a name to her, the absent half brother ten years her senior. At her mother's death twelve years ago, Philip had suddenly loomed large in Julia's life, though still remote, first as her guardian and then as trustee of her estate until last fall, when she'd turned twenty-five.

Although she still barely knew the man, in a few scant weeks she'd learned that he seldom rose before noon, took most meals out, and generally frequented the city's many theaters and concert halls and galleries before lingering at one club or another well into the wee hours. Yet he also had an uncanny way of surprising her, of upsetting each basketful of smug judgments just as she managed to assemble it. Whatever his misgivings about her return to New York, Philip kept them to himself. But then, he owed her no less.

For the hundredth time she rued this imposition on his hospitality. At one point eight months ago she'd vowed never again to darken his door, after he'd nearly usurped her inheritance. Worse, he'd done so in jest, claiming he'd never dreamed the panel of arbiters would accept his specious claims about their father's will. Afterward he'd begged her forgiveness, insisting he'd never have cut her off. But Julia needed time to recover. Once glimpsed from its brink, the maw of poverty was not easily forgotten.

The pocket doors to the library had not been fully closed. Through the gap she saw Philip slouched wearily in his favorite wing chair beside the hearth, legs stretched out across the carpet and fingers knit at his waist to enfold a crystal snifter. He looked half-asleep.

She hesitated. Was he alone? Should she interrupt? She'd like to simply invoke a guest's prerogative—the cheerful claim of a brandy before bed—but their relationship was still tenuous. Lifelong ambivalence (no, call it the wariness it was) and the monstrous scare he'd given her last fall lingered. Growing up, she'd never mourned the absence of his affection, having never had it. But in recent months she'd felt a few pangs of empathy with the man she was finally learning not to fear, if not yet to fully trust.

At the sound of a voice too muffled for Julia to recognize, Philip stirred. He set aside his drink and lit a cigarette. His long fingers moved lazily. Julia held her breath, alert for what came next. Philip's most careless gestures were often his most deliberate. The more idle the movement—the languid heave of a shoulder, a bored sigh—the more he often simmered with some deep annoyance or even anger.

"Don't be an ass," the visitor whined. "You're such a bloody orchid, Kydd."

"So you've mentioned." Philip flicked ash into a saucer.

Oho! Whatever simmered might soon boil. This she would not miss for anything. Julia pushed apart the doors. He *had* murmured something about making herself at home.

"*Ma petite soeur,*" Philip said in an abruptly velvet voice. "You remember Wright?"

Ah. Too clearly. His guest was Willard Huntington Wright, the purported author. A dismal superstition crossed her mind: Had her recollection of his name earlier that evening somehow, genie-like, summoned him? It had been a flippant remark, and she rued it all the more if it had now conjured the odious fellow.

Wright half lay across the sofa, too ill or dissipated to rise at her entrance. He had aged a decade since September. His skin was sallow, his cheeks cavernous, and an odor of stale cigarettes rose from his clothing. Whatever had possessed the man to come calling at this hour, especially in such wretched condition?

Julia nodded. Wright leered, as he did each time they met. He imagined himself irresistible to women of fortune and consequence. "As ravishing as ever, Miss Kydd," he rasped. He meant she passed his muster, an approval she profoundly did not seek. She said nothing.

"Hello, Julia. Nice dress," agreed another voice from near the fire. Philip's good friend Jack Van Dyne rose. He was the most junior member of the Manhattan law firm representing three generations of Kydds, and Julia cautiously considered him her friend as well.

"Looks drafty to me," Philip said, eyeing her beautiful frock. "I'd have thought you could afford something with a bit more cloth. I mean, why else insist on raiding my coffers?"

That was rich. Pure contrarian poppycock, intended to provoke her. She was also learning to read the frivolous undertone in much of what he said and did. Philip could make the most outrageous utterances, and he often did. It amused him to shock and alarm, and nothing delighted him more than a flustered rebuff. His favorite sport was to jab and jab in hopes of rousing a joust. Now that she understood the game, she might soon muster strength to oblige (if not best) him, but not tonight. She swept her shawl from her shoulders, baring her spine, and draped it across the arm of the sofa.

"My sister so enjoyed her last visit that she decided to move back to New York," Philip said before Wright could ask the obvious question. "I humbly bask in her radiance until she finds a home of her own."

More applesauce. He was in a devilish mood. Philip was as likely to grumble at her invasion of hatboxes and shoe trunks as to warble about her company.

"Not that sister nonsense again," Wright snorted. "Spare me the pretense, Kydd."

However tasteless, Wright's skepticism was understandable: Appearances gave no clue that Julia and Philip were even remotely related. He shared his mother's dark coloring, while Julia's blue eyes and fair hair proclaimed her own Swedish blood. Both were lean and light boned, nimble when necessary and naturally graceful. But while Philip tended to slouch, Julia stood straight, her posture the last remnant of a misery of ballet lessons. Jack claimed to detect a resemblance, but more objective observers rarely saw it.

"They really are siblings," protested Jack. "Half siblings, anyway."

"Different mothers," Philip added blandly. Neither man saw his droll glance at Julia.

It was true. Julia—the daughter of Lena Jordahl, Milo Kydd's second wife—had been born a scandalously brief eighteen months after the death of his first wife, Charlotte Vancill Kydd. Philip was the only surviving child of that marriage. There was a deeper truth, however, known only to them: they were in fact unrelated. He'd learned this staggering secret only last fall.

Thus, ironically, Wright's barb scratched a secret truth. To the world Julia and Philip remained half siblings, cautiously circling détente after a lifelong estrangement. To each other they were strangers bound in a delicious irony: a private camaraderie at once more intimate than friendship and less burdensome than blood.

Jack settled back into his chair. "Wright stopped by to inquire whether Philip's working on a good puzzler these days."

This explained Philip's mood and Jack's subdued smile. Wright constantly pestered them with questions about the occasional help Philip gave his uncle Kessler, an assistant commissioner with the police, on particularly baffling crimes. A critic chronically short of funds, Wright hoped to write popular detective novels featuring a clever but insufferable sleuth modeled (inaccurately!) on Philip. Naturally Philip forbade it, yet Wright persisted. For plots he'd even tried to weasel from Julia her knowledge of the truth behind the suffragist Naomi Rankin's mysterious death last fall, an impertinence she had firmly quashed.

"You might at least consider his scheme, Philip," Jack said. "Detective stories are all the rage in England these days. What harm can it do? He wouldn't use your real name, of course."

"So you say. Who am I to be, then?" Philip wondered.

"I could call you Attila the Whozit for all the masses care," Wright said. "As long as I give them a cracking good murder and a walking whirligig of civilization to solve it. A Cézanne collector, no less!" He waved at Philip's lovely little watercolor above the drinks trolley. "You'd be the perfect sleuthing macaroni, Kydd."

The muscles along Philip's thin nose tightened. "Celebrity is the least of my objections. What terrifies me is that this dandified do-gooder might exist at all. So no, never. We tell him nothing, Jack." He slouched deeper into his chair and raised his cigarette to his mouth.

Wright gave a sour shrug and reached for more of Philip's whiskey.

"Out hunting beaus?" Philip asked Julia. "A brace of them bundled in the hall?"

"As a matter of fact, I was at a party. Apparently Paul Duveen's soirees are all the rage. Poets to the rafters and a—"

"Duveen?" Philip said. "That bleached meringue?"

Wright barked out a phlegmy laugh. "More like sycophantic ass. Duveen fancies himself a novelist, but his books are decadent drivel. Now he drapes himself in all manner of outré nonsense and rhapsodizes about the great and glorious Negro. God help us." Wright went into raptures at Wagner and the stomp of Teutonic boots, presumably in literature as well as music. Julia could only guess at the acid he might spew at Eva Pruitt's new novel, with its "jazzy tootles."

She couldn't fault Pablo Duveen for relishing the avant-garde. She too resisted so-called respectability, though for different reasons. She preferred to throw her small weight of influence, when she had any, onto the side of the *im*proper, the *mis*matched, and the *not done*, in defense of those who defied conventional strictures. Duveen seemed a champion mostly for himself. Every rule he broke, every shocking thing he did and said, became another sequin stitched to his name, one more twinkle in the display that kept him forever in the public eye.

"Meet anyone interesting?" Philip asked Julia mildly. "Outré and otherwise?"

"Oh yes." She refilled her glass and headed for the door. "A great and glorious partyful."

∽

It was after ten the next morning when Julia wandered from her bedroom in search of breakfast. Christophine had opened the drapes in Philip's library and left tea and oranges on the table beside the sofa. The carpet was warm beneath her feet. She wore her favorite scarlet satin man's dressing gown, its black-tasseled belt hanging loose at her sides. It had belonged to the man she'd once considered the perfect beau—attentive but not hovering, amusing, generous, discreet—until he queered everything by deciding they should marry. Unfortunately, the prospect advanced his interests while trampling hers.

In a marvelous twist of mutual expedience, he'd secured instead the charms of Julia's friend Glennis, who'd arrived in Southampton on the ticket he'd purchased for Julia. It was all neatly Shakespearean, Julia thought: David acquired the missus he wanted, Glennis got her posh English husband and life on a long leash, and Julia gained a lovely new robe. She considered it a memento of their understanding—a truly open relationship without demands or debts of any kind. At least that had been perfect, while it lasted.

She strolled across the room and into the hall. "Good morning, Christophine," she called toward the kitchen. A muffled reply told her that she'd caught her busy in some task. She would join Julia when she could.

Christophine's presence in the kitchen was another ad hoc arrangement, cobbled together in the tumult of Julia's collapsed housing arrangements. It had been a terrible shock to shepherd her household across the Atlantic and then arrive at the apartment she'd leased, only to be barred by a bellicose agent claiming a misunderstanding. Apparently her Albion printing press and related equipment constituted a commercial venture, which was strictly forbidden in the city's districting codes. When she explained that Capriole was unlikely to generate meaningful revenue—private presses were terribly exciting but invariably led to more expense than income—the fellow only deepened his protest. Profitable or not, her enterprise involved heavy equipment, and that bore the unforgivable whiff of trade or, worse, *industry*. She would have to find another place to live.

Julia had no choice but to redirect her crates to a warehouse, hastily found in Brooklyn, and to book a suite for herself and Christophine in the St. Regis. The next day Philip insisted they stay with him until she could find another home. Of course she was wary, but she could see that he spoke from more than courtesy. He wished for a chance to redeem himself after their battle last fall. He was sincere, as close to serious as he seemed to get, and she relented.

By sheer good fortune, Philip's housekeeper, Mrs. Cheadle, had been longing to visit her sister in Florida. She packed a bag, explained the particulars to Christophine, and left promptly for Grand Central Station. By the time Julia and Philip had returned home from dinner that night, Christophine had had a plate of fresh madeleines and an array of liqueurs waiting in the library.

Christophine's quick step sounded in the hall, and she appeared, wiping her hands on a white apron. Although nearing forty, Christophine looked and moved like the adolescent girl of Julia's earliest memory. She wore her hair, springy as moss, cut close to her skull. Her head seemed all face, a mobile joy of wide mouth, bright teeth, delicate nose and ears, shining eyes, and smooth dark skin over fine bones. Daughter of a wayward Trinidadian cook, she had attached herself to Julia's parents when they'd honeymooned on Saint Barthélemy. When the couple had prepared to leave for New York, the girl had begged to be taken along as nursery maid to the coming child. Now only she and Julia remained from that long-ago household.

She retrieved a tabloid slipped beneath the *Times* and opened it to a page near the back. "You see you in the paper, miss?" She spoke with the bumpy, present-tense music of her Caribbean childhood, a way of speaking that Julia loved as much as the woman herself. She poked at the Tidbits and Tattles column, handed it to Julia, and settled into the facing chair to listen. She was joined by Pestilence, one of Philip's two aging gray tabbies, both battle scarred yet friendly as kittens. The other, Pudd'nhead, already nestled against Julia's thigh.

Few things were more redolent of home and happiness to Julia than reading aloud to Christophine. The habit had begun when Julia was seven or eight, on orders of her tutor. But soon they'd sat most evenings twined together, all limbs and held breath, as the stories unfurled. Even still at times they settled into their more adult— in private—arrangement: Julia reading at one end of a sofa while Christophine sat at the other, Julia's feet in her lap beneath a whirl of thread and pins and stitches. Today they stayed in separate chairs.

"Oho!" There it was: *Miss Julia Kydd* circled in bright-blue ink, midway down the column. It looked to be a rambling report of the goings-on at Duveen's party last night. Julia pulled the spectacles from her pocket (she could bear only Christophine to see her wearing the hated wire-and-glass contraption) and began to read aloud.

"'The West Side apartment of Mr. Paul Duveen, noted author and critic, was again the scene of wit and artistic display last evening. Guests from the theater included the always-striking Misses Pola Negri and Erma Magill'—yes, yes." Julia skipped over descriptions of dull gowns and jewelry. "'The actresses were accompanied by Broadway orchestra conductor Mr. Irving West.'"

She scanned the next few paragraphs, surprised at the names of guests she must have seen but had not met.

"Here we are," she murmured, arriving further down the column. "'New to us was'—listen, Fee—'Miss Julia Kydd, who wore a daring French frock of yellow silk and seed pearls. We understand Miss Kydd is a patroness of Parisian couture, and we hope to see more of her wardrobe from that fair city. We will certainly see, in such fashions, more of Miss Kydd.'"

She lowered the paper. *Stuff!* What cheek.

Christophine tried to frown, but both women's shoulders quivered. "Miss Lila love that."

Lila Cartwell, Julia's London dressmaker, would indeed delight to have her work mistaken for French couture, even though it was Christophine's alterations that had captured the writer's eye. For years she'd doodled, as she called it, with their old clothes, experimenting with overlays and cutaways, appliqué, ornament, and whatever else suited her fancy. Her skills with hats were even more astonishing. She was wildly original—sometimes making dreadful hashes but more often creating arresting new looks. Christophine was an artist, an inventive modiste, though until last night, she refused to let any of her "mending" leave the house. With luck, Julia hoped, this success would loosen her restrictions.

"To Mademoiselle Fee!" Julia raised a phantom glass. "In New York less than a month and already turning heads!"

Fee scoffed happily and knuckled the page for Julia to read on.

She did. "'Never flagging in his enthusiasm for Negroes, Mr. Duveen treated his guests to a show of colored talent. Mr. Jerome Crockett recited his poem "While We Slept," recently published to acclaim in Chicago. Mr. Paul Robeson was persuaded to sing again the selection of Negro spirituals which so delighted guests at the apartment a week ago. The sultry tones of Miss Evangeline Pruitt, noted performer at Harlem cabaret Carlotta's, followed with a moving rendition of "Slave to Love," her signature tune.'"

Julia dropped the paper. "What rot to miss the entertainment."

Christophine pulled her chair closer and peeled an orange. She ate a section and handed another to Julia. It was another childhood routine: as Julia read, Christophine supplied their snacks. She had always slipped fruit to her this way, neatly peeled, sliced, seeded, or cored. Julia could do these things for herself, but with sticky and mangled results. Long ago she'd been barred from the household produce and from the kitchen generally. Though the childishness of the arrangement embarrassed her, she acquiesced as usual. The orange was juicy and sweet.

"'The dramatic high point of the evening,'" Julia resumed, "'concerned Miss Pruitt. Mr. Duveen announced that the publishing firm of Arthur Goldsmith has secured the rights to publish Miss Pruitt's debut novel. Friends tell us the novel will be eagerly awaited for its vivid scenes drawn from Miss Pruitt's stage career.'

"I met her," Julia said. "She's lovely. I liked her, very much." She stretched her arms over her head. "My first mixed party, Fee. It was smashing good fun."

To Julia's surprise, Christophine wrinkled her nose as if the milk had turned and declared herself glad to be nowhere near such an awkward assembly. What Julia had found exhilarating, she regarded with suspicion. But when Julia asked why, Christophine only shrugged and gave her usual end-of-discussion answer: "Just is."

Puzzled, Julia refolded the paper. Her eyes fell on Eva Pruitt's name, and her first impressions, so strong and so appealing, grew elusive. Was the woman a writer or a singer? Was she white or colored? The idea of a life so slippery—its edges shifting, like tide lines on a shore—fascinated Julia. She too longed to live facing forward, each moment erasing the previous. She itched to meet again the mysterious writer with the hidden manuscript. Tonight, she hoped, at Horace Liveright's party.

She was struck again by the idea of debuting her Capriole Press in America with work by the rising new novelist. Julia would watch for the right moment to ask if Eva had a short story or set of poems she might showcase in a fine edition. No need for the explosive stuff Logan Lanier had hinted at—although a bright flash was always better than a pensive flicker. In fact, a nice modern pop might be just the thing.

Yes, indeed. A shot across the Grolier Club's bow!

CHAPTER 4

Something red splatted against the doorframe as Julia entered the crowded reception room that evening. A wave of laughter followed the juicy missile, and she balked on the threshold. Austen Hurd stepped in front of her. "Hey, cut it out!"

They seemed to have interrupted a game that involved partiers tossing what looked to be strawberries at each other. Two shrieking women rushed past. From the commotion, Julia gathered the aim was to tuck the berries into women's bodices and down men's trousers. So this was the famous publishing house of Boni & Liveright, from which were launched eminent works of philosophy, literature, science, and history. And strawberries.

Another couple arrived, pushing them forward into the melee. Austen juked to dodge a woman's attempt to squeeze a berry under his collar, while Julia swatted another's stained fingers from her dress. What a ridiculous business! Before Austen could apologize or explain, someone seized her from behind. Two long arms in a gray pin-striped suit gripped her for several airless moments. "Pardon the hooligans, my dear," rumbled a well-liquored voice into her ear.

The man retreated half an arm's length and spun her to face him. Although clearly drunk, he had a patrician air about him, with fair hair sleeked back from his forehead and a lean, noble nose. No one had dared to so much as smudge his person with wayward fruit. He rolled

Julia's fingers between bony palms. "Horace Liveright, darling. Have we met?"

The great publisher himself. Austen scrambled to introduce Julia, but before he could, his boss nodded to someone across the room and relinquished Julia's hand. Excusing himself with a lush compliment, Liveright departed as abruptly as he had appeared, plumping Julia's derriere as he passed.

Impertinent sod. Welcome to America.

Austen made a wide-eyed mug of contrition. "Sorry for the rummy reception. Actually, the old goat can be a lot worse than that. You got the duchess treatment." He spoke over his shoulder as he led the way through the crowd toward the bar. Most of the strawberry hurlers seemed to be shifting out onto a terrace, where their cries disappeared into the din of snarled traffic on West Forty-Eighth Street below.

The bar turned out to be a wide table covered with bottles, glasses, scattered peanut shells, crumpled napkins, and damp bar towels. It was marginally quieter at that end of the room. Julia had little experience of workplace offices, but she wondered again how serious work was ever done in such a place. Austen handed her a gin fizz. "It's not usually this bad. A lot of new people turned up tonight when they heard Pablo's coming to show off his new protégé."

He dropped his chin. "Oh boy. Brace yourself."

A muscular, dark-haired woman of at least thirty kissed Austen with a loud smack and saluted Julia with her glass. "Wilhelmina Fischer, lamb. Call me Billie." She threaded her arm through Austen's. "Come to hail Pablo's noble savage? Haven't we all? I'd sell my grandmother for a novel that could pry real cash out of Arthur. Hell, I'd even prance around onstage for a weasel like Lenny Timson. Since that seems to be what it takes."

She fished the cherry out of her drink and popped it into her mouth. Her black-rimmed eyes swept over Julia's frock. "Couture, or I'm off my nut." She pinched Julia's sleeve. "Say, bunny, if you're looking for dough, scram now. On a publishing salary, this mutt couldn't keep you in last year's rags. Or out of them." She hooted at her witticism, turning nearby heads, and spanked Austen's cheek before strolling off toward a group of men on the terrace.

"Sorry," Austen said, before Julia could forbid another apology. "Billie drinks like a sailor. She's a theater critic who's discovered she makes a bigger splash panning a show." He made a throat-slashing gesture. "Jugular, every time."

"Ghastly woman." Julia glanced about. "I assume I haven't yet met your friends."

Austen looked around too. "You're right. It's a miracle this place publishes anything at all. Horace's a randy old dog, and he's extravagant to a fault, but he has a great nose for books. I love the man, really. He's been like a prince to me."

A prince with presumptuous paws. "Is the guest of honor here?" Julia wondered. "The author from Nebraska?"

"I was hoping you'd forgotten." Austen's head pitched to the right. Through a half-open door, Julia saw the soles of a man's shoes atop the backrest of a wide divan, as well as a jacket on the floor nearby. Someone in a pastel frock, likely a professional, celebrated the prone author. Julia examined her gin.

"Hold on." Austen sidled over to the room. Keeping his head and shoulders angled toward the party, he reached in, found the door's handle, and pulled it shut.

"Horace likes to treat authors like royalty when they visit, so he throws these parties and lines up, well, entertainment. It's embarrassing, but most of them love it. This fellow's found what Horace calls his casting couch. Sorry."

"Do you think I haven't seen prostitutes? I don't shock easily. And please stop apologizing. What does Mr. Liveright do for his lady authors? Squire them himself?"

Austen blushed. "Horace prefers chorines and actresses to authors, at least to authors he intends to publish. He loves to show—"

A great shout drowned the rest of his sentence. Pablo Duveen loomed in the doorway. "We won!" he bellowed. "We outfoxed you old coots, and we've come for our cackle!" He turned to sweep Eva Pruitt into the room. A stiff-spined, dark-complected man followed.

A crescendo of good-natured curses engulfed the trio.

"Is that Goldsmith?" Julia asked, eyeing the second man.

"I knew it," Austen said with a nod. "I bet a buddy Arthur couldn't resist coming along tonight to gloat. Horace wanted Eva's book too, you know, if only because Arthur had the leg up. Pablo egged him on with all his chirping about New Negroes." He leaned closer. "And I bet Arthur forked over a big contract just to give Horace a good steam. They may be smiling right now, but oh boy, Horace is hating this as much as Arthur's enjoying it. He'd kill to snatch Eva's book for us and wipe that smirk off Arthur's face."

Julia eyed the rival publishers, their hands locked in a pretense of bonhomie. Austen dropped his voice. "I don't know Arthur well, but then I doubt anyone does. He keeps his distance from Horace, treating him like something unsavory. I do know Horace resents Arthur something fierce. Oh, Arthur's a genius for publishing, no doubt about that, but he's such a prig. Arrogant, shrewd, careful to a fault with money and power—don't get Horace started on the subject. They say Arthur's ruthless about getting what he wants, which is always the best of anything."

Julia studied the man as they moved forward to greet the newcomers. Shrewd and ambitious—Arthur Goldsmith certainly matched the description. A precisely tapered black mustache hovered like two sable paintbrushes above his mouth as he accepted the crowd's attentions with small nods. He was dressed every bit as impeccably as Liveright, but with a surprisingly brazen touch: crisp pink shirt, white collar, magenta tie.

Goldsmith's dark eyes assessed Julia during Austen's introduction. His glance swept from her waist to her head before he dismissed her with the conventional courtesies. He'd sized her up—as a female—and decided she merited no further attention. It was true then: Arthur Goldsmith did love books more than women. Julia was far from the most attractive woman in the room, but she doubted any could rival her command of bookmaking. In measuring the woman, he'd overlooked the printer. Typical man. As he turned away, she raised her voice and said, "Stanley Morison speaks well of your work in raising typographic standards."

His gaze returned instantly. It was shameless, of course, to drop the name of Britain's foremost arbiter of typographic taste, and not altogether honest, as Julia had no idea what Morison thought of Goldsmith's books. The important thing was that she'd invoked the fine bookmaking movement, a renaissance in which Julia included her work with Capriole. Anyone who paid serious attention to type, layout, papers, bindings, and so on—as Goldsmith did—would sit up in attention at Morison's name.

As Goldsmith did now. "You know Morison?"

Austen answered with a rousing account of Morison's early blessings on Julia's Capriole Press. "Virginia Woolf with a Gill engraving," he enthused of *Wednesday*, Capriole's (more or less) inaugural title. "Fifty-five copies on Barcham Green, sold out after Morison's good word." Julia failed to tamp down her smile.

"Gill can be an acquired taste," Goldsmith said dryly. Julia nodded, equally circumspect. She admired Eric Gill's sensuous line drawings and humanistic letterforms, as well as his mystical eroticism—on the page. He'd drawn the image for her Capriole pressmark, a young she-goat (Julia herself) in a glade of book-leaved trees, but afterward she'd needed every agile leap of her namesake kid to escape the lusty fellow. Gill the artist was inspired; Gill the man was merely that, in all the usual carnal senses.

The turnabout in Goldsmith's regard was comical. A gaze that had been indifferent now burned with interest. While gratifying, Julia suspected this was fueled more by vanity than collegial respect. He was roughly a decade her senior and clearly more accomplished in the field, but even so. If his attention had to be earned, so did hers. She'd achieved her aim: Goldsmith had noticed.

Duveen lurched off toward the bar, and Julia moved to join Eva, whose smile grew wider at Julia's congratulations. A pale-blue felt cloche nestled over her skull, its brim frosted with silver bugle beads.

She looped her arm through Julia's. "Stay with me. You're my good luck charm." She eyed the hubbub. "Some splash, isn't it?"

"You look awfully happy."

"I am." Eva placed three fingertips on Julia's forearm. "They're taking me to dinner at the Plaza tonight. The *Plaza*, Julia."

Julia felt an unsettling twinge on hearing Eva pronounce her name. Then she realized what had sounded off key: never before had a colored person addressed her with such familiarity. Even Christophine, who knew her more intimately than anyone alive, would not forgo the *Miss* from her name. Julia had always thought of the syllable as merely an affectionate contraction: Julia to Miss as Christophine to Fee. How blind to absorb that social deference as naturally as one's name! Julia's stomach quivered. Did the title endure because Christophine, however loved, was technically her employee and dark as ditches? Would Julia have expected Eva to address her as Miss Julia? Of course not. The very idea was preposterous. But the moment's flash of surprise left a disturbing afterimage of doubt on Julia's mind. Were there more distasteful truths about herself she did not see?

"Since Jerome can't come, you know," Eva added.

Julia nodded vaguely, still disconcerted. Did she mean because he was obviously colored and so not allowed, or because of some other trouble? She remembered the couple's quarrel in Duveen's back bedroom. Was that the problem?

Eva's glow dimmed. "He wouldn't enjoy this anyway. He's glad for me and all, but he's sore about the fuss." As if reciting an assertion she'd heard a hundred times, she added, "He says true writers care only

about writing well, not the fiddle-faddle over their books." She sipped to obscure a new smile. "But I do love this."

Eva's enthusiasm restored Julia's. What good fortune they'd met when they had, each poised on the brink of a new venture. If they joined forces, their aspirations and talents might converge with eye-popping results. She lowered her voice, drawing Eva close, and described her modest but hopeful work as a publisher of handcrafted limited editions. "I'm thinking about my first production," Julia said, "to debut my Capriole Press in New York. I need something special. I know you're busy and excited about your novel, but I wonder if you might have some poems or a story you'd let me read and maybe publish."

When Eva didn't answer, she added, "I'd do my best to make it beautiful, with an illustration or two and handmade papers and brand-new types. A marbled wrapper, maybe?"

Eva shook her head to show that she didn't follow any of the design details. "You'd consider publishing something I wrote?"

"I'd be honored," Julia said. "It would announce us both to the literary world. Look out, Misters Goldsmith and Liveright and Harper and Scribner and all the other misters. Here come Eva Pruitt and Julia Kydd!"

Eva lifted her lovely face. "Eva Pruitt and Julia Kydd," she repeated with a curious wonder in her voice. "I like that. But I don't have any stories, only my book for Mr. Goldsmith."

Not a problem, Julia reassured her. "You could write something new. There's no rush. The shorter the better, actually, because I set my type by hand and have limited fonts. If we do decide to do this, you could help me plan the design, if you like."

"I never thought of books as having design," Eva admitted. "They're just words."

Julia explained that design was everything to fine printers, whose books aimed to exalt their texts by rendering them in beautiful physical form. Unlike more affordable and durable editions, whose purpose was to be read, fine editions were meant to be admired. They were like extravagant gowns for special occasions, made solely to dazzle and flatter.

Eva smiled. "Chambray and double seams for rehearsals, acres of chiffon for the show." She fluttered her skirt of seafoam chiffon with its intricate floral design of sapphire beads.

"Exactly," Julia said. "Now you understand my work better than I understand yours. I have to admit I'd never heard of New Negro literature before last night. What does—"

She stopped. It was an important question. She prayed her ignorance wouldn't offend. "I'm sorry, but what *does* Pablo mean when he says yours is a New Negro book?"

Eva exhaled a bemused snort. "He does carry on about that, doesn't he? He means it's good and culluhed. All jookin' and jelly dippin'." Her expression sobered. "Mostly he means a book written by a colored person that he thinks is worth reading. He means it includes the rough bits. Pablo thinks white people should know about"—she searched for a word—"the difficulties. Not that there's anything new about those."

"Why does he call it new, then?"

"Jerome can answer that better than I can. It means different things to different people. Have you heard of the Talented Tenth?"

Julia confessed her ignorance.

"It's what they call Negroes like Jerome and Logan who are as educated and accomplished as any white person. Upper-crust types: doctors, lawyers, professors, and such. Strivers. That's one kind of new, but Pablo calls new what he thinks Negroes have and white folks don't, some special snap." She slid her feet in a soft dance move. "What's new is white people paying attention, like they just now noticed we have something to say."

Something to say? Negroes had as much to say as anyone else. Julia listened every day to Christophine, though rarely at length or in great depth. Christophine had plenty to say about the price of ivory buttons, the hats pictured in the society pages, or her long walk to the bus stop, but race never came into any of it.

At least that Julia could see. What did she really know of Christophine's life beyond what they experienced together and the stories she chose to share? Julia felt a twist of chagrin. Had she failed to notice what else lay beneath and beyond those stories? Or had she not even bothered to ask? It was a galling thought.

Was this new "something" why publishers were so keen to publish Eva's book? Julia remembered Logan Lanier's bitter mention of coy theatrics with the manuscript, implying Eva was withholding it until money changed hands.

Eva watched Julia's face. "What?"

"I was just wondering if you've given Pablo the manuscript. Logan Lanier thought there might be some trickiness to that."

Eva turned to find Duveen. He stood near the windows, singing falsetto harmony with a woman captured under his arm. They were piecing together off-key phrases of "When My Sugar Walks down the Street," Duveen chiming in on the birdies' chorus with a robust *Tweet! Tweet! Tweet!*

Eva lowered her voice. "Not yet. I had to hide it."

"Hide it from whom?"

Eva ran her tongue along the underside of her lip.

"And why?"

Eva raised her glass to her mouth but left it there, untouched, as she watched Duveen abandon the song and shamble closer. "After Pablo gives me the money, I'll give him the manuscript. Soon."

Julia puzzled at this news. The furtive transaction sounded like something Willard Wright might concoct for one of his detective stories.

Eva's eyes never left Duveen as he headed their way. Her hand trembled as she emptied her glass, one small swallow after another. "First Pablo has to make a special account with me at his bank," she said. "Leonard, I mean my boss, Mr. Timson, takes care of the money he pays me—it's mine, but he watches over it. So we need somewhere else to put the book money so Leonard won't know about it right away. Because when he finds out, oh Lordy, he'll be mad as a wet hen."

Mention of bank accounts and complicated finances reminded Julia of her own years when Philip had held total control over her funds, simply because women were deemed incompetent at managing money. Many women endured much harsher oversight of husbands or fathers or brothers. Women might now have the vote, but many still had to rely on a man for bus fare to the polls. It was unjust and infuriating: the great victory rendered hollow by mundane realities.

"Why would your boss be angry about the money?" Julia asked, but Eva didn't answer, intent on tracking Duveen's return.

He rejoined them and waved Eva's empty glass at the bar, perhaps hoping someone would notice and bring over a bottle. "I've been telling everyone they must come with me up to Harlem. Your new show will curl their cummerbunds." His belly quivered in a dreadful shimmy.

Eva smiled.

"You should see what this Sheba can do," Duveen crowed to Austen and Goldsmith. "I mean it. Come with me sometime, Hurd. I'm a crusader. I lead tours to Harlem for repressed rich white folk. I proselytize for the powers of Negro sass and pep—just the tonic our stodgy old civilization needs. Come tonight."

Austen shook his head, blaming early plans in the morning. Julia might have added that no one here seemed particularly repressed or stodgy. But Duveen insisted, and a date was set for a week from Saturday. Austen and Julia would join Duveen and an out-of-town couple who, he said, had engaged him to escort them into Harlem. Escort? Julia had an absurd image of Duveen leading his timid charges down the street with a well-thumbed Baedeker, as if he alone spoke the language and knew the coinage of the realm. They did know it was New York, didn't they?

"You too, Arthur," Duveen badgered his friend. "She's your new author. Come too."

Goldsmith deliberated. He considered Eva, who returned his gaze with friendly encouragement, and then, at length, Julia. "Coral's arranged something for that evening, but perhaps I could get away for a short while."

"Lemony larkspurs!" Duveen exclaimed. "It's a party then. Come to my place first. You'll meet the mighty Max Clark from San Fran. He's a big player in timber out in Oregon, or is it Ida-hoo? Somewhere wretched and rainy. He wants to dazzle a new wife while he's nailing down deals. He'll burn dough faster than matches while she's watching, so we can scamper along on his dime. We'll start off with the late supper show at Carlotta's; then I'll spin your heads right through breakfast at the Sugar Bowl. Grits and gravy, washed down with their own Seventh Avenue thunder. Regular monkey rum, that stuff."

Julia fought hard not to laugh at his slang-soaked enthusiasm. From the shadow under her hat's brim, she caught Eva's eye. "Pishposh," Eva mouthed, her lips barely moving.

With a throaty *hey* and two sharp elbows, Billie Fischer wedged into the conversation. "This?" she said, eyeing Eva. "This is what all the stink's about?"

She pumped Eva's hand. "Hello, sunshine. Billie Fischer. Glad you could grace our pack of drudges, Miss Pruitt. No one here's written a really grand novel—not even you, Pablo, admit it. We just supply the drivel." Billie twirled her index finger. Julia stepped back to avoid the slosh from her forgotten drink.

"But they say you've got the goods," Billie went on. "Pablo says it's colored fiction we need these days. Hot little souls, prancin' to paradise. Is that so? Will colored fiction set us free, Miss Pruitt?"

Eva stared at her, puzzled. A tentative smile spread across her face, as if she had decided to regard this strange invective as yet another compliment.

"She's drunk," Julia whispered. "Ignore her."

Eva nodded faintly and began to turn away, but Billie stepped closer and laid the back of her hand beside Eva's jaw.

"What do you know?" Billie's coarse voice rose. "Look here, everybody, I'm darker than the darky. So why the hell is Arthur paying good greenbacks for a colored novel from a cow who's no more colored than I am?"

The room quieted. What was wrong with the woman? Did she think she was amusing?

Duveen squirmed. "Cut it out, Billie. Eva is what they call a high yaller, a light mulatto. It's top drawer, the very best kind of colored."

"You don't say. I find it hard to believe this buttercup can dish out hash black enough for your inky tastes, Pepino." Her squint sharpened. She brought her index finger to her mouth and sucked on it noisily. "Maybe under all this powder and shit—" She dragged her fingertip down the length of Eva's left cheek, leaving a slick trail of whiskeyed saliva.

Eva flinched but did not recoil. Julia's breath congealed in her throat.

"Christ, Billie," Duveen stammered. To Eva he said, grimacing, "She's soused. No offense meant, I'm sure."

She meant nothing but! Julia fumbled for her handkerchief, but before she could wipe the smear from Eva's cheek, Billie reared back. Bellowing a profanity, she knocked away Duveen's hand.

"And that's for the hot little colored ass Pablo wants us to dream about!" she shouted, dashing the remains of her whiskey against the back and side of Eva's frock.

The moment swelled like an airless bubble in Julia's ears, squeezing all noise from the room. Goldsmith's upper lip curled and his nostrils flared. Duveen glowed with vast pink chagrin. Billie snorted when he whispered something, still clutching at her swerving sleeve.

"Fuck manners, you obsequious piglet," she roared, "and get me a drink. I need a fucking drink."

CHAPTER 5

Two bar towels draped over her forearm, Julia followed Eva into the ladies' toilet while Austen held open the door and groped for the light switch. He had acted quickly, grabbing the towels and motioning with his head as he led them through the gauntlet of wide-eyed stares, out of the room and down the hallway.

The lavatory was a large space, lit by a single light bulb hanging from the ceiling. Against one wall was an old toilet, surrounded by a short wooden stall. Idle hands had picked away large patches of its chipping white paint. A basket rested on the floor beside the toilet, filled with magazines whose torn covers suggested they'd been old before they'd been put there, and that had been some time ago. On the opposite wall hung a large basin, its porcelain stained by years of drips, beneath a mirror and a narrow shelf covered with an untidy array of combs, face powders, hand creams, tooth powders, and mugs. Julia couldn't imagine conducting one's daily toilette in such communal circumstances. But apparently the ladies of the publishing firm of Boni & Liveright did just that.

Under a soot-caked window sagged a massive sofa. Its once-scarlet upholstery had faded to a patchwork of brown nap and threadbare weave. Long ago discarded by its owner, it now offered comfort for the faint, squeamish, or sleepy.

Eva peered down at her dress. Its beautiful chiffon was plastered against her waist and hip below her left elbow. She lifted her arm and fumbled at the fasteners that lay beneath a placket in the side seam. "Can you help with these?"

Julia bent to open the tiny hooks and eyes. There was nothing she could say to erase Billie Fischer's ugly words, but she might be able to fix the damage she'd inflicted. She reached to remove Eva's cloche before lifting the fine fabric over its sharp beads, but Eva veered away.

"Leave it on, please," she said. She raised her arms, bent over, and wiggled as Julia drew the dress over her head, fingers spread wide to avoid catching the fabric. Eva sat on the old sofa and daubed one of the towels against the wet silk of her chemise while Julia bore the dress to the basin, its airy panels fluttering like scraps of a burst balloon.

They both jumped at a sharp knock on the door. Julia braced it with her foot and peeked out. Eyes averted, Austen handed her two glasses and a nearly full bottle of champagne. "Thought you could use strengthening."

"Good man." Julia thanked him. She filled both glasses and left the bottle on the floor beside Eva.

Bent over the basin, she applied a moistened corner of the remaining towel to the whiskey-soaked frock. In the mirror she watched Eva settle at the far end of the sofa. Wearing only her cloche, pearls, stockings, and a pale-gold film of lingerie, she stretched her legs across the cushions like a modern odalisque.

"I'm hardly a lucky charm tonight," Julia said.

"You might be," Eva said, after a pause. "She could have thrown worse."

"Whiskey was reprehensible enough."

Something about the remark cheered Eva. She smiled. "*Reprehensible.* Ella, my sister, liked that word. She did love her syllables." She clicked her tongue. "Ella was like my smarter, sassier half, the brave one. You remind me some of her. Oh, not to look at, but she talked like you. She loved words like *reprehensible.*" Eva played with the word, repeating it in staccato and operatic variants. "She was the real writer in the family. My book is partly for her.

"Funny, isn't it?" she said, speaking to Julia's reflection in the mirror. "I get as much trouble for not being colored as for not being white.

White people think I'm sneaky, putting on airs, and Negroes can be even worse. I sometimes think it would be simpler just to pass."

Pass. The word hung in the quiet room. Such a short syllable for something so complicated. Julia first knew the term from Christophine's occasional muttered disapproval. She would frown and call it foolish, bound to end badly. Julia always supposed she meant the risks of discovery were too great. Some white people considered it a kind of brazen fraud, like traveling first-class with a third-class ticket. Others viewed passing as a spectator sport, cheering on the rule breakers like schoolchildren urging twins to torment their teachers by answering to each other's names. Pablo's mixed soirees were exactly that, a smug poke in the eye of social norms. And he'd certainly enjoy a good snigger later tonight at the Plaza's expense. Worse, and unfortunately more common, were those whites who feared some kind of contamination, as if Negroes might infect their air or soil their furniture.

For herself, Julia considered passing one of those harmless deceptions everyone, to some degree, practiced. Surely most people hid what they didn't want known about themselves and fabricated or embellished what suited them. Julia had sworn Christophine to secrecy about her reading spectacles. Christophine called her alterations "mending." And good Lord, Philip had not one drop of Kydd blood, and still the name opened every door in town to him. Diverting as those deceptions might be, in the end Julia had always considered them inconsequential and so not worthy of looking at too closely.

"I must admit," Julia said, head down, watching Eva obliquely, "I had no idea you were colored when we met. That is what you mean? That you can pass for a white person?"

Eva's earrings swung as she dipped her chin to one shoulder. The corners of her mouth rippled at some bitter joke. "Oh yes. My mother was light, and my father's a white gentleman. Back in Louisville. Theodore Stillwater Byron Love the Third, if you can believe such a dicty name. We called him the professor."

"You knew him?" Julia asked. "If it's not impertinent to ask," she added, realizing too late what she had presumed. Miscegenation, especially in the South, rarely involved families.

"Yes, I knew him. He cared for my mother for years." She refilled her glass. "I don't mind your asking. I don't get much call to talk about him. We had a little house on the back of his property. His wife was an invalid, and Mama was her nurse. I must say he was good to us, made sure we had nice clothes and things. He even arranged for tutors after he saw what we got in the colored schools. And oh my, the books he gave us. Armloads of books, every year. He even helped me write a little newspaper, the *Deaver Road Occasional*, I called it." She rolled her eyes. "I wanted to be an author even then, I suppose. A little Jo March I was."

Her gaze roamed around the room. She lifted her elbow, patted the towel against her damp hip, and took a long swallow. "When I was fourteen, we had to leave. The professor's wife died, you see, and he remarried. I saw him a few times after that, but he pretended not to recognize me. He had to, really, to please his new family."

Julia knew the sting of a father's rejection. Her own had died when she was six, before she was old enough to garner his interest. But Eva's story was worse. To be loved for years and then spurned in public? Unthinkable.

"I don't understand," Julia said slowly. "You look utterly white. Why don't you just call yourself white? No one would know."

Eva's beautiful mouth curved in a wry smile. "It's not that simple. I can pass, but Ella was too dark. It happens. Even just a touch of the tarbrush can sometimes show. I know a man who threw his wife out into the street after their third baby turned out colored." Her long fingers stroked the back of her neck. "She let him think she had a Negro lover rather than tell him the truth. To save her other children, you see. She was crazy, having those babies. It's kin that counts, not skin."

One sister dark and another light? Julia was taken aback. Then she remembered that of course skin color could be as unpredictable as that of eyes or hair. One sibling among several might sport Grandfather's freckles or Grandmother's olive complexion. As Billie Fischer had so crassly demonstrated, white people came in many shades too. Julia wondered vaguely who decided who was "white."

"Yet it must be tempting," she said, "to go anywhere, to just . . ." The sentence trailed off. She meant simply to live unencumbered, in the ways that had always seemed ordinary—for her.

She knew of course about race segregation and the great disparity between what was accessible to white Americans and what to coloreds. "Separate but equal" was anything but. The inequality was no secret; in fact, it was the point. Yet many white people, including Julia and likely everyone else at the party, lived peaceably under the system not because they endorsed it but because they never thought about it. Race separation made Negroes invisible to many whites. They literally never saw colored people except as maids, cooks, groundskeepers, bellhops, porters, and the like, roles that seemed to fuse race with subservience. The system was pervasive, which made it seem inevitable: as natural a feature of American life as celebrating Thanksgiving or motoring on the right-hand side of the road. If asked, many whites might rue its unfairness, but mostly they just forgot. They didn't see it. Julia saw their blindness but wondered now about her own.

Maids, cooks. The words snagged like a thorn in Julia's mind, with their guilty afterthought: Christophine. They were both grown women now, bound less by an employment contract than a mutual devotion. But however much they shared an unwavering sense of home, they were neither family nor, in the social sense, friends. Beyond the walls of their apartment, each went her own way.

Julia had always supposed this stemmed from their differing tastes. Christophine would rather chew nails than compose a colophon in ten-point type, just as Julia would slump in clumsy confusion at one of Christophine's daylong quilting parties. Christophine relished Sundays with her West Indian church friends, while Julia preferred to play at the typecases with drop caps and letterspacing and new combinations of fleurons. These differences seemed straightforward, as natural and benign as those between Methodists and Anglicans or cat fanciers and dog owners. She and Christophine simply chose their separate pleasures. Or so Julia had always thought.

Eva watched as Julia explored her naivete with growing chagrin. "It is tempting to pass, and terribly convenient," she said, with a note of weary patience. Julia wondered how often she'd tried to explain these things to other oblivious Nordics. "But it's lonely too. You have to leave your colored friends behind, yet you don't dare cross over until you've thought up a new past and family for yourself. That's risky and exhausting. I'm not clever or careful enough for it. When I pass, it's only to fool a waiter or clerk, just to buy a pair of stockings and use a clean toilet. My fay friends"—she hesitated before continuing quietly—"like you, all know what I am."

Friends. There was the rub. *Friends.* By every measure of taste and style, she and Eva Pruitt were naturally suited to be good friends. She had no doubt they would enjoy talking for hours over lunch at Sherry's, visiting the salons, or strolling the shops along Fifth Avenue. Julia would relish Eva's company at a gala evening at the Met or poetry recital in the back rooms of the Swetnam Galleries.

But none of that was possible unless Eva passed. Negroes were not welcome at any of those places. Most of Julia's public life (How did she not think of this every day?) transpired in places and events where the only Negroes were usually silent, deferential employees. No matter how knowledgeable, talented, cultured, or wealthy Eva was, race limited her movements.

As a woman Julia knew something of such bitter exclusion, barred as she was from attending Harvard or Yale, from lunching weekdays at the Plaza, and from a myriad of other activities. Worst of all, she could never hope to join the Grolier Club. To its members and other serious bibliophiles she dared to consider her peers, she was a *lady* fine printer, a *female* book collector—and as such barred by definition from their inner sanctum. These policies were justified as self-evident:

women lacked the capacity to appreciate, much less achieve, the loftiest reaches of culture and commerce, and their presence would disrupt the established order of things. The same reasons—and worse—were used to bar Negroes. But Julia's frustrations were, yet again, nothing compared to all that was closed to Eva on double the grounds.

If Eva noticed the turmoil beneath the blue georgette frock bent over the basin, she gave no sign of it. She savored a mouthful of champagne. "I can pass, easily," she reflected, "but I'd rather not. I always feel a bit disloyal to the race."

"What do you mean?" Julia said, grateful to refocus. "Other Negroes are offended?"

"Mmmm," Eva murmured into her glass. "It's more than that. I'm not ashamed of my family or my friends. Just because I can walk away from them doesn't mean I ever would." Her tone shifted. "Never. Especially now. It's Jerome I think about now."

Julia glanced in the mirror. Eva had leaned a shoulder into the cushion and was studying the bubbles in her glass as she spun it.

"I'm sorry he was rude last night," she said. "He wasn't comfortable. People think he's snooty, but he deserves to be proud. He doesn't like Pablo's parties. He doesn't like it when Negroes are paraded about. That's what he calls it."

Julia looked down at her stilled hands, pressed into a meager froth of soap. Had it been a parade? Was her pleasure last evening merely the thrill of a spectacle? Was the party no more than some kind of human zoo, where if you ventured close enough, the bars seemed to disappear but of course remained? The idea shamed her. She stared at the dress in her hands. What on earth was she doing? She'd never laundered a garment in her life. She knew nothing of the chemistry of fabric and water and soap. Perhaps this was futile or, worse, destructive.

"How did you come to New York, Eva?" It was the first benign thing she could think of. She might not know how to clean Eva's frock, but she could try to get it dry again. She refolded the towel to a dry patch.

Eva's swirling slowed. A clamor of horns and shouting drivers over on Broadway drifted into the room while she drew in her cheeks, pensive, silent. The interval grew so long that Julia was startled at her abrupt words: "Mother and Ella died after the war, from the influenza. This seemed as good a place to go as any."

She stifled a cough with a long swallow. "I'd done well in school. I thought I could work in a library or an office, someplace clean, respectable. Naturally I knew no colored girl, no matter how light she is, can work with white girls unless she's passing. But colored bosses wouldn't hire me either—the darker girls would call me hincty, think I'd get special favors, that sort of thing. Finally someone told me about a job for light girls like me—in one of the new nightclubs. I was desperate. I couldn't afford to be proud, so I went to see about it."

She coughed again. "And that's how I started. I couldn't hoof worth a lick, and my singing wasn't much better. I could carry a tune well enough back at Ninth Street Baptist, but believe me, I was nothing special. You know what it was, Julia? I matched. All the girls had to be tall and light. Big smile, good skin and teeth, no habit. If you could shake your tail like you meant it and more or less keep your dogs in step—twenty-six dollars a week, plus a place to live, if you needed it." She sighed. "Thought I'd gone to heaven."

A minute or more passed, filled with only the pulsing din of traffic and the light swish as Julia blotted and rubbed Eva's dress between two layers of toweling. Her mind pulsed as well, recalling her own recent struggle to imagine how she might earn her way in the world. She too was only generally educated, with few marketable skills. It had been dispiriting, yes, but how far more dire Eva's situation had been. Though bred to similar sensibilities, she'd been barred even from Julia's humble options, and ironically on both sides of the race barrier.

"The boss put me in front," Eva abruptly resumed, "and customers liked me. They didn't care I'm no Florence Mills, as long as there's something nice to look at, you know. Then, oh, a few years ago, I had a little trouble, and they moved me up to Carlotta's." Another cough. "My, now that was prosperity. By then I knew exactly what to do, and I might as well get paid all I could for it. I don't even think about the nonsense anymore. It's like I'm not even there. It's not really me onstage, just what I do for my job. Don't believe it for one minute."

"Believe what?"

"You'll see. It's just a job, Julia. I'm part of the show, doing what I'm paid to do. That's all. And it's so easy." She raised one leg off the cushion and arched her foot, turning it to admire the curve of calf and ankle. Her glass rested on her stomach. "Leonard once gave me a gold bracelet just to sit on an alderman's knee for ten minutes, let him drool on my earring." Champagne swayed at the memory.

"He can be a stinker sometimes, but mostly he leaves me be. I just keep tucking away those little gifts. I always figured someday I'd go home to Louisville, get married, have a few babies, sing in a church choir, join a reading society. Well, until Jerome."

Her smiling mention of the brusque poet jarred loose a nugget of caution in Julia's mind. She barely knew the man, but his evident displeasure at Eva's success struck her as ominous. Julia had seen before the dangers of men who needed to feel superior to women. She asked in an even voice how the couple had met.

Eva thought for several moments. Her reply began with an easy chuckle. "It was at the library, a Sunday symposium about a year ago. Lots of people come, all dressed up, real honest-to-goodness Strivers. They talk about literature and Mr. Du Bois and politics and racial uplift. Sometimes they get going in French. I love to hear them, even if it's too fast for me.

"So one day, there was Jerome. Logan introduced us, but every time we tried to talk, someone interrupted to declare what a fine family Jerome came from, how his father *and* his mother are fine teachers, how he's sure to be a fine teacher himself.

"Well, pretty soon Jerome looked like he was going to punch the next person who said one more word about his prospects. He spouted off something in French—oh, it sounded glorious—and out the door he went, taking me with him. It was rude, but I loved it."

She beamed. "We walked and walked, all the way to my flat, but Leonard has rules about visitors, so then I walked him home. We drank a little wine, and then we walked back to my place. We never stopped talking."

Julia smiled. She knew those happy first hours when every word, every glance, was a marvel of discovery. A deep laugh rumbled in Eva's lungs. "I was in love before the sun went down. We told each other everything we could think of. He has a scholarship to go to the University of Chicago and become a literature professor. And he wants to, but first he wants to be a poet."

Eva's smile faded. "It's hard for him, Julia. He's too proud to ask his parents or uncle for help with a job. He wants something respectable, but the only work a copper Negro can get is servant work. He tried that, but the other boys hate him because he's educated. You can't imagine how frustrating it is. So I made Leonard hire him. He didn't like to, and Jerome isn't keen either, but at least he gets time to write.

"His book is beautiful," she said, watching Julia's hands move. "It's much more important than mine, with deep ideas." She took a deep swallow without, Julia imagined, tasting much of it. The bottle was nearly empty. "Now I'd trade all this, oh, in a—" She snapped her fingers, a click so sharp that Julia's head jerked up.

"For what?"

"What?"

"You'd trade your success for what?"

Pink splotches spread across Eva's cheeks and throat. "I shouldn't have said that. I'm sorry." Her gaze dived to her lap. "It's a secret."

Her finger circled the rim of her glass. In a low, defiant voice, she said, "Maybe I can tell just one person. You won't tell anyone, will you? I can tell *you*."

Julia nodded vaguely, neither encouraging an indiscretion nor resisting a confidence.

"As soon as I get this book money, we're going to Paris."

"Paris!"

Eva twisted upright. "Please don't tell. You can't tell a soul."

"I won't. But why on earth would you rush off to Paris?"

Eva set her glass on the floor and stood. "I've said too much already. Please forget I said that. I have to go. Is my frock dry yet?"

Julia looked down at Eva's dress, dangling forgotten from the towel between her hands. She lifted it slowly. The peaty aroma was gone, and the large splotch was more or less dry. The water and rubbing had ruined the chiffon's smooth lie, but that couldn't be helped now.

She slid it over Eva's bent arms and head, fastened the tiny hooks, adjusted the fit over Eva's hips, and stepped back to look. From her lower back to her left hip, a faint island the color of tobacco juice floated in a sea of blue and violet.

Eva peered at her backside in the mirror. "Looks li—"

The door hurtled open, bouncing against the peg in the floor, and Billie Fischer rushed in. She pulled up abruptly, her left heel wobbling. "What are you staring at? Can't a girl pee?"

She pushed into the stall and noisily relieved herself. Julia and Eva looked away, their eyes meeting in the mirror.

"Thought you'd left ages ago," Billie complained as she rattled out a length of tissue. "Christ, this place is a bore. Gotta be a better party somewhere. Vincent's usually good for a laugh; guess I'll mooch on over there."

Her hatless head rose above the rickety wall. She yanked the chain and emerged.

Squinting at her reflection, she puckered her lips and reached for one of the lipstick applicators on the shelf below the mirror. Her lips stretched and twisted to receive the swath of scarlet. She smiled at her reflection and tossed the applicator back onto the shelf. "White

Negroes," she said, tucking a strand of black hair into place. "What a load of crap."

With a wave over her shoulder, Billie swaggered out, her collar and hem awry.

Julia turned to Eva, unable to speak. What could she say? Billie's banal scorn chilled her most. The critic's impersonal cruelty.

Eva made a wry face. "I've known worse." Arm raised, she twisted and looked again at her blighted dress. "How low are the lights at the Plaza?"

Julia swore softly under her breath. "I'm a dunderhead. Wait here."

She slipped out and returned a minute later with her shawl. She fluttered it over Eva's shoulders, blazing a salvation of purple and yellow and blue embroidery across her back. She tied the shawl into place with a loose knot, and the stain receded from view. It was still there, if one knew where to look, but Eva's radiant face would distract any gaze. Her dress, at least, would have no trouble withstanding the Plaza's scrutiny. Eva dipped to swish the fine silk fringe against her calves, but instead she unleashed a loud hiccup.

Two fingers flew to her throat. Then she laughed, mouth open, round as a sunflower. *Ha ha ha ha.* It flowed from her in low pulses, an old-fashioned, resonant laugh, nothing like the twittering arpeggios practiced in more fashionable circles.

"Thank you, thank you." She squeezed Julia's hand and pulled her into a close embrace, the knot of the shawl disappearing into the soft warmth of their waists. "No one will ever know."

For the second time in as many days, Julia was struck by how unafraid Eva was of touching and being touched. Touch was both the first human bond and often the most fraught. Women could be lovers, of course, but this wasn't that. This was trust, pure and unembarrassed. It was friendship claimed and clasped, a gesture both innocent and brave.

As she watched Eva leave, fresh admiration swept through Julia, trailed by a vague fear. Innocence and courage could be precarious partners. She looked down. This time the trembling hand was her own.

CHAPTER 6

"I wonder how Eva will fare at the Plaza tonight," Julia said. She cradled her sidecar.

She and Austen had settled into a booth in one of the several speakeasies on West Forty-Eighth Street—an essential neighborhood amenity, according to Liveright. Austen had greeted the doorman by name, and the familiarity was returned. Now that Julia had been admitted in the company of a regular, the door would be opened for her in the future too. She must remember the fellow's name. Benny. Benny.

Austen shrugged. "Since Pablo dines there all the time, I doubt she'll be questioned. Anyone who knows Eva's colored either doesn't go there or would get as much satisfaction in the stunt as Pablo will. I bet they'll fidget more over Arthur. Jews aren't welcome either."

Two bowls of onion soup arrived, thick with croutons and bubbling gruyère. With the tip of her spoon, Julia poked the crust. "At least Pablo has the face to defy the rules."

Austen lifted a spoonful of broth, but it was too hot, and he returned it to the bowl. "I'm not sure what Pablo's up to half the time. He's so besotted with Negroes right now that he claims he'd love to be one."

"What does Pablo do, if he doesn't actually work for Mr. Goldsmith?"

"Good question, bean." He tapped her forehead as if she'd said something clever. "I suppose you'd call him a writer. He's written three or four novels, nothing great, but entertaining enough. He writes articles on art, theater, music, that sort of thing. It wouldn't pay his bills, but I gather he has a fat bankroll on the side. Arthur publishes his novels, though they say Pablo's better friends with Coral, Arthur's wife. She's the one who really sails that ship, from behind the scenes. And for all his silliness, Pablo is a shrewd reader. Arthur knows his modern Russians and Italians and other Europeans, but he scratches his head over some of the American stuff. So Pablo helps him out, and in return he gets to dispense fame and fortune, or at least fame."

Julia watched the fragrant steam rise. "How do you know him?"

He tried another spoonful of soup with more success. "From parties, I suppose, mostly Horace's. Pablo turns up anywhere there's book talk and liquor. Which means everywhere."

Book talk and liquor. Parties where writers and editors and publishers mingled almost daily. Artists and printers and binders too, possibly. Julia quelled a growing excitement. Austen's interests dovetailed with hers, and he moved in the circles she most hoped to join. It was impossibly lucky they should have met again. "How about you?" she asked. "Russell Coates told me you started out on Wall Street. How did you make your way to publishing?"

That crooked smile. "I bet your real question is why," he said. "Everybody knows there's no money in books, and folks are starting to roll in it on Wall Street. Easy. I was bored. Screaming bored. I think I have a pretty good nose for books. Pop thought I was daft, but he let me cash in what my mother left me to buy a job with Horace.

"He's always short of cash," he explained. "He stays afloat by taking in what he calls college boys like me with more money than patience. If we put twenty grand into the coffers, voilà, we get a fancy title and an office where we can do as little as we please. The less the better. I drive him crazy because I want to do more than flirt with the secretaries, and he'd rather I didn't muck about. So I stay out of his way but watch like a hawk to see how he does it. Old Horace really knows his onions when it comes to books."

Julia sipped her soup. "He'd better watch his back."

Austen laughed. "I'm not after his job. I want to start my own imprint someday, like you, only more in the trade. I think there's a real market opening up for limited editions, but Horace won't give it a try, except for occasional esoterica. Blue limericks in ten-dollar bindings, that's it. Anonymous authors too. Grievously underpaid. All the money goes to the glamorous ones like Eva Pruitt."

Julia wondered again how Eva was faring. If anyone at the Plaza detected the ruse, would they challenge her? Julia suspected Pablo's regular patronage might be enough to forestall a scene. Yet he'd relish the stunt regardless—he had nothing to lose. Should disaster strike, he could protest in noble indignation; Eva would bear all the humiliation. Julia felt a sympathetic heat in her cheeks. "I wonder what I'd do," she said, "if I were asked to leave a restaurant because of my race."

"You'd live. I've been through it."

Julia lowered her spoon, dumbstruck. Austen? It had not occurred to her. She had to ask. "Are you colored too?"

His face curled in pleasure. After a moment's thought he said, *"Oh, what does it mean to be dark?*

"Colored mama, perhaps? Saint-Tropez on a lark?"

He lifted a palm for patience. *"He might be a Negro—he don't care a fig, though—"*

She grabbed his wrist. *"Stop! Julia withdraws her remark."*

He grinned, eyebrows raised appreciatively. "Colored? Next to Eva, it might seem so. But no. My mother was Jewish, Pop too, more remotely, from one of the murkier Russian provinces. We weren't religious, though. I remember asking if I could have a bar mitzvah after some older boys said it was a great way to get gifts."

"What happened?"

"Not a chance, when I found out about the Hebrew. Later I figured out being Jewish mostly works against you. Yale wouldn't take me, since they already had their quota. Same with Dartmouth and Princeton."

He rolled his eyes. "But then, I was no prize. Luckily Columbia wasn't so picky."

Julia nodded. Life in London had taught her plenty about how Jews could be treated. Fortunately, in the more bohemian art circles she frequented, no one made any distinction. In fact, most writers and artists she knew wore their social "flaws" like badges: they were proudly Jewish or Persian or Zoroastrian and so on, and more than a few such distinctions seemed hastily acquired. Julia was merely left handed and nearsighted, minor demerits, but enough.

"After college," Austen went on, "it's mostly been little things, like clubs I can't join. Some high-hat restaurants won't have me—but I can't afford them anyway. Nothing too painful. My story's nothing compared to the race rules and nonsense Negroes face."

Nonsense was hardly the word. Julia shook her head in protest. "That Billie tonight—what a vicious creature. Imagine hurling such abuse at another person. Literally."

"Inexcusable," Austen agreed with a grimace. "Writing is like giving birth for Billie—she screams and curses the whole time. She can't stand for anyone else to suffer less than she does. Eventually she sweats out a story and passes round cigars, but then someone else's work is smarter or funnier or more successful, and she hates them for it. Same in the romance department. She's always going on about what louses men are, or they're married or swishes. That's good for a daily pint right there."

He chased down the last spoonful of soup. "How about you? What's your story, bean?"

Julia thought for a moment to distill the old narrative. "I'm on my own and have been for years. I have only a vague sense of my father—he owned a shipping line, mostly in South America, but it was sold before I knew anything about it. He died when I was six."

She frowned at Austen's consoling murmur. Her father had receded early from her life, well before his death. Even in her earliest memories, Milo had been perennially out, taking meals and passing hours at his clubs.

At the rare times when he'd been home, he'd withdrawn to his library and other distant quarters of the old house, far from the rooms where she and Christophine had played. "I hardly knew him," she said. "My mother died too, when I was thirteen. Struck down by a motorcar in Stockholm."

Her gaze strayed as she thought of the thunderclap that had dispelled her childhood in one sentence. She could still hear Christophine's voice splinter at the calamitous news. "She was much younger than my father and infinitely more interesting. I wish I could have known her longer."

At the look on Austen's face, she added, "But I had my old nursery maid, Christophine, who still lives with me. And I have a half brother, Philip, who's ten years older. He lives here in New York, but I don't know him well."

How much more she might have said. Philip had been packed off to boarding school before she had even been born. For years they'd rarely seen each other, and then across a gulf of grievances. Appointed her guardian after Lena's death, because there had been no one else, he'd dispatched her to her own exile of schools, travels, and so on. For the next twelve years they'd exchanged only the most intermittent and efficient courtesies, in the end from separate continents.

"I'm temporarily staying with him, but I'll have my own place as soon as I find an apartment that will accommodate Capriole."

Austen pushed away his empty bowl. Leaning an elbow on the table, he propped up his head. "I have to ask. Fraternizing with a Jew would be verboten to some girls. It doesn't seem to bother you, but would your brother object?"

The question disheartened her. She answered to no one, particularly in respect to whom she could or could not befriend. Surely they were both well past the age of family approval. She shook her head, as much to dismiss the question as to answer it.

Her dismay deepened to see Austen's dark eyes swim with a new warmth. "Russell Coates was squiring you about last fall. Is he still in the picture? I mean, are you free?"

Oh dear. Julia felt her cheeks cloud. While it was true she'd enjoyed a few lovely outings with Russell, their pleasure in each other's company stemmed mostly from a shared love of books. As Julia was often the only woman in bibliophilic circles, her book friends were invariably men— but not de facto prospective lovers. Why would people always hobble friendship between the sexes with romantic expectations?

Much as she liked Austen, whatever romantic feelings she might have harbored for him—mild to weak, she realized in that instant— withered in the glare of what his question assumed. Austen was, perhaps unknowingly, in search of a wife. As far as Julia could tell, marriage was a bargain in which the woman paid dearly for dubious benefits. Ready as she was to again enjoy a man's company, Julia would never relinquish her freedom for it. She must be as free within love as without it.

"He's in New Mexico, I believe. I'm not attached, if that's what you're asking. And I have no wish to be. I much prefer life without corsets of any kind."

Curiosity lit his smile. "*Très moderne*, Mizz K.," he said, in a voice thick with a charming huskiness. "*Très moderne.*"

As she expected, the light was on in Julia's bedroom when she returned. Christophine would be sitting upright on the bed, notions and bits of fabric spread out around her. For years that had been how she liked to work, and the bed in the maid's room here was too narrow. The initial inconvenience had quickly become a companionable pleasure, reminiscent of those distant days when the top-floor nursery had been their private domain. Julia made two weak gin fizzes (which was all Christophine would drink) at the library trolley and joined her.

Christophine mumbled a greeting through lips bristling with pins. She was freshening a hat; already she had a new gentleman friend to impress. Every Sunday she stepped out with friends at the Church of the Freedom

Road to Glory Everlasting, a dozen jubilant West Indians who met twice a week above a barbershop in Brooklyn. Her new gentleman was a fellow Trinidadian named Calvin Otto, a widower with two grown daughters.

"Divine," Julia said about the hat, setting Christophine's glass on the bedside table.

"Hmmm," Christophine agreed as she laid the hat aside and transferred the pins to her left cuff. She sipped her drink, then yelped. Eyes wide, she exclaimed that she'd forgotten to get fresh eggs for tomorrow morning.

The mention of domestic duties startled Julia as well. She waved it away, reminded of her earlier observation about Negroes disappearing from white minds beneath invisible roles as maids, porters, and such. She hadn't immediately thought of Christophine at the time, remembering her only tardily on reflection. In truth she rarely thought of Christophine as either a Negro or domestic help. Was that good or bad? She did pay attention to her, often deeply, but how much did she truly register of Christophine's life, her hopes and fears and all else she held close inside herself?

She sat on the edge of the bed and lifted one of Fee's feet, rubbing her thumb along the arch, where an ache often settled after a long day. "If you could change anything in your life, Fee, what would it be?"

"More hands," she joked as she resumed sewing, needle moving in smooth arcs above her lap. "Or better toes." She nudged Julia with her free foot.

"I'm serious."

"Why you be serious? My life be fine, thank you." Then her needle paused. "Why?" She studied Julia's face.

"I've been thinking about last night's frock, how people noticed it. Your talents are wasted doing housework when you could be doing this." Julia stroked the hat's embroidered brim.

Swift currents glinted beneath Christophine's dark eyes. Julia was prepared for the usual skepticism but went on when she heard none. "We can find someone else to help with the household when we're settled again."

Still Christophine said nothing. Julia massaged her other foot. "You know there's nothing you'd rather be doing or that you're better at."

Joy flared in Fee's eyes. She loved compliments as much as anyone.

"You're a modiste," Julia said. "Or you could be, if you accepted clients." They'd often danced around this point in the past, each time Christophine yearning for more to do but then drawing back in fear of public scrutiny.

Christophine took in a sharp breath, a Scandinavian tic she'd learned from Julia's mother. It was an emphatic but also reluctant yes. Agreeing and resisting in one gulp of air.

"I have my best job already," she said. "Fancies just my fun."

Julia heard anxiety beneath the usual protest. It was easy to forget that Christophine was nearly forty. The prospect of a clean slate, the fresh horizons that so energized Julia, might loom as a frightening uncertainty to her. Christophine had always been one to avoid surprises, reduce risks. She was the one who made careful arrangements, ensured the larder was stocked, watched the clock when appointments loomed. She valued stability, even predictability. Her sewing came out only when the household was in order. No wonder the idea of forgoing her easy and familiar job to instead take in work, especially work that depended on taste and fashion, seemed a mad, unnecessary plunge.

Julia jiggled her ankle. "Of course you'll have a home with me—forever, I hope. Always. But we both made this move to see if something new and wonderful could happen. You might just try it, like I'm trying to make something of Capriole. It could be better, Fee. You could take only as much work as you'd like, and for good money. I'd insist you charge not a penny less than what I paid Lila."

As she spoke, a rare thing happened. Christophine's busy hands slowed, then lay lax in her lap. Fingers stalled inside the forgotten hat, her gaze softened to a smudge. It meant she was far away in her mind, thinking hard, but whether she was looking back or looking forward, Julia could not tell.

CHAPTER 7

"Swish it like there's no tomorrow, Mrs. Clark!" Standing well clear of his guest's flying heels, Pablo Duveen assessed the whisk of her backside. "All elbows and feet. Those knees will take care of themselves. That's it. Now you've got it. Faster! Let's hear those tassels hum." Jacket off, cuffs dangling loose, Duveen stood panting as his pupil pumped her arms and legs in a commotion of crepe de chine and swirling strands of twisted silk.

A week had passed since the party in Liveright's offices. Julia gripped her drink and leaned away from the Charleston lesson gathering force on the oriental rug in Duveen's apartment. She and Austen sat on a narrow green velvet sofa pushed to one edge of the large rug, across from Max Clark, the other half of the tourist couple from San Francisco. Short and muscular, with gray temples and eyes the color of stone, Max looked at least twenty years older than his wife, Dolly. He'd waved off Duveen's fulsome introduction and said he was in forest products.

"Let's go." Duveen grabbed Dolly's hand, spun her around, and matched her pace, eight limbs akimbo. They pounded and flailed, too intent to speak, until the phonograph record ended in a scratchy whine. Duveen collapsed into a smoking chair.

Dolly fell onto the Chesterfield sofa, bouncing against her husband. Her mauve dress was an expensive confection of beads and tiered fringe, cut low in both front and back. Without a flattening bandeau, her plump cleavage jiggled about with unfashionable freedom. Alerted by the dip of Julia's eyes, she tugged her bodice back into place. "Just wait'll my friends see this. They'll think I picked up a touch of something colored, like measles, only fun." She flopped back, heels sprawled out across the rug, fanny in danger of following them with a thud onto the floor.

Duveen mopped at his forehead, gasps hissing through his teeth. "Your turn next, Miss Kydd? I'm an excellent teacher. Learned it straight from a Negro myself."

Julia thanked him but declined. Six years of ballet study—indifferently pursued and happily abandoned—had ruined her taste for anything so riotous. She liked the more vigorous dance steps but seldom entered the sweaty fray herself.

Duveen placed a different record on the phonograph, releasing the mournful wails of a blues ballad. He refreshed the Clarks' drinks while the eerie keening filled the room.

"Mamie Smith," he said. "'Crazy Blues,' the first big race record. I'm learning everything I can about Negroes these days—I'll be a professor of all things Ethiop soon, and even then it won't be enough." He took a gulp of his gin. "I'm quite addicted."

Julia imagined Eva's beautiful eyes rolling heavenward. Dolly's remark was ludicrous enough, but Pablo's zeal reminded Julia of the most extreme bibliophiles who loved books so much they called their favorite volumes mistresses and their libraries seraglios. Such outsize obsession was skin crawling enough for inanimate objects, but Duveen was extolling the supposed attributes of an entire swath of humanity. In idolizing all Negroes, he seemed not to truly know a single one.

Dolly asked, "What got you so interested in coloreds, Mr. Duveen?"

"Pablo," he reminded her. He rose and searched along the lower shelves of the bookcase. "I've known them all my life, naturally, but I never gave them much thought until last fall, when I read the most extraordinary book. Walter White's *The Fire in the Flint*. Do you know it?"

He pulled out a book bound in purple cloth with orange-and-turquoise artwork stamped on its front board and spine. Its bumped corners were badly frayed. "I've badgered so many friends about it that my copy doesn't look like much anymore," he said with a wink at Julia as he handed it to Dolly, "but this book showed me a new kind of Negro. It's about a colored physician in the South, facing *affreux* obstacles and injustices. Sensational stuff—you must read it."

Dolly turned it front to back. She stared at its title page as if it were in Greek.

"Turns out the author lives up in Harlem, so I had to meet him straightaway. To my amazement the man can chat as easily about Proust or Debussy as any Yale man. He and his wife gave the most elegant tea party for me, where I met a crowd of Negroes every bit as intelligent and cultured as you or I. All the talk about natural Nordic superiority is sheer horsefeathers—as anyone would see if they spent an hour with these people.

"But here's the remarkable thing. I also rediscovered Harlem. Just a taxi ride away and yet another country, full of marvelous things. Not only French-speaking, Schubert-playing doctors and lawyers but endlessly fascinating ordinary people too. They can turn squalor and vice into an eye-popping, head-spinning party. Just walk into any Harlem club after midnight."

"They can sure dance," Dolly said.

"There's more to it than that." Duveen took his book from her hands. "Even the most cerebral Negro's soul is fired by passion. They can create art with their bodies, from some deep, primitive instinct for it, without first thinking it to death." He returned the volume to the shelf, then turned and punched out his words like a roused preacher. "We've become all brains and no bodies. We need Negroes to sound a drumbeat in our blood. I'm telling you, we should watch them, learn from them— we should honor and applaud them—we should shine *their* shoes!"

Julia studied her drink. She didn't dare meet Austen's eye. It was hard to know how much of Pablo's evangelism to take seriously. He did nothing by halves. He spoke to startle and amaze, to keep his name forever fresh in gossip columns and cocktail conversations. This speech would certainly make the rounds in San Francisco soon.

Max Clark flicked ash into a heavy cut-crystal tray. "You're some booster, Mr. Duveen."

"Can't we get a wiggle on?" Dolly hugged her arms.

"Soon, Dolly, soon." Duveen took a framed photograph from the piano. "But first consider," he said, thrusting it at the Clarks. "That's Walter and Gladys."

He towered over them as they peered. "But Pablo," Dolly said, "they're white people."

Duveen whooped. "A tickle, no?" He showed the photograph to Julia and Austen. "Race is a funny thing. Just like us, Negroes come in all shades. Mulattoes like the Whites—and I swear that really is their name—are called yellow or tan. We call them olive if they're a tad darker, like Mr. Hurd here."

An obliging smile dented Austen's left cheek. Julia looked away quickly to stifle another laugh. Who was more ridiculous at the moment, Duveen flourishing his self-anointed mantle of authority, or she and the others lined up like schoolchildren gaping at his earnest lecture?

"The medium shades," Pablo went on, spouting his new expertise, "range from copper and cocoa to nut brown and seal, plus chestnut and coffee and even maroon. The poor darkest ones are called blue, charcoal, or ebony. You may think these are just a dozen clever ways to split those nappy hairs, but those shades matter—right up and down their own tough little social scale. It's quite a caste system, as you'll see tonight. Virtually everyone working in the clubs will be colored, but many will look utterly white. Chorus girls are strictly tans or yellows. Waiters might be coffee colored or sealskins, and the door boys and hounds in the kitchen might be so dark they're called eight balls and inks."

Max Clark rattled the ice in his glass as the ponderous lesson settled over them. Julia pinched her wrist and ignored the jitter of Austen's shoulders. Duveen beamed to display his prize nuggets of knowledge—a smug grin—yet Julia knew from Eva's account of these color strictures that the social hierarchy could be oppressive indeed. She had to wonder again at the paradox: so many whites were naturally darker than Eva, including Austen and Philip, who'd turn a good olive or even copper after a few weeks on the Riviera. Something else, more inscrutable and important than skin color, determined race. It made the whole notion suddenly feel specious, a grand and preposterous hoax, and yet the stakes could not be higher.

"So then." Duveen returned the photograph to the piano. "Our first stop tonight will be Carlotta's. You'll feel plenty of steam when Eva Pruitt sings, Dolly. She's a scorcher. She's also written her first novel—not for the faint of heart. It's got a taste of the more scabrous Harlem goings-on, not just the razzle-dazzle. For people who can't get there in person, Eva's book will be the next best thing. We're hoping it really pops some corks, and I don't just mean sell lots of copies." He rapped his knuckles for luck on the gleaming wood.

Julia remembered Eva's anxious precautions about the manuscript. Presumably by now the necessary bank accounts had been set up, the funds transferred, and the manuscript safely delivered to Goldsmith's offices.

"Before we go, a quick word about Carlotta's. The owner is a dicey fellow named Leonard Timson. Like most of the bosses in Harlem, he's up to his eyeballs in shady doings. He did a couple of years in Sing Sing, for God knows what, and is not to be trifled with. Filthy rich too, but one doesn't ask about that."

Shady doings? Eva had only called him a stinker. Perhaps the "filthy rich" part was meant to impress the Clarks.

He shot Max a pointed look. "Timson loves to show off his club to bigwigs. When I told him I was bringing you tonight, Max, he invited us to sit at his table—quite the honor. You'll be expected to spend lavishly, but then you'll be entertained royally in return."

Max nodded, and Dolly squeaked. Her third martini was nearly gone. At this rate she would remember little of her excursion.

"Carlotta's is the swankiest club we'll see tonight. From there I thought we'd move on to Bamville or the Band Box. We'll finish up at a shocking little place called the Sugar Bowl to catch their breakfast show. I promise a night you'll never forget."

The Clarks looked heartened by the pep talk, as if they were heading into battle.

Duveen clapped his hands on his thighs. "Shall we be off? The sirens of Harlem beckon."

Dolly sprang up like a college girl after a touchdown. "Oh yes, oh yes," she chanted as Max draped a silver fox across her shoulders. "Sirens, Maxie!"

⁓

The street in front of Carlotta's was clogged with expensive motorcars arriving from the south. Duveen's entourage rode in a spacious limousine the Clarks had hired for the evening. Their driver maneuvered into the line of cars disgorging bejeweled occupants, and within a few minutes they too stood on the pavement of West 135th Street, inhaling the exotic spring air of Harlem. Duveen spoke to the driver, and the motor pulled away, to await them later.

Dolly looped her hands around Max's forearm and gazed up at a marquee lit by thousands of yellow bulbs proclaiming CARLOTTA'S in a florid script. Austen leaned toward Julia. "I was born in Harlem," he whispered. "Think they'd pay for my autograph?"

Tented sidewalk boards boasted that inside awaited "the cream of Harlem's creole talent, the finest sepia stars, and a chorus of bronze beauties!" Down the block two more clubs thrust bright canopies over the sidewalk, luring in patrons like bees to lilies. Between the cabarets the pavement receded into shadow, obscuring the hand-lettered signs of daytime commerce: affordable shoe repair, men's shaves and haircuts for a dime, and the services of a beautician trained in the patented hair-straightening system of Mrs. C. J. Walker. But at midnight the street blazed with brilliance, mirrored in the slow glide of passing windows, the swirl of beads and gems, and the glint of silver flasks consulted one last time before their owners disappeared under the clubs' awnings.

The crowd jostled them forward. Julia stepped aside to pause before a large poster announcing, CARLOTTA'S OWN HARLEM ANGEL . . . EVANGELINE PRUITT! A soft-focus painting depicted Eva in a provocative profile, her head arched back as she balanced on a floor cushion, arms around one raised knee while her braceleted other leg extended out. She wore a filmy gown that fell open to reveal an unblemished thigh. Her head was wrapped in a gold headdress with tall white feathers, and enormous gold hoops hung from her ears. The artist had painted the phantom shape of large, unnaturally upturned, and cone-like breasts, adding the clear thrust of massive nipples beneath the sheer wash of gold. It was impossible not to stare at the anatomical absurdity. Although skillfully rendered, the painting's taste was brazen, even vulgar. Julia's cheeks heated. Eva was beautiful enough. Why graft her gentle face onto this parody of a body? The answer streamed past: customers, wealthy and eager, crowds of them.

Duveen swept past the poster, probably for the hundredth time, a Clark tucked under each arm. Two stony doormen scanned them and stepped aside as Julia and Austen followed, inside and up a flight of carpeted stairs to a second set of doors, opened for them by another imposing pair of uniformed Negroes.

"That was easy," Austen said. "Good thing you wore all those diamonds." Julia wore her mother's engagement ring and her favorite sapphire earrings, but her jewels fell far short of Dolly Clark's—or those of many patrons, she realized, as they adjusted to the club's dim light and babble: voices, laughter, and occasional rockets of champagne corks.

The room was much larger than the street front had suggested. A low stage jutted into the center, surrounded by a giant horseshoe space filled with small tables, all draped in white cloths. Two steps up, a mezzanine of upholstered banquettes ringed the club. Several tall replicas of palm trees spiked toward murals of a forest canopy overhead. Suspended fans stirred the palms' fronds, their shadows, murky with smoke, moving across the painted ceiling like the ceaseless current of a Manhattan Amazon.

In the noisy buzz between shows, the floor teemed with waiters bearing silver trays laden with orders or cleared debris. Austen and Julia were ushered to a round table in the center of the room, directly in front of the stage. Max and Dolly Clark were already seated, a silver ice bucket beside them. Duveen greeted Goldsmith and gestured him into the adjacent seat. Ogling the room, the Clarks paid no attention when Austen and Julia were served champagne from their bottle.

Austen lifted his glass and touched its rim to Julia's. "To Oregon timber."

"And Harlem hoopla." They spoke sotto voce, even though no one was paying them any attention. If the Clarks were tourists, Julia felt like a stowaway on their voyage to the Camelot Pablo called "Ethiop," watching their fawning delight from the forgotten shadows.

"Here we go," Austen whispered, eyeing a corpulent man about to join their table. "The dicey fellow himself."

Duveen scrambled up more quickly than his bulk might suggest. "Mr. Timson. It's an honor."

Timson positioned his chair with his back to the stage and welcomed them to Carlotta's, "the finest entertainment this side of Paris or Berlin." He was middle aged, with a cowlick pushing sand-colored hair up from his right temple. His eyes were small and wide set. Between his brows ran a strong vertical dent that suggested either perpetual confusion or anger. There was something ominous to the look of Eva's boss. Julia was no shrinking violet, but she was beginning to understand that Eva, despite her trusting and gentle demeanor, was far more seasoned than she in the rough ways of the world. Eva apparently took men like Timson in her stride.

Timson lifted his hand, and a waiter materialized at his shoulder. "Like our champagne, Mr. Clark? That one's on the house. Want more?

Good. Keep it coming, Leroy. And tell the kitchen to send whatever's particularly fine tonight."

They were beset with another ice bucket and two more bottles, each uncorked and poured into shallow glasses all around. An array of dishes followed, including platters piled with deep-fried chicken and pork ribs bathed in a red sauce. Dolly Clark exclaimed at what she called the jungle food and filled plates for herself and Max. Julia chose a small tournedos of beef, wrapped in fatty bacon. On closer inspection it was overcooked.

She was still chewing when the lights dimmed. A tuxedoed orchestra at the rear of the stage awoke with a wailing high note, trumpets over winds. The crowd instantly quieted.

Julia had no sooner wondered why champagne had been poured for the vacant place to her right than a figure eased into the seat. In the fading light she saw a man of about forty, blond hair brilliantined back from his forehead. His evening jacket was perfectly cut and pressed. When he reached for the glass, a starched white cuff, anchored by a gold monogrammed stud, emerged from his sleeve. He leaned a shoulder toward Julia and whispered a brief apology for his late arrival. She nodded, observing the complex scent borne by his cheek. French.

The man twisted to look at her. His arm moved across his lap, and he took her hand. "Martin Wallace," he breathed. His eyes were blue, alert. He did not smile. He continued to hold her hand as Julia murmured her name in reply. He leaned closer to listen. His grasp faintly rolled her fingers like the swell of an ocean wave. The scent brushed her again as he repeated her name before straightening to face the dark stage.

Without moving her eyes from the spotlighted orchestra, Julia saw every contour of his immaculate head, motionless beside her. She registered the spotless gleam of his collar, the heat of the shoulder not two inches from hers. When she reached for her glass, he mirrored her movement—the stretched arm, the lingering sip—but his eyes also never left the stage.

The fabled Carlotta's floor show had begun.

CHAPTER 8

The orchestra settled into a lively jazz melody, and a column of pink feathers streamed onto the stage from each far corner, joining in front of their table. Costumed in lavish headdresses, skirts of three-foot-long feathers, and glittering halters, twenty or more dancers whirled and dipped through a complicated pattern of maneuvers. They seemed almost printed, to Julia's bookish mind, each was so alike: tall, lithe, and pale. Arms linked, they ebbed and flowed toward the audience, huge smiles and high-focused eyes never faltering.

Applause swept the dancers back through the curtains as the music shifted. Two comical figures in padded raggedy clothes and tar-black painted faces bounded toward center stage, bellowing an exaggerated dialect. After their nonsensical repartee set the audience to laughing, the comedians broke into a more intelligible but still dizzying dialogue. Each wore a huge wig of woolly Negro hair. Pointing to her partner's nest of kinky curls, the woman bawled, "Man, you got mailman hair!"

"Mailman hair?" the man shrieked. "Whachu mean, inky pink?"

"Each knot's got izzown route!"

The audience roared. The man pranced around his partner and sang, "Child, yah hair looks mighty good."

The woman patted the stiff hanks, ironed flat in the current fashion, covering her ears. "Yeah? Well, Madame Walker just been over."

Her partner gripped her shoulder and spun her around, where the back of her hair was every bit as full and springy as his own. "Yeah? Well, she fuhgot t' walk through yuh kitchen."

Her hands flew up to wrestle the wad into a bandana scarf, the audience hooting and clapping. The act went on for several more minutes, their mugging and startling slang reducing the crowd to helpless laughter.

Julia had been to several cabarets in Paris and London. This show was similar in its pace and kaleidoscopic variety, with lavish chorus numbers blending into dancing blending into a ballad blending into comedy, and so on. She knew that, as a headliner, Eva would have the most extravagant number, likely near the end.

In fact, when Eva did appear, Julia did not at first recognize her. Following the tap-dancing Barney Brothers—who repeatedly leaped high into the air, newsboy caps secured low over one eye, and landed with heels skating in opposite directions across the polished floor—the stage went dark and silent.

The lights came up on a tight huddle of half-naked men in the center of the stage. They made a great knot of muscle and bone that began to throb to a low drumbeat, soon joined by a clarinet's sullen sob. As the men began to dance, writhing as a single pulsing form, their deep voices wordlessly echoed the drum's throb in a counterpoint rhythm. Bare feet sliding in an intricate weaving motion, the circle slowly released first one thrusting arm and then another, and another, each fissure revealing glimpses of something shiny and motionless in its center. The mound began to sway in a slow-drifting circle, then spin. In some impossible choreography, the men danced faster and faster, heads and arms still knit together at the shape's center. The pounding of their feet rocked the floor. Julia steadied her chair's slight wobble. The whirling form seemed about to fly apart when, with a clash of cymbals, it suddenly froze. The men sprang up to their full heights, arms outstretched. With another cymbal strike they lunged toward the center again, then arched back, their thighs straining as shoulders hovered over heels. They teetered in tense balance, spines curved in crouching backward Cs.

Julia realized her mouth was open. Her heart hammered. It was impossible not to be caught in the swirling web of energy. It was a human fountain, a spring of life and power bubbling up out of some inchoate form and finally bursting free. A creation myth? There was something frightening in the sheer power of this potent mass blooming into men. Julia moistened her lips and folded her hands, glad for the darkness. She was an adult. She mustn't gape like a five-year-old at whatever spectacle came next.

Another keening high note from a single clarinet. One thin white arm, its hand splayed wide, rose from a folded mound of flickering gold. Slowly a head appeared above the men's splayed forms. Beneath a fantastic headdress of heaped gold chiffon, fixed by thin gold chains draped across her brow and over her ears, Eva's face emerged. A few loose layers floated to her shoulders. Expressionless, eyes closed, she rose, slowly unfurling her body's full length. Her shoulders and arms were bare, but her torso and legs were swathed in more gold chiffon, secured by long coils of chain that circled her hips, waist, ribs, and throat. From each chain-wrapped wrist hung a polished gold ball the size of a tangerine. No part of Eva moved. Except for a faint pulse at the base of her throat, it was as if she'd left her body.

Julia felt a painful dissonance in her own shallow breathing. Her cheeks burned. She tried to see Eva through the dramatic lighting, tried to separate her from this unsettling scene. It was as if Eva—no, her body—had become a thing, some kind of trophy offered up for the spellbound audience. Two emotional undercurrents swirled in Julia's pulse. One was horror that the Eva she knew had been so effaced. The other was a subversive pleasure to think Eva had retreated, that she was distancing herself. It was her body, her performance, but it wasn't *her*. She'd even said as much the other evening. In a way, the scene enacted the humbling impotence everyone felt when forced to yield to those with greater power: the child asking pardon from an unjust adult, the doorman thanking a rude guest. Retreat—holding back one's *self*—was the only sanctuary. No wonder Eva dreamed of going to Paris. Of taking her money and escaping into the relatively benign life of a writer.

The room fell silent. Eva stood erect, both arms raised, the gold balls swaying from her hands. She began to sing. The sound came from deep in her throat, a wavering moan to answer the men's throbbing chant. Her eyes drifted open, their gaze fixed high over the audience, and the music focused into song. Her voice had an ethereal quality, gaining clarity as it rose. The words of her song were so lost in the extraordinary timbre of her voice that only occasional fragments crystallized into a language Julia could understand. Over and over the phrase recurred: *I'm just a slave of love.* A dozen variations of it flowed through Eva's lungs, her voice at times seizing, at other times rumbling.

I'm just a slave to love
Why do I crave his love?
I can't be saved by love
Only betrayed by love
I'm just a slave to love

She began to move, the billow of weightless chiffon a cruel contrast to her chained torso. Bending back into the arms of two men, she thrust her right leg high and laid her ankle on the lowered shoulder of one of the dancers so that the chiffon fell away to her hip. Glinting in the harsh light was a thick gold cuff locked above her ankle. The slow dance continued, accompanied by a single drumbeat, the men's chanting, Eva's cries and moans, and the metallic clink of chains. As the pace quickened, two of the men took hold of her arms and seized the gold spheres swinging from her palms. They began to circle Eva's outstretched arms, gradually unwinding the coiled chain as they danced. The choreography grew more frenzied, and the music, including Eva's voice, gained power.

I'm just a sla-a-a-a-ve to love.

Soon all the dancers were leaping in tight circles around Eva, who dipped and spun furiously. Yards and yards of the thin, gleaming chain tumbled into the arms of her attendants.

The frenzied music and motion held the audience spellbound. Julia too caught her breath as she realized Eva's shroud would drop to her feet when she was freed from the final loop of chain.

The scene froze. With agonizing tenderness a single dancer completed the last three circuits of Eva's now-motionless body. She stood with her back to the audience, feet apart and arms again raised high, palms upturned. The last swath of chiffon slipped and wobbled. Finally, in silence, it drifted to the floor. Eva stood still as a statue, her back white as marble. She wore only her headdress and a thin halter and loincloth of pale-gold silk.

Julia wanted to look away but could not. Silence roared in her ears. The room was too hot. She felt as trapped as Eva, seduced by the luminous beauty of this terrible dance of conquering power. Facing Eva and the rapt audience, the dancer held out his armload of gold chain, which spilled over his forearms. A rustle swept the room: the end of the chain did not hang free. It was still connected to Eva. As the murmur grew, she threw back her chin. She shook her head to loosen the filmy chiffon of her headdress and rattle the chains draped over her ears. At last she turned to face the crowd.

For one stunned moment in the narrowed spotlight, everyone saw: the remaining chain dangled from a gold loop sewn to her halter so that it appeared to be pierced through Eva's left breast. Then she grasped the chain coiled about her ear and tugged it free. The piled chiffon floated down, hiding her features in a diaphanous cloud. Gasps and cheers erupted.

A shower of gold rings clattered at Eva's feet. Julia twisted her jaw to ease the pressure inside her ears, like after a sudden plummet. Her bones felt hollow, pliant, as if she might slither to the floor if she foolishly tried to stand. What exactly had she just witnessed? For a moment she was aware of nothing but that last searing vision.

A whirlwind seemed to buffet the place. Julia registered the visceral power of dance and music and theater to commandeer the breath, and also a fresh wave of horror. It wasn't the erotic aspect per se—Julia had seen other risqué acts on the burlesque stage—but the scene itself, so enveloping one might not see it at all. There was something abhorrent about this gilded evocation of slavery, performed by Negro artists at the direction of rich white men who grew richer from it every night. That was the true obscenity. Julia cooled her face with her palms. It was almost another kind of slavery, violence disguised as art. She couldn't make more sense of it than that. Not yet.

Everywhere around her patrons were flinging tiny rings onto the stage. Shouting "E-va, E-va," they stood and cheered. Duveen reached for a small bowl of hollow rings in the center of the table, apparently provided for this purpose, and gleefully tossed a handful toward Eva's shrouded form. Both Max and Dolly welcomed the supply Duveen emptied into their palms and wildly threw them into the melee.

Wallace simply covered his champagne glass as errant rings bounced onto their table. Julia reached shakily to do the same.

The stage lights faded into darkness, and thunderous applause broke out. Shouts pulsing Eva's name brought her back through the curtains. She bowed her head twice and disappeared again as the house lights came up.

Timson sat back. Looking squarely at Max Clark, he said, "What'd I tell you? Hot show, in't she? Only in Harlem, folks, only in Harlem."

Dolly swallowed. "Oh my." Dark spots on her cheeks mottled the rosier tints carefully laid on earlier that evening. "It's so, so—" She struggled to find a bold word.

Taking her discomposure as a compliment, Timson brought his heavy forearm down on the table with satisfaction. He nodded as Duveen added exuberant praises. Goldsmith said nothing, but his color had deepened. But then no one could remain unaffected by what they'd just witnessed, so close they could see the trails of perspiration disappearing into the folds of performers' costumes and smell the sweat that misted the air with each kick and spin.

"Pure jungle energy!" Duveen crowed, to no one in particular. "Primitive splendor, jam-packed in one spectacular show!"

Timson acknowledged this with a wave. "Hey, folks, want you to meet an old friend, Martin Wallace. Watch this fella. He'll be Senator Wallace one of these days. It's a real honor to have him join us."

Wallace demurred at the praise and circled the table, shaking hands as Duveen introduced their party. Resettling beside Julia, he refilled her glass before his own and told Clark he'd done considerable business out West. This and that. Clark's interest was reply enough, and the two men conversed across the table for a few minutes.

Leroy appeared at Timson's elbow. Following his employer's nod, he silently circled the table and slipped a folded bill beside Max Clark's glass.

"I understand you folks intend to visit some of our more quaint neighborhood establishments tonight," Timson said, standing. Around them other patrons milled about, greeting friends, placing orders, and seeking the lavatories. "But you're welcome to stop by my private rooms upstairs, meet my little songbird. You too, Marty, if you got a minute. Let's show Clark here some Harlem hospitality. I'll tell Eva to come up."

Duveen sent a furtive look of triumph toward Max Clark, who nodded to acknowledge that the rare privilege might cost him. Duveen thanked Timson and promised they'd be up shortly.

Timson grunted and walked away. Clark dismissed the hovering Leroy with a careless toss of bills onto the table.

CHAPTER 9

One didn't simply stop by Timson's rooms. A pair of guards, guns bulging visibly beneath their open jackets, barred the stairs. They slid rough paws over the men's torsos and thighs, taking brusque inventory of seams and accessories. Just as coarsely they palpated Julia's and Dolly's small handbags.

Julia had never been so close to a gun. Duveen's mention of Timson's shady past had been offhand, as if warning them of a limp or tremor one mustn't stare at. But there was nothing benign or simply awkward about the guns less than an arm's length away. They were worn openly, not even buttoned inside a coat. In one swift motion these men could become killers. More importantly, those guns were the first (and only) thing you understood about them. They wanted you to be afraid. And she was—of anyone who wielded fear as a weapon more powerful than the gun itself.

When satisfied no one posed a threat, one of the guards escorted them up another long flight of stairs. A landing halfway up opened to a narrow, dim hallway, silent but for the flutter of costumes and scurrying heels. Another sentinel stood at this landing, arms crossed and feet planted. He too scanned them carefully before allowing them to climb the last dozen steps up to Timson's private sanctum.

Baroque sconces bathed the room in the greenish light of a troll king's grotto. Two sofas faced each other across a low table, and an oak bar festooned with sinewy carvings bracketed the far wall, an opulent altar promising refreshments as bottomless as those downstairs. Behind the bar hung a large painting of leering satyrs and taunting nymphs in the overwrought style of Böcklin or Rops, in a massive gilt frame. Julia fought not to smile. How Philip would yelp at the sight of it. Only yesterday he'd neglected his lunch—Christophine's salmon terrine—for a spirited diatribe on such symbolist claptrap, whose emotional excesses he despised (though not more, he'd decided, than Boucher's insipid cupids). His tastes in art were more modern than Julia's—a bracing discovery, clarifying as a splash of ice water—yet even Philip would appreciate the sight of this voluptuous painting presiding over the lair of a Harlem gangster. She couldn't wait to tell him.

Wallace stood near the bar, deftly pouring champagne into waiting glasses. He greeted them all by name with an expression that was cordial yet composed, neither guarded nor eager. He looked directly into Julia's eyes as for the second time that evening he spoke her name. It was quiet, respectful. "Miss Kydd." Did she imagine a resonance? In the next moment he greeted Austen, Duveen, and Goldsmith. She wished there had been time to talk with him earlier, downstairs before the show. What might they have said to each other, in that instant when their hands had met?

Timson scooped up the glasses, spilling what his friend had so skillfully poured, and distributed them to his guests. The second bottle had just been opened when Eva emerged from a door painted to blend into the adjacent wall, trailing Jerome Crockett behind her. Dressed in the blue uniform of the hall guards, he slipped behind the bar and took up a small white towel. Wiping the spotless counter in slow circles, he avoided Julia's eye and gave no clue that he knew at least three of the guests in the room.

Eva greeted each guest with dazzling warmth. She embraced Duveen and kissed Julia's cheek. When they settled onto the couches, Jerome remained behind the bar, silent and forgotten. Wallace too remained apart, leaning against the bar as he rolled the thin stem of his glass between his thumb and forefinger. Timson sat on the arm of one of the sofas and pulled Eva to his knee, her chiffon dressing gown lapping over his shoes.

"You were swell tonight, baby," he said, planting a loud kiss on her cheek. He ran a finger along her throat. "Pretty neck needs something more. One of those nice necklaces you got."

"They're at home, Mr. Timson." She smiled and pushed his finger away.

"You got some beauties. I bet Mrs. Clark here would love to see one of them dazzlers."

"You know they're not here, Leonard."

Timson drained his champagne. "You earned those fancy rocks, you oughta show them off."

She demurred again, but he rose and sauntered to the bar. At his approach Jerome stepped back, receding into the farthest corner. Timson swung aside the Böcklin painting, revealing a square wall safe. He twisted the combination lock, opened the door, and pulled out a large, ornately inlaid wood box. He lowered it onto the bar with a show of caution. "Open it, punkin seed."

Eva stood, her face stormy, all gracious charm gone. "How did you get that? It's mine, Leonard. You had no right to take it. Give it back."

She took a step forward, and he swung an elbow, as if to fend her off. Whatever he had taken was important to Eva. Her jewelry? The room quieted.

"Who pays the rent for that place, punkin? That's all the right I need." Timson played with the lock as he spoke, and then he flicked aside the latch. It was broken, hanging from a single hinge.

"No!" Eva jerked out a hand in protest. "You can't do that. You can't go through my private things. That case was locked. It's mine, and everything in it is mine."

He lifted the lid, set aside the top tray of brooches, and drew out a sheaf of papers, tied with string.

"Wait!" Eva cried, but without effect.

The manuscript. It had to be. Eva's hidden treasure. Julia had seen plenty of manuscripts before, and this one was ordinary enough, a stack of typewritten pages, corners bumped from handling. But the way Timson gripped it made Julia hold her breath. Something about it angered him, just as Eva had feared.

"No!" Eva objected. "That's private."

He waved the bundle in the air. "*Harlem Angel*, by Evangeline Pruitt. Real special, huh?"

Her novel. Eva's prize, the achievement that would proclaim her name in print by Christmas. Julia held her breath. There was a perilous vulnerability to manuscripts that only those in the book business truly understood. Those papers represented hundreds or thousands of hours of thought and effort, of writing and rewriting, of doubt and despair and determination. Yet all that creative labor was only as secure as the paper it was typed on. Unless Eva had made a carbon copy—Julia fervently hoped she had—Timson held absolute power over the fate of all that work, that unrepeatable labor. Thank God there was no fire in the room, or Julia might faint from fear of it thudding into its flames.

Duveen must have felt the same terror. He leaped to his feet. "Thanks! We've been dying to get our hands on this. Eva's going to be our next big thing." He extended a hand for the manuscript as casually as if Timson had just found his lost umbrella.

"Think so, Duveen?"

Duveen hesitated, stalled by the menace in Timson's voice. Sweat began to prickle Julia's scalp. Were the radiators on?

Eva reached for the manuscript, but Timson pulled it to his chest. "You take me for a grade A idiot? I hear you wrote a book—you think I'm not gonna wonder what's in it? You think I'm not gonna figure out where you stashed it and see for myself?" He chuckled. "You probably think a businessman like me ain't gonna read a goddamn book. But this one, now, it was—interesting."

"We can't wait to read it," Dolly Clark boomed, then giggled into her palm at the blast of her voice. "Pablo says it'll make you famous."

Eva forced a brittle laugh. "It's just a story, Leonard. Mr. Goldsmith and Mr. Duveen think it's good enough to publish. Isn't that wonderful? It might bring in more people, like the lady said, even though it's not *about* Carlotta's. Just something like—people will know that."

Timson smiled. "You think so? I ain't so sure. I bet folks will think exactly that you're talking about Carlotta's. About me."

He slapped the manuscript down onto the bar. The muscles in his jaw worked. "What's all that crap about dope and messin' up people? You know I treat my niggers just fine." He spat the vile word in Eva's face.

Julia choked on a gulp of air. Dolly Clark yelped like a startled parrot, splashing champagne onto Max's shoe.

Eva shot a nervous glance at Jerome, who watched in alert silence, his dark face melting into the shadows behind Wallace. "It's only a story. I made it up. It's not Carlotta's, and the owner, that Mr. Coburn, he isn't you."

"You'd be a pinked-up quiff if it weren't for me, and your boy'd be pushing a broom." Timson stabbed a squat thumb over his shoulder toward Jerome. "Some gratitude!"

Arms crossed, hands gripping his sleeves, Jerome dropped his eyes to the floor. Nothing in his face moved. Jerome the lauded poet. What language must be roiling in his mind, imperceptible beneath that smooth, subservient mask? Was it poetry or something more inchoate? Julia couldn't imagine the strength needed to accept one's own powerlessness. Yet she felt trapped too, pinned to the sofa as the drama played out in front of them.

Timson turned toward his guests. "Jungle energy, my ass. It's her job to grease your pants, and she's paid plenty to do it."

Eva composed her face. "Please, Mr.—"

"And that god-awful crap about that Coburn guy screwing her with his gun." His nostrils flared. "That's disgusting. That's—"

Julia's stomach flinched as she registered the obscene menace of Timson's words. It rustled through the others as well, with a chorus of disgusted coughs and snarls. Wallace took a deep breath, then lowered his chin and settled his gaze on the carpet. Behind him, Jerome's cheekbones seemed to contract, squeezing his eyes into black marbles.

"It's a story!" Eva spun toward Jerome. "It's *fiction*. No one will think it's true. I made it all up."

"Yeah, well, these babies don't know that." Timson waved toward the Clarks, whose eyes were large as coins. "They'll think Leonard Timson is some kinda monster who screws his gals with a gun."

Eva looked wildly around the room. "No, no. I promise they won't. No one will think that."

Timson pitched the manuscript back into the safe. He shoved the jewelry case and its tray in on top of it, spilling a pearl earring onto the floor, and slammed the door shut.

"Please, *please*," Eva begged. "That's mine. I need it. You can't just take my things!"

"You got a job, girl, and it don't need your brain. Stick to what I pay you for." He swung the heavy picture back into place and turned to his guests with a grim smile.

"But we've paid for that manuscript," Duveen squeaked. Julia wondered that he could speak at all. A snake of fear had closed around her own throat. "It belongs to Mr. Goldsmith now."

Timson's smile ripened. "No one paid me. It's in my safe; looks to me like it's mine. You been swindled if you paid this doll for something she don't have to sell." He paused. "But I'm a reasonable man. What's it worth to you, Goldsmith?"

Goldsmith sat on the edge of the sofa, his back rigid. He had not yet spoken, and he was the only man in the room whose forehead was not blistered with perspiration. "A manuscript belongs to its author, Mr. Timson."

Timson chortled. "That so? Let her sue me for it."

Goldsmith rose. "You will hear from our lawyers." His voice was cold and precise. "We will do everything in our power to secure Miss Pruitt's property for her. We will seek prosecution if necessary, despite the ridiculous cretins behind whom you attempt to hide."

"Ain't that just dandy. Some sissy kike in a purple shirt thinks he can talk like a big boy. You're never seeing that manuscript, fella. It's mine now. Wave it bye-bye." Timson flapped a toddler's gesture.

"This is not over." Fury whittled Goldsmith's words into needles. "Pablo, deal with this person."

With a slam that shook the doorframe, he was gone.

Duveen swiveled. "I'm afraid Arthur is right, Mr. Timson. Legally the manuscript is Eva's, and she's sold it to us." He swallowed and persevered in a high, pinched voice. "Our readers are sophisticated folks. They don't assume what's depicted is literally true. Good writers set a realistic stage, but what happens there comes from their imaginations. That realism is what gives good literature the power to resonate in readers' memory and to move them to sympathy."

This discourse on literary method sounded an absurd note in the hot room. Timson stared as if Duveen were a new comic auditioning to join his show.

Duveen took this as encouragement. "What's important is that such violence as Miss Pruitt depicts could happen, not that in fact it did. That rape scene is horrifying, yes, but it conveys the circumstances and dangers that a young woman might face in today's Harlem. Readers will have no reason to suspect the Coburn character is real, Mr. Timson. But it's vital that they believe such a fellow could exist, that such unspeakable acts could happen." He paused and added dramatically, "And even that they probably do."

Timson clapped twice. "Very pretty, Mister Professor. But full of crap. Could, would, did—makes no difference to me. Who cares about teacher ladies in Cleveland? Anybody in New York will sure as hell think she's dishing the hash on bad old Leonard Timson." His eyebrows rose as if challenging anyone to deny it. "Except they won't. Because they'll never read it." His triumphant gaze traveled from one face to another before reaching Eva. "No one will."

She met his eyes squarely. Julia saw determination in them, a resolve to reclaim what was rightly hers.

Then she sprang at him. Timson caught her raised arm and wrenched it behind her back. He gripped her hard against his chest, and she stilled. A gun was wedged under her cheekbone.

Julia heard herself gasp. Dolly Clark slapped both hands to her mouth. Duveen made a strange gulping noise. Jerome swallowed, but otherwise he remained motionless, still hidden behind Wallace.

Julia didn't see where the gun had come from. One instant Eva had been about to slap him, and the next she was pinned into place by a muzzle. When she tried to move, Timson drove the gun in deeper, pinching her eye into a terrified wedge of flesh. Then her eyelids sank shut. Her face went lax.

Julia could not pull her horrified gaze from Eva's limp face. Was this the look of someone who knew she was about to die? Was this how Julia's first sweetheart had looked as he'd resolved to kick away the chair? After three long years of fighting a war that would never end inside his head, had poor Gerald's face collapsed like this, in such fear and sorrow?

"Come, now."

Wallace's voice was like cream poured on a fiery dish. He moved from behind the bar and walked slowly toward Timson and Eva. Five soundless, patient, measured steps.

"Come now, Leonard. She meant no harm. Let her go." He reached for the gun.

Timson regripped. Eva squeaked like a pinched rabbit. Or perhaps the noise came from Dolly, or even Julia's own lungs.

Wallace scoffed gently. "You two need each other, am I not right? Forget that book; forget this little scene. Take a deep breath, both of you." His fingertip reached Eva's face. "Back to business? Eh?"

He slowly turned the gun away. Her jaw sagged to her shoulder, eyes still pressed shut. With a last twist Timson released Eva's arm and jabbed the gun back into its holster under his jacket. Wallace nudged Eva's chin, coaxing her to open her eyes and meet his own.

Timson shrugged. "Yeah, sure. Forget about that crazy book. No harm done." He wiped his palms. "Hey, folks, didn't mean for you to see a squabble. Employees, huh?" He reached for another bottle of champagne. "How about another drink?"

No one moved. Timson receded like a buzzing insect to the periphery of Julia's vision as she watched Wallace slip his arm around Eva. When she finally looked up, it was to Jerome. Both blood and expression had drained from her face.

"Eva, baby, go get ready," Timson said. "Take these ladies with you."

Wallace squeezed Eva's elbow before releasing it. "It will be all right," he said into her ear. She nodded once and disappeared through the side door without looking back. Julia followed, with Dolly Clark dragging on her arm for help in navigating the tilting floor.

Timson shooed them on and refilled the men's glasses. "More trouble than the little monkey's worth," he complained with a gusty chuckle.

CHAPTER 10

"Oh, sweetie, not so fast." Dolly Clark listed heavily against Julia, engulfing her in a cloud of Guerlain, perspiration, and belched champagne. "I'm not feeling so pink." Her cheeks had drained to a grayish white beneath a film of rouge. Julia struggled to keep her from drooping to the floor as they two-stepped into the back room. Someone shut the door behind them.

"Ohhh." Dolly surged forward when Eva stepped out of a lavatory. Dolly rushed to the toilet, shuddering with imminent sickness. Julia turned on a tap and closed the door to give the miserable woman some semblance of privacy.

Julia took Eva's hand and moved them away from the wrenching noises. It was clammy, despite the heat. Eva's eyes held the same deadened chill. Did she understand that her dreams might soon dissolve? "Did he hurt you?"

A muzzle-shaped pock flamed high on Eva's cheek. The answer was more air than sound. "Not really."

They were in some kind of exotic bedroom. A large bed dominated the far wall, piled with pillows. Everything was covered in black satin. They sat on its edge with a small bounce. Eva's hands shook as she opened a carved box on the nightstand and pulled out a fat hand-rolled cigarette. She lit it and inhaled, holding her breath for some moments before releasing a thread of smoke and extending the cigarette to Julia.

Eva kicked off her mules as Julia declined. She sat back and stretched out her legs, her turbaned skull settling against the black padded headboard. She drew deep puffs into her lungs, savoring every vapor. From hips to head she was completely pillowed in black satin, as if laid out at an undertaker's. She lay motionless, spine curled, eyes closed, breath faint.

"Eva?" Julia jiggled her friend's hand to rouse her from a dangerous lethargy. Was she in shock? Did she not fathom the dire reality of Timson's threat? He'd shoved a gun into her face.

Several seconds passed. When Eva opened her eyes, they were sheened with tears. Her voice was a mournful whisper. "Oh Lordy, I've queered that something royal."

Did she mean losing her manuscript? Surely Timson and his gun posed the greater concern. "Eva, you're not safe here. He might have killed you. You have to get away from him."

Eva looked as if Julia were the one who didn't understand. Her chin rose, and she spoke to the ceiling, her voice returned to its normal register. "I'm sorry you had to see that. But I'll fix it. I have to get my book back." She slid deeper into the bed's dark meringue and crossed her legs. One bare foot brushed Julia's calf.

"I don't see how you can, unless you know the combination to that safe." Julia lifted her voice—was there any chance?—but Eva simply closed her eyes. *No.*

"Do you have another copy?" Julia asked.

Eva's jaw swung to one side. "I should have. I know that. But I didn't think it was important, and Pablo kept suggesting things to add or take out. Carbons are just too much work, Julia. And messy." She lifted her fingertips. "One smudge, and Leonard would have asked what I was up to. And it was hard enough to hide one copy. Where would I have tucked another?"

Julia nodded. There was nothing to be done about it now. "Is there anyone who can help you?" At Eva's puzzled face she added, "Can

Jerome do something?" She forced it into a question, though she knew the answer.

Eva gaped at her with disbelief. "Jerome? He's a poet, not a fighter. And he's colored, Julia. If he'd raised so much as a finger in there, he'd be dead now, shot from three directions. He loves me, but he can't help with this." She squirmed. "Now Mr. Goldsmith's hopping mad too."

At least that was simply a business problem. Authors reneged on contracts all the time. "If you return his money," Julia suggested, "he'll just have to accept that the book's no longer available."

"I've already spent it. I bought our tickets to Paris. We're sailing next Thursday." Eva wiped her eyes. "One or two more days. I was going to give Pablo the manuscript on Monday, just as soon as I made a new dedication page. It's still dedicated to Jerome, but I want to change the wording, add something. I can't tell you what. Not yet."

Julia bit back a groan. Had the wording on one page cost Eva everything? If she'd simply given the manuscript to Duveen the moment the money was deposited, Timson would never have found it, never have read the passage that sent him into a rage. It was terrible to think of the small differences that could ripple out into massive consequences, but Julia kept this thought to herself. Eva would have to live with this particular regret all her life.

Eva's foot thumped against Julia's shin. "Why did he have to do that? I thought he'd never know. Now he thinks I betrayed him." She pressed both hands over her mouth. "Oh Lord."

"He might return it if you promise to take out that rape scene," Julia said. The book was still only in manuscript. If Timson feared readers would guess he was the novel's rapist, he might not object if she deleted the most repugnant scenes.

"What?" Another frown curdled Eva's forehead. "It's too late. I can't, anyway. Pablo thinks it's the most important part." She took a powerful drag. "Damn damn damn *damn*. He'll be so angry."

Who would be angry? Timson? Pablo? Goldsmith? Puzzled by the shifting pronouns, Julia watched Eva inhale the calming fumes. She remembered Eva's fearful glances toward Jerome and the stony countenance that refused to meet them. Maybe it was Jerome's anger she feared. Like so many women, Eva saw her lover's brilliance, not his demons. Men like him always had demons.

"It's so unfair," Eva said. "Jerome writes beautiful poems and gets a drawerful of fancy awards with ten-dollar prizes. But it's nothing to what people pay to see my titties. That's really what Pablo wants too. Only he wants it in writing. Even in books, they think Negroes are best for this." She patted her crotch. "Not decent things, not fine, decent literature." She pronounced the word with four syllables.

"Then just go," Julia urged. "Get away from this place. Worry about Goldsmith's contract later, once you're safely across the Atlantic. Maybe you could write another novel there. He'd have to wait, but at least he'd get what he paid for. Are you working on anything else?"

Eva squeezed her lips together. *Nothing.* "I suppose I could try. But wouldn't that be dishonest? Like stealing?"

Julia felt a sting of surprise. Goldsmith had witnessed Timson's crime; surely he'd understand Eva's predicament, that she was the victim, not the thief. Eva's concern for honesty seemed a dubious virtue in the circumstances, like patriotic honor to those soldiers flinging themselves over the trenches at Gallipoli. Didn't protecting yourself come first? Wasn't that more important, more morally imperative, than the harsh laws demanding all debts be paid?

Eva took a quick, deep breath. "No, I'll just have to ask him. Leonard's not afraid of my book, not really. He only made that stink because he heard Mr. Goldsmith wants it, and he hates to think I might work for anyone else. Like he owns me or something. But I know what he likes. If I beg right, he'll give it back."

She lifted her arm and touched the greenish thumb-shaped bruise emerging above her elbow, visible through her sheer chiffon sleeve. "This will help."

An image of that unspeakable rape in Eva's novel swept unbidden into Julia's mind. Was it true? Had that actually happened? "Does he . . . ?" Julia hesitated before choosing the least ridiculous euphemism she could think of: "Does he force himself on you?"

Eva's forehead puckered, the first harsh expression Julia had seen her make. But before she could answer, the toilet erupted in a noisy flush. Over its rush of water they heard Dolly's muffled exclamation. "Jeesh!" And a moment later, "Doll, you're a mess! Jeesh!"

Eva pushed two fingers up from the bridge of her nose, smoothing the furrows in her forehead. "I can't think about this now. I have to get ready."

She lowered her feet to the floor and watched the transfer of weight, as if uncertain they would hold her. Without a murmur of modesty she slipped off her gown and let it fall across the bed. She wore nothing beneath it but the gold loincloth. Where the halter had been were etched raw grooves across her collarbones and reddish slashes alongside her breasts. She crossed to the dressing table's white padded bench. She switched on both lamps flanking the table and peered at her reflection in the huge mirror looming like a vacant halo before her.

Julia was not new to public, even casual nudity. In London and Paris she'd frequented avant-garde theaters and cabarets. She'd observed models sitting for painters and had once briefly modeled herself. She saw beauty in the honest human form, freed from the sheer volume and poundage of Victorian modesty. But this was different.

Eva's body had a false pallor to it. Her skin looked waxy, dull, with the artificial sheen of something lifeless. Except for the chafed stripes, her torso was a single tone, molded by layers of stage paste as if she were a mannequin. In contrast the areolae of her breasts—stained or painted a garish dull black—seemed frightening, brutal. Onstage her body had looked elemental, a gilded Venus, but here was only the artifice. She'd become a kind of high-style Hottentot, a carnal exotic wrapped in chiffon, satin, and ruby lipstick: styled by men and for men. She'd been made into a caricature of everything female, effacing everything human. Eva the person was as submerged beneath this costume of sculpted flesh as she'd been by yards of chiffon and hollow chains.

"I'll get it back," Eva said matter-of-factly, examining the pink welt beneath her cheekbone. "Even if Leonard's a beast, I'll get it back." Raising her right arm, she peered at the bruise. "I'll do whatever it takes." She mouthed a silent *Paris* and smiled at Julia in the mirror.

She shook lotion from a tall opaque jar onto her palm and feathered it over the red blotch on her cheek. A fine layer of face powder followed. She twisted to check the results from several angles, inhaled, and, apparently satisfied, arched her shoulders. Then she clapped her hands softly and poured more yellow lotion into her palm. With long circling strokes she smoothed it onto her shoulders, arms, breasts, and down over each hip, under the lip of her gold loincloth. Hidden beneath it was an odd pattern of five pea-size scars on her left hip. Eva covered them with extra lotion and a dusting of powder, rendering them almost invisible, and tugged her waistband back into place.

"That's a strange scar," Julia said.

Eva quickly covered it with her hand. "What? Oh no—"

The lavatory door opened, and Dolly Clark pitched into the room, a white hand towel over her mouth. "Holy Toledo," she said. "I feel better. But how do I look? Am I an abso*lute* wreck? Max hates it when I'm sick."

She lowered the towel. Her dress was bunched at her waist, and her headpiece was askew, but her eyes had cleared. Fresh lipstick restored some color to her face.

Julia offered to straighten her dress. Dolly lifted her arms as Julia did her best to tug down the fabric puddled above her hips. They were simply too wide for the cut of the frock. There was nothing Julia could do but sweep a hand across the back of the skirt and hope the seams survived the night.

Dolly mumbled her thanks, staring unabashedly at Eva. "I guess you must be used to it, huh? I'd be bawling my eyes out if some guy pawed my boobs and stuck a gun in my face, but not you." Dolly leaned close as Eva outlined her eyes, painted her lips, and dusted more fine powder over her whole body. "You're cool as custard."

She watched Eva massage her feet and legs with generous slatherings of the yellow lotion. The scent of lemons was powerful. "Hey, are you really colored?"

Eva raised the stout jar. "I cheat a little. I'll bleed lemon juice someday."

Dolly belched. "That's a good one."

Julia steered the drunken woman toward the bed. "Try to rest, Mrs. Clark." Dolly flopped down in a graceless heap, mugging to an imagined mirror.

Eva slid to one side of the bench and patted for Julia to join her. From a small icebox under the table, she drew out a glass bowl filled with shaved ice. "I hate this part," she whispered.

She lifted her left breast and tucked the bowl around it, as if nursing a baby. Her head pitched back, and she inhaled sharply through clenched teeth. "Makes them hard," she said through a grimace. She switched the bowl to the other breast and again recoiled from the painful shock. "A girl on the line showed him this trick. I could kick her."

"Sex-y," Dolly sang, dimpling at herself. "Sex-ex-ex-y lemon sexy custard."

"I'm glad you're here," Eva said quietly, under the off-key drone. "My new publisher. My friend who doesn't care stink about all this. You know, the other night at Pablo's I felt like I recognized you, or that I would recognize you once we met. Now it feels like we've known each other for years."

Julia nodded. She remembered her own tingle of recognition when they met, her inkling that Eva and she shared some unspoken clarity, some kindred way of yearning to be in the world. She relished again the surprise, that thrill of discovering a rare new friend.

Eva glanced at the clock. She nudged closer, resting her hip against Julia's. Watching in the mirror, she threaded her fingers through Julia's and lifted their linked hands. They made a bouquet, her pale, creamy fingers mingled with Julia's faintly yellow ones above the slim stems of their wrists.

"Ella and I used to braid our fingers together like this," she said. "She said it was like stirring milk into roast yams. Do you know some say you can tell a colored person by their palms, their fingernails?"

Three raps sounded on the door. Timson's voice broke Eva's reverie. "Showtime, punkin seed."

CHAPTER 11

A sharp thump lifted Julia's face from the pillow. She floundered up from sleep. It came again, three brisk raps.

"Julia?" Philip's voice pulled her upright.

"What is it?" she croaked.

"You have visitors."

A hulking shape loomed up from beyond the foot of her bed.

"Of a constabulary sort." Philip's amusement wafted through the door. "They insist on speaking with you."

She stared as the shape resolved into a disheveled and blurry Austen Hurd, struggling to sit up from the small divan where he had, apparently, been sleeping.

For heaven's sake. "Ask them to wait. I'll be out in ten minutes."

She sat up. She was wearing last night's chemise and step-ins. Both stockings and her evening frock lay in a shocking heap on the vanity chair. Everything came back to her in a rush. Harlem. Eva's show. Her locked-away manuscript.

They'd returned quite late (or early, judging by the orange gleam on the horizon) in a dizzy swirl of too much liquor and music. Austen had wobbled into the apartment with her, but when she'd offered him a harmless half of the bed, he'd mashed his lips against her forehead. With a muffled, "Thanks, but no. Night, bean," he'd dropped—shoes, braces, and all—to the tufted divan under the window. Ten seconds later he'd been fast asleep, left arm and leg spilled over onto the carpet.

Now abruptly she'd been pulled from sweet oblivion into two strange puzzles. The police visit was clearly ominous, but Austen on her divan? She felt equal parts bemused and annoyed. While she wanted nothing amorous from him, surely she warranted at least a glimmer of manly interest to rebuff. Did he fear for her virtue? Worse, did he fear for his own? It was vanity, she knew, but still his tumble straight to sleep rankled.

"Fiddlesticks!" she sputtered. "What the blazes do they want?"

She stumbled across the room to the wardrobe. Austen heaved himself toward the wall, shielding his eyes from the sight of her in crumpled scanties. *For heaven's sake.* She gazed stupidly at the array of frocks, blouses, skirts, trousers. Dressing meant fresh underthings, stockings, shoes—altogether too much work after what felt like ten minutes of sleep. She pulled out her scarlet dressing gown and wrapped herself in its heavy satin. "If they insist on disturbing a lady at first crack on a Sunday morning, they must accept me en déshabillé." Muttering bolstered her courage to face whatever calamity had brought policemen to her door.

She slipped into her mules and nipped her cheeks. Her face in the vanity mirror was the color of chalk, tinted only by smudges of last night's mascara. There wasn't time for cold cream. She scrubbed with a tongue-moistened corner of a handkerchief and still looked ghastly.

Two men stood peering at the two oil portraits above the mantel in Philip's library. They turned when she entered. One was young, with unruly red hair, pale-blue eyes, and a pocked complexion. He wore a starched policeman's uniform. The other was an indeterminate age with a bristly brown pompadour and a wide, florid face. He was dressed in a tweed jacket and ill-pressed white shirt, its collar straining to encircle his neck. "Miss Kydd? Miss Julia Kydd?"

Philip entered bearing a tray with a full coffee service. Julia remembered that Christophine was out all day, no doubt beguiling Mr. Earl with her beautiful hat. Remarkable that Philip should step so ably into her shoes. She knew he could pour, but brew?

He placed the tray on the low table in front of the sofa and wordlessly retreated to the far, shadowed corner of the room, to which he had apparently been banned. Twisting sideways in his chair to ensure he heard everything clearly—unbeknownst to all but his closest friends, he was deaf in his left ear—he shrugged and touched a finger to his lips. Consigned to silence as well?

Julia offered the men coffee. When both refused, she poured herself a cup, hoping it might jolt her brain into clarity. "What brings you here, gentlemen?" she asked, bracing herself.

"I'm Sergeant Millard Hannity of the New York Police Department," the older man said, "and this is Officer O'Leary." He jutted his thumb at his companion. "Homicide bureau."

Homicide. Julia sat carefully on the sofa. This might be bad. Possibly very bad. He hadn't answered her question. She was desperate to know why he had come, and yet a small part of her was relieved, hoping to be spared bad news. His ominous manner might be a ruse to frighten her, though for what purpose she couldn't imagine.

"Are you ill, Miss Kydd?"

"I'm well, thank you." The cliché bred into her from childhood limped out. Of course she looked awful, but it was a ghastly question to ask a woman, whatever her appearance. He'd already knocked her off balance. Her vanity in shambles, she needed to preserve at least some semblance of dignity. She must concentrate, take better heed of whatever the man was here to say. He seemed determined to make her guess the trouble, which hardened her caution. Until she knew what had happened, she needed to speak with care.

"My sister was fast asleep a few minutes ago, Sergeant," Philip said from the corner. It was a mild rebuke for such an affront, but welcome.

Hannity fingered his left cuff. "No offense, miss. It's just, well, the time." He turned to his assistant. "O'Leary here and I figure ladies are receiving visitors by now, that's all. Don't we, O'Leary?"

The boy dragged watery eyes from Julia to his superior. "Right, sir. We do, sir."

Why was he fussing about the time? What did it matter if she was a dissolute layabout, as he clearly inferred? She tried again. "How can I help you, Sergeant?"

"Did you go out last night, Miss Kydd?"

Last night. Julia hoped her dismay did not show. Something terrible must have happened. Had Pablo's bawdy tastes landed him in the soup? Had someone strangled poor Dolly Clark? Julia had seen Goldsmith's hands twitching once or twice in her direction. But that was nothing compared to the real violence of the evening: all those guns. Particularly the one shoved hard into Eva's cheek. Dear God. Had she gone back upstairs? Without Wallace there to intervene, anything could have happened. Had Timson made good on his threat? Had he shot her?

Julia's heart pounded as she waved her hand to convey a calm she couldn't trust her voice to achieve. "Last night? As a matter of fact, I did go out."

"Mind telling me where?"

"Harlem. With several others." She swallowed. "Why do you ask?"

"We'll get to the others in a minute. Go any place in particular?"

"A club called Carlotta's. What's this about, Sergeant?"

"And after the show? What did you do then?"

Julia took a hasty sip of coffee and burned her tongue. This was like watching disaster unfurl in slow motion and being powerless to intervene or look away. Hannity was determined to reveal nothing. She managed to answer somewhat steadily, "The club's owner invited us up to his private rooms. Why?"

Hannity roamed the room, stopping to study the brooding African tribal masks mounted on the crimson wall behind Philip's piano. "And what happened there?"

She risked another scalding swallow. "We chatted, as one does." He couldn't mulishly continue to ignore her questions and expect her to fully answer his own.

Hannity sauntered back to the sofa, stopping behind her. He bent abruptly and whistled into her ear, startling Philip and O'Leary as much as Julia. "I wouldn't advise you try that la-di-da with me, Miss Kydd," he said. "Fact is, you're mixed up in some nasty business."

Julia stood, scattering the remnants of her composure. "For pity's sake, what's happened?"

Hannity studied her, face to face across the sofa. His wordless scrutiny was unbearable. To busy her hands, she helped herself to one of the Régies from Philip's cigarette case on the mantel and bent gratefully over O'Leary's match.

Hannity waited until she looked at him. "Please sit down, Miss Kydd."

She shook her head, rustling the skirts of her dressing gown to hide her still-trembling knees. She needed to sit, but not at this man's command.

Hannity shrugged. "So you say you chatted about nothing special. We'll try that again in a minute. Who was there?"

Julia lifted her eyes toward the ceiling, as if to reconstruct the scene from a hazy memory. In truth, in her growing dread she wasn't sure she could remember her own name.

"I was there, Sergeant." Austen strode into the room, hand extended in introduction. His wrinkled evening suit and collarless white evening shirt told an embarrassing if familiar tale.

Hannity watched Austen pour himself coffee and join Julia beside the mantel. "Well, how about that? Mr. Hurd just saved us a trip uptown, O'Leary. Isn't this cozy?"

"The gentleman is our guest," Philip said from his corner, into the uncomfortable silence. "I trust you're not here to investigate our social calendars, Sergeant."

A dull flush spread across Hannity's throat. "No, Mr. Kydd. Sorry, sir."

Did they know each other? Did Hannity work with Philip's uncle Kessler?

Hannity wiped the corner of his mouth with the back of his hand. He straightened his shoulders and started again. "So who else, Mr. Hurd?"

"Let's see. There was Paul Duveen, a pretty well-known critic and writer. And a couple from California. San Francisco, I believe. Max and Dolly Clark. I'm sure Duveen can tell you—"

"Just tell me what happened last night."

"We were invited upstairs after the show. Duveen and the Californian couple were there, and Arthur Goldsmith, the publisher. The owner, Leonard Timson, was there, of course, and his friend, a Mr. Wallace, who shared our table during the show. Shortly after we arrived, the headline performer, Eva Pruitt, and her escort, Jerome Crockett, joined us. I believe that's everyone."

"Now we're getting somewhere," Hannity said as O'Leary hunched busily over a notebook, scribbling. "Had you been to Carlotta's before?"

At their denials he continued, "Any special reason why you went there last night? Just curious about coloreds?"

He meant to goad them. Julia bit back a testy reply, glad when Austen answered. "I work in publishing, Sergeant. The big buzz last week was Eva Pruitt's new novel. Arthur Goldsmith just bought the rights to publish it. We thought it would be fun to see Miss Pruitt's show."

"You work in publishing too, Miss Kydd?"

"Not as such, no." Even though she considered her fledgling Capriole Press a venture every bit as serious as Austen's work at Boni & Liveright, Hannity would never understand.

"So what happened in Timson's apartment? After the chitchat. Miss Kydd?"

Julia sat, not too gracelessly, she hoped, as a new thought struck. Did Hannity suspect *her* of something? Was that why he refused to answer her questions? The notion was absurd, but she'd heard tales of innocent people nattering on unawares to policemen, delivering all sorts of information that could be construed as incriminating. She desperately missed a hat brim, so useful in shielding one's face while allowing a good view of others'. Until she knew more, she needed to be cautious. "After Eva and Jerome arrived, we drank champagne. Talk turned to her novel."

"First names, huh? You're pals with Pruitt and Crockett? Met them before?"

"Last week," Julia said carefully, "at a literary party."

"What exactly do you mean, 'talk turned to her novel'?"

"Apparently Timson learned about Eva's book and stole the manuscript," Austen said. "He had no right, of course, but wouldn't listen to Eva's objections. He made something of a show in locking it away in his safe."

"You saw him lock the papers in the safe? Her jewelry too?"

They nodded. So he'd already talked to others, if he knew about her jewelry case.

"What did Miss Pruitt do then?"

Julia's heart plunged. As she'd feared, he was focusing on Eva. If only Julia had worked harder to dissuade her from returning for that manuscript. Without Wallace to calm him, Timson's fury might have boiled over if she'd confronted him again about it. Had he pulled the trigger this time? Good God, was Eva dead?

"It's what Timson did that matters," Julia exclaimed. "He drew his gun and threatened her. He's a ruthless man, Sergeant. Ruthless and violent. If anything's happened to her, he's the one you—"

Hannity made a maddening tsking sound, as if Julia were a child speaking out of turn. "So they quarreled. Then what?"

Julia's fears burst out. "Why are you asking these questions? Is Miss Pruitt all right?"

Hannity strolled to the windows. He looked down over the quiet courtyard. "So when did everyone leave Timson's rooms?"

Julia saw again Eva's lax face, surrendering to whatever fate the gun in her cheek might deliver. Had she felt a premonition of what awaited her later? An inadvertent twitch and—Julia twisted for breath as her mind braced for the fatal explosion. She only faintly heard Austen explain that Goldsmith had left first, followed by Wallace. Jerome had escorted Eva downstairs, and the rest of them had left soon after.

"What time would you say that was?"

"Maybe two thirty? Before Eva's last performance, whenever that was."

"Where'd you go next?"

"Julia and I parted ways with Duveen and the Clarks. We left them waiting for their car."

"You both came back here?"

"Not directly. We went on to a club near where I work. We had a few drinks and settled our minds after what had happened. It was quite late before I saw Miss Kydd home. Around five, I think."

Hannity made a sour face.

"Did either of you go out again after that?"

Austen shook his head.

"Have you seen or heard from anyone who was there last night?"

Again, no.

Hannity paused to make sure O'Leary recorded every scrap of information. "Timson was alone when you left him?"

"Quite alone," Austen said.

Julia couldn't bear it any longer. "You must tell us what's happened, Sergeant." She was reduced to pleading. *"Please."*

"I must, must I?" He eyed them for several long seconds. "Well, you'll read about it in the papers soon enough. Last night someone shot Leonard Timson. Put a slug right between his eyes."

He smiled at the noise that escaped from Julia's lungs. Into the silence he added, "And one other thing. His safe was standing wide open, empty. Bare as a baby's bottom."

⌒෧

Julia marshaled every strength to fathom this news. Eva was alive. Timson, not Eva, was dead. But his safe was empty. The implication was monstrous.

"So it's only natural to wonder," Hannity said with exaggerated patience, "if Pruitt's manuscript has something to do with it."

"Surely not." Julia jumped up despite herself. "That place was filthy with guns. We saw at least half a dozen on our way upstairs. Who were those guards protecting him from? Not from the likes of us. Timson was probably thick as thieves with all sorts of unsavory types. You can't ignore that, Sergeant. He was a bully surrounded by bullies, and every one of them had a gun." It poured out of her. Eva and her book could have nothing to do with that man's death.

Hannity smiled again. "Nice speech, miss. Sure, there's johnnies who'd plug their mamas as soon as sneeze, if the price was right or their heels hot enough. But we know how they work, and this just don't have that feel."

"If the safe was empty," Julia said, scrambling for alternatives, "then her jewelry case is missing too."

Philip spoke thoughtfully, as if puzzling out a riddle. Julia turned to see he'd risen from his corner, apparently risking Hannity's ire to enter the fray. He'd heard her speak of Eva; he would know the extent of Julia's alarm. "From what I understand, the lady is a true star in the nightclub firmament. She no doubt had some expensive pieces, much more valuable than any novel. A thief could have been after them."

"Maybe so, sir," Hannity conceded, in a new respectful tone. "We're checking on it."

"But Sergeant," Austen said, "you can't seriously think people murder for novels. They're not like bootleg rum or crooked numbers. Nobody kills for them. And besides, Eva's book might not even sell. Publishers are incurable optimists—we always think our next titles will sell up a storm, but they almost never do. Most likely Eva's book will get a few good reviews, probably written by Goldsmith's friends, and a respectable but hardly spectacular sale. It's her second or third book Arthur's really investing in. That's the way it works. There's little money or power in the business, believe me. Definitely not worth killing for."

"Why on earth," Julia added, "would you go after writers when the man's world was crawling with criminals?"

"Who said anything about going after writers?" Hannity said. "Though now you mention it, we wouldn't mind talking to Miss Pruitt. But it's a funny thing. She's done a bunk. No one's seen her since about four this morning."

CHAPTER 12

"She's missing?" Julia stumbled as she caught her toe on the leg of the coffee table. "She could be hurt, or in danger. And you're wasting time with this twaddle? Why aren't you trying to find her?"

"Oh, the boys are doing their best," Hannity said. "But it looks like she's hopped it. Her boyfriend too. Timson's got a hole in his head, and the Queen of Sheba and her manuscript are nowhere to be seen. We figure she's holed up somewhere working like mad on the last chapter, the one where she dreams up how she didn't pop the guy."

"No. Eva Pruitt is not a killer, no matter what it may look like."

He snorted. "They never are. Just tell me, you know where she might be?"

If she did, she'd be on her way to dress and go find her herself. But she could only shrug.

Scraping his thumb along the corner of his mouth, Hannity sized up her poker skills. He handed her a small card. "Well, if you hear from her, telephone this number in the next tick."

❧

Julia covered her mouth as Philip showed the policemen out. "Good God."

Austen let out a low whistle. "Poor Eva."

"You don't think she killed him, do you? No. I don't believe it for a minute."

Philip returned and fetched the empty cup from beside his corner chair. "So much for Sunday ennui. You've rattled the day something fierce, my dear. Who could read Herodotus after that?"

Julia scoffed. Eight months ago she would have seethed at such a cavalier remark. Now she understood the teasing in fact revealed how clearly he perceived the trouble. She introduced Austen, and the men nodded to one another.

Philip poured himself coffee. "What now, young ones?"

"Actually," Austen said, wincing at the mantel clock, "I need to find a taxi. Though I'll look a sad rummy heading home like this." He smoothed a hand over his rumpled sleeve.

"Hardly the first gent to do so," Philip murmured.

"You don't have to leave yet?" Julia's thoughts were still whirling. After leaving Duveen and the Clarks, they'd steadied their nerves over passable gin fizzes and talked over the stormy scene they'd witnessed. Now, in the sober light of day, she hoped Austen could help her make some sense of this new thunderclap. Timson's death was a shock, but Eva's disappearance was more disturbing. Hannity had stirred up a hundred questions and provided precious few answers.

"Afraid so," he said. "I'm boarding the *Aquitania* tomorrow. I'll be gone for eighteen days, and I have loads to do before then. Lousy timing!"

Julia had forgotten about his imminent trip. But he was already palming smooth his tousled hair, and there was nothing to do but wish him a good journey, escort him to the front door, and send him off with a distracted farewell.

When she returned to the library, Philip sat slouched in his usual chair. "I leave you unattended for one evening," he said, "and you land yourself in another murder. What a menace you are, my dear."

Eerily enough, he was right. Just last fall they'd sat in this very room discussing another sudden death. Timson's demise, however, was a very different kettle of fish from Naomi Rankin's.

She dropped onto the sofa. "It may be amusing to you, but Eva Pruitt is a friend. Timson's a brute who's probably dispatched a few men himself, but I'm sick for Eva. She may be hurt, or—" She tried to pick up her coffee cup. It rattled in her hand, and she returned it to the saucer.

Her mind raced with thoughts of her enigmatic new friend. How their arms had brushed in conspiratorial closeness the night they'd met—a scant week ago. The easy intimacy of their conversation as Julia had attempted to clean Eva's dress, and their mutual delight at combining talents for Capriole's American debut. They'd spoken privately on only three occasions, yet Julia felt, like Eva, as if they'd been friends for years.

And also that she barely knew Eva at all. With each new glimpse into Eva's life, Julia saw more clearly their differences. Wealth, family, education, and especially race carved a deep chasm between Julia's world and Eva's. By those measures Eva should be a novel exotic to her, as she was to Pablo and his tourists. From where Julia now sat, secure in the beauty and comfort of Philip's fine apartment, Eva's friendship might easily recede into some hundred-dollar Harlem souvenir. Already she sensed the story of Eva's misfortune becoming gasp-worthy entertainment at parties.

Julia drummed a useless fist against her thigh. If she stood by and watched that unfold, she'd betray not just Eva and their budding friendship but everything she dared to believe about herself.

Philip's wry smile faded. For several seconds they held each other's gaze. They'd been through a crucible together last fall, one of Philip's careless making. They had been adversaries then, but the experience had left them with an oddly shrewd understanding of each other. He seemed to be measuring her now, as she was measuring herself: the direction of her next move.

"Come," he said.

She absently followed him into the hall but balked when he pushed open the kitchen's swinging door. The thought of food made her slightly ill.

Philip, however, took hold of her elbow and guided her into the room. Spacious and tidy, it smelled of peonies and bread. A fresh loaf lay on a board beside a block studded with knife handles. Philip asked her to slice it as he poured water from a simmering kettle into a teapot.

Julia considered the knife handles. The first she pulled out had a short tapered blade, not big enough. Her second choice produced a cleaver, no better but perhaps serviceable.

"May I?" Philip extracted a long serrated blade with a rounded tip. He cut off the heel and two thick slices and carried the board to the table in the center of the room.

They sat on two stools. "I gather the sordid gist," he said, "but perhaps you'd care to fill in the more vital bits?"

She hesitated. She desperately wanted help in making sense of what she'd just learned. But from Philip? He'd proved helpful before, in his needling and contrarian way, as she'd grappled with the conundrums of Naomi Rankin's death. And he'd kept his word, leaking nothing to his uncle Kessler. When he put a cup of fresh tea before her, she managed to lift it to her lips without a splash. She could do this. She had to.

Where to begin? Only twelve hours ago she'd expected to be regaling him with Timson's penchant for Böcklin. Now his hideous art was not worth mentioning.

"I told you about Eva Pruitt. She's the author I met last week at Pablo Duveen's party. There was a great to-do because Arthur Goldsmith bought the rights to publish her first novel. Apparently Pablo brokered the deal. He certainly took great glee in announcing it."

"Championing New Negroes."

Julia nodded. "He invited Austen and me to go with him to Harlem last night to see Eva's show. She's a singer, it turns out, at one of the posh clubs. Afterward the owner, Leonard Timson, invited us to his rooms to meet her."

"So you told the sergeant. It's what you didn't tell him I'm craving to hear." Philip nudged forward the remaining slice of bread, generously buttered.

"Timson stole Eva's manuscript and then quite viciously refused to return it. He put a gun to her head, Philip. Apparently there are some vile scenes and characters in it, and he feared it's a roman à clef. Eva objected bitterly, of course, but he wouldn't budge. He threw it into his safe and swore he'd never let her have it."

Philip nodded to register this. "And then?"

Julia told him how she'd followed Eva into the back bedroom but found it difficult to describe what had happened there. She recalled some moments vividly but also remembered sensing that much was beyond her grasp, that her mind had not been subtle or perceptive enough to notice, much less understand, all that she was witnessing. "She wasn't murderous but erratic. Talking to herself as much as to me. She was disheartened more than angry. I tried to think of ways out of the dilemma. I thought she might return Goldsmith's money or just write another novel for him instead."

"Spoken like a publisher," Philip said.

"She's already spent the money."

His eyebrows rose.

"She knew Timson would be difficult, but she seemed confident she could retrieve the manuscript. She seemed to know what it would take to mollify him." Julia squirmed at a rude noise from her stomach.

"Keep talking." Philip tied on one of Christophine's aprons, rolled up his sleeves, and explored the Frigidaire again, pulling out eggs, milk, butter, and cheese.

"You can cook?"

"Another legacy from Aunt Lillian." He whisked the eggs, added milk and herbs, and lit another ring on the range. Julia remembered the cantankerous old woman she'd met last fall, the maiden aunt who had been his childhood playmate, teaching him to jest and joust and to skewer staid respectability with a gimlet eye. Upon her death he'd learned that Lillian, his surrogate mother after her sister Charlotte's death, was in fact his natural mother. It was still too tender a knowledge to mention.

Tossing butter into the heating pan, he said, "On Cook's days off, she trussed me into an apron and stationed me at the stove." He poured the mixture into the hot pan and adjusted the flame. "Mind you, I couldn't bake bread to save my life. But a good roast chicken or omelet or stack of griddle cakes—I'm your man."

He shaved cheese onto the board and brushed it onto the firming eggs. After wrapping a towel around the pan's handle, he shook it gently. "You say she was determined to retrieve her manuscript. Sounds incriminating."

Julia felt oddly calmed watching him work. "No, she meant she would get it by pleasing him in some way, reassuring him of her loyalties. I'm sure of it. She was thinking about coddling, not violence."

"That's a thin line. She might have gone back armed with feminine wiles—plus a gun, just in case."

"Don't even say that. I don't for an instant believe she'd shoot anyone."

Philip folded the omelet, divided it in half, and slid each portion onto a plate. A sprinkle of herbs, two forks from a drawer, and he set the plates onto the table with a flourish.

"Goodness." Julia wondered if she could eat any of it.

"Appearances do suggest she's the killer, my dear."

She wanted to denounce him for allowing the thought to form, but she could not. Though he could be exasperating at times, Philip's mind was always sharp. He made no judgments; neither did he simply accept Eva's innocence. Was Julia rushing too blindly to her friend's defense?

She remembered Eva's eager secret about her trip to Paris with Jerome. There was something poignant in her urgency, as if she were trying to outrun fate, to affirm their bond before anything could sever it. Beneath her preoccupied calm, had Eva been afraid? How excruciating to have reached the very brink of her dream. She'd nearly bubbled last week with the jubilant sense that she was about to break free into something new and wonderful. Her new life, her literary arrival, was so close. Timson's anger about the manuscript had seemed only an obstacle to Eva, not a defeat. Why would she destroy all that by killing Timson, especially when she felt confident she could appease his anger?

Julia forced herself to taste the omelet. That was the wrong question. Instead she should ask, Was Eva's envisioned future—a published novel, marriage, and a new career—worth risking everything for? Would she have killed Timson rather than let him crush her dreams?

At first Julia had felt certain that no, Eva's gentle nature and decency made such a thing unthinkable. It was the pretty answer, but was it entirely honest? Any human heart was a maelstrom of raw and even base impulses. Julia had faced difficult choices herself last fall. Then she'd considered her situation dire, though now Eva's crisis put that dilemma into perspective. Her choice between marriage or accepting Philip's control of her purse strings hardly involved the risk of prison or death. Maybe Eva's options had truly been unthinkable: kill a man, or let him destroy everything that mattered to her. How would Julia choose? How would anyone? Gentleness and decency might be no match for such a choice.

Julia managed a second bite, barely. "At first glance, perhaps. But that oaf of a policeman seemed ready to string her up without bothering to look beyond those appearances."

"I know Hannity," Philip said. "I'll grant you he has ham hocks for manners, but he's not the buffoon you suppose." He cored several strawberries and slid the plate toward her. "Is the manuscript valuable?"

"Goldsmith paid her an advance for it, so he must figure it will sell well. Valuable in that sense, I suppose. But surely her jewelry is worth far more, and it's easily turned into cash. The novel makes money only after it's published."

"That does seem to be the kicker," Philip agreed. "Hannity's probably right. No thief would haul away a bunch of papers unless he was after them. Most likely the jewelry was just gravy. It's hard not to assume Timson was killed by someone who wanted that manuscript."

Julia bit into a huge strawberry. At its sweet and juicy perfection, tears welled in her eyes, which she brushed away.

Where was Eva? Was she hiding or abducted? Was she injured—or even alive? That was the most painful question of all. Something deadly had occurred in Timson's rooms last night. Had Eva found her way to safety, or had she been caught up in his violence?

Julia pushed away the berries. "She's in terrible trouble. How can I help when I know almost nothing useful about her? I don't know where she lives or whom she might turn to. Pablo boasts about discovering her, but I'm not sure he'd dirty his precious hands for her now. I have to do something, Philip. But what?"

He didn't answer for a moment, perhaps discarding one of his usual flippant replies. There were many clichés available. Mercifully he offered none of them. "If she's found," he finally said, "and she says she's innocent, you can believe her."

"That's not enough."

"From a top-drawer white woman, it can be a great deal."

Julia stared at him. How easy it was to reduce others to convenient categories—Negro writer, Jewish publisher—but she seldom thought of how neatly she too fit into a conventional box: top-drawer white woman. Reduced to wholly impersonal features. And yet without even noticing, she moved, as did everyone, in a world that treated her accordingly. How easy to believe the world was simply as it was for her, a woman for whom doors were whisked open with a deferential nod or quiet *miss*. Philip's words reminded her that she too was forever sized up and sorted, no less than the blackest Negro or the most orthodox Jew. The difference was that doors swung open for women like Julia; they slammed shut for women like Eva.

"I'll believe her." Julia's voice dropped. "And do what I can to help her."

Philip looked at her thoughtfully. "Are you sure she needs your help? Or even wants it?"

Julia had a sudden memory of Austen holding her back when she'd have rushed to Eva's defense that first night in Duveen's apartment, after they'd witnessed anger flaring between Eva and Jerome. He'd been right: Eva could steer her own course through whatever tension simmered there. But this was different. It wasn't a matter of respecting Eva's right to speak and act for herself. From the hard set of Sergeant Hannity's jaw, she feared Eva would not get that opportunity.

"I don't mean fight her battles for her. I just want to make sure she gets the chance to tell her side of whatever happened."

Philip watched her face. "Wading into this could get unpleasant. People will wonder what you're up to. You might as well think it through now, because everyone will ask. Why involve yourself?"

She felt a flush of discomfort. Her first response was indignant. Wouldn't anyone? Who could abandon a friend to such misfortune? But he was right. Natural empathy carried one only through the immediate crisis. Philip was asking about what came after that—the decision to do more, which only rarely followed the initial sympathy. Why insert herself into Eva's trouble, and on such relatively skimpy footing? A fortnight ago they hadn't even met. In short, why did she care so much?

Julia sat back. It was hard to explain. She knew only that a fist was clenching inside her chest. It pained her to imagine Eva's anguish. Even if she was safe and unhurt (please, God), her future might be shattered. Weren't friends bound by their troubles as much as their joys? Eva had shared with Julia her soaring triumph and her jubilant hopes, and now

Julia would not flinch from sharing her horror too. She opened her mouth to answer, but no words came out.

Philip peered for a long moment into her face and nodded.

಄

The telephone bell was ringing. What time was it? Julia sat up in her bed, pushing back the heavy coverlet spread across her. She'd meant only to take two Spartans and close her eyes for a minute in hopes they might ease her raging headache. But now the drapes were drawn against a weak morning light. She pulled the clock to her face. Seven forty. Had she slept straight through?

The ringing stopped, and Philip's voice sounded from the hall alcove where the instrument was kept.

Was this news about Eva? Was Eva herself calling? They hadn't exchanged numbers, but it was easy to try the few Kydds listed in the directory. Julia flung off the coverlet, scrambled into her dressing gown, and stepped into the hall to listen.

"I see," Philip said three times, at longish intervals. "Yes, all right. Frightfully grateful." After another maddening silence, he rang off. He turned and saw her.

"That was Kessler. Evangeline Pruitt was located at 5:17 this morning."

"Alive?" Julia stammered.

"She's being questioned downtown as we speak."

Her breath rushed out, as if stoppered for hours, in an exclamation of relief.

"He suggested I might commune with *la femme* this afternoon. It seems she ain't inclined to warble for her hosts. He thinks my dulcet charms might persuade her to confess."

Before Julia could protest the vile assumption, Philip added, "If I can find a sufficiently sturdy pair of coattails, you might care to ride along."

CHAPTER 13

At two that afternoon they were ushered into Kessler's offices on the fourth floor of the police headquarters building on Center and Broome Streets. It was a bleak place, oppressive with the remnants of a former elegance. The plaster wore the soot of a thousand cigars. The brown rug and draperies seemed to leak their brackish color into the room. Heavy oak woodwork was yellowed with varnish, and a bronze-and-china chandelier hung morosely overhead.

Kessler was speaking on the telephone, his chair swiveled toward the tall windows behind his desk. Over his shoulder he waved them in. They idly toured the room. Philip narrated what he could about the artist, unknown to Julia, who had produced a pair of bronze statuettes of warring Indians mounted atop a long oak table.

Kessler ended the call and spun his chair to face his guests. He began to greet Philip when he saw Julia and froze.

Philip shook his extended hand. "You remember Julia, my wayward sister? I thought I'd bring her along."

"Miss Kydd." Kessler inclined his head. "Please excuse us."

To Philip he said, "Are you mad? She's involved in the case." He hurried around his desk and grasped Julia's arm. "I'm sorry, Miss Kydd, but you can't be here."

"You can't believe I was involved with that man's death?" Julia protested.

"Don't be an ass," Philip said. "She's discreet. She might even be useful to you."

"I'd like to talk with my friend," Julia said, shaking free of Kessler's hand. "Not long, just for a quick word. Please?"

He eyed her. "I don't yet know where you fit into this case, Miss Kydd. Until I do, I will ask the questions. And under no circumstances will you be speaking with Miss Pruitt. Not until we have a great deal more information ourselves."

"I've already told your sergeant everything I know."

"Then I'll know more after I've read Hannity's report. Until then, please wait outside."

"Just grill her yourself, old man," Philip suggested. "Plumb the depths of her nefarious soul if you must. But do it now, or we both leave."

Kessler frowned at this but returned to his desk and found his pen to take notes. Julia marveled at Philip's pull with the man. She knew only that they'd known each other for years. More than that, Kessler was married to Philip's aunt Arlene, the youngest and now only surviving Vancill sister. Even so Kessler must value Philip's occasional advice highly enough to defer to the younger man's judgment. That she was still in the room at all was testament to that.

Kessler's questions covered much of the same territory Hannity's had. Julia recounted her tale with what she considered heroic patience. Philip had heard everything before but listened attentively.

"There," he said when she'd finished. "As I said, she's a better witness than suspect. Let her stay."

Kessler still balked. "It's a stretch having even you here, Kydd. This isn't some three-ring circus to entertain your idle friends and family. I can't risk her chattering about this at her next mah-jongg luncheon and jeopardizing my investigation."

"My concern here is hardly idle," Julia objected, "and I never chatter, as my brother can—"

"We're a package set," Philip said. "Two Kydds for the bother of one."

"Good God. One of you rooting around in police business is bad enough."

"Don't forget how useful this old snout has been to you. Accept our terms and get on with it."

Kessler dropped into his chair. "I suppose she can stay, but only until Hannity brings up the suspect." He eyed Julia uneasily. "You're to be well out in the lobby before he comes. On no account do I want you speaking to or even seeing Miss Pruitt. Is that clear, Miss Kydd?"

Julia nodded. Infuriating, but clear.

"Agreed. Now, what can you tell me about the case thus far?" Philip motioned Julia into one of the deep leather chairs facing Kessler's desk and drew up another for himself.

Kessler hesitated, scowling at Julia. "We found Timson just before seven yesterday morning, after a call came in to the local precinct. We all knew the man, of course. He's heavily involved in backroom stuff—mostly numbers rackets. Not one of our more illustrious citizens."

"The man was a skunk," Julia said. "Anyone could see that." She scooted forward. "I suppose you're honor bound to investigate all murders, but if ever there was a case for skimping, this has to be it. Can't you ease up and consider Timson's death a favor to the city?"

Kessler bristled. "The law doesn't work that way. No one deserves to be murdered."

For an awful moment Julia feared Philip would argue the point—Bluebeard? Jack the Ripper? Attila the Hun? She could almost see his mind rising to the juicy bait. But before he could disappear down that rabbit hole, Kessler spoke again.

"As I was saying, Timson's crooked, but he's always been careful to keep Carlotta's high-class downtown clientele happy. And that clientele includes a pretty elite swath from city hall. So when the boys got the call, they knew it could be a tickler and alerted me first thing. I got there soon after Hannity."

He extended his humidor to Philip, who declined. Kessler lit a Corona Perfecto.

"Who called it in?" Philip asked.

"Carlotta's manager, a chap named Bobby Hobart. He called us, and then he called Martin Wallace, asking for help in case trouble broke out downstairs."

Julia dipped her head to shade her eyes beneath her hat brim. She didn't want either man to notice her interest at the mention of Wallace's name. The mysterious blond man with a quiet power she didn't yet understand.

"Now why would he do that?" Philip stretched his legs and lit one of his own Régies. "Why would he phone the enterprising Mr. Wallace?"

"I suppose because he has one of the few level heads up in that neck of the woods. Wallace understands the sensitive nature of the situation. Both colored and white club owners listen to him, and that's no small testament to his reputation as a square dealer."

"So first on the scene, or nearly. A prime suspect, surely?"

"He certainly knew Timson moderately well. They had a few business dealings in the past, but nothing special. He's known as a tough but honest businessman, the sort who sees that giving others a fair shake pays dividends down the line. You've met him, at the Stuyvesant? We've golfed together on occasion. He owns a few of the smaller Harlem clubs, but he's mostly involved in commercial real estate. Something of a fresh horse in politics as well. He sits on a passel of those citizen committees the governor likes to ballyhoo. They say he's caught the eye of the party bosses in Albany. Rumor has it he may take a run at Wadsworth's Senate seat next year."

"A criminal profile if ever I heard one," Philip said.

Kessler ignored this. "But we questioned him at length yesterday. Wallace has no connection to the missing manuscript, and a dozen witnesses confirmed his whereabouts all night. Seems he met no less than Senator James at Carlotta's that night, and together they went on to one of Wallace's clubs on Seventh Avenue. Neither left until Hobart telephoned.

"And he's helping us now. I've asked him to talk to the locals, keep a lid on things. Time is of the essence here. Too many short tempers in the mix."

He glanced at Philip, who for once sat mute. "This needs to be handled carefully. Plenty of unscrupulous people are angry about Timson's death, and they're itching for vengeance. I imagine Eva Pruitt seems as likely a killer to them as she does to us. Whether she knows it or not, she's far better off in here with us than out on the streets, where a justice much rougher than ours often prevails."

"You mean some kind of vigilante violence?" Julia's voice rose.

Kessler grimaced at the term. "That's why we need to wrap this up quickly."

"At least the papers aren't yet hounding you," Philip said. "Maybe they're sensible enough to see the city's better off with the johnny dead. As long as you keep the race element quiet."

"What do you mean?" Julia's chest constricted again. But she knew exactly what he meant. *The race element* was a sanitized euphemism for the violence burgeoning throughout the South and elsewhere. Race per se wasn't the problem. The problem was the Ku Klux Klan's crusade to punish colored people for failing to respect the "God-given rights of white folks." Sometimes that meant neglecting to step back when white ladies wished to use the pavement; sometimes it meant laughing too loud when a white gentleman was listening to the wireless. If a mob believed Eva had put a bullet in a white man's brain, their retribution would be swift and terrible.

"Wealthy white boss dies at the hand of colored employee," Kessler muttered, translating the danger into the kind of headline that would stoke virulent righteousness—and sell great stacks of newspapers.

Philip watched the smoke curl from his cigarette. "Unfortunately, just the thing to quicken the newshound's pulse."

Kessler swept his hand across his mouth. "That's the last thing we need, and you know it. Race had nothing to do with this case. Pruitt's the obvious suspect for all the usual reasons. But yes, that's another reason we need her to talk. I'm counting on you, Kydd."

"What's your case against her?"

"They argued violently when Timson refused to return her book manuscript and jewelry. A few hours later, both are missing and so is she. She had easy access—came and went from that apartment all the time. We haven't formally arrested her yet, as we're still looking for the murder weapon and any witnesses, but my men are searching. The sticking point is that she refuses to answer questions—not one word. I'm hoping you can dazzle her into talking."

"The almighty confession?" Philip smiled. "You Torquemadas love to badger the magic words out of a suspect. Never mind that people blurt out just about anything for all sorts of reasons that rarely include a sudden taste for veracity."

"Everything points to Pruitt," Kessler insisted. "She had motive and opportunity and no alibi. You may wrinkle your nose at confessions, but they work wonders with a jury."

As Philip lifted a palm in acquiescence, the bespectacled young man stationed in Kessler's outer office knocked and thrust his head into the room.

"Sergeant Hannity is here, sir."

Kessler pushed back his chair and swore under his breath. "Have him wait, Jones. Give me one minute."

He glared at Julia as he spoke to Philip. "I wanted her well away before this. Damn." He looked about and motioned Julia toward a small door near the entrance to the office, obscured behind a thicket of Boston ferns. "In there. I think you can squeeze in. You must promise not to move or make a sound. If you hear anything, which I hope you can't, you must swear you won't repeat any of it to anyone. Is that clear, Miss Kydd?"

Julia peered into the cramped space he proposed she enter. It was a shallow supply closet lined on three sides with narrow shelving. If she stood very upright and held her breath, she might fit. The situation was ludicrous, but at least it meant she could stay. She intended to listen with every possible care.

"Not a peep," he reiterated, watching her edge in. "I can't have Pruitt know you're here."

She nodded as the door closed against her knees. Kessler dragged over the massive fern's pot to make sure she stayed hidden.

She heard him move away and a moment later call out, "Thank you, Jones. Send him in."

As he spoke, Julia cracked open the door the inch or so allowed by the heavy pot. Without a trace of fresh air, she might gag on the fumes of cleaners and disinfectants stashed around her. Furthermore, as she'd hoped, she had a narrow but clear view of Kessler's desk.

Hannity strode into the room. He greeted Kessler and nodded to Philip. "This Pruitt gal's a tough one, sir."

Behind him came a uniformed policeman, pushing Eva forward. Julia bit her lip to keep quiet. She hardly recognized her friend. Without her heeled shoes and proud posture, Eva's height seemed merely gangly. She wore water-stained slippers, the back of one squashed flat as if it had been too much effort to slip her foot fully into it, a black scarf tied over her hair, and a blue dress made shapeless by its missing hip sash. A green bruise seeped from below her left ear, and a more colorful bruise crowned her swollen left cheek. Her lips were a pale-liver color. Without fresh makeup and likely without sleep, she looked ghostly, as if wrapped in a stagnant fog.

Her hazel eyes were hard with fear and something else. Anger. Hurt. Worry. Despite the walnut-size lump that squeezed her left eye partly shut, she gazed at the men warily. She lowered herself into the chair Kessler indicated, facing his desk. Hannity flanked her on one side, Philip on the other. Seated, her back was to Julia, who saw surprise in Kessler's face. He was expecting a colored woman.

"I understand you tried to elude my men, Miss Pruitt," Kessler began. "Hiding only heightens our resolve to find out what you know.

Please tell us about Saturday evening and yesterday morning, after you challenged Leonard Timson about the papers in his safe. Describe the events of that night for us."

For two minutes the room was still. Eva didn't stir. A typewriter clattered in the outer office.

Why didn't she speak? Julia struggled not to twist with anxiety. This was Eva's chance to tell her story, explain her innocence. Why was she hesitating?

Kessler leaned across the desk. "A man has been murdered, Miss Pruitt. A man you argued with just hours before. A man who refused to return items belonging to you." He waited for nearly a minute. When Eva gave no sign of answering, he went on in a low voice. "You were seen going to Timson's rooms early yesterday morning."

Julia gripped the nearest shelf edge. Was she? He hadn't mentioned this. Or was Kessler bluffing, trying to trick her into thinking her situation was hopeless, that they already had evidence of her guilt?

His voice rose with a hint of impatience. "A short time later he was found dead. I need you to tell us what happened, Miss Pruitt. In your own words."

From her cramped closet Julia saw his hand close around his pen and his knuckles whiten. In that moment she saw what Eva saw. She saw Kessler's anger, his determination to draw from her mouth the words he would use to hang her. He had hemmed her into an impossible position. By declaring her involvement with Timson's death, the only space in the story his questions left for her was the details. He wanted to know how and why, not if his narrative was accurate. Eva's only power lay in refusing to enter the story he framed.

Julia understood: to speak and be deliberately misheard was worse than saying nothing. She cheered Eva's silence. What Kessler interpreted as insolence or guilt, she knew to be self-defense. If Eva said anything at all, they would find a damning subtext in it, something to bolster their beliefs of her involvement.

"Silence suggests you have something to hide," Kessler said. "You'll fare much better if you tell us what happened rather than force us into guesswork."

Another silent minute passed. Julia's stomach ached from the tension of listening, each passing moment of Eva's resistance a small victory. Philip continued to wait, but Hannity blew out a loud breath. The typewriter fell silent too.

"For Pete's sake," Hannity burst out, "don't you understand simple English?"

Julia squeezed her lips together, stifling her own combative reply.

"Sergeant." Kessler shook his head slightly.

Hannity cocked his jaw toward the windows.

It seemed to Julia that an eternity passed, and still Eva made no sound. Apart from the rise and fall of her shoulders with each shallow breath, she might have been a statue. Julia wondered if her eyes were open or closed.

Kessler sat back. Hannity swung his knees toward Eva.

She remained motionless.

"May I have a word with the lady?" Philip spoke to Kessler, but his eyes never left Eva.

He drew out his sterling cigarette case and offered Eva one of his finest rose-tipped Régies. She ignored it.

"I understand you're quite the diva, Miss Pruitt. The toast of Harlem, I'm told. Admirers fawning at your feet, champagne by the bucket, fresh flowers every hour."

He smiled at the ridiculous picture. "But it's not all wine and roses, is it? The stage life is not for the faint of heart. Theaters are full of modern Svengalis. Owners, managers, bosses—they all exact their toll. Hardly fair or right, eh? All your talent and years of hard work going mostly to boost a man's vanity and line his pockets?

"Beastly rotter, that Leonard Timson," he said. "Now there's a brute no one will miss. He had no right to take what belonged to you, did he?"

Despite Eva's silence Philip continued in the same desultory tone, as if making small talk over sweet tea on a Georgia porch swing. Julia recognized the cunning behind his ambling drawl and silently urged Eva not to be fooled. Anything she said would be whisked away and typed up in triplicate for prosecutors, the rest of her story disregarded as so much chaff. *Be careful, Eva. Answer only the fair questions, the ones assuming your innocence, not your guilt.*

"I imagine his taste in literature was abysmal," Philip said with a knowing sigh. "He had no idea what it meant to garner a contract from Mr. Goldsmith, did he? It's an extraordinary honor, a greater thrill than a lifetime of applause at Carlotta's, am I right? A literary coup. It will carry your name not just through Harlem but the whole city, the whole country. *Quite* a prize."

Eva's shoulders gave a sudden jerk. Hannity scooted forward in his chair, and Kessler straightened. Only Philip did not move. All three men watched her, waiting for something more.

She slowly crossed her arms, and her shoulders resumed their adamant set.

Hannity glared at her. Then his patience snapped. He snarled into her face, "Say something, you little—" and slapped her hard above her ear, spinning her sideways in her chair.

Julia gripped the nearest shelf edge, holding on to anything that would keep her from bursting out into the room, her impulse to escape mirroring what must have been pulsing in Eva's veins. Hannity was a burly man. He could break Eva's arm with one sharp twist. Yet she was trapped, unable to run from his blows. It was outrageous! How dared he strike a woman, or anyone so defenseless?

Eva slowly righted herself and made a noise in her throat as if gathering phlegm to spit. Hannity hit her again, knocking her scarf to the floor.

"Stop that!" Philip protested. Julia bit her cheek, wishing instead he'd returned the blow with a good old-fashioned slug. The ferric tang of blood flooded her mouth.

"Back off, Sergeant," Kessler said, frowning. "We were just starting to get somewhere."

Julia was astounded. Kessler faulted Hannity for breaking the spell Philip was beginning to weave? What about the violence? His sergeant had struck a prisoner! No, *not* a prisoner. Eva wasn't under arrest. She was an American citizen, entitled by right to be treated with respect—and every other tenet of basic human courtesy.

Hannity gave a sulky shrug and edged back in his chair.

With a low moan Eva tried to cover her exposed head. Her arms swarmed to hide her hair. A dull milky-brown color, it was coarse Negro hair, lying in stiff, flat sheets like slabs of dried mud. She bent for her scarf.

With a scornful belly laugh Hannity kicked it under Kessler's desk. "Not so easy to fool the suckers now, is it?"

Eva gave a plaintive gasp as Philip stirred with a sharp "Sergeant!" Kessler seconded the rebuke with an inarticulate growl.

Julia clutched the edge of the door, her fingers wedged into the narrow gap. She wrestled back a need to scream or shout. She could barely watch as Eva bent forward and Hannity rose again, towering over her. He muttered something through his teeth, and Eva cowered, swiveling toward Philip. Before Hannity's fist could slam into her shoulder, Philip threw out an arm to deflect the blow and seized Hannity's wrist.

"That's enough!" bellowed Kessler. He slammed his pen down on his desk. "Looks like we're done here."

Hannity shook off Philip's grasp. Eva squirmed, turning toward Philip so that Julia could see her give him one quick, inscrutable look. It pierced Julia. As cautious as it was intense, it implored yet defied him to read what was there. What did it mean? What was she trying to say?

Hannity clamped down on Eva's forearm. "I'm not convinced this canary won't sing. My boys know how to make her squawk. Let's go."

Eva struggled to keep her flattened slippers on her feet as he yanked her out of the chair and pushed her out across the room ahead of him. As soon as the door swung shut behind them, Julia smacked her own prison door into the heavy fern pot. Philip dragged it aside, and she burst out.

"Good God!" Julia exclaimed. "What did he mean by that?"

"Don't be naive," Philip murmured.

He was right. She knew what Hannity meant. But she couldn't fathom that an officer of the law would strike Eva—or any woman, any person, of any race. Julia knew terrible things were done in corrupt places like the rural South or foreign countries ruled by dictators. But this was New York, one of the world's great cosmopolitan capitals, beacon of enlightened culture and society. Of course it had its share of lawless violence, but surely those in power sought to curb such violence, not wield it—with impunity—themselves.

The police were meant to be a cornerstone of civilization. In dark past times the powerful had routinely preyed upon the weak, but now laws, not brute force, prevailed. Didn't every child learn, as Julia had, that one could turn to the police for help in times of fear or trouble? They were pledged to serve and protect, not terrorize. Julia trembled to comprehend what she'd just witnessed. Those hooded Klansmen and their ilk were bad enough, but clearly Eva had good reason to fear the police too. Where would she be safe, much less find justice?

"Take your sister home, Kydd. Now." Kessler's eyes had gone cold and small.

To Julia he said, "You're to say nothing about this to anyone, Miss Kydd. Not one word."

"Or what, Mr. Kessler?" Julia shook off Philip's restraining hand. In a weaker voice than she'd have liked, she added, "You're afraid I'll squawk?"

CHAPTER 14

Julia insisted she be let out of the taxi at Brentano's. She hoped an hour of wandering among its congested shelves might calm her mind, but the shop's dusty hush only amplified her unrest. She bought two books in gratitude for the refuge and retreated to a nearby tea shop, where fragrant steam and clattery commotion slowly eased her agitation. Only when she felt sure Philip would be gone for the evening, out to dine at one of his clubs and then off to the theater or concert hall with Jack, did she return home.

She was removing her hat in the vestibule when Christophine called out from the kitchen. Julia knocked twice and waited—well trained—for the quick *yes, yes* before pushing open the door. Christophine stood covered to her elbows in flour, two soft balls of pie dough plopped on the table in front of her. A stew of vegetables, chicken, and spices simmered on the range. Mr. Otto, her new Trini beau, was coming over for dinner later. Julia had promised to go out or spend the evening in her room, leaving the apartment free. "Smells wonderful," she said.

"How be she?"

Christophine was asking about Eva. That morning over breakfast Julia had told her all that had happened since Saturday evening. She'd told her about the terrifying scene in Timson's apartment, his theft of Eva's manuscript, and the shocking news of his murder. She had explained the day's errand, her anxiety about seeing Eva in police custody, and her determination to make sure Eva got a chance to defend herself. Christophine had listened with a deep frown, one cheek sucked into her mouth.

When Julia didn't answer, Christophine whisked a palm across her apron and tapped her above the wrist, an old trick to catch Julia's attention. "What happen?"

"Oh, Fee, it was—" Julia stopped. "You're busy. You have your beau coming soon. We can talk about it tomorrow."

"Here," Fee said, handing Julia a spoon.

Julia took up the long-handled spoon and began to stir the stew. She'd been relegated to stirring early on, after episodes of dropped bowls, sliced fingers, and—twice—burned eyelashes. Each circuit of the deep pot made a soothing rhythm as she struggled to lasso her thoughts about the disturbing interview.

"The policeman struck her," Julia blurted. "As if she were a dog. She was just sitting there, not moving or speaking at all. That made him angry, and he lashed out and hit her. Right there in the assistant commissioner's office!"

Fee pinched both lips under her teeth. "It happen, miss. It happen all the time."

"But she did nothing to provoke him. She has a perfect right to say nothing."

Fee shook her head. Her rolling pin thumped and spun, thumped and spun. "Them police not so nice nice as you think. You see whitelady police. It be different for your friend."

The spoon slowed. Julia winced at her own naivete. She stared at the flecks of flour on Christophine's cheek, the glaze of perspiration along her hairline. She was wearing the opal earrings Julia had given her last Christmas. Once her mother's, they glowed more richly against Fee's skin than they ever had against her own. Christophine was angry but not shocked to hear of Eva's treatment. The police she knew were not white-lady police.

It was a horrid term, crawling with implications. It suggested there was no such thing as what Julia had always referred to as simply "the police." (Didn't everyone? Or, rather, didn't every white person of her acquaintance?) The definition she considered standard and universal—a helpful force for public safety and well-being—was apparently only one version of a widely varying reality. Even more unsettling to consider: Eva's experience might be the more common, and Julia's the more rare. The notion upended something foundational.

Christophine set aside the rolling pin. She lifted the limp circle of dough and laid it in the pie plate. Watching her, Julia felt something tighten inside at the thought of anyone laying a threatening hand on Christophine. "I swear, if anyone ever struck you or treated you badly in any way, I'd send up a howl so blue they'd hear it in China."

Fee smiled and smacked her rolling pin across the center of the second mound of dough. "I got some good howl in me too, miss."

Julia had heard that howl, and it was fearsome. Her stirring slowed again. "I can't stop wondering what might have happened if Philip and I were not there." She paused. "Or what probably happens all the time that I never knew about. It was as if the police could say or do anything and Eva had no way to stop them. That sergeant had no right to strike her, and yet he did. He's supposed to enforce the law, not break it himself."

Fee's hands worked rhythmically, the rolling pin creaking from the force of her strokes. The dough spread quickly into a smooth circle. "Who be telling they no, huh?"

She wiped her hands on her apron before spooning chopped rhubarb into the piedish and deftly unfolding the top crust over it.

What Julia had witnessed that afternoon had to be illegal. It was certainly a travesty. But Fee was right: Who be telling they no? The police? Hardly. Kessler's anger at her objections still rang in Julia's ears.

A politician? Ensconced in their own bureaucratic fortresses, they were even less concerned than the police. A judge or lawyer? For a significant fee, perhaps.

It was a brutal question, both in the abstract and in practice. If she protested, who would listen? Like Kessler, most authorities would dismiss her as yet another dewy-eyed female sheltered from the ways of the world. Christophine's words, and what Julia had now seen for herself, shook her blithe confidence that the law in action much resembled the law in principle.

Christophine pinched together the two crusts rimming the pie and forked a pinwheel pattern across the top. She moved it to the counter, wiped the table with a folded rag, and began to scrub potatoes.

Abruptly, her hands stopped moving, and her chin came up.

Julia let go of the spoon. "What?"

Fee gave her head a small shake but didn't answer.

Julia moved closer and brushed her forearm. "Tell me."

"Bernice." Fee's voice had gone small.

Bernice. The name dislodged something inside Julia. It rose like a fist to her sternum. It was the same tight pain that had swelled in her chest yesterday, as if hatched under Philip's gaze, when he'd asked why she felt so compelled to help Eva. *Bernice.* The day she'd first felt that stiff, suffocating fear.

It had been some twenty years ago. She'd been very young, no more than five or six. She'd been in the park. Christophine had sat on a bench with her friend Bernice, the only other colored nanny. Julia had been peevish that day, sulky at being forced to put on her ugly boots and go outside. She'd been standing near a knot of rowdy children she didn't know, watching them tussle. A fight broke out, and one of the boys pushed the littlest girl, grabbing her hat. Its chin strap caught on her coat button, briefly choking her, and the girl shrieked. When her nanny—Bernice—ran to her and retrieved the hat from the boy's fists, he too started to scream. Another nanny, tall and fierce, swept in to comfort him. With a piercing Irish brogue she berated Bernice and slapped her hard across the face. Before the startled woman could react, the angry nanny grabbed her arm and pulled her toward the benches, shouting for the police.

Julia watched stupidly as the boy wailed ever louder, insisting Bernice had attacked him. A policeman came running, and soon he dragged her away, despite her frantic protests. Everyone had seen what happened, but no one said a single word in the innocent woman's defense. Julia had felt Christophine gripping her from behind, forbidding her to make a sound. "Nothing we can do," Christophine had hissed into her ear, voice prickly with fear. She was only nineteen or twenty herself.

When the others had all whisked away their charges, Christophine corralled the hatless little girl, rigid and dry eyed with alarm, and the three of them hurried out of the park in a tight, stumbling huddle. Julia didn't remember where they'd taken the little girl, whom she'd never seen again, and they had never spoken of it again. Until now.

"Bernice be from Jamaica," Fee said. "Them white gals be vex with we, think we take they jobs. I never see she again after that."

The recollection flooded Julia. She remembered the children's cries and that tall nanny's powerful slap. In breathless silence she remembered the strange brew of confusion, fear, and shame that had filled her throat. It wasn't the child's accusation but the onlookers' silence that had betrayed poor innocent Bernice.

Fresh fear squeezed Julia's chest as she thought of Eva. Fear that Eva's innocence wouldn't matter. That even if she swore she hadn't killed Timson, the police wouldn't listen. Speaking was one thing; being heard was another. Fear that unless others spoke up too, insisting on better answers, Eva's fate was already sealed.

"Yesterday," Julia said, nearly into Christophine's ear. They were leaning into each other, almost as they had been on that terrible day. "When I heard about Eva, something started to hurt. It was the same pain I felt when we watched Bernice being taken away. I couldn't remember where the feeling came from, but it was that fear of watching her go. How not one person told the policeman what really happened. I knew, but they wouldn't have listened to me. I was just a child—" Julia stopped. The accusing boy had not been much older than she had been. If his word had carried weight, hers might have counted for something too. She felt sick to think maybe her silence had not been as powerless as she had thought. She'd been one of those silent onlookers, standing by and doing nothing, as if she'd had no choice. But there had been a choice then, and there was a choice now, with Eva. There was always a choice.

"You were terrified too, Fee," she said. "Why? You know my mother would never let them cause you any trouble."

Fee swallowed and gave Julia's hand an excruciating squeeze. For a small woman she was ferociously strong. She began to peel the potatoes, long brown strips curling into the sink. "Maybe yes, maybe no. That day I pray so hard no one rough me too, say I hurt you like they say Bernice hurt that white child. Even your good mam not be standing up to that."

Julia balked in disbelief. "But they couldn't completely make something up, say whatever mean and untrue thing they wanted, could they? Not without some kind of proof. I know things are terribly unjust for Negroes in the South, but this is New York." She looked around the spacious kitchen with its sparkling Frigidaire and its gleaming white cooker, as if only reason and justice could prevail in such an orderly and modern place. "I'm sure they couldn't just outright lie. It doesn't seem possible. Not *here*?"

The certainty faded as soon as it left her lips. She felt a second flush of shame at her own reluctance to believe something so loathsome. Hadn't she just witnessed Eva's violent mistreatment? Didn't everything she'd seen and heard confirm what Fee had told her, that Julia's New York was not Eva's New York? She couldn't keep peppering Fee with questions. She ought to start facing those questions herself, learning her own answers.

Fee swallowed again. "Here, miss." She began slicing a waterfall of potato disks into a pan of water. The pieces fell in a calming, steady stream.

Julia stepped back. She understood. Fee tried to take things in stride. She was a "just is" pragmatist, accustomed to disappointments and obstacles Julia would protest if she knew about them. Yet indignation was itself a kind of luxury, an indulgence of time and effort that only those with plenty of both could afford. To Fee, negotiating a path through the troubles was achievement enough. It was a good day's work not to be nearby when a scuffle broke out, or not to be accosted in that moment between bagging the vegetables and paying for them.

Fee lit the gas ring under the potatoes and adjusted the flame. As she turned to Julia, she untied her apron strings. "Oh yes, miss. Very right here."

CHAPTER 15

The sentence passed beneath Julia's eyes for the third time, and still she did not follow it. Something about Countess de Kerninon, likely to be convicted for shooting the count. Yes, yes, of course she was. Julia dropped the newspaper into her lap with an exasperated rustle.

Philip's voice sounded in the hall. He'd been out since well before noon, leaving no hint of when he might return. After yesterday's debacle in Kessler's office, she was strictly in for the day, still feeling unsettled. She had time only to throw off her lap shawl before he pushed open the library doors and joined her.

"I'm beastly company," she warned.

"Thought you might be."

She grimaced. "I have every right to feel aggrieved. I was whisked into a closet like a bad puppy and then made to witness my friend being harassed and attacked by men claiming to 'interview' her. I've never seen such flagrant abuse of power."

"I did warn you the law's gloves come off when there's a dead body to account for. Fighting crime is not always pretty."

It was true he had said something about bracing herself for strong language and the reek of cigars, but she'd never expected outright violence. She scoffed at the word *pretty*. "Don't patronize me. Eva was treated like a convicted criminal, as if she had no rights at all. You tried to confuse her with your mumbo jumbo. That's only marginally better than Sergeant Hannity's outright thuggery. You both wanted to make her say what Kessler wants to hear. How is that possibly right, or even legal?"

Philip dropped into a facing chair. "I'll concede it was a bad show. Hannity had some bee in his bonnet; I don't know why. I suspect he was irked she didn't look like a Negro. He felt tricked, and no one likes to be made a fool of."

"She never denied she was colored. She tricked no one. Only the police did that."

Philip lifted his hands in surrender. "I suppose I'm jaded, having seen how this works too many times. There's a certain latitude, shall we say, when investigating major crimes. Timson was dispatched violently, so surely his killer can't whimper about a bit of rough treatment in return. That's the thinking, anyway," he added, seeing Julia's brewing retort.

"Hannity was beyond the pale, but you, Philip? I expected better of you."

He sighed and lit a cigarette. "Then you'll be pleased to know I've spent the morning making a great nuisance of myself on behalf of your unforthcoming friend. Kessler's seen the wisdom of releasing her."

"She's not arrested?" Julia sat upright. "No longer a suspect?"

"No longer one in custody."

"You persuaded him? How?" Given Kessler's certainty that Eva was only a confession away from a murder conviction, this seemed miraculous.

"I pointed out the flimsiness of his case. A premature arrest would only make it weaker. I think he relented in order to entice me to help."

"He wants you to help with his investigation?" It was the most cheering news she'd had in two days. With Julia to hound him, Philip could make sure they kept searching for other suspects. "That's marvelous."

"I told him no."

"Philip! You have to help. You know otherwise she won't get a fair shake."

He lifted a hand. "Not my patch, either the Harlem set or your literary crowd. Kessler needs fresh eyes and ears for this, but mine won't do."

Julia's brief pleasure sank. "Let me do it, then."

His eyebrows rose. "You? You hardly endeared yourself to the man yesterday. He'd never agree."

Julia was astonished at the notion too. But once it sprang out, she warmed to it. There were ways around Kessler's rigid fussiness. "Don't tell him. Deputize me, Philip. Tell him you'll talk with Eva again, but let me do it instead. She'll speak with me, I'm sure of it."

"No doubt—because you'd help her run the other way. The point is to gain her cooperation, not fuel her resistance."

Julia cooled her gaze. "I thought the point was to find Timson's killer."

He exhaled. "You know what I mean. Murder is serious business. Your friend is thick in the middle of a very explosive situation. She's as answerable to the law as any of us."

"But you saw how she was treated. The law doesn't seem much interested in protecting her rights. How lawful were those punches? The police assume she's guilty. All they want is proof or a confession—even if they have to beat it out of her."

"What they want is the truth. All Kessler has is a dead man, a missing manuscript and jewelry case, and their silent owner, who disappeared for twenty-four hours after he was shot. Given her refusal to speak, Kessler would be a fool not to suspect she's involved."

"Which is why he needs me to talk with her."

Philip drew a knuckle across his brow as he thought. For a full minute neither spoke. He crushed out his cigarette. "If I agreed—and I'm not yet convinced I should—you'd have to promise to tell me everything you learn, with the understanding that I'll pass it along to Kessler.

Perhaps with a *little* discretionary editing, but only a little. A solemn promise, Julia."

She was torn too. Only the chance to hear Eva's account of events was worth joining forces with the likes of quick-fisted Hannity. She answered slowly. "I won't trick or betray her. I must have your assurance that no matter what we learn, she'll be treated with respect. If she played any role in that man's death—*if*, Philip—she'd have had powerful justification. You must promise to remember that."

Philip considered this, head down. He looked up. "All right. You have my word." Beneath his bland expression his eyes spoke a steady, even adamant assurance. For all his trying qualities, Philip's honor seemed sound.

"Then I promise too. I'll be exactly as candid and forthcoming as you are." She extended her hand, and he shook it. "So how can I reach her?"

"Don't you want to know more about the investigation first?"

"I want to hear what she has to say first. Where can I reach her?"

Philip took a small card from his breast pocket and handed it to her. "I was told someone at this number would know."

Julia hesitated. Her role suddenly felt underhanded, deceptive. "Is this what they mean by being a snitch?"

Philip smiled. "Merely a sleuth."

Julia went to the hall alcove and dialed the number on the card. It rang fourteen times before she disengaged the line. She tried the call again, with the same results. Wherever it was ringing, no one there seemed available or inclined to answer it. Julia slowly put down the receiver.

"Setback?" Philip said when she returned. He lit a fresh Régie.

"Temporary." She looked at his cigarette case. "Are you sharing?"

He obliged, and she savored the first vapors. "So what do the police know so far?"

Philip settled into his chair and gestured her back to the sofa. "Timson was shot once at close range. Killed instantly with a bullet through the forehead—"

"All of his men carried guns. There are your obvious suspects."

"—and his empty shoulder holster was found hanging over the arm of a chair."

"He was killed with his own gun?"

"Hard to say—because it's missing. Fortunately it's a distinctive thing, with a turquoise-and-silver inlay on the underside of the handgrip."

Odd. Julia wondered if he wore matching spurs. "Do they know when he was shot?"

"Between four and six at best estimate."

"What do the guards say? We saw at least three of them on those stairs."

"They swear no one came or went that way after your party came down."

"Did anyone hear the shot?"

"Unfortunately, no. The man at the landing claimed he never left his post, but he reported several disturbances that could have distracted him from noise upstairs. The others were farther away and say they heard nothing."

"They could be lying."

"Which is why Kessler's had a squad of men there since Sunday, going over everyone's story backward and forward. So far it all squares. Seems no one trusts anyone else, which means they keep a close eye on each other."

"So what are the cops doing now?"

"They're thrashing about in the usual thickets, poking around for that sparkly gun and the other stolen goods. I also suggested they look for—unless they think the killer could fly—the swinging bookcase or secret stair that got her in and out." He lifted a hand to stay Julia's pro-test. "Or *him*. Tap the walls, twist the finials, that sort of thing."

"So apart from the obvious horde of gunmen about, who does Kessler suspect?"

"He reasons—rightly, I think—that the missing manuscript is key to this business, so he's focusing on those who learned its whereabouts that night. Including you."

Julia did a quick calculation. "There were ten of us in the room. Timson and Eva, Goldsmith and Duveen and the two tourists, plus Austen and me. Martin Wallace and Jerome Crockett were there too. So nine, subtracting Timson. Seven, eliminating Austen and me."

Philip smiled. "Keep going. You'll have this wrapped up in no time."

"Surely Kessler has no reason to suspect Austen or me."

"Little to none, as it turns out. Someone confirmed you were seen at a midtown speakeasy until after four, and good Mrs. Lewiston down-stairs reported your less-than-stealthy return at a quarter to five. Really, Julia, think of my good name."

She demurred with a look of injured reproach. So much for disap-pearing into the city's bosom of anonymity. Was it Benny who'd ratted on them? And she'd thought their return exceptionally stealthy.

"Make that six," she said. "Kessler said yesterday that he grilled Mr. Wallace and decided his alibi was strong too."

Philip nodded absently.

"Assuming Kessler's right about the manuscript," Julia went on, "who might have wanted it badly enough to kill for it?"

Before Philip could repeat the obvious answer, she provided two alternatives. "Goldsmith and Duveen stood to lose money and face."

Philip nodded. "Goldsmith will lose a packet if the manuscript isn't found and published—which gives him ample motive. But Kessler says his wife swore he returned home that night about two thirty and never left again. Paul Duveen and the Clark couple returned to Duveen's building after seven Sunday morning, which the doorman recalls all too vividly. Duveen claims they were in Harlem all night, though he can't reconstruct an itinerary from two thirty to seven. Kessler hasn't ruled them out, but they're hardly obvious suspects."

He sent a quivery smoke ring into the air. "All of which is why he's most interested in Eva Pruitt. She argued with Timson. He'd confiscated her property, which then disappeared. No one saw her from about four a.m. Sunday, when she was seen arguing outside her dressing room, until she turned up at the local precinct early yesterday morning. And she refuses to answer questions."

"Arguing with whom?"

"Top suspect number two, Jerome Crockett, who also had motive, opportunity, and no alibi after that argument. His flatmates claim they heard him come in sometime around dawn, but at ten when Sergeant Hannity went round to question him, he found evidence of hasty packing but no Crockett. No one's seen him since."

Julia recalled the proud, arrogant man. "He's Eva's lover. He's a poet, a rather fierce one, and an intellectual. She'd deny it, but I think Eva's a little afraid of him. I am. When she and Timson were arguing over the manuscript, she gave Jerome several panicky glances. I think she was warning him not to lose his temper. He looked like he might explode. A few minutes later he had to stand by and do nothing when Timson held a gun to her head."

Julia considered this. Jerome Crockett must have seethed with fury and hatred. "Wouldn't that drive any man into a rage? If he loves her as much as she believes, maybe he sneaked back later to get her manuscript. Or maybe he shot Timson simply as a jealous lover. This could be a simple crime of passion."

"If Crockett restrained himself during the actual abuses, why wait and lose control later?"

Julia didn't know. She ran her fingers through her hair. "At least we're down to just four plausible suspects."

Philip quirked an eyebrow.

She lifted one finger at a time. "Goldsmith, Duveen, Eva, Jerome. All had a strong motive to retrieve Eva's manuscript, and all had at least theoretical opportunity to kill him. As soon as I've had a chat with Eva, I plan to cross her off the list too. My money's on Jerome."

Philip made another face of astonishment. "Culprit by dinnertime?"

"I certainly hope so."

He shooed her toward the telephone alcove with a flick of fingers. "By all means then, extract her story. Wrap up this pesky business."

She tried the number again, but with no better luck. From the hall she asked, "Do you know where she went? After the police released her?"

"Wallace came to fetch her. He promised to set her up in a private place to stay, out of view. He's the one who gave Kessler that number."

Julia considered who might know Wallace's friends and associates. She could only think of Pablo Duveen, whose taste for gossip was nearly as avid as his appetite for all things Harlem. She returned to the telephone, consulted the directory in the drawer, and dialed his number.

Duveen had much to say, but eventually Julia was able to thank him and end the call. "Bother."

"Thwarted again?" Philip asked when she flopped back down onto the sofa.

"He knows less than we do."

"Pity. Though hardly a surprise."

The doorbell rang. "I'm not home, Fee," Julia reminded Christophine as she passed by from the kitchen to answer it. "You saw how terrified Eva was yesterday. There must be something more I can do, other than keep dialing that number."

"You could try to find out what or whom she's afraid of." Philip paused. "Other than Timson."

"Jerome." Each mention of his name deepened Julia's suspicion. Like a gun, he was cold and hard, taut with suppressed inner violence.

Besotted with his literary prowess, Eva saw only the poet beneath the pride. But if he'd cracked and killed Timson, she might suspect or even know as much and now be hiding from him as much as from the police.

"Or Wallace," Philip suggested.

Julia threw up her hands. He was right. At this point all she had was speculation. "Or Goldsmith, or some complete stranger. At least I can start at Pablo's salon on Thursday. I'm sure it'll be humming with talk of Eva. Someone there might know something."

Philip sent another lazy smoke ring drifting into the air. "What do you know about this Wallace fellow?"

Julia recalled the fair-haired man with the gleaming cuffs, French scent, and steady nerves. "Very little. He calmed the situation when Timson drew his gun. But if he's a friend to Eva, I like him too."

Philip's voice grew serious. "I realize you prefer to fling mud in the eye of prudence, my dear, but be careful there. He's not what he seems. He courts half the city's debutantes each year, and their mothers no less openly. He relishes nothing better than a fresh conquest. Watch out for that chap."

Christophine entered with a tall vase of apricot roses. Precisely the shade of the frock she'd worn to Carlotta's, Julia thought as she glanced down to read the card.

Her laugh startled the day's grim mood. It was ten years too late for brotherly advice in that or any other department. "Oh, I shall, Philip. I'll keep a very close eye on him." She laughed again. "He's invited me to dine on Saturday."

CHAPTER 16

Billie Fischer's voice sailed as Julia accepted a martini and moved into Duveen's dining room. "They say Arthur's blown a fuse—all that fol-derol, and all he got was a Harlem hangover." Surrounded by rapt lis-teners, Billie sucked on her cigarette. "I'll bet she never even had a manuscript. Not one pretty page." She flung back her head and expelled the smoke through scarlet lips. "What a fraud."

"She wasn't a splash for long," someone agreed. "Pablo's sure lost his gloat."

Julia stepped between two admirers to join the circle. Billie was the last person on earth Julia wished to see again, after the appalling scene she'd made at Liveright's party. But now she'd gladly stomach the vitriol if it led to helpful news about Eva. Her quick prowl through the apart-ment had spotted any number of acquaintances, but no sign of either Wallace or Eva. The chances they'd be there were slim to vanishing. But still, she had hoped.

"The Miss Kydd *formidable*." Billie craned her jaw toward Julia's cheek. "Taken a fancy to us lit'ry worker bees? Every now and then something tasty buzzes along." She nipped at the trousers of a passing fellow carrying two empty glasses. He swerved and exhaled an affection-ate vulgarity.

"Have you heard anything about Eva Pruitt?" Julia asked, shame-lessly inviting gossip.

Billie exchanged her glass for a full one from a nearby tray. "Disappeared. Melted right back into the muck. Pablo's moping, but he should have known better. I mean, who was she? Who'd ever heard of her a year ago? She just wiggled what she claimed to be her darky ass and mentioned a manuscript, and the boys went wild to buy it. It smelled funny from the start, you know. I don't just mean her ass."

Julia submerged her revulsion in a prolonged consideration of gin. At least Wallace, it seemed, had been good to his word. He'd found her a deep hiding place, well out of harm's way. Julia was glad Eva was safe, but also troubled. For the past two days she'd repeatedly dialed the telephone number that supposedly would reach her, and each time it rang unanswered. At Philip's badgering, Kessler had confirmed its accuracy but claimed he didn't know whose number it was, only that it reached someone who could relay a message to Eva. Except that it hadn't, and no one had relayed a word. Julia knew little more than Billie and the others. If that route was closed to her, she'd have to find another.

Today was Thursday. In a wild fancy Julia imagined Eva and Jerome were missing in the best possible sense—onboard a ship as planned, bound for Le Havre. Julia wished she had somehow found a way to honor those tickets, paid for at such a dear price. They'd be sipping champagne before dinner, celebrating their first day of freedom— in a sense of the word far beyond what Eva had meant that night in Liveright's bathroom.

"Nothing else?" Julia prodded Billie. "Any other suspects?"

Billie watched a striking dark-haired woman cross the hall toward the piano. "Who cares? Timson was a shit. Pruitt's finished too, and they can cuddle up in hell together if you ask me." She waved when the woman turned. "Nice chatting, peach fuzz. We both have quarry yet to bag tonight. Just don't cross my line of fire." She winked.

Billie made straight for the brunette now beckoning to her with a gesture as much command as welcome. She was older than Julia, thirtyish, and like Billie attractive in a predatory sort of way. Duveen materialized to light the cigarette she appended to a long ivory holder. Her very glance, or hint of one, seemed to telegraph her wishes. Hatless, her hair was sleek and smooth, cut in a longish bob. Not a strand strayed from its assigned position. She wore a deep-blue ensemble dress with a narrow pleated skirt and double-breasted jacket that reached her thighs, the garb of a woman not to be trifled with. A lady banker perhaps, Julia mused, or lady lawyer—if such creatures existed in America.

"Good to see you, Miss Kydd," a formally polite voice said over her shoulder. "I hoped you'd turn up again at one of Pablo's Thursdays. No one else talks so prettily about the Cuala."

Julia met Logan Lanier's greeting with genuine warmth. The earnest young poet touched something in her, and she hoped they could become friends. Part of her was thinking as a publisher, always alert for promising writers not yet able to command high prices for their work, but a greater part simply liked his boyish face. She handed him a small parcel from beside her handbag, stashed beneath one of the dining chairs. "It's only a trifle, but I thought it belonged in your collection more than mine."

Folding back the protective glassine, Lanier gazed at the bright blues and reds of a pamphlet in a new wrapper of French curl marbled paper. He opened to the title page of Yeats's *In the Seven Woods*, a slim thing produced in 1903 by the Yeats sisters at their Cuala Press studio in Dublin. His cheeks swelled into dark plums of embarrassed gratitude. "It's beautiful, Miss Kydd."

She asked him to call her Julia. After the caustic vinegar of Billie Fischer, his company was clear, cool water. His regard was pure, his interests genuine, his manner attentive. With a pang Julia missed Eva, whose company in this very room two weeks ago had moved her in the same ways. Both Eva and Logan had a depth, a quiet glow of intelligence, that was easily lost—and doubly appealing—in the garish *too much* of Duveen's parties.

He nodded with courteous gravity. "Then Logan, please."

This pact of at least a desire for friendship pleased Julia. "It was languishing in a box of my father's old ephemera," she explained. "I'm glad to find it an appreciative home. I have drawers full of these Cockerell sheets, which make lovely new coats for such little orphans."

He seemed about to expire from a mixture of pleasure and excruciating shyness, so she went on. "It's a token of congratulations as well."

They edged away from the jostling traffic. Ten minutes earlier, Duveen had crowed to announce Logan's recent second-place poetry prize from *Opportunity* magazine. His poem would be published in the August issue.

"Thank you." Eyes downcast, their gaze as velvety as his voice, he added that the prize carried no monetary reward.

Even so, national recognition was a triumph for any young poet, particularly a colored one. "Pablo's certainly proud. He's a great champion of your talent. I gather he's urging Goldsmith to publish your first book. That must please you no end."

Logan held the pamphlet to his chest. He seemed to struggle over how to respond. "I'm grateful for Pablo's help with the prize, but I'd actually prefer he not do anything for me with Goldsmith."

Julia cocked her head.

"This may sound churlish, but I want to be published because my poems are worthy, not because Pablo fixes it with his friends. I'd like to catch Goldsmith's eye on my own, Miss Kydd. Julia." He looked up, almost defiantly. "I want to be a great poet. I want to be a professor like Longfellow or Lowell and write poems schoolchildren learn and then recite to their children. Poems of America. Poems of all men. For everyone."

"And this prize is a lovely way to begin," Julia said stoutly. She felt honored by his confession, his cautious admission of what modesty insisted one deny. There was something fragile about Logan in his youthful yearning for greatness. She understood both the yearning and the pressure to subdue it. She knew about ambitions. She knew what it was to hunger for an excellence one had been taught was by definition beyond reach. Truly great poets were never colored. No woman could master fine typography. *Appreciate the masters' work,* one was told. *Never aspire to transcend it. Speak softly, or the jackals will devour your confidence, leaving you with only shame.* It was a bitter thing to be made ashamed of your dreams. Julia felt an urge to throw wide her arms and protect Logan Lanier from the jackals, the sneering Billie Fischers of the world. She couldn't, of course, but her heart swelled for him nonetheless.

Reluctant or unable to say more, Logan slid the pamphlet into his coat pocket and took up his glass. Pearls of perspiration crowned his hairline. He couldn't bear another moment of this conversation. Time to change the subject. Time for the more vital questions.

She watched the ice cube circle his slowly revolving glass. "I'm worried about Eva Pruitt. Have you heard where she might be?"

He blinked. "No. Nothing."

Julia waited, expecting at least some murmured lament for their friend's dilemma. But Logan's mouth had gone flat, his eyes murky. Puzzling. Billie's schadenfreude she understood; Logan's reticence baffled her. "I understand Jerome Crockett is missing too." Her voice lifted, edging into her real work.

With each passing day Julia's conviction had grown that Jerome was a far better suspect than Eva. Unfortunately, Philip had quashed her reasoning with news that witnesses had seen Jerome early that morning, several blocks from Carlotta's at the time Timson had been shot. Worse, this meant the police were no longer searching for him, figuring they already had their killer. With Eva sequestered firmly under Wallace's watch, they were simply looking for evidence to convict her.

Julia didn't believe those witness reports for one minute. Witnesses could be bribed. They could lie for any number of reasons. In her mind, Jerome's apparent alibi only made him more suspicious.

Logan scowled. "I wouldn't know."

His denial was too quick. "But he's your friend," she said. "You must know where he might be." If she could tip off police, they could at least question him, find some cracks in his convenient alibi.

"If he's smart, he's in Chicago, registering for fall classes," Logan said in a rush, as if his friend might overhear and object. "There's nothing he can do for Eva. I just hope he has the sense to save himself."

"Save himself from . . ." Julia's thought trailed as she hoped Logan would explain. That prospect disappeared when a curt interruption severed their conversation.

"I understand you're to be congratulated, Mr. Lanier." The lady banker stood beside them. The woman's sharp features softened, but not so far as to yield a smile.

Logan squared his shoulders and thanked her as if she'd offered extravagant good wishes. "It's a great honor," he said carefully. "I hope I can fulfill its expectations."

Julia wondered at the somber clichés, but the woman wasn't listening. She had already turned her green-gray eyes to Julia.

"Might I ask you to introduce your friend, Mr. Lanier?" she said.

"I beg your pardon, Mrs. Goldsmith," he replied with a hasty solicitude that pained Julia. "May I present Miss Julia Kydd?"

"Coral Goldsmith." The woman extended her hand. "Would you excuse us, please, Mr. Lanier? I'd like a private word with Miss Kydd."

Logan was no less astonished than Julia, but more accommodating. Julia bristled at his dismissal, but before she could think of a civil objection, Pablo Duveen quieted the party with ringing crystal.

"Lanier!" he bellowed from the living room.

Logan straightened. He took two quick breaths and fingered his cuff links.

"Logan? Where are you, pet? Where's my prize poet?" Duveen clapped as Logan stepped into view, and the guests joined in amiable applause. "Every pawty needs a pwize poet." Duveen splashed a kiss on the younger man's cheek. "Isn't he luscious?"

Low laughter skidded through the room.

Duveen pulled Logan toward the piano, where people made room for them. "We must have a poem," he announced. "No, three."

More applause, as well as rustling to retrieve drinks or take up fresh ones.

Logan turned to the crowd. "First, I'm grateful to Pablo, who put in a good word for me with the judges."

"A thundering good paragraph."

Logan blushed. "Yes. A great help."

Several seconds of silence followed. Just as a current of resuming conversations began to hum, a sonorous "On Lazarus's knee" rolled from Logan's round face. With that single slow, six-jointed note, a poem had begun.

Julia had often seen poets recite their work, but never in such an intimate setting. From her place at the edge of the dining room, she watched Logan's gaze sweep the corners of the ceiling, then settle above the bookcase as his voice swelled. He spoke as if without breathing, each word melting into the next like notes from a pensive cello. It was beautiful.

A warm grip closed around her right wrist. Coral Goldsmith's voice slid into her ear. "Would you be so kind as to step with me into Pablo's study?"

Julia stiffened. Whatever power this woman commanded over the others, she had no right to compel Julia as she pleased. Then opportunity quelled indignation: this imperious stranger was Arthur Goldsmith's wife. She might have a great deal to say about the recent debacle.

No one seemed to notice the noiseless wake of two retreating women.

Duveen's library was chaotic. This was his working space, its jumbled shelves a stark contrast to the pristine collection of valuable books kept behind glass in the living room. Papers and books covered a large desk. More books, some laid open facedown, were strewed across the floor and cushions of an old-fashioned green velvet sofa. The ginger tortoiseshell cat lay curled on the center cushion in a nest of someone's white cashmere shawl. The room was stale with odors of cigarettes and recent meals.

"I take it you're not married, that you are indeed a Miss Kydd?" Mrs. Goldsmith fit a fresh Lucky Strike into her black holder and lit it with a match from Duveen's desk drawer. Seen close up, her hair had a reddish cast to it, like a rich Bordeaux.

"And planning to remain so for the foreseeable future," Julia admitted, curious what the woman was getting at. She wanted to talk, but not about herself.

"Wise." The older woman exhaled and continued briskly. "I have no particular interest in your acquaintance, Miss Kydd, and shan't keep you long. I merely wish to warn you of a possible annoyance to us both. My husband is Arthur Goldsmith, as I'm sure you realize. I have reason to believe he is attracted to you and that he may even muster some effort to pursue your favors."

Julia trusted her composure to hide her surprise, but her face must have betrayed something, because before she could speak, Coral broke into a wide smile. "Yes," she said. "The notion appalls you, naturally. Arthur's prospects as a lover are quite ridiculous, despite his occasional glimmers of charm."

Her smile subsided, but the clipped edge to her speech did not return. "Oh, humor him if you like, Miss Kydd. A bit on the side is no threat to me. In fact, it would be rather a holiday." Another smile spread across her meticulous features. "But while you're welcome to a liaison of the more"—it widened—"strenuous variety, I will not allow it to interfere with our business. Do you understand me, Miss Kydd?" She paused, expectant.

Julia's first thought was to wonder whom she might regale with this extraordinary warning. Austen would relish it, but he was midway across the Atlantic. For the moment, Julia only nodded. Bizarre as the notion was, she understood it clearly enough.

Coral continued, her words crisp. "As far as I know, you have no literary ambitions, beyond your hobby press. But I won't risk not making myself clear. If you hope to parlay Arthur's admiration into any favored consideration with our firm, for yourself or for someone else, you will find me a formidable opponent. Arthur may have few, mercifully few, weak moments of judgment, but I do not. I am not to be trifled with in this matter. I will crush any effort that might sully the Goldsmith imprint, Miss Kydd."

Terms laid out, she again waited for reassurances. It was a remarkable performance, though Julia bristled at Capriole's demotion to a hobby, as if she were a bored countess arranging types and papers instead of flowers or decorative bijoux. She subdued a fitting retort, however. She had her own agenda yet to pursue.

"You may be right, Mrs. Goldsmith," Julia replied, "but I've seen nothing to cause you any worry." Far from it. Her husband had barely deigned to notice her when they'd met at Liveright's party, and had said nothing at all to her that terrible night at Carlotta's. Julia couldn't imagine what Coral Goldsmith referred to.

As Coral's eyes narrowed, measuring Julia's meaning and her tone, Julia helped herself to one of Pablo's cigarettes from a rather squashed packet of Raleighs. Coral made no effort to pass along the matches, so Julia rooted in the drawer for another box. She lit her cigarette and drew the smoke deep into her lungs before releasing it. She *must* ask Philip to teach her how to blow smoke rings. She wished desperately for the skill and resolved to start practicing tomorrow.

Coral seemed about to speak when Julia inhaled sharply through her nose, turnabout being fair play. "But if he should develop an interest," Julia added, with a stretch of syllables, "or I should sprout new literary aspirations, I'll consider myself forewarned."

Coral Goldsmith recognized this as the treatment in kind it was. For a long moment she eyed Julia, scanning for signs of insurrection. Julia returned the assessment.

Coral stiffened. Was she going to walk out? Julia feared she'd gone too far, alienating this arrogant woman before she'd asked about the situation with Eva. But before she could speak again in less chilly tones, Coral gave a bark of pleasure.

"God, I rather like you," she said. "Arthur may cast his seed upon the rocks, but Christ, I'd go straight for you." She laughed, a rich and lingering sound that explained much about her power. "How did you ever find your way into this day nursery of sycophants, Miss Kydd?" She tapped off her ashes into a saucer from the desk.

Julia did the same when she extended the saucer. "The usual way. I enjoy book people."

Coral nodded. She cleared space on the sofa, pitching the cat to the floor, and sat. She patted the space beside her for Julia.

"I've only met your husband twice," Julia said, easing the conversation around a bend. "On both occasions Eva Pruitt was the center of attention."

"Christ. That fiasco."

"I suppose you've lost money?"

Another crisp blasphemy. "A sure thing. Pablo swore it. Arthur trusted him, agreeing to a tidy advance on royalties before we had the manuscript in hand, and the little minx played us for fools. Now we may wind up with nothing at all. I suppose you know she blew that fellow's brains out and disappeared herself, with both the manuscript and our money."

Coral repeated Billie's cavalier assumptions with a blasé resignation. As Julia had feared, in these people's minds Eva was as good as arrested and convicted. Coral cared nothing for that, only her own business troubles. She leaned back into a needlepoint pillow and crossed her legs. One expensive blue shoe swayed above the other. "I was not consulted on the initial arrangements. But I certainly made it my business to be involved in the matter this week. We've been swindled, to put it succinctly. Against my better judgment I've allowed Pablo one more week to retrieve either a manuscript or our money. How he tracks her down isn't my concern. But should he fail, our lawyers will see she's charged with fraud and theft, quite regardless of that other business. She's in one pretty pickle, I must say." She paused thoughtfully. "If only I could have a chat with her."

Her cold resolve made Hannity's threats seem like the spleen of a petulant altar boy. Julia forced herself to match her sangfroid, inspecting the glowing tip of her cigarette as she searched for the right indifferent words, hoping to earn the woman's confidence. "I know her a bit. I doubt it was a scam. I saw the manuscript last weekend. You might yet get it when everything is sorted out."

"You sound like Pablo." Coral sighed in disgust. "If it exists, if it's found, if we can get hold of it—it may still be worthless nonsense. What the hell was Arthur thinking?"

"I can't imagine he was happy about that little scene after the show." Julia smoothed her skirt, careful to keep their dance moving but not lead too forcefully.

Coral surprised her with another low, melodic laugh. "He was furious. Stormed about like a guilty schoolboy—to beat me to the punch, of course. We'd been to a party at my sister's that night, but Arthur just had to slip off to see the creature's show with Pablo. I was getting ready to leave when he returned with the news that that madman wouldn't give us the manuscript. There was a terrible scene, naturally, and Arthur skulked out of the house—sensible alternative to sharing a taxi home with me, I'll grant you—and crept off to who knows where."

Julia mustered a laugh to disguise her spike of interest. This was not what the Goldsmiths had told the police. Kessler believed Goldsmith had been home by two thirty. This woman had confirmed it and assured police he'd stayed in for the remainder of the night.

Why would he lie? Why would she? More importantly, where had Goldsmith gone—at the very hours in which Timson had been shot?

"Poor man," Julia said. "Was he out long, and in all that rain?"

Coral released a tendril of smoke. "Oh, my dear, I have no idea. His bedroom and mine are miles apart. I didn't see him until the next afternoon, when neither of us was in a mood to speak of it, especially with policemen demanding details. But he was perfectly dry and rested. Believe me, Arthur is not one for troubled breast-beating through deserted city streets. I expect he hopped straight into a taxi and sneaked up to sleep at the office. Yes, that's about right for Arthur."

She laughed again, the rumbling of a patient volcano, and covered Julia's hand with her own. It was cool and strong. "But don't pay much heed to my jaded opinions, Miss Kydd. I rather hope he does set his cap for you. A tangle with a clever beauty might do him some good, restore a bit of the old boy's flair. Just don't turn his business head."

Her crush of Julia's hand was brief but sufficient. Their meeting was concluded.

CHAPTER 17

Two nights later Julia stepped into the magnificent Twilight Lounge of the Hotel Astor. Wallace brushed a bill into the maître d's palm, and they followed a pair of slim white-jacketed shoulders into the plush room. The hour was late, but it was filled with other partiers in formal attire. The Twilight was a favorite meeting place for those who held regular boxes at the opera, and those regulars gathered now in convivial groups of six or eight at clustered tables and drawn-up armchairs. Most were men, but intermittent blooms of colors, glowing like candles in the lush decor, revealed women too.

Despite the dozens of people in the room, nothing so vulgar as a commotion escaped it. Several large oriental rugs covered the floor, cushioning footsteps and sliding chairs. Burgundy velvet draperies softened the paneled walls, and white damask puddled from every table. The long mahogany bar was inset with padded leather, muffling the clink of glass and china. Even the small orchestra in the far corner of the room discreetly muted its labors.

A fire flickered under a wide mahogany mantel in the center of one long wall. It faced the bar, from which white-jacketed men delivered endless rounds of beverages in delicately painted bone china teacups. The china disguise was a droll touch, since the Astor faced no danger of surveillance from Prohibition agents. The lieutenant governor himself sprawled in one of the fattest armchairs, a cigar in one hand and a brimming teacup in the other. No doubt half the men surrounding him were civic luminaries.

"You've been a marvelous sport," Wallace said into Julia's ear. "Now we get better acquainted." His hand rode her hip as he guided her forward.

She longed for the intimate hour ahead. Despite her best efforts to subtly raise the subject of Timson's murder, she and Wallace hadn't spoken of it beyond a few guarded clichés of shock and horror. When she'd tried to spark a conversation, hoping he'd confide his role in protecting Eva, he'd merely said he hoped she was safe, wherever she was. In the next breath he'd waved over a friend he'd introduced as the city's next mayor, and the subject of Eva had disappeared.

It was frustrating. If he'd confided in her, she could have asked directly why she'd had such trouble reaching Eva. After four futile days, an unidentified woman had finally answered the mysterious telephone, on Julia's third call yesterday morning. She'd promised to relay a message asking Eva to return the call. Thus far she hadn't, despite two more pleas the woman had sullenly agreed to pass along. Did Eva receive the messages? If Wallace had overseen the arrangements, why was this intermediary so elusive and unhelpful?

Oddly, his reluctance to speak of the situation also deepened Julia's regard. He might have abandoned Eva to her great fall like so many others, but he'd chosen instead to catch and cushion her. Julia admired that his caution in preserving Eva's safety was stronger than his desire to impress. He could be trusted. Eva was well sheltered. For the first time in days, Julia could relax, even enjoy the evening's glittering pleasures.

When Julia had learned they were going to a gala dinner to benefit the Saint Patrick's Cathedral Roof Restoration Fund, she'd understood the agenda. As a rising political prospect, Wallace wanted to be seen widely and well, and female company was part of the desired tableau. It had been an evening of opulence, as events spawned by charity frequently were. Julia thoroughly enjoyed the clothes, the jewels, the effusive alcohol, the course after course of culinary objets d'art. She even relished the insipid chat, the vacuous pleasantries, the social fawning, the political pretenses. It would be a pleasure to recount everything over the next several days to a rapt—if blushing—Christophine.

Julia wore the latest of Christophine's reworked gowns. It was a cornflower-blue satin sheath with a fistful of fabric gathered bustle-like at her bum, a fluid satinfall that murmured as she moved. Christophine had cut a new deep V neckline to echo the wedge of bare spine in the back, then inserted a triangle of chartreuse organdy along one side so that it swept in an asymmetrical panel above her left breast, covering what might have been (on another woman) décolletage. It was a fine joke, to hide what was not there. On the organdy she'd stitched a single meandering line of tiny gold beads, as if a gilded ant had wandered by in search of a picnic. A dozen women had remarked on her frock, which alone testified to its success. Julia could hardly wait to relay the compliments to Christophine, to whom they were really directed.

Wallace and Julia had dined at a large round table with three other couples in one of the hotel's grand ballrooms upstairs. During the meal her unspoken job was to divert the husbands while Wallace enchanted the wives. The real work came afterward, when the women receded to a salon with music to oblige the men their cigars and brandies. Over thimbles of sherry Julia endured innumerable recommendations of clubs and societies to which she really must belong, as well as endless pecking at the edges of her mildly worrying pedigree. ("Milo Kydd's daughter? Was your mother the foreign girl?") The tedium was rewarded when Wallace bagged—Julia's term—invitations to three country weekends, two debutante parties, and one new advisory board. A successful night's work.

Now the personal pleasures could begin. Or as soon as they could reach a private table. Every man rose to greet Wallace as they moved through the crowded lounge. At each stop Julia met another middle-aged, wealthy, and no doubt powerful businessman or lawyer or banker or industrialist, each alike in easy yet hungry confidence. She understood that every compliment paid her was deposited straight into Wallace's treasury. She didn't mind. His luster enabled her to shine. They could share the profits.

Julia saw them before they noticed her. Sunk into a trio of armchairs in a distant bay between two columns, in a companionable haze of smoke, sat Philip, Jack, and Kessler. They'd chosen a spot farthest from the orchestra, where its efforts would not ruffle what looked to be an intense conversation. Julia had no doubt of the subject: Leonard Timson's murder—still unresolved. As each day passed without an arrest, the newspapers' clamor grew. Unfortunately, every day she asked Philip if there was any news, and every day he sighed and answered that Kessler remained as baffled as ever.

She began to angle a path away from them, but a pressure at her waist objected.

"I see the assistant commissioner is here," Wallace said into her hair. "I'd like a word with him, if you don't mind. Just to say hello—not long."

Did he have some information about Eva to pass along to the police? He'd dodged Julia's efforts to learn of how she was faring in whatever shadows he'd created for her, but surely he'd speak more plainly to Kessler. Julia readily led the way to the sequestered men in the rear alcove. Kessler greeted Wallace with a distracted handshake, clearly troubled to see him with Julia. He began to introduce Philip and Jack when Wallace interrupted. "I had no idea you had a sister, Kydd, and such a charming one. Kessler's bringing out his secret weapon?"

Philip dismissed this with a skewed eyebrow. His occasional help on Kessler's more baffling murder cases was not exactly common knowledge, but rumors—no doubt inflated—abounded in places like the Twilight Lounge.

A waiter slid two more chairs into the alcove. Additional brandies arrived. With the usual banter they agreed to a foursome of golf at the Marylebone Club. Julia appreciated Philip's acquiescence, as he enjoyed mocking the sport more than playing it, but he wouldn't miss the likely discussion of the Timson case. The golf course was as bad as the smoking lounge or steam room (or Grolier reading rooms)—each a place for discussing vital business or legal matters shaping daily lives. When men returned from their afternoon on the links, often all that remained was to announce their decisions. Those excluded from those places, including women, could only protest the done deals—even (especially) those directly governing themselves. Kessler wrote the agreed-upon date in his pocket calendar, and banal civilities petered out to silence.

Surely everyone was ready to burst with the obvious questions. Julia looked to Wallace, who dropped his eyes. All right then. She would have to ask them herself. "Have you found Eva Pruitt's novel manuscript yet, Mr. Kessler? Or Timson's gun?"

So much begged to be discussed, yet hesitation reigned. Kessler inhaled, his lips compressed. He merely shook his head, refusing to answer. Beside her, Wallace cleared his throat. For heaven's sake!

She looked to Philip. He alone returned her gaze. It took a moment before she could read his look: *Leave it to me.* Kessler would not speak of the Timson case in Julia's hearing, but he and Wallace clearly had something to discuss. Beneath Philip's atrocious posture, melted lazily into the cushions of his club chair, and his indolent air of supreme indifference, she now knew he was more alert than ever. *I've got this,* his manner telegraphed. He'd listen on her behalf and share everything at first opportunity. A mole! A partner in espionage. The small thrill of it eased the sting of the role she knew she must play.

"Oh, gentlemen." She sighed. "Does chivalry never rest? I may as well take my nose off for a long powder." She excused herself and threaded a slow, circuitous route to the ladies' lounge, bracing for the noisy and meddlesome crush she'd find there. For every cigar-congested lair where men congregated, there was an overmirrored, overscented, and plushly decorated lounge where women held court. Men might rebuff her questions, but women might gush with answers, most of them spontaneous and, if possible, titillating.

She was right. The ladies' lounge was crowded with a dozen or more avid conversations dissecting the social niceties of who had spoken with whom at which restaurant last week, of whose daughter had caught the eye of which up-and-comer from Yale or Princeton or Wall Street. Julia settled onto a padded velvet stool beside the long marble counter, drew an ashtray close, and commenced to enjoy one of the Régies she'd filched from Philip's unattended case. To her surprise, another woman edged in beside her and spoke her name.

It was Mrs. Macready, whom Julia knew only as Philip's mysterious friend. They'd met in a predawn encounter last fall in Philip's library when neither woman (nor Philip) had been dressed in more than a hastily pulled-on dressing gown. Clearly she was Philip's lover, of sorts, but beyond that Julia couldn't discern and Philip would not say. All she knew was that their relationship seemed intensely private.

She looked radiant, her beautiful hair a more auburn shade than Julia remembered but still lustrous, dressed in a becoming loose chignon. She wore a stunning gown of ivory chiffon with a collar of rubies at her throat.

"Leah Macready," she said, as if Julia might not recall their extraordinary acquaintance. "You look ravishing tonight, my dear." She squeezed Julia's hand. "You have an exquisite dressmaker."

Julia repaid the compliment. She hesitated and then decided the shroud over Christophine's talent would combust if she didn't lift it just a bit. She admitted that she had the rare good fortune to employ one of New York's undiscovered talents. She lifted the underside of her frock's hem, where Christophine had stitched a slender curl of the chartreuse organdy across the blue satin. No one could see it, except in a swirling flash as she danced.

"That's marvelous," Leah Macready breathed. "I'd love to see more of her work."

Julia explained her modiste's preferences for anonymity but said she hoped to soften those restrictions. She'd already confided too much. Mrs. Macready sighed, thanked her for her candor, and lamented that she'd be missed if she didn't return to her party. Julia waited another ten minutes and followed her out.

She rejoined the men in time to hear Kessler grumble cryptically, "Two weeks, then. Not a day more."

Julia had no sooner caught Philip's eye—*Anything?*—and perceived a satisfying glimmer in reply than she heard with alarm a voice approaching from behind, slurred with alcohol and venom. She recognized it with dread: Willard Wright. He must have seen her crossing the room and followed. She dropped quickly into a chair, but his weaving rant drew closer. Detestable man. He was known to hover like a vulture, sniffing out any fresh morsels of gossip about the city's latest salacious crime, and Timson's murder would be a banquet. He pestered even vague acquaintances in search of fodder for those infernal detective novels he kept threatening to write.

"Gentlemen," Wright said, leaning over Julia's chair. "Drumbeats in Harlem? Murderous moll on the loose? Do tell."

Kessler reached for his brandy. "You know I can't comment."

"Go home, Wright," Philip said, twisting to turn his good ear away from the man. Julia suppressed a smile, knowing how Wright would interpret his subsequent failure to hear properly as a personal affront. She'd done as much—understandably!—last fall before Mrs. Macready had enlightened her to Philip's deafness.

Jack added, more kindly, "You're drunk."

"I've neglected my lovely guest," Wallace said abruptly, touching Julia's arm. "Please excuse us."

Julia thought the men did so with unusual alacrity. Perhaps to protect her from Wright's baiting, or perhaps to dispatch him in terms they'd rather she not hear. It didn't matter. She too wanted well away from the unpleasant man.

Wallace danced beautifully. Time and the simple immediacies— that French scent, the muscles beneath his jacket—ought to have dissolved all cares for the world beyond his arms, but Julia resisted long enough to ask, "Two weeks?"

Wallace considered her with an expression she couldn't interpret. Apology? Pity? Regret? "Nothing to trouble you, my dear."

"Is it about Eva Pruitt?" Her feet slowed. "Is she all right?"

He regripped her hand, caressing her fingers. "I admire your concern for our mutual friend. I can only say I'm doing everything I can to protect her. Trust me. There's nothing to worry about." His other hand resettled too, cupping the bare curve of her lower back, and the subject was closed.

∽

Later, as the heavy Duesenberg moved through a plum-streaked Manhattan daybreak, the weight of countless champagne toasts and a blur of brandies drove Julia's head into the smooth leather upholstery. Her thoughts spun with the turn of the motorcar. What had Philip said? That Wallace preferred debutantes and their mothers. She was nothing like either.

The liquor pinned her eyes shut, but every thought in her head tracked his attentions traveling her throat, ear, cheekbone, nose, lips.

"I'm told to beware your seductive charms," Julia teased. His scent was intoxicating.

Wallace drew back. Jaw in his palm, his elbow sank into the cushion beside her head. He stroked the skin behind her ear. "Seductive? Not at all. I defer to your wishes." His fingers slid into her hair. "What would you have me do next, Miss Kydd?"

Julia tasted the warmth of his cognac. Desire twisted awake, curling her spine and lifting her chin. Her eyes opened with the deep pull of it. Stately stone buildings, glowing in the early dawn, slid past the car's window like fat pink pearls.

"Say good night, Mr. Wallace."

CHAPTER 18

"At last," Philip said late the next morning when Julia pushed open the library doors. "I was about to crash a few minor chords to rouse you."

It was just before noon, hardly cause for comment. Julia suspected the coffee in his cup was freshly brewed, not stale and cooling as he'd have her think. She yawned and filled a cup from the pot beside his chair, remembering it was Christophine's Sunday out. Apart from any other qualities the man claimed to possess, knowing his way around a kitchen seemed to Julia among the most useful.

Philip watched her with maddening attention. Was her hair standing upright? Her robe's collar askew? His eyebrows rose in comical inquiry. Damn him. What was so funny?

It took just one swallow, and her focus returned. Last night. The conclave between Kessler, Philip, and Wallace she had not been allowed to join. Philip was mocking her slow-awakening wits. Wasn't she perishing to learn what he had heard? The apartment had been dark last night when she'd returned, and she'd assumed he'd retired—or was still out.

"Yes, yes—so tell me." She pulled up a chair. "Has Kessler found Eva's manuscript?"

Philip shook his head. "Not for lack of trying. The poor man is flummoxed. He's had men combing the neighborhood, inside and out, but no scrap of it's turned up. He did discover how the killer got in and out, though."

"Not the obvious way?" Julia sat forward. "Is there another?"

"Turns out there's a second stairway. Not surprising, really, in those old buildings. It leads from the back alleyway—a painted-over door behind the rubbish bins and coal chute—up to the apartment."

"I saw only two rooms, the office and a little bedroom Eva used to get ready between shows. There was nothing even resembling a door. Where is it?"

"In the lavatory, apparently. I suppose a well-directed tap or firm twist to some finial, and the linen cupboard swings out to reveal the passageway. Hobart danced a fine jig as Kessler's men turned the place inside out, and no wonder. Turns out they use the passage to stash bootlegged liquor. Crates and crates of the stuff."

Julia considered this, not the bootlegging but the secret passage. Why was it there at all? She could think of several possibilities, well beyond providing access to a commode for the distressed pedestrian below. Most obviously it offered access to and from Timson's rooms without alerting his guards. The killer had to be someone well acquainted with the club's layout and operations. One of those armed brutes seemed most likely.

"It's quite the spice route," Philip went on. "One door opens into a coat closet in the manager's office downstairs—"

Julia interrupted. "Bobby Hobart. I knew it. Or one of Timson's guards. I saw it in their eyes, Philip. They're killers. Probably many times over."

"In their eyes?" Philip leaned close to peer into hers. "A wild glint? The pallor of a dead soul? The smudge of eternal damnation?"

She clapped a hand over her eyes to thwart his mocking gaze. "Something. Killing changes a person. It must."

He sat back, briefly somber. "You have no idea."

For a fraction of a second she wondered if he'd ever killed a person. Shocking thought! In the war? She knew only that he'd served as some kind of attaché, far from any actual shooting. But before she could ask, he said, "Kessler needs more than garrulous peepers. He's checked those fellows' alibis a hundred times, and nothing has budged yet, but I agree there's nothing more intriguing than the airtight alibi. Still, I'm afraid that deuced passageway keeps meandering. There's another entry point behind a mirror in the biggest backstage dressing room. Eva Pruitt's dressing room."

"Damn!" Julia didn't apologize for her unseemly outburst. Her heart fell. This explained how Eva and Jerome had gotten upstairs that night. They'd arrived after Julia and the others but come in through the back bedroom. She had wondered only vaguely at the time. "I bet Kessler leaped to all sorts of conclusions about that."

"Only the obvious ones. And theories, not conclusions."

"But anyone could have used those stairs, coming from the alley or from Hobart's office."

"Or her dressing room. Much as you want to see your friend exonerated, Julia, you have to think like a detective and look at all possibilities."

He was right, of course. Moving on, she asked, "What did Mr. Wallace have to say? He seemed intent on talking to Kessler about something, I assumed about Eva. Is she all right? He wouldn't tell me much, only that she was safe."

Philip rolled his lips between his teeth for a moment. "Your aging suitor—"

"Philip! Don't be absurd. He's not much older than you."

"And he preys on young—"

"Please. Just what did he say?"

"When Kessler needled him for doing too good a job of keeping Pruitt out of the public eye, Wallace hemmed and hawed—"

Julia coughed in exasperation. The man she knew was incapable of hemming and hawing.

"But finally he confessed that he's lost her."

"Lost her?"

"She's given him the slip. Disappeared. Gone."

Julia tried to smother her reaction before Philip saw it. As an unofficial deputy to Kessler's unofficial deputy, she'd agreed to help the police discover Timson's murderer. Kessler wanted evidence to convict Eva, but Julia (and Philip, she hoped) was determined to look more widely and to ensure Eva got every benefit of the doubt. But now a new possibility surged. Was there any chance, any shred of hope, Eva had escaped? Not simply from Wallace's supervision but from New York? Had she somehow managed to sail away to France as she'd dreamed? It was a tantalizing vision: Eva and her precious Jerome halfway across the Atlantic by now.

Philip watched Julia's reaction. "Kessler was less sanguine than you at the news. His reaction involved a few choice invectives. Wallace let him down rather badly."

"Or Eva proved more resourceful than anyone gave her credit for. She's an intelligent and determined woman, Philip. She'd know exactly the dangers she faced. She wouldn't simply put her fate in a few men's hands and trust them to take care of her." Julia spoke with conviction, though at some level she was voicing hope more than certainty. She and Eva seemed to share many instincts; surely an impulse to take charge of her own fate would be one of them.

"She did manage to hoodwink your admirer, it seems," Philip allowed, his inflection suggesting Wallace's dim wits were as much to blame as Eva's cunning.

"How did it happen?" There was no point in tussling over blame (or credit). Julia needed to know what Wallace had told the men.

"He said he took her to his home on Tuesday to bathe and rest. His housekeeper went to fetch some things from Eva's apartment—which had been turned over pretty well by Kessler's men. She reported that hoodlums had been there as well, defacing her things and leaving nasty messages on the walls."

Julia grimaced. She'd known Eva wouldn't be safe there, but even unseen the graphic assault unsettled her.

"Unfortunately, that led to new problems. The next morning, his housekeeper, a Mrs. Hoskins, laid down a law of her own. Apparently she refused to countenance Miss Pruitt living under her roof. Wallace said she feared it put them all in danger—though the man must live in a virtual fortress, given the circles he moves in."

Before Julia could challenge his unsavory insinuation, Philip went on. "But it turned out the real rub was that she did not care to be waiting on a colored guest, even though she's black as coal herself." He smiled at the absurdity.

It made sense to Julia, though, after hearing Eva's tales of being resented and mistrusted by some darker Negroes. She'd explain it to him later. "What did he do?"

"When a good housekeeper says jump, one jumps. He moved Miss Pruitt into a vacant apartment in a building he owns up on West 141st. He claimed the tenants there keep to their own business and thought she'd be safe there. Kessler was none too pleased he hadn't been consulted or even informed about the move."

Julia could well imagine his outburst at the news, and she silently applauded Wallace's initiative. Kessler would have simply taken her back into custody. Once Eva entered a cell, Julia feared she'd never be allowed to leave it. "For her own safety" would become a prison sentence of its own.

"And that's when she got away?"

Philip nodded. "Vanished, according to Wallace."

A terrible thought occurred. Surely he would have said. But she had to ask. "Was there any sign of trouble? That she'd been forced to leave? That maybe Timson's men took her?"

He shook his head. "Wallace swore he saw nothing untoward." The vague word encompassed a multitude of scenarios best left unimagined, and Julia was grateful for its abstraction, leaving her thoughts clear for the immediate purposes.

"So what happens now?"

"Shall I quote?" Philip lit a fresh Régie. "After the juicier expletives, I believe *cherchez la femme* crossed a few lips. Kessler turned a few shades closer to scarlet, and I had to remind him to breathe. He blamed me, complaining that no one would have to *cherchez* at all if I hadn't badgered him to release the lady."

"Thank God you did, or she'd be pilloried to high heaven by now." A week without an arrest had the newspapers in a frenzy, as Wright had pointed out.

She glanced at the mantel clock. "Sergeant Hannity must be spitting daggers." A week ago the man had been prowling about this very room badgering her for information about that evening at Carlotta's. Seven long yet fruitless days ago. "What does Kessler intend to do?"

"Oh, he wants her found pronto, as you'd expect. Wallace did some pretty fancy talking, claiming he's in a better position to retrieve her with no one the wiser. He swore he'd see to it himself."

"He's right. Wallace knows those neighborhoods. He can make sure it's done on the sly, with a well-placed word here and there."

"Quite possibly," Philip agreed, "though Kessler's understandably more chary of his word this time around. Still, what choice does he have? He's in a tough spot. A beefy platoon of Hannity's boys tramping around would only throw off all sorts of delicate balances. He's convinced there are still too many raw suspicions and itchy trigger fingers in the mix. One blunder and he'd have anarchy on those streets—Timson's aggrieved men seeking retribution wherever they can find it. Kessler's worst nightmare."

"No one mentioned this to Wright, did they? He'd love nothing better than to see Kessler raked over the coals in the press for losing a suspect."

Philip shook his head. "But Kessler knows it's only a matter of time before the press cotton on to it, and the commissioner will demand an arrest."

"We all know it," Julia said. Arbitrary and expedient though it was, she knew how public officials could sacrifice almost any nicety of justice and fair play to appease a bloodthirsty public. "So what did he do?"

"He relented. It nearly choked him to say, but he gave the fellow permission to try to find her himself."

"Was that what he meant by 'two weeks'?" Julia asked, remembering his cryptic last comment as she'd rejoined the men.

"Precisely. Kessler gave him one week, but Wallace talked him up to two. He has two weeks to find what he so carelessly misplaced, or Kessler sends in his troops."

"It's not funny." Julia protested the frivolous language. "Eva's missing, Philip, not misplaced. She could be in danger."

"Danger?" Philip tapped off his ashes. "I doubt it. Unless Wallace is more cold blooded than even I suspect, nothing about his demeanor last night suggested he feared she was in mortal peril. I think she simply gave him the slip, as he said."

He sat forward. "Think about it. Maybe she's simply on a walkabout, for reasons of her own. Or she's bolted to join her paramour. Crockett has vanished too, remember? Maybe the two of them are holed up together, hoping to ride out the storm. Regardless, she can't go far without money or passport."

No passport. That meant no champagne, no shipboard dinner, no triumphant arrival at Le Havre. "How do you know that?"

"I don't. I'm just repeating what Wallace said."

Julia's brief hope of Eva's escape sank as fantasy gave way to reality. "Walkabout" was Philip's airy gloss on the situation. The fact remained that she now had no way to reach Eva, no way to speak with her and hear her account of that night. Wherever she was, Eva was not safely hidden under Wallace's care.

Wallace. The lovely glow of their last hour together dimmed. Why hadn't he told her any of this? She'd asked him directly, and he'd assured her he'd protect Eva. *Nothing to worry about.* Was that mere bravado? The male impulse to shield women from bad news? Did he really think she'd bruise so easily? Eva's disappearance gave her a great deal to worry about, yet his deceit, even by omission, was troubling too.

During her silence Philip refilled their empty cups. He lifted his to his chin but for several seconds simply contemplated her over its rim. "I take it, from your face and from your questions," he said, "that your friend did not share this information himself last night?"

Her cheeks flooded. That realization had been rising in her thoughts as well, cold and rank as a marsh fog.

He sighed. "Trust is like glass, you know. Once broken, it can never be mended."

Julia scowled and turned in her chair. She remembered the deep solicitude in Wallace's eyes as they'd traveled home, his eerily somber *What will you have me do, Miss Kydd?* As if honoring her wishes were all. His face, full of respect and deference, was not the face of a liar. Her trust was cracked, perhaps, but not broken.

Yet if he'd told her the truth, if Eva was still in his care and safe from danger, then he'd fabricated the story he'd told Kessler. It would be fantastically bold, as well as risky, to hoodwink the New York Police Department in such a high-stakes matter. Wallace was no fool, especially if he was about to launch himself into public service. No, Julia had to admit that any romantic interests he hoped to pursue with her paled in comparison to his civic responsibilities to Kessler. Wallace was smart and ambitious; his priorities must lie with his career, not a brewing dalliance (however delightful) with Julia. Kessler would get the truth, not her.

She set aside her cup and saucer with a hasty clatter. Wallace's deceit was not her first concern. She had a more urgent new truth to face: Eva had disappeared, and every hour she remained missing deepened

Kessler's conviction of her guilt. Unless she could find Eva herself and learn what had happened that night, Julia's only hope of helping her evade Kessler's grip was to present him with a plausible alternative suspect. Her instinct's favorite candidate, Jerome Crockett, remained elusive, which left her with few options. Best was to follow the spider of interest that had traveled her spine at Coral Goldsmith's news that her husband had lied about his alibi.

Arthur Goldsmith's disappearance that night might be as innocuous as Coral suspected—a taxi ride to his office sofa. But he'd witnessed Timson's violent resolve to keep the manuscript, and he'd seen where he'd put it. Beyond Eva, no one had more stake in the fate of that manuscript than Goldsmith. His anger had been righteous, frightening in its suppressed fury. He had paid for that novel; by rights it belonged to him. And he had raged out into the night, alone, during the very hours Leonard Timson had been shot.

Julia's forgotten cigarette smoldered nearly to her fingers. With a start she ground it out. She would have to come up with a pretext to talk with Goldsmith. However contrived it might be, she needed to sustain the ruse long enough to gauge his temperament, to see if she could imagine—or convincingly portray—him as Timson's murderer.

CHAPTER 19

Arthur Goldsmith rose when Julia was shown into his third floor office above West Forty-Second Street. He buttoned his fawn-colored jacket over a turquoise shirt with a white collar and deep-emerald tie. The ensemble, paired with his olive skin and gleaming black hair, carried a Mediterranean élan, as if he had just stepped from his yacht off the coast of Capri. The eminent publisher greeted her with a mix of curiosity and condescension. Julia accepted this. She deserved as much, given the flimsy reason for her appointment. She carried her blue leather portfolio, posing as a prospective designer in search of commissions.

She accepted the brief grip of Goldsmith's hand and followed its courteous sweep toward a pair of tight-backed upholstered chairs facing his desk. She crossed the room with languid care, chin high and shoulders relaxed. Her frock suited her beautifully, a cream silk day dress edged in pale pink with a low suede belt. Its fluid skirt moved with every sway of her stride. She'd worn her finest pair of Italian street shoes, pale-rose suede and snakeskin with silver buckles.

Anything? She turned, alert for some inkling of interest. Coral Goldsmith's astonishing claim of her husband's attraction amused Julia. Could there be even a grain of truth to it?

No, she decided. Not one glimmer of lusty interest, which was just as well. Whatever desire this man might feel, it would be bloodless and shrewd, like the calculating drive for a good price or sound investment.

Julia imagined sex between the two Goldsmiths must resemble the labors of unoiled machinery, steel grinding against steel.

So she had only one card to play, his passion for typography. She was more than knowledgeable in that arena herself and could easily match his enthusiasm. She hoped it might again overcome his more general disregard for her as a young person of no significance.

She was in luck. Several framed type specimens and broadsheets were arranged on the back wall. With an avid click of her tongue, she moved to admire them. Goldsmith hesitated, no doubt totting the moments he'd allotted for this interruption and calculating the cost of any digression. Then he followed her to the display.

The type specimens drew her eye first. She admired his copy of the 1734 edition of William Caslon's proud exhibition of his foundry's wares, as well as a striking broadsheet of Rudolf Koch's bold new Neuland. Koch was an accomplished lettering artist, and his type designs captured his calligraphic skills.

The other sheets were title pages, all American of recent vintage. She recognized Goudy's *Elements of Lettering*, featuring his long-limbed but endearing Kennerley types, and Bruce Rogers's recent confection for the Grolier Club, *The Pierrot of the Minute*. Goldsmith identified other pages as Rogers's work, and a handsome selection of Elmer Adler's ephemera work from the Pynson Printers. As she perused this gallery, he narrated its treasures with growing animation, encouraged by the informed dips and nods of her salmon-pink cloche.

"None of your own books, Mr. Goldsmith?"

He tipped his head with satisfaction, explaining that framed selections of the firm's own publications were displayed in the company library down the hall. Six of his books, he added, since she was interested, had been selected among the nation's fifty most handsome productions for 1923 and 1924. He hoped to notch an even bigger proportion in the next judging. Any number of other Goldsmith titles, he noted, deserved honor as well. He credited the several designers to whom he entrusted their books, Rogers and Adler preeminently. "And this good man."

A smiling fellow with a shock of unruly white hair strode into the room. Introduced as Mr. Dwiggins, he handed Goldsmith a pencil-rendered title page board for Willa Cather's *My Mortal Enemy* and immediately excused himself. It was beautifully hand-lettered. Of the many arts she longed to master, Julia said truthfully, calligraphy was high on the list. But being left handed, she might as well wish to dance on the moon.

"It's always a pleasure to share an interest in typography," Goldsmith said, resuming his business day with tact. "But I understand your visit has another purpose?"

Julia retrieved her portfolio. Oh yes. She too had work to do. And now he looked to her with genuine interest. She realized with a pang that he was a true comrade. In simpler circumstances she would love to talk shop with him about the exciting new typefaces being resurrected from past eras, when the human hand had guided layout and design, before the last century's shift to soul-killing industrial bookmaking. She dreaded to think what today's ruse might cost her in future opportunities for such pleasures.

She settled into one of the low-backed chairs, and Goldsmith sat in the other, hands folded around one knee. His fingers were lean, nails buffed to a spotless sheen. He wore no rings. Julia crossed her legs, slowly, discreetly, just to double-check.

She heard the faintest shift in his breathing. His eyes remained lowered, and she knew. He was aware of her legs now. The man did love books more than women, as Austen had joked, but not strictly instead of them. Julia—that rare combination of a reasonably fine-featured young woman with a bibliophile's heart and mind—had indeed aroused his interest. That gave her a second card to play. With luck it would keep her in the room long enough for her planned gambit.

Goldsmith waited, impatience fading his smile. Julia swiveled to better display her ankle.

"I was told you're a serious bibliophile, Mr. Goldsmith," she said, "and now I've seen for myself the care that goes into the design of your books. They're consistently handsome, as attractive as they are legible. I particularly admired that pretty little edition last year of Mrs. Browning's *Sonnets* and that stunning title page of Mr. Hergesheimer's latest. And how refreshing to see colophons in trade books. I wonder why more American publishers don't follow your lead in this. Colophons can make such a difference in raising readers' awareness of type, don't you think? We both know standards could bear a good deal of raising."

Goldsmith accepted this meandering speech with grace, shadowed by puzzled boredom.

"It's no secret I'm a fine printer myself," Julia hurried on. "I was hoping you might look at a sample of my work. It would be a great honor to design something for you—something small, a pamphlet or catalog, perhaps. It would be an honor to play even a tiny part in your distinguished company, Mr. Goldsmith." She readied the blue leather portfolio in her lap.

Goldsmith listened, dark eyes alert behind hooded lids. He straightened. "Thank you for thinking of our firm, Miss Kydd, but Mr. Adler supervises all of our typographic work."

"Will you at least look?" She patted her skirt, smoothing it toward her knee.

At this he extended his hand and accepted the portfolio. Julia continued to smile, willing him to glance through the entire stack of sketches. Fortunately, her examples were credibly informed by the latest developments in type design and typography. She'd handed Goldsmith half a dozen title page drawings modeled on recent editions from French and British publishers of the sort she thought Goldsmith might like. She wanted to pique just enough interest to make sure he scanned all six designs.

Her smile was in preparation for his reaction to the final sketch. He was about to close the portfolio when he saw it, a bold rendering of *HARLEM ANGEL* in forty-eight-point Goudy caps letterspaced in two lines spanning the width of the type page.

He snapped the portfolio shut. "Your final sample is premature, Miss Kydd. It's also, under the circumstances, in deplorable taste."

Good. She needed to provoke him beyond his cool, arrogant aplomb. She met his reprimand with confusion, then apologies. "I didn't mean to offend you, Mr. Goldsmith. I sketched that before the troubles and must have forgotten to remove it. I've been so distracted, worrying about poor Eva Pruitt. Please forgive me."

This wheedled a tense conciliatory nod out of him. She leaned forward. "You must be upset too, at all the things they're saying. Is Eva's manuscript really missing?"

"I don't know what gossip you listen to, Miss Kydd, but yes, the manuscript is gone."

"How awful. You paid for it, and then to get—nothing."

He stood and moved to his desk, where he picked up a pocket appointment calendar.

Julia rose as well. "You must feel cheated."

At last he seemed discomfited. His eyes dropped to the floor, or perhaps to Julia's ankle.

She shifted her weight to suggest the hip beneath the drape of her dress. "Leonard Timson was a ruthless, dishonest man. He stole from you. You had every right to be furious." Julia did her best to rekindle that angry spark. Anger might rock him further off balance, spur him into an indiscreet account of that night.

"Indeed," Goldsmith said. "But the man is dead now. His crimes are no longer relevant."

His words had the tone of a dismissal, but beneath it Julia heard a chilling, almost boastful ring. Was this some kind of Machiavellian assertion that Timson had paid for those crimes, that the two men were now square? Was Goldsmith implying he'd returned early that morning for the manuscript—and revenge? This was the possibility Julia had come to explore, but now that Goldsmith was suggesting it himself, she was too startled to pounce.

The moment passed. When he lifted his gaze, she saw nothing but cool control. His brazen composure made it clear there would be no further discussion, much less any reckless blurting. He wished to be done with the subject.

But not necessarily with her. A new glint of humor shone in his eyes. He was enjoying this. Their conversation had become a sport to him, a tussle with a playful puppy or willful child. A game—with shapely ankles in the bargain.

Julia, however, could not be turned aside so easily, not on the brink of a breakthrough. She tried again. Her shoulder brushed his sleeve, in case that still carried a trace of charm. "I can't stop thinking of poor Eva. I understand she's missing again."

He nodded. Wisely he forbore mentioning the breach of contract suit Coral had initiated.

Julia winced. "Aren't you worried for her? One of your most promising authors?"

"A tender heart will get you nowhere, Miss Kydd," he counseled, "should you seriously pursue thoughts of becoming a publisher."

His words as good as patted her on the head. He was now simply milking the company of a softheaded woman. Yet Julia plunged ahead. Her pride was already damaged; she had little more to lose.

"I was thinking of those awful policemen who questioned me after Mr. Timson was shot. Thank goodness I could tell them I was at home in my bed. Did they hound you as well?" Her sentence trailed off.

Goldsmith gave a short, incredulous laugh. "Are you interrogating me?"

Julia faltered. "I only wondered—"

"You can't seriously think *I* murdered the fellow."

At his bark of astonishment, she realized how ludicrous she was. Hopes of his guilt had blinded her to the obvious. Goldsmith was a fastidious man, vain and precise. Such a man would never abide the messy drama of a point-blank gunshot. He channeled his aggression into clean, bloodless assaults—legal, moral, and economic. Wherever he had gone that night, Goldsmith had not returned to gun down Timson.

He strode to the door. "Audacity does not become you, Miss Kydd."

Cheeks burning, Julia gathered up her portfolio.

"I will tell you this," he said. "Miss Pruitt is in a volatile relationship with a difficult man. If you're searching for villains, I suggest you begin there."

He grasped the doorknob. "And I assume you have no interest whatsoever in designing for us, so we'll say no more of that either. Don't ever waste my time again, Miss Kydd. Good day."

The puppy had been scolded, the child sent to bed.

He held open the door with perfect manners, and Julia passed through the reception lobby clutching her last tatter of dignity. She'd sacrificed a great deal of pride and gained precisely nothing. Only after she reached the hall and called for the elevator did she realize that her fists were clenched, more from his echoing amusement than his anger.

CHAPTER 20

"Do you remember Arthur Goldsmith, Eva's publisher?" Julia asked Wallace the following evening. She spoke lightly. It must be a delicate, careless overture. The time had finally come for such talk, and she couldn't risk crushing it with urgency. After an evening of all things Schubert in *Blossom Time* at the Majestic, they were settled on the banquette cushions in a private dining alcove at Chez Mareille.

Lifting a finger for patience, he squeezed a lemon wedge over the last two oysters. He carried the smaller one, plump and mottled in its shell, to her mouth. Julia accepted the morsel and dispatched it quickly. As usual the experience was tolerable but hardly transcendent. Nevertheless she smiled and prepared for the kiss that followed. A kiss always followed.

"Julia. How lovely to see you." Julia looked up to see Mrs. Macready. "Welcome, Mr. Wallace," she added coolly.

"Leah." He doused the final oyster with an extra squirt of lemon.

"Enjoy your meal," Mrs. Macready said, already moving away to greet another party.

How very odd. Her tone was unmistakably chilly. Julia turned to her companion and tipped her chin in silent query.

"We go way back, Mrs. Macready and I," Wallace said.

"Who is she, exactly?" Julia had longed to know this from the moment they'd met.

"She owns this place. Or rather her late husband did, and she enjoys his fortune, as you see."

"You don't seem on very good terms."

"She snubs me, you mean? At every opportunity."

"How unpleasant."

"Quite."

"She's been kind to me." Julia remembered Mrs. Macready's recent friendly company in the ladies' lounge and her soothing reassurances last fall, helping Julia to understand Philip's lashing mood the night his aunt Lillian had died. He'd been stung to lose the irascible old woman of whom he was inordinately fond; Julia could only imagine his grief at later learning she was his natural mother. On that and so much else, Philip remained quiet.

"Long ago I offended her in some way, and now nothing I can do or say can atone."

Julia nodded, even though she remained curious why Wallace's experience of the woman was so different from Philip's. Was it also romantic? Wallace no doubt had many former paramours in the city. Had something gone badly wrong between them? Or a business deal gone awry? That too she could imagine.

Wallace smiled, reclaiming her attention. "You asked about Goldsmith. We met that night at Carlotta's. Beyond that, I don't know him. We move in different circles. Why?"

"I wondered if he might be the murderer. He certainly had good reason." She hoped Wallace might offer up some good cause to overturn her dismal conclusion that Goldsmith by nature was not a killer, at least not by a close-range gunshot.

Wallace laughed softly. "Plenty of people had reasons to wish Leonard harm, and most had very good reasons. By all means add Goldsmith to the list if you like. Anything to find Kessler a better suspect than Eva. Preferably one who confesses or hauls out that tatted-up gun."

A silver tureen of *consommé brunoise* arrived. The waiter ladled the steaming broth into two china soup plates, and the sommelier replaced their champagne with a bottle of 1899 Château Tujean from Wallace's collection in the restaurant's cellars. Both men disappeared again, pulling a heavy velvet curtain across the entrance to their booth.

Julia took a deep breath. She'd intended to follow his lead in speaking of Eva, as if she didn't know what he'd admitted to Kessler. But in that moment it seemed only to add a second deception between them, when she much preferred there be none. For better or worse, she put down her spoon and said, "I know she's missing. Philip told me."

Wallace laid down his spoon as well. He examined her face for a good ten seconds before dropping his eyes. "I apologize. I should have told you the truth. I had hoped to spare you the worry, as there's nothing you could do." He gave a small smile. "Though I must confess it's nicer not to have to sidestep the issue. She is missing. I don't know where she is. But I also don't think there's serious cause for worry."

"If only I could talk with her," Julia said. "I just want to know she's all right." She wanted to ask Eva a great deal more, but that agenda was best left covert.

"We all do," Wallace said. "But in this case, no news is good news. She's safe as long as things stay quiet. The boys at Carlotta's are starting to settle down. I'm lending them Ethel Dunway for a few weeks, to get their floor show back on track. Ethel's may not be a household name to you, but in that neighborhood he's quite the celebrity." He gave a hollow laugh. "Eddie or Ethel—it all depends on the whim of his wardrobe. Quite entertaining in a strictly late-night sort of way, but he packs the house. The best thing for Eva would be to get Carlotta's up and running at full power again. Busy cash registers to keep Leonard's men occupied."

"You did that to help her?"

"Keeping a lid on things is good for me and mine. But yes, for Eva too."

"You've been a good friend to her."

Wallace leaned back. His voice dropped to a quieter register. "I've known Eva for a long time, since she was a kid just up from the South somewhere. I've seen her grow up, turn into a real swan."

Julia poured him more wine to encourage the story. This was something she wanted to hear, in as leisurely a fashion as he cared to tell it. She suspected there was a good reason he'd stepped forward to help Eva, and perhaps this would explain it.

"It's not that much of a tale. Ours is strictly a business acquaintance. I could see early on that she had talent, deserved better than the small stage where she worked. I persuaded Leonard to take her on when he opened shop, even though she'd never worked one of the big clubs before." He smiled. "I doubt she even knows that."

Julia wondered, "If she could lie low until Kessler finds the murderer, or at least a better suspect, do you think she could ever work again, at another club? She's beautiful and talented. With time, couldn't she pick up where she left off?"

"It's nice to think so."

"You helped her before. Could you help her again, once all this is sorted? I mean hire her?"

He watched the colors of the Bordeaux splintering in the candlelight. "Even assuming the business of Timson's murder goes away, hiring her would not be as simple as you think."

"I understood you owned a few clubs."

"I keep a hand in just three. Only one might be a possibility. It's called the Half-Shell." He gave Julia an amused glance. "You see how partial I am to oysters. It's a small place but gaining a fairly select clientele. The better downtown sorts, who expect to pay what I'd charge for a show with Eva. The place is more, shall we say, discreet—for those who enjoy what needs discretion—than the flash and strut at Carlotta's.

"I suppose we could make a place for her, eventually, after everything blows over," he mused.

"What about your other clubs?"

"The Tupelo Room on West 143rd, and Slim Sal's even further up Lenox. Rough and rougher. Both are for coloreds, and frankly, I leave them to my managers. Eva wouldn't last long in either place. She needs to play to folks like us."

He touched the curve beneath her jaw. "Like you."

Did Eva need a white audience? Would colored patrons resent her? Julia remembered Eva's trouble finding work, the rejection she'd faced for being too light and yet not white. Or might colored audiences bristle to see images of slavery bathed in glamorous golden light? Julia wished she could ask Eva what went through her mind to be part of that spectacle, gaped at by throngs of what could be the wealthy descendants of slave owners, pelted by their gifts of worthless rings. It was yet another conversation she longed to have with Eva.

Later, after the *filet de boeuf en croûte* had been served and cleared away, Julia's thoughts returned to the arrogant amusement in Arthur Goldsmith's eyes, and then for the hundredth time to Eva's broken hobble as she'd been yanked from Kessler's office. This last image of her enigmatic friend troubled her, and she flinched. The wine in her glass swayed.

"No news might be bad news," she said. "Don't you have *some* idea where she is?"

"None, I'm afraid."

"What if she's trapped somewhere? What if someone forced her out of that apartment?"

Wallace's head rocked back in exasperation. "Julia, please. Leave it. I will find her."

"I wish there was something I could do."

"Do not even think of looking for her yourself. You could stumble into any number of hornet nests. More than that, you could make things worse for her."

What did that mean?

"I'm serious. It could be dangerous. You can't take risks you don't understand."

Julia willed reticence into her eyes. She was not a child. She understood the risk. The danger was precisely why she wanted to find her friend.

Wallace took the glass from her hand. He drew the inner length of her forearm across his chin, lingering at the crook of her elbow. Her hand dangled above his right ear. Julia watched the slow turn of radiant colors from the diamonds in her bracelet, as if she were deep underwater. "Do not involve yourself. Do not ask questions you don't understand of people you don't know."

He lowered her arm and slipped it inside his jacket. Guiding her palm across his crisp shirtfront, over the steady postprandial thump of his heart, he pressed it hard onto a gun sleeping against his ribs.

She jerked upright and tried to pull free.

His grip tightened, forcing her fingers over the contours of the weapon. "Good. You should be frightened. Guns are everywhere, Julia. This"—he jiggled the weapon beneath her hand—"gives everyone time to think. And if it fires, I've lost, not won."

The curtain stirred, and beyond it a throat was cleared with forced vigor. "Telephone call for you, Mr. Wallace, sir."

He squeezed her hand before lifting it for a kiss. "Trust me on this."

With a wry half smile Wallace slid along the cushions and disappeared. Julia gripped her water glass and took several calming sips. By the time he returned, she had gathered her handbag and resigned herself to the conversation, and likely the evening, being over.

"I must apologize," he said, settling beside her. "I had hoped to advance my cause with you this evening. But it seems that hope must wait."

"Your cause?"

"My suit, if you prefer."

"Your seduction. Let's be clear about these things. Your conquest."

She spoke with a facetious lilt, but Wallace's nose tightened in distaste. He laid his palm flat against the white linen tablecloth and tapped twice with his forefinger. "I loathe those terms. Any intimacies I enjoy are freely given. I despise any notion of *conquest*."

Julia felt chastened. "I'm sorry," she said. "It was glib of me."

"And I'm sorry for abandoning the evening." He brushed a knuckle across her cheek. "A problem has come up at the Half-Shell I must attend to. I've called for the car. Edgar will take you home. I promise fewer distractions next time."

He helped her from the booth and guided her through the hushed room. Reaching the entrance, he kissed her cheek and transferred her to the waiting doorman.

Julia felt every moment of his gaze as she descended the seven steps to the pavement and the solicitous Edgar. When the Duesenberg eased into traffic, she smiled. Although curtailed and unsettling, the evening had deepened her interest in Martin Wallace, and she felt certain the attraction was mutual. He would be an exquisite lover.

The familiar ache tipped her head back into the smooth leather. But something else eluded her, perplexed her. She wanted more than his carnal attention. She could dance that dance, but why settle for the pastime of the bored and disillusioned?

Yes, Wallace desired her. But she was still a bauble to him. A prized bauble, one whose qualities he discerned and valued, but a bauble nonetheless. She would be patient, relish the wait. Soon they'd understand each other. She smiled at her reflection in the window. At last. What a pleasure it was to finally know such a man.

Even if he carried a gun.

CHAPTER 21

The following afternoon Julia paid the driver and turned to the entrance of the handsome West 135th Street branch of the city's public library. Four young Negro boys in enormous caps sprawled with tangled legs across the steps. One tried to whistle at her, but what emerged was a high-pitched *hoo-hoo*. They rolled from side to side, laughing and pointing.

"Hot choo," another called out. "Whatchu jig chasin'?"

They hooted as she crouched to see their faces, shading her eyes from the glaring pavement. "Them rags some scratch. To da bricks, looksa. Ooo-wah." Their glee was like a new kind of mysterious music. Were they mocking her? Cursing her? Possibly both, but they were right to laugh at her. She was dressed for Fifth Avenue; here she was a ridiculous sight. The smallest boy, whose crooked spectacles magnified a lazy eye, brushed the peacock feathers stitched to the brim of her straw cloche. The others crowded around. Hand after hand petted the exotic feathers, straying to her crepe de chine hem, the picot edging of her sleeve, and even the tiny clocked chevrons marching down her stocking toward her ankle.

Julia removed her hat. With a swift tug she dislodged one of the feathers—for which she'd no doubt paid a premium to Mademoiselle Reynard in Rue de Phénicie last winter—and laid it in the child's dirty palm. Christophine could replace it in a trice and otherwise improve the hat while she had her needle handy. The boys whooped and escorted Julia with two-booted hops up the steps to the wide front door, but they scattered when she motioned them to join her inside.

It smelled of lilacs, newsprint, and floor wax. A fistful of languid blooms drooped over the oak counter of the circulation desk. The large room was quiet, bathed in warm light streaming in the tall windows. Some half dozen women were working at small desks behind the counter. She approached and waited. One of the women hobbled forward as if her shoes were too small.

"I wonder if I might speak with a young man who works here," Julia said in a low voice. "Mr. Logan Lanier?"

The woman glared at her. "He's working, miss."

"Yes, I understand. I won't take but a few minutes of his time."

"This is no place for that. You can talk to that boy all you want on his own time, honey."

"Could you at least tell me when he'll take a break? I'll wait." Julia folded her hands on the counter.

"Can't say."

An older woman approached. She patted the first woman's arm. "I'm sorry, miss, but employees are not allowed visitors during their shifts. Too many distractions here as it is."

Julia offered a sympathetic nod and leaned forward, resting her forearm on the ancient wood. "I'm here from *Vanity Fair*," she whispered. "I'm under an awful deadline and really must speak to Mr. Lanier today. I haven't been able to reach him any other way."

The woman looked more flustered than stubborn. Julia heard a rustle from the workers seated behind the counter, but when she glanced at them, their eyes dived elsewhere.

"May I simply—" Julia began again when a door at the back clanked open and Logan hurried over. He must have been alerted that someone was asking for him.

"I've been here since eleven, Mrs. Crowder," he said. "I'm due for a break. Or," he continued, nearly stammering, "I could sort out the retrieval baskets that came in last week. She could talk to me—whatever this is about—while I work down there."

"I decide when you're due for a break," she said. "And what tasks you boys take on."

"Yes, ma'am." He had not yet looked at Julia.

"But those baskets have gone unsorted long enough," the woman conceded. "She can go with you, but make it quick. Answer her questions and get back to work. I want her gone in fifteen minutes. And see me before you leave today."

"Yes, ma'am." He turned and signaled for Julia to follow. As they passed through the flotilla of small oak desks, the staff twittered, bosoms bouncing in a hiss of whispers. It was English, of course, but like nothing she'd ever heard. "She yo Sheba, *Mistah* Logan-berry?" "Dinge got hisself a pinktail." "Ain't yo arnchy!" She understood only that the barrage was demeaning.

Julia followed him down a flight of linoleum-covered stairs, bristling at his meek obedience and acceptance of those women's scorn. He deserved respect, not derision. In silence he led her to a basement room with a cement floor and two small windows, cased in heavy grillwork, high on the wall. He yanked the string hanging from a light bulb in the center of the room, releasing a weak yellow light and a galaxy of dust. Several baskets full of books sat under a table beneath the windows. At last he turned. "What in God's good name are you doing here?"

His tone startled her. "I'm sorry. I never meant to cause you any trouble. I wouldn't have bothered you, but it's important, and I don't know who else I can ask."

"Stick with Pablo, Miss Kydd. Do your sightseeing with him." Logan heaved one of the baskets onto the table and upended it. *Miss Kydd*, not *Julia*. He was angry indeed if their fragile start of a friendship meant nothing now.

"Stop that." Julia reached to break the fall of books. She straightened those that had fallen spine up, their pages buckling open. "You're angry with me, not them."

Logan tossed the empty basket beneath the table. He pulled books out of the jumble and began to set them on their fore edges. "You shouldn't have come here."

Julia righted the books more carefully and ordered them by the Dewey numbers penned on their spines. Something more was tormenting him. "Why do those women taunt you like that? Don't they know you write prize-winning poetry?"

Logan swung his jaw in frustration. Footsteps shuffled in the hall. He waited until the stairwell door banged shut. "You have no idea how ridiculous I am to most of the folks up there." He swung his fist toward the street beyond the narrow windows. "Poetry! Jesus! It will be bad enough explaining you."

Logan paced across the room and back. When he spoke, the words nearly choked him. "You know what? I can speak three languages, write a damn decent villanelle, and lecture on Shakespeare or Yeats, but in the end I'm still just a sorry-ass buck to those hyenas. And I'd better never forget it. Those women make damn sure I don't."

Julia didn't understand. Logan Lanier was a talented poet and scholar. It pained her to hear anyone, least of all Logan himself, refer to him with derision. In each of their conversations, she'd felt a growing regard for his intelligence, his brave aspirations, his gentle demeanor. He deserved respect, yet somehow her visit—and her presumed friendship—had instead stirred others to scorn and ridicule him.

"I'm sorry." She was sorry for her apology too. It was feeble and thin, unequal to the embarrassment she'd caused.

He shook his head to cut short her apology, to change the subject. "Why are you here?"

"I need to talk with you."

"Ask Pablo. He's the expert." Logan emptied a second basket of books onto the table, less violently, and began to sort them into place with the first batch lined up against the wall.

Julia helped when he edged aside to allow it. "Do you know where Eva Pruitt is?"

He punched out a sharp breath and kept working. "No."

"Haven't you heard anything? A rumor? A suspicion?"

"No."

"Eva needs your help, Logan." Julia kept her voice low. "You must have some idea where she's hiding. Or Jerome Crockett?"

"Nope. None."

The spilled books made a puddle of scuffed and fraying buckram in drab shades of green, blue, tan, and maroon. Library bindings, they were called, corners bulging with an extra thickness of the sturdy, starched cloth. They reminded her of children muffled beneath layers of coats and scarves, unable to play or dance or speak. "She could be in terrible danger."

"Leave it alone, Julia. Wherever she is, Eva Pruitt got herself into this mess, and she can get herself out of it."

It was a brutal thing to say. Julia remembered Eva's fond introduction at Duveen's party, her generous words. "I thought she was your friend. She had only good things to say about you, about your poetry. And now she's in desperate trouble."

He glanced at the dusty clock on the wall above the door. Twelve minutes had elapsed. "I'm sorry for her. I am. But all along she let everyone know she didn't need anything from us. She just started announcing that, oh, by the way, she was writing a novel—in her spare time, on top of being a big glamorous star at Carlotta's, making more money in a week than I make in a month. Then she waltzed straight to Pablo, straight to his power and purse strings, to sell him exactly what he wants—his precious finger-snapping tell-all of low-down jigaboo life."

He turned to face Julia, forehead creased. "Why do you care?"

Before she could answer, he began transferring the ordered books into one of the emptied baskets. He brushed Julia's hands away. "Just please, *please* don't tell me you fancy yourself one of those rich white lady patronesses. Another sweet little Miss Anne swooping in to rescue deserving Negroes." He paused. "For one thing, Eva's the last person who needs that kind of help. For another"—he glared at his feet—"I thought you had better sense."

Rich white lady patronesses? It took Julia a moment to figure out what he meant. Then it incensed her. When he lifted the basket, taking her silence for guilt, she gripped his wrist. "How can you possibly think I'm out to collect writers, like some pompous dowager?"

"Then why are you here?"

"She's my friend and I want to help her. That's all."

"That's never all." He gave a bitter smile. "There's always something more when white folks say they want to help. Pablo wants to plant his flag smack in the center of all things Negro. Arthur Goldsmith wants profit and prestige. Austen Hurd hopes some of it comes Liveright's way. Martin Wallace is real helpful, as long as he gets to be the big man calling the shots around here. What's in this for you?"

His accusation stung. When Philip had posed the question, it had been cautionary; Logan's was suspicious. What *was* in it for her? It was an appalling question. She saw again Bernice being led away in a rage of tears as the others said nothing. In part that was what was in it for Julia—the need this time to not be one of those silent watchers. They could have stepped forward. *Only* they could have intervened. Would it matter less if it had also helped them sleep better that night?

"I'm a publisher," she said. "Not much of one yet, and not in it for profit like Goldsmith or Liveright, but all publishers need writers. Does that make me selfish and insincere? I thought we were friends, Logan, and not simply because I'd like to publish your poems someday."

Logan looked down. "Would I have a say in the matter?"

Julia still clutched his wrist. Without thinking, she'd jerked it back and forth in her agitation. She dropped it and tucked her arm against her waist, mortified.

"Sorry," she said quickly. "I would, though—want to publish your work. You're a promising New Negro poet."

"Poet. Just poet. No modifiers."

He was too modest. "That's not what Pablo says."

"Pablo's nothing but modifiers. *New* and *Negro* say it all for him."

"He means it as a distinction, something to be proud of."

"Does he? Tell my friends upstairs. You have no idea what it is to be a Negro, often *the* Negro, in a white world. It qualifies everything. I'm a *Negro* student, a *Negro* poet."

"You're a Negro and a poet. Isn't that the point? Negroes can be poets—and doctors and scientists and lawyers and such."

"Of course we can and are. But what do I know about Africa? Pablo thinks colored skin means you hear drumbeats in your blood. That you can't help but hoof the Charleston while you're cleaning your teeth. No matter what you do, it's doing it as a Negro that interests him. Phi Beta Kappa with jazz in your belly—that's Pablo's perfect Negro.

"Now he thinks he's discovered us. It's better than having doors slammed in our faces, but not much. Now editors want only our *Negro* poems and stories. Now the door slams if they're not colored enough."

"Isn't it good more editors want your work? That they want to publish your perspectives, your experiences? It's recognition, Logan. Publication. I thought all writers jumped at that. I don't understand."

"Because you're white. You can be just *you*. But if an editor knows I'm colored and I send him a regular poem, about some regular thing like sunsets or daffodils or a Grecian urn, he turns it down and asks for something colored. He means something about last night's rent party or my people's struggle. Even platitudes of racial uplift will do. Especially those." He watched the clock's minute hand jump forward. "I want to be just me. All me. A poet. Full stop."

He took a sharp breath. "It's the same for Jerome. Whatever he writes, it's never colored enough. We have better luck with pseudonyms." Logan's cheeks puffed with the brittle joke. "He's Jervis Carter, and I'm Leopold Lenox—just a plain old pair of buckras from Boise or Omaha or anywhere other than Harlem." His humor faded. "He could really be something. He has a letter from T. S. Eliot saying his poem was very good. From Eliot."

Julia had once met the proud and proper Tom Eliot at a party in London. She could understand how he and Jerome would share literary tastes.

"If I'm not a poet, I'm nothing," Logan said. He raised a hand to stay her objections. "Forget the fancy education, the damn foreign languages. I'm colored, and that's all anyone can see. We thought big changes were coming after the war and all. A new day, right? Yeah, well, what's new is how fast the doors slam shut when we come knocking. Ballot box? Union hall? 'Sorry, boy. You're not eligible.' There's always another fee you can't pay, another requirement you can't meet, all of it perfectly legal. Those shiny new office buildings shooting up all over town? The ones looking for lawyers and accountants and brokers and all? 'Not hiring today, boy. Try the custodial office. The kitchen might need help.' 'You think your money's good enough to live in our neighborhood? We'll burn your house down before letting you set foot in it.' It goes on and on and on."

Julia swallowed. She traced a line of perspiration blooming along her scalp. Tears pricked her eyes, which Logan pretended not to notice. They weren't tears of sympathy, though she felt that, but of shame. Shame at her own proud eagerness to embrace the modern new world, believing it bright with promise and possibilities. She'd thought that was what *modern* and *new* meant.

"I didn't know," she said. She had known, vaguely, but thought those things were the backward remnants of the old world, the world that had died in the great slaughter. Wasn't a new society meant to rise from the war's rubble? That promise of a more wise and just future was the only thing that made memories of the war bearable.

"So what's left?" Logan said. "If Negroes want to show we contribute to this country too, on a par with whites, the only place left is Culture, with a big *C*. Art, music, theater, literature. For me it's poetry. On the same level, just as good, period. Not good 'for a Negro.'"

"But you are on the same level. Those prizes prove it. Jerome's letter from Eliot."

Logan thumped the table. "And look what the fool did with it. When someone like that says you've got talent, wouldn't you leap at a fellowship to Chicago? That's where Jerome should be, not hiding in some hellhole. Instead he follows Eva around like a lapdog. Her book's shim-sham compared to his, and they both know it. But she waltzes to the bank while he sweeps floors for a snake. Just to hang around her.

"If they get out of this thing alive, I'm afraid Eva will ditch him," he said more quietly. "She'll decide poetry is boring and breeze off to write more Hot Harlem hooey. It's all about Eva. Now he's going down with her ship. And for what?"

The clock ticked. Dust sifted through the jaundiced light. Eva would never abandon Jerome. Wise or foolish, she'd stick by her man. Julia thought of that fateful manuscript page. If Eva hadn't wanted to embellish her dedication to Jerome, Goldsmith would have the book now, Timson would be alive, and Eva and Jerome would be strolling the sidewalks of Paris.

"Where is she?" Julia said.

Logan sucked his lips. "I told you. I have no idea."

Julia listened with every muscle, but she heard only truth. He didn't know. Her one friend who knew these neighborhoods, Logan had been her last hope, and he didn't know.

That left dread. The sole remaining route to finding Eva was through the person Julia most feared, Jerome Crockett. He too had vanished. He too had powerful reasons to take Eva's manuscript. Despite

Eva's denials and Logan's regard, Julia saw violence beneath the man's stony countenance. Give him a gun and time alone with Timson—Julia could almost hear the shot. Why else had he disappeared that morning? Chances were good he was hiding somewhere in a nearby warren of back alleys and back rooms. If anyone knew where Eva was, Jerome would. Possibly they were together.

"Jerome, then. Do you know where he is?"

She waited.

"Logan?"

He hoisted a basket of books onto his hip.

"No one's seen him since the murder," she said. "He looks more guilty than Eva."

"Jerome is not a killer."

"The cops are looking for him. If I can talk to him, I may be able to help them both."

Logan shifted the heavy basket to his other hip. "He's dead if they find him."

"Maybe not, if I reach him first."

He squeezed his eyes shut.

"Help him, Logan. Where is he?"

"I got a note last week."

It was so low she could barely hear.

"He's holed up backstage over on Seventh Avenue. At a joint called the Half-Shell."

CHAPTER 22

The entrance to the Half-Shell was a short flight of stairs down from the noisy pavement on Seventh Avenue. Smaller and more intimate than Carlotta's, it was unremarkable in its plain decor. No paper-and-glue jungle vines, no white plantation pillars. The dim stage was barely large enough for seven or eight performers. A dozen or more round tables, each with four chairs, filled the dining room. A few musicians at the rear of the stage played a muted melody, making just enough noise to blur conversations.

Julia led Philip and Jack to a table at the far side of the room, where the shadows suited her purposes. She'd have rather come alone, but an unaccompanied woman would attract too much attention. Philip had agreed, and Jack was content to spend an evening anywhere that promised his good friend's company. The Half-Shell was a far cry from the pair's usual haunts—recital halls, art galleries, theaters, followed by brandies in Philip's library or at one of their clubs. But they'd accepted the outing without a murmur.

Dispatching a waiter for glasses and soda, Philip produced his flask. At least they knew what they would be drinking. Whatever liquor the Half-Shell was likely to offer might be dubious. Julia was dismayed at the conventional look of the place and the tedious loop of music. Unless the place filled soon and a show began, the men would begin fidgeting for a speedy departure, and she would have to think quickly to disguise her intentions for the evening. She nursed her drink in exact proportion to Philip's restlessness. She ought to have told him what she hoped to do here, but even Philip—not one to fuss without good reason—would make a powerful case against her plan. And he'd be right. It was foolhardy. Possibly futile, possibly even dangerous. Julia needed all her wits and courage to grapple with her own misgivings. Facing Philip's too would defeat her for certain, and she had to do this. It was her only remaining idea.

A familiar-sounding commotion at the entrance turned her head. Sure enough, Pablo Duveen stood in the open doors, his West Indian poet friend tucked like a child under his arm. Another pair of men tumbled in behind them, clinging together in an unsteady mix of affection and alcohol. Searching for a table, Duveen saw Julia. "Butter my asparagus! Look who's here. *Quelle surprise.*"

They descended with a clatter on the adjacent table. Duveen introduced his friends: Carl Sweeney—*remember?*—and Edwin and Jay, visiting from Miami. He pushed his chair close to Sweeney's and yipped small bites at his ear. *R-r-ruff, r-r-ruff.*

"Are we too boisterous, Miss Kydd?" Duveen leaned across the narrow space between the tables. "Boys, boys, boys, boys—these are boisterous times."

"You're drunk, Pablo."

"I've been drunk since 1922. True, true, Cruel Sweet Pea?" He nuzzled Sweeney's chin. "I'm obscenely happy tonight. I'm celebrating!"

Julia's hoisted eyebrow was inquiry enough.

"Fortunes have shifted," he exclaimed. "*Harlem Angel* flies again. We're publishing a murderess! Even if she's not."

"What?" Julia's voice sailed on a gust of wild hope. "You've found her?"

Duveen's white head rolled backward, and he belched a laugh that might have danced plates in the kitchen. "No, no, no, no. Not Eva."

"You said *Harlem Angel* flies again. You have the manuscript?"

Another blast of merriment. "Not flying, not yet." He stretched his lips across his protruding teeth in an effort to smile mysteriously. With a trill of fingers he teased, "But a flutter of wings."

∽

A clarinet's high yowl extinguished the house lights. At the show's first raucous notes, amid scraping chairs and hectic orders for fresh ice and soda, Julia bent toward Philip. "I'm off to the ladies'. I may be a while." She tapped his sleeve—*Enjoy the show*—and hurried away.

In the service hallway she twisted to smooth her skirt and look behind her. No one. She strode past the entrances to the toilets, past the telephone table, and past another closed, unmarked door. She squinted in the deep murk of a second corridor: unlit, drab, unfurnished. She edged forward, toward the low light and bustle that came from the opening at its far end. Backstage, she hoped.

She slid along the shadowed wall until she could see. Bodies moved back and forth through the smoky haze. A couple of musicians strolled past, peeling off their jackets. Boxes, cartons, and odd chairs and other furniture were piled haphazardly, leaving no clear path for performers and stagehands. They moved in all directions like insects, sidestepping obstacles and each other.

"Hey-ya, lady. You lost?" A boy sat smoking on a nearby crate, watching her. He couldn't have been more than ten years old.

"I'm looking for someone. Can you help me?"

"Maybe."

"Is a man named Jerome Crockett here?"

He shrugged, peering hard at her handbag.

Of course. She drew out a quarter. The boy hopped up, stubbed out his cigarette, and laid it carefully in the center of the crate.

"Jerome Crockett?" she asked again.

His nose wrinkled. He wanted that quarter but shook his head.

For heaven's sake. Not ten hours ago Logan had said Crockett was here. He had to be somewhere in this backstage hive. And if she was lucky—please, God—so was Eva.

She had an idea. "How about Jervis Carter?"

His eyes sparked, fastened on the coin between her fingers.

"Take me to him and it's yours."

The boy dashed away.

"Wait!" She mustered the closest thing to a run her shoes would allow. Their course churned up a colorful wake of expletives and cat-calls, but no one tried to stop her. She glanced about as best she could, scouting for signs of places to hide. In the dim congestion, possibilities abounded—but not opportunities to explore.

"There." The child skated to a halt at the end of another unlit corridor. He pointed through an open doorway at a solitary figure bent over a newspaper spread across a table. She could see him only in silhouette, backlit by a yellow light from behind a brick chimney. It was hot. Some kind of laundry room, Julia thought, as the boy snatched the quarter and fled.

She waited until the commotion swallowed the sound of his footsteps. Cautiously she retraced her steps, dipping into the shadows when someone passed nearby. There were jumbled crates and a few rusty racks holding costumes, but no other doors or even alcoves where someone could hunker unseen for more than a few hours. If Eva was sheltering in this building, it wasn't here. *Damn.* Julia couldn't simply poke around, not without raising suspicions. She needed some clue, some direction.

Confronting Jerome was her only option. She had to return to that stifling laundry room. If she kept her distance, he couldn't hurt her, at least not before she could get off a good scream. She crept back along the dark corridor to the door propped open by a rusty iron. The stooped man was still there. He didn't notice her. She was only half-certain it was Jerome. His once-white undervest was wet with perspiration and stained from several soakings. He was thinner than she remembered.

Brown trousers, rolled at the top, sagged from his waist. Barefoot and bent over as he was, she couldn't gauge his height. This man could be anyone—anyone with reason to cower in a backstage oven.

She had no choice. She gripped her handbag, metal clasp facing out, preparing to swing it with all her strength if he came at her. A dozen people were close enough to hear her scream. "Jerome?"

The man turned. His eyes were veined with pink, and his stubbled cheeks seemed to sink into his face. He backed away, scrabbling across the table for something. One hand braced against the bricks behind him; in the other he wielded a dull pencil stub like a knife. "What the hell?"

His voice was ragged, harsh and then cracking, as if he'd just woken from a deep sleep.

But it was Jerome's voice: low and wary.

Julia edged into the doorway. The room was hot, the air congested and thick. "I'm Julia Kydd. Eva's friend."

"Back off." He waved the pencil stub. A colony of pimples swarmed across his neck and chest, beneath the filthy cotton vest plastered to his skin. When had he last bathed? This poet, this promising scholar with a letter from Eliot? Two weeks ago he'd carried his future high on confident shoulders, shoes shone to glass. If this squalor was now his shelter, how much more noxious was the place where Eva—the greater quarry—hid?

"Where is she? Just tell me, and I'll go."

"Leave us alone."

"Tell me where she is."

"Get the hell out of here."

"I saw her in the police station," Julia said. "I know she didn't kill anyone. I want to help."

At *police* he dipped into a crouch. He regripped the blunt thumb of the pencil. It was short and dull but still a weapon. With enough force, it could do plenty of damage. Julia took a quick step back, raising her handbag and bracing her heel should she need to turn and run. Her voice rattled. "Please, where is she?"

He swallowed. His jaw creaked, but no words came out.

She tried again. "If you care about Eva, tell me where she is."

He shook his head. Did that mean he didn't know, or he would never tell? Perhaps he felt he was protecting her. Regardless, he seemed adamant.

"I just want to talk to her," Julia said. "Find some way to prove she's innocent."

He paced toward the back of the cave-like room, shaking his head like a bear tormented by flies. "You live on another planet. If Timson's dogs don't get her, the cops will. Either way, it's just one more New York lynching. She's good as dead."

Scraping sounds rose from his lungs, the empty husks of tears. Julia could hardly bear it. Eva was right. This man did love her. He might be persuaded to help her in some other way.

"You can still help her get out of this alive," Julia said.

His head came up, eyes narrowed. "How?"

"Give yourself up. You can't hide forever."

His forehead pleated in disbelief.

She pressed the point. "Confess, Jerome. At least save her."

With a guttural moan he took a step closer. She raised her handbag like a shield, flashing its sharp clasp. He stared at it, then at the remnant of pencil in his fist. He barked a hoarse laugh and dropped it onto the table. "Really?" he croaked. "You're afraid of *me*? Filthy and rank, I know, but frightening?"

His unshaven face convulsed in disbelief. Another wrenching sound came from his lungs. "You can't think *I* shot Timson."

Couldn't she? An hour ago she'd been certain of it. Now that certainty was melting fast. A fugitive killer with nothing more to lose would never make that anguished sound. A murderer would never accept a slow descent into this backstage hell. No killer would wonder at her fear.

Julia regripped the handbag at her waist, as if to ward off the terrible sound. She had come prepared for anger, even violence, but not this. Not such tormented grief.

"Do you know where she is?"

Another gust of despair. "I don't know one damn thing. Not one!"

Julia's heart lurched. This man was broken. Grief leaked out of every pore. She wanted to flee his misery but couldn't. She had to stay, try to learn anything she could. But when she asked what he knew about that night, his jaw sagged in scorn.

"Why the hell would I tell you anything? *You?*"

"Eva trusts me."

His eyes narrowed. He didn't believe her, or he didn't care.

"I'm her friend," Julia pleaded.

He swayed, thighs bumping against the table edge. "It's too late."

"Not as long as she's still hiding. Tell me, Jerome."

He bent toward her. Their noses six inches apart, his dark, hard eyes bored into hers. She blinked at the noxious smell of uncleaned teeth and endless cigarettes.

"You think you can just waltz in anywhere—her life, my life, this hellhole?" He gave a ragged sweep of his arm. "I may be a pathetic wretch, but you can snap your fingers all you want, and I still don't have to jump. Not for you. You don't get to tell me what to do." He lifted his chin. Dirt lined the creases in his neck.

Sweet Jesus.

Julia! What a dunderhead she was. He was right. She'd done exactly what Logan had warned her against. She'd sailed into his hiding place like a meddling Miss Anne, one of those righteous white women determined to rescue Negroes from their woes. She'd mistrusted Jerome from the start, wary for Eva's sake and put off by his haughty pride. What about *her* arrogance? She'd presumed much and understood little. He had every reason to mistrust her.

"I'm sorry," she said. "I truly am. But I can't do anything without your help, and you can't do anything without mine. Please trust me, for Eva's sake? Please?"

His eyes darted across her face as if searching for chinks of treachery. At last he turned and shuffled into a tiny side chamber created by a thin wall of rough boards. This hiding place had been partitioned off from the laundry, sharing its heat and moisture but not the basins. A grimy window, covered with an iron grille, was pushed up as far as it would go. But it admitted only the stench of stewing garbage from the alley. Beneath it was a cot with a bedsheet tucked neatly into place. A single metal chair, its white paint chipped and scratched, held a folded shirt. Was this tidiness the last vestige of his pride? He moved the shirt to the bed and sat beside it, slapping the chair for Julia.

A distant roar reached them from the stage. The show must be coming to its headline acts. Jerome slumped, elbows on his knees, forehead in his palms. Perspiration beaded and trickled on his skin. She tried to ignore her own.

"She wouldn't shoot him," he said wearily, as if for the thousandth time. "No matter how vile he was. She hates guns. She's terrified of them."

"Did she go back up after her last show?"

Jerome raked fingers over his spongy mat of hair. "She wanted to get that damn manuscript. I thought it was a terrible idea. But she wouldn't give it up."

Julia considered. "She went back?"

His head sagged into his hands. "I don't know."

"What happened?"

Jerome sank as he spoke, until his chest lay on the planks of his thighs. "I went home. Next thing I knew, some white men were hauling me out of bed and saying Timson had been shot. That was all. They gave me about two minutes to get some things together, then dumped me here and said I'm a dead man if I try to leave. As if I killed him!"

"Have you talked with her?"

"Once, that night. They took me into Wallace's office. I guess he owns this place. I got on the line, and her voice was shaking so bad she couldn't put more than three or four words together. I've never heard her like that."

"What did she say?"

"That Timson was dead and we both had to hide. She was crying about how we were in terrible trouble. She fussed about losing that damn manuscript. Like I care two beans for that now."

"Do you know where she was?"

"One of Wallace's buildings, I don't know which. She said he told her he'd help if she went to the cops, so she was going to do it in the morning. I think maybe he was there."

Jerome looked straight at Julia. "She never said she killed him, and she never said she didn't. She knew it was hopeless either way."

"She went to Wallace for help?"

"Yes." The word gushed out in a sluice of pained disbelief. "Why him? Why not me?"

Julia understood why. Eva had gone to someone with the power to help her. She swallowed and asked her next difficult question, praying he wouldn't get angry. "When I saw her on Monday, she had some nasty bruises. Do you know how she got them?"

He coughed. "You mean, Did I beat her? Just say it. Yes, we argued. I told her it was crazy to go back upstairs. You saw what that man was like. But I would never, ever lay a hand on her."

He exhaled another foul breath. "It was probably the cops. They like to remind us who's in charge."

"They said she'd been beaten before she came into the precinct."

"Timson then. Bastard."

"Except," Julia said slowly, thinking, "those bruises could prove Timson attacked her. She could say she acted in self-defense."

Jerome snorted. "Says a white lady in a ten-dollar hat. There's no such thing as self-defense if you're colored and a white man's dead."

Julia felt something slip inside her, her moral logic wobble and crack. He was right. How could she keep forgetting? Her map of the world was the wrong map. Here she was a ridiculous stranger. How absurd was she at that moment, formulating a logical defense in her smart Agnès hat and Callot frock, now sodden with the perspiration of a backstage laundress?

She found her small handkerchief and lifted off her hat. She ran the cloth around her hairline, pushing back the curls stuck to her face. "Eva loved your plans for Paris."

His eyes sparked. "She told you about that? Seems like a million years ago. We're not going anywhere now. Not to Paris, not to the toilet, nowhere, without checking six times that no one sees us."

Julia refolded the cloth and wiped the hollows of her throat. She hunched her shoulders and jiggled her dress before daubing the trickles between her breasts. *Sweat is a great equalizer,* she thought as she sacrificed dignity for relief. "Why was she so keen on Paris? Wouldn't it be simpler to stay closer to home?"

A wry smile crossed his face. "She was keen, wasn't she? It made no sense. But when I told her about the time I was there on a fellowship, she decided it was the perfect city, perfect for us. With a little money, the world was going to be at our feet."

The smile faded, but his eyes kindled with a new warmth. "She started scheming how to get us there. That's why she decided to write her book, to give Pablo Duveen what he'd been babbling for, the whole gaudy, glittering rara avis of Evangeline Pruitt, in prose just purple enough to make him pry open Goldsmith's wallet and dig deep."

"She wrote it for the money?"

Jerome smiled again, and Julia saw a tenderness so acute she dropped her eyes. "Hopeless romantic," he said, cheeks buckling. "Did she tell you? We got married two weeks ago so we could share a cabin on the ship."

Julia's throat swelled. She clamped down against tears. Married. Oh, Eva. That was why she'd wanted to change the wording of her dedication page. The irony was unbearable.

"She wanted the ship's captain to perform another ceremony," Jerome said, "for pictures to send out with the announcement. We were going to stay in Paris as long as the money lasted. It was to be our honeymoon, but what she really loved was the idea of afterward, being a teacher's wife, having a few babies, singing in a choir, writing some. She has talent, you know, not that you'd see it in that damn novel. She has a nice vernacular style, an easy, clean voice."

"I'd have thought she had plenty of money," Julia began, until she remembered that Timson controlled Eva's bank account. Good God. When would men and banks trust women to manage their own funds?

"That's what Timson wanted everyone to think. He bragged about her big salary like he was so generous, but he took most of it back for rent and 'security' fees. He actually charged her for the goons he hired to make sure she toed the line. She got just enough cash to keep herself looking good, which was all he wanted to pay for anyway."

Julia's sense of Eva's elegant life slipped even further. "What about her jewelry? Couldn't she sell some of it to buy those tickets?"

"He watched what she wore. She was like his expensive pet—she had to look rich to show how rich he was."

"No wonder she wanted out."

"And she was proud of that book money, thought it was respectable. She wanted to show my parents she could measure up to their Strivin' standards."

They sat nearly knee to knee now. In the linty heat Julia's slippery legs eased apart. Another few degrees, and she'd be no better than a slumbering grandma. "Where is she, Jerome?"

He took the hat from her lap. In his dark hands, his fingernails rimmed with dried blood from cracks and fissures, the thing looked as ridiculous as Marie Antoinette's towering powdered wigs. He made a fist and hung the limp pouch of straw, felt, and Belgian ribbon from it, like a foppish head on a bloody pike.

She hiccuped a weak laugh.

Jerome made a kind of laughter too. Julia tasted salt. She sponged at her face with her scrap of lace and linen. Jerome wiped his with the crown of her hat.

He laid the sticky wad in her lap. "You need a new hat."

She caught his thumb. "Where is she?"

"I do not know. Honest to God."

Julia let go of his thumb.

"You could ask your boyfriend."

"My boyfriend?"

He swiped his face again, with the back of his hand. "I saw the way you looked at him. Wallace knows. He's the one who stuck me in here. Some child brings me cigarettes and vile stuff they call food, and I just piss away the days in this oven. Might as well be in prison."

Julia barely heard him over the shouts in her brain. Wallace knew where Eva was?

Wallace knew. He'd lied to her. Each time he'd said he didn't know, he'd been lying. Each time he'd listened to her worry and speculate, his silence had been another kind of lying.

She straightened. "Can you communicate with her?"

"I write notes, but who knows what the boy does with them. I know one got out—" He stopped. "Lanier. It was that sap who told you I was here."

"I made him tell me. Don't blame him."

"What a gent. He'd twist his knickers to please a pretty girl who talks Yeats."

"What about Eva? Have you heard from her?"

"Two notes, both queer, both begging for that damn manuscript. How the hell do I know where it is?"

Julia considered this puzzling news. "May I see?"

He stood. As he moved, the cot's thin mattress shifted, and something clattered to the floor. Julia nearly gasped when she saw it: the barrel of a gun, poking out of a small chamois bag. She shrank back, thinking wildly of what to do. Was it better to try to dive for the thing before he could grab it, or run like mad?

Jerome made a startled noise too. "Damn thing. It's not mine." Julia spread her palms in a ridiculous semblance of a shield as he picked up the bag with two fingers and folded it shut.

"Wallace's men gave it to me, in case someone comes nosing around. As if I'd last two seconds in some shoot-out. I'd feel safer without it."

He pushed it back under the mattress and pulled a small leather satchel from under the cot. He lifted out its contents: a few framed photographs she didn't have time to see and two folded letters, both typed. One fell open long enough for her to read its letterhead: *The Criterion*. The letter from Eliot. Of course he'd save that. Before the pain of its new irrelevance could unsettle her, she watched him remove a pile of old newspapers, limp and wrinkled in the heat. They were covered with blue ink, written in columns across the length of the pages, perpendicular to the print: palimpsests. The script was swollen and distorted, possibly no longer legible on the unsized paper. From beneath them he handed her a square white card.

The card stock was heavy and expensive with a mouldmade deckle. In a large spiking hand, each stroke like a wayward arrow, was written: *Baby, it's important! Please give my book to Mr. Wallace's boy. XO! E.*

"The other one's just like it."

Julia read the note again and turned it over. The back of the card was covered with a dozen or more lines written in a tight, crabbed cursive of blue ink, spattered with blotted-out words and webbed with lines threading substitutions to be inserted. A poem in progress.

Jerome returned it to the bottom of his satchel. "I might as well use the paper."

"You're writing?"

"What else can I do?"

"On newspapers?"

He cocked his head. "You never think about all the clean white paper at your fingertips. I had to leave so fast I didn't even have time to grab a book, much less paper. Well, when you're ready to scream for something to write on, newspaper works just fine. But all I could find in this hole was that sorry stump of a pencil. That's why I had to ask Logan for a pen."

He exhaled. "It's almost out of ink now."

Julia's thoughts churned. Those notes meant Eva didn't have the manuscript. It wasn't exactly proof of innocence, but it made Kessler's assumptions much shakier. Why would she want it so badly? Was she frightened by Goldsmith's ultimatum? More importantly, why did she think Jerome had it? Did she think he'd killed Timson?

Good Lord. Had he? Had Julia's first instinct been right after all?

Too many questions swarmed in her melting mind. Another blast of wailing trumpets meant the show would be ending soon. She had to get back before the performers returned backstage. She stood and peeled her dress from the back of her thighs. "I have to leave. But I'll do everything I can to help."

Jerome pulled himself to his feet as well, stirring a wake of nauseating odors.

Julia reached the door before she thought of it. She turned back to hand him the pen from her handbag, a slim silver Waterman. It had been a gift from a long-ago friend who called himself a writer but would never understand how scraps of newspaper could be enough.

She nearly ran through the Half-Shell's backstage cavern. She ignored the whistles and grunting laughter. Music caromed off the walls, peppering her temples with its hot tempo. Philip would be wondering what had become of her. She broke into a faster trot. A single thought drummed in her mind to the music's beat: Wallace knew where Eva was. Wallace *knew*.

She reached the corridor that led to the carpeted hallway. She spun around the corner and smacked straight into a wall that hadn't been there before. She'd have been knocked to the floor if the man had not caught her elbows.

"Pardon me," she gasped, then recognized Martin Wallace.

In an instant she saw. He knew where she'd been. As she dug for breath to speak, he steered her through the unmarked door.

CHAPTER 23

It was an office, beautifully furnished with a settee and two wing chairs facing each other across a low table. A massive desk presided over the far end of the room, beneath a gloomy New England landscape in oils. Two lamps glowed on a sideboard, giving the windowless room a genteel warmth cruelly unlike the clogged heat of Jerome's cell.

The door closed on the orchestra's wild thumping. Wallace released her arm.

He knew where Eva was. He'd known all along. Julia slapped him hard across his right cheek.

He rubbed the spot as he poured out whiskey from a decanter on the sideboard. "So you've flushed out Mr. Crockett. I assure you it would've been better if you hadn't."

"You lied to me."

"I lied to you." He rested his glass against his chastened cheek.

"You've been hiding Eva all along?"

He took a swallow. "I have."

"I want to see her."

He touched the damp skin beneath her ear.

Julia leaned away. "I want to know what you know."

For several seconds he considered. "All right. We'll talk about it. But not here."

∽⊙

Julia slipped into the chair beside Philip. If he'd wondered about her long absence, it was far from his mind now. He lifted a forefinger to register her return but kept his narrowed eyes on the stage. Jack was even more absorbed in the show. He sat on the edge of his seat, elbows splayed over the table and hands framing his head, blinkered like a dray horse to focus wholly on what lay ahead.

The orchestra seemed to burst from its corner: trombones poking their snouts into the spotlight, cornets and clarinets squalling in counterrhythms. In the vortex of all that sound, impaled by a shaft of white light, danced a man and a woman. Both wore huge headdresses transforming them into fantastical strange birds with human bodies, all eight limbs painted shades of green and banded with rows of gold bracelets. Their bones throbbed from one erotic posture to another, arms and legs swarming and humming, shoulders ever squared beneath the weight of their bird masks.

The audience had swelled. The Half-Shell was now jammed with watchers, some unable to stay in their chairs. They pounded tables and stomped on the floor to the beat of music and muscles. Their energy inflamed the performances of both the featured dancers and the impromptu ones.

Behind the costumed pair, half in and half out of the stage's shadows, another couple cavorted. Pablo Duveen and Carl Sweeney drew shrieks of laughter as they mimicked the dancers' movements. Both men's jackets were gone, and Duveen's white dress shirt gaped open to his belly. Slabs of pale flesh quivered as he pranced into and out of

Sweeney's embrace, his white hands graphic claws against the younger man's black trousers.

As the music reached a crescendo, the masked dancers swung apart. The man sank onto his back on the floor, and the woman knelt in triumph over his mask, its sharp beak thrusting explicitly between her parted thighs. Beside them, Duveen also tumbled to the floor and pulled Sweeney to his knees, haunches hovering over Duveen's panting face. The final cornet note screamed, and Duveen waggled his tongue like a randy snake. Julia had never witnessed anything so obscene.

The houselights brightened onto bedlam. Weirdly severed from the masks left lolling on the floor, the dancers flung up their arms to receive the adulation, then followed the sweat-mopping musicians back through the curtains offstage. Duveen and Sweeney retrieved their jackets and slowly made their way through the crowd toward Jay and Edwin, who stood clapping and barking.

Philip sat back with a wry smile, but Jack sat motionless for several seconds. Then he pulled a handkerchief from his pocket to wipe his face. His mottled cheeks spoke to the pace of his heartbeat.

"I'm going to leave in a few minutes," Julia said. "With Martin Wallace."

Philip rose half out of his chair, but before he could implode with objections, Duveen and Sweeney returned, stirring commotion with every cackle. Jay and Edwin embraced them with all the affection of a six-hour acquaintance. Duveen poured gin straight from his flask into his throat, burbling what he couldn't swallow.

"We're off to worship Gladys Bentley." He reached across Philip to tug at Jack's sleeve. "Van Dyne, you virtuous daisy. Come with us. You too, Kydd."

So they'd become acquainted while she was away.

Sweeney giggled. "She's the queen of the life. Biggest bulldagger in Harlem."

"Two hundred pounds of sugar!" Duveen's arms swarmed to find the sleeves of his jacket. His shirt still hung open, and his pale breasts sagged like an old woman's. "You haven't seen Harlem till you've seen Gladys stir her vat. Come on, daisy. You'll love her."

Julia eased away to the ladies' room to freshen her wilted countenance. Which terror would Philip choose, she wondered: Gladys Bentley, or contemplation of her departure with Wallace?

$$\infty$$

The Duesenberg rolled through the streets of Harlem like a great stalking cat. Julia watched scores of people, mostly colored but some white, walking, dancing, arguing, singing, weeping, laughing, and being sick on the sidewalks as they glided by. It must be three or four in the morning, yet no one was sleeping. A breeze stirred her hair and chilled her scalp. It brought fleeting smells of garbage and gasoline.

As they headed south, the streets grew darker and quieter. Soon Central Park loomed black on their left, and slumbering apartment buildings towered on their right. They crossed the park and headed north again on Fifth Avenue. Edgar turned the motorcar smoothly onto one of the residential side streets, then right again into a small narrow lane along the rear east side of a handsome brick building. He eased to a stop in front of a sidewalk that led to a recessed private entrance framed by two conical shrubs in urns. A red-jacketed doorman held aside the door, then pushed the button to summon the elevator. After relocking the entrance behind him, he turned to join them, but Wallace waved him off.

"I can manage, Archie," he said, maneuvering the iron gate closed. He eased up the controls, and the machine lifted them into the building. Its only stop was at the top. They rode in silence. Wallace kept his eyes down, his thoughts veiled. If he was feeling half as chastened as he ought, Julia wanted to see it. A subdued spirit was not enough. She still seethed. She'd been played for a fool. She had hoped they'd become allies in Eva's cause, but if he intended simply to lie to her, he was only another obstacle to be overcome. A formidable obstacle, made more so by her smarting heart.

Julia stepped into a marble foyer. A Venetian chandelier shimmered overhead. On facing walls stood identical polished mahogany harp tables, topped with vases of fresh white roses, each beneath a similar but not matching large gilt-framed mirror. She saw her reflection in the nearest one and observed her back reflected in the opposite glass: an infinity of Julias. As many Wallaces lifted the Spanish shawl from her shoulders.

The foyer intersected a long hall lit by sconces. When she stepped onto its plush carpet, patterned with elaborate Celtic knots, she smelled a faint aroma of lemons. It swept through Julia like a flame. Eva. Wallace had told Kessler he'd brought her here at least once, when the police had released her into his care. Was she still here? Every nerve strained for some clue: a sound, another whiff of that sweet citrus lotion. Nothing. She smelled only the roses from the foyer behind them.

Ahead lay the living room, one step down. Tall windows spanned the opposite wall, each draped with burgundy velvet. It was a grand room, some thirty feet or more in length. Several lamps provided ghostly pumpkins of golden light.

"This place was built for Andrew Millbank," he said, glancing to see if Julia recognized the name. She did not.

"Are these family things?" Julia asked, amazed at the room's abundance of paintings and sculptures and bibelots.

Wallace laughed. "No, no. This is what fortunes are for. My father kept books for a button-making firm in Queens. But anything can be bought these days, including family heirlooms. I merely hired someone to put it all together. But I like it. It's mine now."

To their left the wide corridor led to several closed doors, but Wallace showed Julia to the first door on their right. It was a beautifully appointed bathroom. Fresh towels lay on an ebony sideboard. "You can freshen up in here."

She opened the taps to run water into the basin, then peeked into the hall. With Wallace moving about in the living room, she could only explore to her right. She slipped out. Directly opposite was a spacious room swathed in shadows. Silver candelabra glimmered in the dark, ghostly reflections across a long polished dining table. It was huge, easily seating two dozen. An enormous silver samovar stood like a proud flagship on a walnut sideboard.

The hall jogged right and narrowed, the carpet changing to maroon linoleum to mark the service end of the apartment. The first door opened to a large kitchen. Julia counted five closed doors along the long wall opposite and three on the kitchen side, plus an opening to another corridor. As she crept forward, she heard someone grunt and punch a pillow with a low epithet. She froze to listen but heard nothing more than the trickling water. No scent of lemons, no further sounds, but at least one person was awake behind these doors.

She hurried back to the bathroom. No sign of Eva's lotion, no earring escaped behind a vase or jar of bath salts. Julia laid her frock over the side of the bathtub and swabbed herself with a wet cloth. It seemed an age since she had sweltered beside Jerome in that backstage hell. In lieu of a more thorough wash, she dusted herself liberally with the perfumed powder offered in a decorated tin. She smoothed her step-ins, trimmed in deep bands of ivory Valenciennes lace; straightened her stockings; and drifted her dress back over her head. She pinched her cheeks and shook her hair to loosen the way it fell about her face. Christophine would despair, but it would have to do. Wallace would expect a leisurely toilette, but she couldn't wait another minute to demand answers.

He was standing beside a large turbulent seascape painted in oils in the last century. Below it, on a massive credenza, stood two filled champagne flutes and a bottle diapered in linen in a silver bucket. An excellent vintage. Avize, 1911. He handed her a glass, its crystal etched with his elaborate monogram, an interlaced *M* and *W*. Brushing back the hair that curled about her hatless face, he said, "Did Mr. Crockett clear things up for you or only confuse you further?"

"Where is she?"

"I can't tell you."

"Is she safe?"

"As long as no one knows where she is."

"Is she here?"

He smiled. "She is safe. Location secret."

He nudged Julia's hand, encouraging her to taste the champagne. "If Eva is to have any chance, she needs to disappear. No one, not even a well-meaning friend, can know where she is. Everything is on the line for her, Julia. For me as well."

He met her gaze. His eyes were nearly the color of hers, dark blue without a hint of gray. She saw no shadow, no hitch in their steady overture. Yet he had lied, deliberately deceived her. Deceit was a slippery slope. Unless he could convince her otherwise, it now shadowed everything she knew and felt about him.

"Why did she go to you that morning?"

"That troubles Crockett, does it?" Wallace led her to a plush burgundy sofa. "I did promise you some answers. Which you shall have. I'm a man of my word."

She sat warily, waiting.

"There are two answers to your question. Neither is short." He removed his jacket, loosened his tie, and unfastened his top collar stud. "We may as well get comfortable." He sat and stretched an arm behind her.

Julia sat forward. Wallace gave a soft laugh.

"The first answer is that she trusts me." He tapped faintly along the ridge of her collarbone. "Unlike you."

She brushed his hand from her shoulder. "You lied to me. Repeatedly."

"No one is entirely honest, my dear. No one. You and I both have many secrets. You're clearly interested in mine, and I hope to discover a few of yours."

"Why does Eva trust you?"

"She and I have known each other for a very long time. She worked in a little club I owned with some other people. It was a pretty rough and common place, mainly for coloreds. It was managed by a terrible boozer named Rudy who scraped along just under the law, but he kept the place profitable, and we didn't ask many questions. Eva was tall and skinny but light skinned enough for what passed for a chorus line— tans, they call them."

He paused for a few swallows of champagne. "Well, Eva was sweating away for her twenty bucks a week in the Calico Club. Then one night I noticed how the other girls looked like whores in that cheap getup, but not Eva. Even then, hoofing away on the end of the line, she had that *something*. So I asked Rudy to let her try a solo number, and right away, she's a hit. People started coming round to that dump just to see her."

Julia remembered Eva's mesmerizing performance. She was graceful and lithe but not a natural dancer, and her singing voice was passable but nothing remarkable. Yet she held the spotlight, captured a roomful of eyes, better than most stage performers. Her *something* was powerful and seductive. It was, Julia realized, the subterranean flow of interest that had so captivated her that first evening they'd met, at Duveen's party. She felt a stab of gratitude that Wallace had noticed it too, despite that club's drab squalor. How much more grateful Eva must have been. It had opened up a new life for her.

"That started her career?"

"It seemed so. Until one night when I stopped by and some West Indian girl was doing her number. I found Eva backstage with bandages wrapped around her head." He circled his own, drawing an imaginary swath across his hairline and over both ears. "There'd been a blowup. Rudy was a worse stinker than I thought."

Julia wondered if this was the source of the scene in Eva's manuscript that had sent Timson into a fury. If it had actually happened, Eva must have been desperate to escape. "Did he rape her? That terrible scene in her book, was it him?"

Rising with an exaggerated creak of his knees, Wallace carried his glass to the credenza and refilled it. "I've asked myself that question a hundred times these past few weeks. I don't know. She said nothing then and won't talk about it now. But I saw that gash on her head, clean through to her skull. If he had raped her, and I'd known about it, well." He stifled the rest of the sentence with a hand across his mouth. "As it was, I knew he'd continue to hurt her if she stayed."

"How did she get away?"

"I struck a deal with Leonard Timson. He was a rat too, but a bigger, smarter rat. He'd just bought the old Shalliwag Club and renamed it Carlotta's. He was putting in a lot of money to make it the best. Best music, best clientele, best entertainment. I told Leonard if he gave her top billing and treated her well, she'd fill that place for him."

So Wallace had brokered Eva's escape. Not only that, he'd made sure she moved into a bigger and better spotlight. He'd possibly saved her life. At the same time Timson had gained his biggest star. This explained why both he and Eva had yielded during their intense confrontation after Eva's show.

But Wallace was no simple country parson urging peace and harmony. Julia remembered the gun sleeping against his ribs. *Firing means you've lost, not won.* He emanated power more than he exercised it. Julia wondered if there was more to the deal than he'd mentioned. Had he included incentives or threats to induce Timson and Eva to accept the arrangement? Where was his gun now? Perhaps it didn't matter. Wallace was a pragmatist in a way that Julia was coming to better understand.

In a way, she was too. Power could be a force for good as much as for evil. No wonder Eva trusted him.

Julia drank her champagne. It was cold, sweet, delicious. "So he hired her at Carlotta's?"

"It was just the ticket for her," Wallace said, resettling beside her. "Leonard was still a rat, but he knew if he went too far, I'd hear about it, and I could make things miserable for him."

"What do you mean?"

He kissed the top of her head. "I don't break thumbs, if that's what you're thinking. No dungeons down the hall. I meant I have connections downtown, among the clientele Leonard depended on. I have the ear of influential men."

"It didn't stop Timson from treating her viciously that night."

"Leonard could be nasty, but that was a performance. He was too smart to foul his own nest. Not with her." Wallace's voice rumbled into Julia's hair.

This was what Eva had said too. But Timson had been livid. Julia remembered the tension of that night, the squeeze at her windpipe. She couldn't know his usual temper, but when he'd spoken of the manuscript, and particularly that scene, his rage had seemed white hot.

Wallace lifted her chin, but she turned aside, and his lips brushed her cheek.

Something more, something deeper, had disturbed Timson. "Could Timson be the rapist in her book?"

Wallace let out a heavy breath. "Quite possibly. I don't know for certain."

"You could ask her."

"I could." He kissed her nose. "I did. But she won't say. She says very little these days."

He pulled back to look into her face. "Which is wise. Until the police find something that points them elsewhere in the next few days, she's square in their sights."

Julia finished her champagne in one swallow, cutting short the import of his words.

"I'm doing all I can to protect her from Hobart," Wallace said quietly, moving her glass to the floor. As he bent forward, she marveled at the gold luster of his hair, swept back over the crown of his head to a precisely shaved edge at his nape.

"But unless you trust me, I can't keep her safe from the courts." He caressed her shoulder and edged aside the strap of her frock.

His mouth moved to the hollow below her throat. *Not yet,* she told her spine, helplessly arching. *Listen. Concentrate.* She felt his hand slide to the top of her stocking and knew in a moment she would be lost.

A strange sound escaped from her lungs. "Wait."

He recognized it as a word before she did. He breathed deeply and sat back.

She swallowed. "You said there were two reasons Eva went to you. What's the second?"

"Ahhh." Wallace dropped his chin. "The second reason."

He lifted the fallen strap of her dress.

"She didn't exactly come to me. When I went up to see what had happened, she was there. Kneeling beside his body."

CHAPTER 24

Julia jerked upright. "What?"

Wallace clasped her knee. "You must swear on whatever's holy that you won't repeat any of this. It would only make things worse for Eva. I'm serious, Julia. Promise me."

"Of course." She twisted to face him. "What happened?"

He took another deep breath, gathering his thoughts. "When I left Carlotta's that night, I ran into Senator James. He and I went on to the Half-Shell. After Eddie's late show—he was in fine form that night— we retired to my office to discuss a few matters over an excellent bottle of Scotch. The next thing I knew, Bobby Hobart's on the telephone. I could hardly understand him. He said Timson was dead, shot. He wanted my help."

So Kessler had been right about Wallace's political ambitions. No wonder he was circumspect about helping Eva.

"I rushed back there, grabbed the keys from Bobby, and ran upstairs. I unlocked the door and saw Leonard, obviously dead, with Eva beside him."

Julia held his forearm as she listened.

He stroked her fingers, perhaps to loosen their grip. "Poor kid. She was hysterical."

"Did she have a gun?"

"No. I didn't have time to think of much, but I did check that. I told her to hide in the alley until I could get to her. She ran into the bedroom and disappeared."

"So you knew about the back staircase?"

Wallace massaged his jaw, roughening the new day's beard. "I did then. She told me that's how she got in."

"Any sign of the manuscript?"

"No. Leonard's holster was on the chair, but his gun was gone and the safe was empty. Otherwise the place didn't seem disturbed. I hustled downstairs to send Edgar around for Eva in the alley. I had him take her to a flat in the Lester, a building I own on West 146th."

He smiled faintly. "It's a flat I keep as a favor for friends who need a place their wives don't know about. The car had just turned out of sight when the cops came roaring up, as they do. I told everything—almost everything—to the precinct men and then to the detective from the homicide bureau."

"Hannity," said Julia. She felt herself relaxing. Everything Wallace was telling her matched what she knew from Kessler and Jerome. He might have lied to her about his roles—his quite illegal roles—in helping both Eva and Jerome escape, but he hadn't. True to his word, he'd shared everything about his involvement in the matter, which was considerable.

In doing so, he'd placed complete trust in Julia. She now knew enough to destroy his reputation and credibility, at least with Kessler and the police, which would cripple his political ambitions. It was a gift, she realized, a gesture of good faith in her and in their budding relationship. He was repaying her suspicion with humbling candor.

"Hannity," he affirmed. "Then Kessler showed up, and he wanted the whole story too. They were nervous as cats, knowing the place could blow sky-high."

As if remembering that fear, he wrapped a protective arm around her.

Julia breathed in a lungful of that intoxicating scent, then freed herself and stood. Not yet. She couldn't think clearly when he was so close. "You didn't tell the police you saw her?"

"No. She was terrified, but not with guilt. I'm convinced she didn't kill him."

So he'd lied to the police too. Of course—his own neck was on the line for helping her escape. Even so, that lie had saved Eva from certain arrest, and he'd freely admitted it. His trust was breathtaking.

Julia felt an urge to take his face between her hands, to feel the muscles of his jaw. She turned and paced to the windows. "When did you see her again?"

"I had to bide my time. Until they checked with James, I was a major suspect. When he finally cleared my story, Kessler asked for my help. I promised I'd try to keep a lid on Bobby and his men. The place was a tinderbox."

She nudged aside the heavy velvet. The sky was starless. "And Eva?"

Wallace joined her and swept back the drapery. They were high above the park, above cresting waves of treetops. On the avenue below, a few headlamps plied the dark pools between streetlights. "I got to the Lester about nine that night. I told her I could help only if she let the police question her. It was risky, but we had no choice. The next morning she walked into the local precinct like she'd promised, and they carted her downtown."

He let the curtain fall into place with a dustless rustle. "You know the rest."

Julia rested two fingertips in the gap between her lips as she thought. She barely registered the faint pressure when Wallace kissed her hair. "What about Jerome Crockett?" she asked. "Where did he fit in?"

"My men got him out of sight that morning too, because Eva begged me to, but I'm not convinced he's as clueless as he lets on. He's a smart man. He could be playing a hand I can only guess at. But as long as he stays put and keeps his head down, he can't do her any harm."

"What do you know about her manuscript?"

"I know it's missing. I know Eva's worried about it. Beyond that, nothing. Why?"

"That manuscript has to be the key. It must be why Timson was murdered."

He brushed hair back from her face, fingers lingering above her ear. "If I knew anything, I'd tell you. We just have to hope, for Eva's sake, that Kessler turns up something." He tilted her face to make certain she understood the import of his words.

She did—the all-important *we*—and met his kiss. But before a corner could be turned, she pulled back. "And now?"

"And now each day Eddie does his Ethel magic, Carlotta's settles down a bit more. I doubt they care much anymore who shot Leonard— or why, for that matter. Sometimes it's best just to move on, as I keep trying to convince Kessler. But if I can't, and nothing turns up by next weekend, you heard me say I'd help them search." He touched his nose to hers. "I lied, Julia. A whopper."

She smiled.

"I plan to prove remarkably inept at finding her. I hope she can rely on your bungling as well."

She smiled again. At last they were where she'd hoped to be from the start, on the same side, working together to find a safe path forward for Eva.

The joke faded as somewhere water pipes labored awake. Someone was about.

"Mrs. Hoskins," Wallace said. "She gets up at a ghastly hour every morning to take care of God knows what all."

Julia thought of the hallway of closed doors. "You must have a large household."

"Just four. Mrs. Hoskins, plus Edgar and Archie and my man Farraday, but he sleeps at the other end of the apartment."

"It seems large enough for more."

"There's space for six, I believe, though for all I know Mrs. Hoskins grows orchids in those rooms. She'll be bustling in here soon." Wallace took her hand. "Come. Let me show you the rest of the apartment."

He led her down the long hallway with its ornate wainscoting to the north end of the apartment. As they approached a beautifully carved pair of walnut doors on their right, he swept open a door to their left. Julia admired a large windowless billiards room, pungent with tobacco. He gestured her around the hallway's bend. The carved doors remained closed, ignored. Why? Surely another wondrous room lay beyond them. Why pass it by? Was this the place? Was Eva inside, just yards away?

Julia steadied her voice. "What's in that room?"

"Only my library. Off limits, I'm afraid. My important papers are in there." He led her on to a final pair of even more magnificent carved doors. These Wallace swung open. It was a grand bedroom, presumably his own. The bed was gargantuan, a continent of ecru satin that may have once served a French duke or Italian count. Here were more seascapes, one almost certainly a Turner, and a collection of Chinese bronze figures Philip would envy.

Wallace watched as she moved about the room. A deep oriental carpet hushed all sound. As she loitered in front of the Turner, he joined her, hands on her shoulders. "Satisfied?"

She laid her cheek on his knuckles. "Why won't you tell me?"

He laughed. "Because I care about her, and you." More quietly he added, "Julia?"

Even now it was a question. The choice to stay or go was hers.

Oh yes. She was past the point of rational choice, except for one thing. She drew him back down the hall to the locked doors. "In there."

He gave another short laugh. "Curiosity over comfort?"

From his pocket he pulled a ring of keys. They jangled loudly as he sorted them. Was it deliberate? Julia strained to listen but heard only the rattling keys. Was Eva crouching on the other side, afraid? She couldn't know who was coming or if it meant Wallace's betrayal. But if she was there, she was silent.

Wallace found the key. He threw back first one heavy bolt, then a second. He pushed open the doors, and Julia saw a magnificent panorama of red streaks bleeding into the predawn sky. The drapes had not been drawn, and a chill glazed the air. Nothing stirred. No one was there.

Arms folded, Wallace watched her slowly circle the large room with tall windows on two sides. A massive desk faced them at the far end, its surface orderly. On the floor lay a great white bearskin, its head toward the desk, fanged in a perpetual roar.

"An indulgence of questionable taste," Wallace murmured.

Julia completed her circuit, avoiding the bearskin. The two interior walls were lined with eight-foot walnut bookcases, all with locking glass doors. They held a mixture of moderately valuable old tomes—no doubt imported by the cubic yard from some destitute European estate library—and several shelves of purely functional volumes: New York state and municipal civil codes and statutes, books pertaining to business and financial regulations and procedures. Dozens of custom-bound file boxes, their leather blind-tooled with Wallace's distinctive mirrored monogram, filled the lower shelves. Each was neatly identified with a handwritten paper label. His business documents: the leather-coffined ranks of loan contracts and mortgages, the clean carnage of modern hunters.

This was indeed his inner sanctum. A fine layer of dust confirmed no housekeeper had entered in some time. Even so, the man was as orderly and exact in his business records as in his person. Only a few boxes showed signs of recent activity—the dust swiped from the shelf's edge—yet they were aligned in perfect symmetry with their fellows.

Julia scanned the room again but saw nothing else. No hairpins, no overlooked glove, no trace of face powder.

Wallace unfolded his arms. "Mistrust does not become you, my dear." He took her by the shoulders for a kiss that pitched her head back, stopped her breath. It was swift and powerful. This time there was no question. No solicitude, no choosing. He thrust his knee between her thighs, and she would have fallen had he not gripped her so tightly their hearts beat like trapped birds against each other. This time was all decision: he'd paid penance enough.

Her dress fell to the floor in a few deft gestures. Gravity shifted, and she too went down, to the island of white fur at her back. The beast beneath her roared. She saw the arch of its tooth, the arch of her foot. With a seize of air, she felt its clench in her belly and its claw in her breast. Then all thought narrowed to the silk sweeping down her calves, the hands sweeping up.

She lurched at the sudden clatter of a telephone bell. Wallace swore, a harsh and vulgar growl. His jaw tightened; his eyes narrowed in subdued fury.

A man's reluctant voice—the unfortunate Farraday?—came through the door: "Very sorry to disturb you, sir, but Mr. Kessler says it's urgent."

CHAPTER 25

Edgar delivered her home, maneuvering the Duesenberg through the maze of dairy trucks and bakery vans. Julia could barely stammer her gratitude before fleeing up the steps to Philip's apartment. Her head pounded in turbulent confusion—at Kessler's cryptic summons, at Wallace's terse retreat, at her need to muster composure (please, God, let her clothing not be too askew) and follow a sleepy Edgar down into the breaking dawn. Every nerve felt stretched to thrumming, tuned to the brink of a great chord and then abandoned.

Not one word had been spoken beyond that profane snarl of frustration. Wallace might have glanced an apology at her, but his weight had already shifted to his knees, his mind already turning to trouble's greater urgency. His desire had been real, but was it also unremarkable? She felt foolish and unsteady.

She let herself into the dark apartment. From the library came the eerie trickle of a Chopin nocturne. Philip!

Had Kessler found Eva? Was Philip up at this appalling hour to share the news that Wallace hadn't?

Julia pushed apart the doors. Philip sat in the dark, hunched over the keys. He finished a phrase and lifted his hands. "Good morning," he said.

"Any news from Kessler?"

He looked at her quizzically. "Should there be?"

Her hopes fell. Kessler would have called Philip had there been a breakthrough. His business with Wallace must have concerned something else. She felt dismay and relief in equal measure.

"Why are you up?" she asked. Her tone was curt with a new suspicion.

"Can't a man inspect his soul in a private hour?"

Not with her foul temper in the room. "Were you waiting up for me?"

When he lowered his eyes to the keyboard, she leaped at his presumption. "How dare you! I'm not a child. You have no right to monitor my comings and goings. Who I see, and when and how, is of no possible concern of yours. None!" It was histrionic, as shrill as the prickling nerves that Wallace had so powerfully awakened.

Philip swiveled. "I may not be a blood relation," he said, "but I'm entitled to concern for a friend, a friend who is foolishly straying into territory whose hazards she cannot begin to fathom."

They rarely spoke of their sibling charade. Until now they'd sidestepped the consequences, or limits, of that ruse. Was she fair to enjoy Philip's generosity as a brother while forbidding him to behave like one? But surely a brother's prerogative was grounded in trust and regard more than blood ties per se. Which raised the more fundamental question: They were not related, but were they friends?

It was a question that could only answer itself.

"I am acquainted with men, Philip. I have known many, a few quite well indeed. I can judge for myself who will suit. I can perceive hazards for myself—or declare them to be no such thing."

She dropped onto the sofa and saw that her left stocking was spiraled hastily up her calf. She crossed her legs, hoping Philip wouldn't notice. But he would. No one had a keener eye. And even a child could see she'd had a disastrous night. She'd lost her hat to the Half-Shell's hellish heat, and her crumpled frock no doubt reeked of perspiration and cigarettes. She couldn't bear to face his wry teasing about her failed evening.

But he said nothing. He looked rough too. Barefoot, he wore loose trousers under a black dressing gown. His hair fell into his eyes, despite frequent swipes to push it away. He too had not slept, or only badly. They were a fine pair, and yes, she realized, however unlikely and uncertainly, they were friends.

"I am an adult," she repeated, temper mostly spent. "Why is it so hard to trust a woman to choose her own company? I might choose badly, as anyone might. But let me choose for myself. I can survive mistakes. I have survived plenty already."

"No doubt. It's this particular mistake I cannot swallow. I'm sorry, but I can't say more than that."

As he spoke, his eyes rested on the large oil portrait of Lillian Vancill hanging over the mantel, beside that of his putative parents, Milo and Charlotte, with him as an infant. The sisters had always struck Julia as two versions of the same brunette beauty. Lillian glowed with a robust energy, glinting with defiance as if daring the painter to capture her unladylike forward tilt and slightly parted knees beneath a bright-red dress. In contrast, Charlotte was almost ethereal, a guttering flame (she'd be dead seven years later) to Lillian's blazing torch.

"It must be terrible to grieve in secret," Julia said quietly, not sure if this was a subject she was allowed to broach. They'd never really spoken of his true parentage.

Philip nodded so slowly she might have imagined it. "She claimed to be a hussy, you know, at least in her diaries. She brandished the word like a trophy. I can only imagine how she earned it."

"By speaking her mind," Julia said, remembering the sharp-tongued old woman. "Breaking the rules. Even the biggest rule of all—the one you saw fit to remind me of just now."

"Celibacy, you mean?" Philip colored slightly. "You know that's not my concern." Julia marveled: the man who could stare down most social conventions blushing at the delicate subject.

"But yes," he went on, "she broke the rules." He dipped his head to acknowledge himself as living proof. "And with considerable relish, it seems."

Julia hesitated. This was fragile territory; did she have the right to nudge into his privacy? No—if he wished to say more, he would. She would welcome his thoughts but not prompt them.

"She was a wily thing, sly no end." He contemplated the glowing tip of his cigarette. "What secrets the old gal had. And like a puffed-up young strut, I never thought to ask about them. 'Spinster aunt,' my eye. What rubbish to assume she led a dull life."

His expression was solemn but not guarded. The usual hank of black hair hung down his forehead like a stiletto grazing his right eyebrow. His cheekbones cast sharp shadows in the low light. It struck her again that with a slick of oil he could pass for Nijinsky himself.

"You might be the son of a sheik," Julia said.

Philip's eyes widened at the teasing speculation. "Old Milo would turn in his grave. Imagine leaving his fortune to an Arab urchin." He coughed through a wry smile. "Pardon me. Half his fortune."

Julia smiled too. They'd come a long way, to speak lightly of their old battle. "Reason enough for her silence. Just think of the scandal." *And the swooning,* she added silently.

He gave a soft chuckle. "No end of wagging tongues. Though with a bit of a Valentino swagger, my stock might go up, not down. At least with the ladies."

A frisson of interest sharpened Julia's ears. Philip was intensely reticent about his private affairs. Apart from the enigmatic Mrs. Macready, she had no clue about his romantic interests. They were either exceptionally discreet or quite laissez faire, or possibly both. "Your stock there is blue chip already, I'd imagine," she said.

He quirked one cheek and said nothing. He'd seen the bait and spurned it. The subject was not one he wished to discuss.

How easily he drew the curtain across his private life. Yet she was not allowed to do the same? The injustice of it stung afresh, reviving her original grievance. "It's unfair, Philip. Why should I be denied the same freedom Lillian sought, to enjoy love and intimacy wherever I may find it?"

He studied her, saying nothing. They both understood it was a rhetorical lament. He had never challenged her right to form liaisons, though for maddeningly opaque reasons he objected to Martin Wallace in particular. Even so, she chafed at society's double standard. For him such liaisons burnished his social mystique; they threatened to tarnish hers.

"It's not unreasonable," she said. "I simply want to find someone. Not a husband and not forever, but someone, for a while. That's all." She gave a despairing laugh at her twisted stocking and ruined frock. A fine speech for a woman in her state, her proud confidence of eight hours ago now a disheveled mess. She'd regroup tomorrow, but at the moment a good wallow was in order. "As if it were so simple. Look at me. Would you look twice at such a creature? A woman's charms are precarious enough"—she lifted her shin to display its laddered silk— "without a hovering brother."

Philip smiled. "You're tired and have had a vexing night. As have I. With a bath and a rest, you'll be back to form. As you well know." He played a delicate ascending scale.

"And yes," he added, "I would look twice, though it may not be quite brotherly to say so."

They gazed at each other through the predawn murk. Neither flinched from the frankness of it. Then a spot of color appeared on his unshaven cheek, and Julia felt an answering heat on her own. He was right. It was time they said good night.

CHAPTER 26

For three long days Julia sputtered, uncertain of what to do next. She wandered Philip's apartment, checked on her crated household and studio in Brooklyn, and listened with half an ear to an interminable Wagner recital all Sunday afternoon, yet nothing could distract her from her own uselessness. Since her graceless exit early Friday morning from Wallace's home (and arms), she'd had no word from him. Someone had telephoned on Saturday to say he'd been called away to Albany and was not expected home until late next weekend. She'd felt a chill at the news. On Sunday Kessler's grace period would end.

How could Wallace leave the city with just seven days remaining before a horde of police swept through Harlem for the fugitive Eva and Jerome? More troubling, why hadn't he telephoned? She knew his affairs were many and widespread, some perhaps as pressing as Eva's fate, but surely he understood the depth of Julia's concern—not to mention the privileges of their new, if yet unconsummated, intimacy.

On Monday Julia accepted that she had no choice but to trust Wallace's word that Eva was safe somewhere. All she could do now for her friend was distract Kessler with a better suspect. That pitched her back to the vexing mystery of who had killed Timson, which led to the missing manuscript. Her best guess—Jerome—had fizzled. She'd seen his desperation. He'd never write across old newsprint if he had a stack of blank verso pages to hand. But neither Eva nor Wallace had it either. Goldsmith? She had no way of knowing.

Julia's best—her only—lead was to follow the thread of Duveen's drunken boast that *Harlem Angel* had resurfaced. He'd denied it in the next breath—*No, no, no, only a flutter of wings.* Was it gibberish? Possibly, but beneath his antics Duveen was remarkably canny. She needed to poke around in his apartment for some clue to what he'd meant. Did he have the manuscript or know who did? Was he in touch with Eva? "A flutter of wings" was not much, but it did stir a faint breeze. In danger of screaming if she didn't do something soon, Julia spent the afternoon walking to Central Park and back, formulating an idea.

The buzzing doorbell raised muffled sounds from deep inside Duveen's apartment. Several moments passed before the door opened a crack. Duveen peered through.

"Jaunty Kippers," he said. "*Quelle surprise.* But not a good time." He began to close the door.

Someone else was there. A wild thought occurred: Eva?

Julia put out a hand to stop the door. "Wait." A glissade of falsetto laughter—definitely not Eva's—from at least two rooms away gave her a pretty good idea of what she'd interrupted, and her cheeks heated with embarrassment. Still, she had to get inside. In just six days Kessler would launch his angry search.

"I think I left something important here last week." She slid her foot forward.

"Come back tomorrow," Duveen said. "Toodle-oo!"

"It's a copy of my first Capriole book. I brought it to show Logan Lanier and think I left it behind in your study. I've been frantic to find it. I can't rest until I know it's safe."

"If I see it, I'll give you a jingle." He bobbed a fingertip at her as he eased the door shut.

She gasped when it pinched her shoe against the jamb. Duveen released her foot with an apology, but through the same four-inch gap as before.

"You'll forget I'm even here. I'll look quietly, and when I find it, I'll let myself out. Please, Pablo." She resorted to a face of hapless innocence, a look she carried off rather poorly but which could still wilt men over forty, even men like Duveen.

He chewed his lower lip, not persuaded. In fact, he looked on the verge of genuine irritation, in which case she'd never get across his threshold.

"I thought I might also take a look at that essay you asked me about," she said. "The piece you thought might be right for Capriole?"

His eyes brightened. "Really?" Then they clouded as a distant voice whined for him to come back. "Lunch tomorrow?" Duveen suggested.

"I'm not free tomorrow," she lied. "I'm meeting with another author, a poet I'm quite keen to publish. If she likes my work as much as I like hers, well, then I won't need to see your essay. I just thought that since I was here anyway—" Her sentence had nowhere to go, but fortunately it was snatched up by Duveen's vanity.

"Right," he said, opening the door. "One's art must come first."

He swept the orange-lined skirt of his silver dressing gown to welcome her in with a matadorian flourish. Voluminous pyjama trousers flowed out from below his robe. "We have company, Sweet Pea," he called out.

It was a conversation from a few weeks back that normally she'd make a point to forget. When he'd asked about her Capriole Press, she'd replied with ruthless modesty, saying only that she hoped to commence with a fitting new project once her studio was ready. She spoke obliquely because she feared how he might react.

As he did. Like most writers, his eyes bloomed with avarice. Would she consider something of his? A frightfully special piece. "It's about my late cat, Leopold. A majestic fellow. Readers will adore him," he cajoled. "A prince among pookins. That's my title, you know."

At that Julia had latched onto a passing conversation, hoping the flow of gin would rinse the notion from Duveen's memory. Now she was glad it hadn't.

"Someone else who remembers conversations," Duveen marveled as she stepped into his grand apartment. "Clever Pookins. You'll love him. I have drawings too."

Carl Sweeney padded on bare feet into the living room. He wished her a good morning. It was nearly four, yet he too wore a dressing gown. She hadn't seen either man since their frenzied hijinks at the Half-Shell the other night.

Duveen rolled his head toward Sweeney. "Would you mind, swee-tums? This won't take long."

"Don't let me interrupt," Julia said. "I'll just look for my book, quiet as a church mouse."

"Nonsense." Duveen led Julia back to his library just as Coral Goldsmith had, but without the imperious grip. The room seemed even more disheveled in the gray light of a wet May afternoon. Books lay everywhere, flat and upright, in the familiar jumble of a well-used collection. The cat—not Leopold but his lazy sister Artemis, Duveen said in a babyish coo—watched them from a needlepoint pillow. Julia's heart soared to see all sorts of typed pages lying about too, covering the sofa, his desk, a chair seat, and the top of his typewriter. If a clandestine *Harlem Angel* had somehow surfaced in Duveen's world, it would be here. Some of the stacked pages looked cleanly typed, and others were covered with corrections scrawled in bright-green ink.

"Looks like you're starting a new book," she said.

He dropped to his hands and knees to search for his essay manu-script along the bottom shelves of the bookcases. "I'm going to write a Harlem novel myself. If Eva's kaput, someone has to do it."

With Duveen distracted, Julia lifted splayed magazines on the sofa, searching for anything—pages, a letter, a note—that might suggest a connection to *Harlem Angel*.

"There's material for a whole storm of novels," Duveen continued, his silver rump swaying like a baby elephant, "but most colored writers don't even notice the gold mine under their noses. I may be only an honorary Negro—the world's first!—but I know better what to do with it than all those natural-borns sweating out sonnets while jazz drips away through their fingers."

As she scanned the papers on Pablo's desk, Julia thought of gentle, earnest Logan, who aspired to sonnets above all else. So it was just as he'd complained: Pablo was keen to celebrate Negro poets, as long as they not stray from their own neighborhood. The only thing that had changed was his opinion of that neighborhood.

His desk was covered with several piles of pages loosely stacked crossways. They could all be part of his new novel, layers at varying stages of completion. She saw a long letter to "Crispy Violets" and a half-finished review of *Gentlemen Prefer Blondes*. "Is that why you don't care much for Jerome Crockett's work?" she asked to keep Pablo talking.

"Perfect example. Crockett's sitting smack in the middle of the most original material of our time, and all he wants to do is heave his soul onto the page like young Werther. In iambic pentameter, no less. God help us!" Duveen's backside juddered, but his head stayed down. "No wonder he's stewing in a funk. Well, Eva will have the last laugh there."

The only one laughing was Pablo. Eva had never said one unkind word about either Logan's or Jerome's work, however much it differed from her own. Julia left her indignation unsaid and sidled toward the chair to peek at the papers jumbled on its seat. It appeared to be the draft of an essay extolling the genius of Negro music.

"It's here somewhere. Here, Pookie Pookums," Duveen cooed. "Come to Daddy. Have you read my latest book, Jaunty? It's selling like hotcakes."

Julia admitted she hadn't as she skimmed the papers beside his typewriter. They were notes, some sort of cryptic outline or musings.

"It's called *The Tattooed Dachshund*. Silly thing, really."

Julia was glad he could not see her reaction. "I'll look for a copy next time I'm in Brentano's." She turned over a pile that appeared to be another, more detailed outline. Probably plans for his new novel.

"Oh, I'll give you one," came the muffled reply. He moved farther along the base of the wall, his massive rump trailing. "Remind me when I'm upright."

Julia peeked and scanned as quickly as she could. Pile after pile appeared to be Duveen's work, more letters and notes and drafts of various works in progress. She was carefully restoring their jumbled order when she noticed a few sheets peeking out from beneath the typewriter. She saw at once they had been produced on a different machine. She pressed her lips together to silence any sound of reaction and nudged the machine aside for a better look.

"Gotcha!"

Julia wheeled. From his knees Duveen waved a manila folder. Gripping a shelf, he groaned to one knee and then to his feet. "Here's my naughty fellow."

Julia took it from him. "Oh, good," she said faintly. "I'll just sit quietly and read. You go on back to your friend. Forget I'm here."

"Take the beast home with you," Duveen said with a shooing motion toward the door. "We'll lunch next week, yes? I'll bring your book if I find it."

Julia stiffened. She couldn't leave. Not with those intriguing pages within arm's reach. She needed a closer look. If they did appear to be from Eva's novel, she'd have to find out what Duveen knew about them. She could ask him outright, but at the Half-Shell he'd balked into coy silence. Sober, he might resist the subject even more firmly. She'd be ushered straight to the door, and all hope of discovering something would vanish.

No, she needed to examine them first on her own, without his knowledge. Mustering a daffy smile, she said, "It's much better to read in situ, if you don't mind. Absorb the ambience of the subject, you know." It was perfect blather, and he fidgeted, unconvinced. "I'm more inclined to publish work I can commune with," she added. "Privately." She folded her fingers over the bundle and mimed transported bliss.

She was spared any more of this charade when Sweeney appeared in the doorway, dressed and shaved, to say goodbye. Duveen's clucking embrace nearly swallowed the younger man. "Don't forget dinner at Reynaldo and Claire's at eight," Duveen reminded him, following Sweeney down the hall. "Excuse us, Julia." His voice trailed off toward the kitchen. She heard their idle banter rise and fall. Sweeney was in no hurry to leave, nor Duveen to let him go.

Julia quickly set *Pookins* aside and sat at his desk. She lifted his typewriter and pulled out the pages beneath it.

It was a section of something, pages eighty-seven through ninety-five. On page eighty-seven, the text began in the middle of a sentence. She began to read, eager to get a sense of the text before Duveen returned. She turned each sheet over with as much care as if it had been a da Vinci manuscript. The gist was soon clear. It was a story set in Harlem with Negro characters: A cabaret singer named Marie was devoted to a writer named Byron Love. They were at a dance, where Byron lavished attention on a seductive stranger. Marie was humiliated and Byron resentful. They quarreled violently.

Julia listened—Duveen's hearty laugh rang out from well down the hall—and skimmed the pages again, perplexed. This was clearly fiction set in Harlem, which meant it could be pages from *Harlem Angel* or material for Duveen's own new novel. Yet it had been typed on a different machine. Was that enough evidence this was Eva's? Julia scanned again.

A phrase snagged her eye. One of the characters' names. Byron Love. It sounded familiar. Where had she heard that name?

She remembered in a rush. The ladies' lavatory in Liveright's building. Byron Love was the name of Eva's father, the white Louisville professor with the invalid wife in the big house and his mistress's family in the caretaker's cottage. Something something Byron Love.

Julia sat back. This must be part of Eva's manuscript.

How had Duveen gotten it?

Where was the rest?

"What do you think?" Duveen stood in the doorway. He had changed into brown trousers and a yellow shirt, but over them he still wore the silver dressing gown. He'd shaved, and his white hair was smoothed back from his face in its usual soft poof. How long had he been there?

"Thank you for letting me consider Mr. Pookins," Julia said, squaring his essay's pages to steady her hands. "It's charming, Pablo, but I'll need more time to consider. I'll have to see."

Duveen folded his arms. "I'd be a lamb of a client. Delightfully docile. A mewling kitten!"

She couldn't natter on about his damn cat a moment longer. She gave a theatrical sigh and blurted out, "The truth is I'm terribly distracted these days, thinking about poor Eva Pruitt. I thought a new printing project would help, but I can't stop worrying."

"You mean about the murder?"

"And her disappearance. Have you heard anything?"

Duveen shook his head, juddering his loose cheeks. "Nada."

He showed little concern or even interest in Eva's predicament. Nor did he repeat his claim of the other night at the Half-Shell. Not even a flicker of dissembling. Either he'd been so drunk he didn't remember his joyful hints about *Harlem Angel* flying again, or he now wished to quash all references to it.

A blinding new thought occurred. Duveen had said he was writing a Harlem novel himself. Was he planning to appropriate Eva's? No one else had read it entirely. With Eva out of the picture, dead or hiding or in prison, did he intend to claim the novel as his own? It was a powerful motive to kill Timson and to let Eva take the blame.

Before she could stop herself, Julia looked down. Eva's pages were plainly visible beside the typewriting machine. Aghast, she pushed her gaze to his *Pookins* folder, attempting an appreciative expression, and then to Duveen.

He saw. He saw everything. For a moment they measured each other.

Duveen? Would he kill for that novel? Beneath his outré clownishness, was he capable of such ruthlessness? He studied her with an alarming sangfroid. Without shifting her gaze, she gauged how far she'd have to lunge to reach his letter opener, upright in a glass jar of colored pencils and pens.

Did anyone know she was here? Sweeney did, of course, but he'd hardly speak out. She'd told Christophine only that she had an errand to run and would be home before dinnertime. It would be two hours at least before she'd wonder if something was amiss. And even then she'd wait another few hours before considering raising an alarm.

Duveen narrowed his eyes. His gaze burned into hers. What a fool she'd been to insinuate herself so carelessly like this. Her nerves were not made for such subterfuge.

Duveen's lips parted, and his teeth sprang out in a beefy laugh. "You've discovered my secret, you sneaky girl. I told you Eva's manuscript was less missing than before."

"How did you get it?"

The question hung in the air. Was it too blunt? A mistake, revealing her suspicions?

"The mailman brought it!"

He scrambled around the desk to paw gleefully through the mess for it. "Last week."

"Who sent it?"

"Eva! Who else? I mean, who else cares so much about getting it published? It's her ticket to literary Easy Street. More than ever now." He did a lumbering jig with imaginary castanets.

"Where is she?"

"No idea."

"Did she include a note?"

"Just those pages." He stirred about in the wastepaper basket and extracted a large envelope, neatly slit across the sealed edge.

Julia examined it. No tucked-away note or even a return address. Duveen's address had been typed across the front. The franking mark was smudged, making it impossible to identify the post office station where it had been mailed. She sat back to stare at the mysterious pages, sensing something ominous. "What does this mean?"

He blew air out of his cheeks. "It means the manuscript is safe, not moldering to pulp at the bottom of the East River."

It meant more than that. The police believed—everyone believed, including Julia—that Timson had been killed for this manuscript. If Eva had it, the conclusion was obvious.

Duveen barreled on, right into Julia's unspoken fear. "It doesn't necessarily mean she killed him. He could have given it back to her later that night. And then by sheer rotten luck someone else came in and shot him. He was a crook. His friends are crooks. They kill each other all the time. It's possible, and that's good enough for me."

Such a contrived scenario would never dissuade Kessler. If he knew these pages had surfaced, he'd send in his troops tomorrow. Jerome would be run to ground, and quite possibly Eva too. Not even Wallace could hide her forever from a freshly galvanized police force.

"The way I see it," Duveen persisted, "the gangster stuff will settle down pretty soon, and the cops will hie off after some new heinous criminal. Before you know it, Eva will be back in business, turning cartwheels of happiness—in time to sign copies of her first edition."

Foreboding gripped Julia. "Don't say anything to anyone about this, Pablo."

He comically turned a key to lock his protruding lips. "Look at the bright side," he said. "If she can keep the manuscript coming, it will sell like mad. A runaway hit!"

How easily he dismissed Eva's dilemma, finding specious ways to keep it from spoiling his vision of brisk sales and reflected glory. Julia recrossed her legs to disguise her anger. It wasn't simply that she cared more about Eva. Too much about the whole situation was unsettling. Unlike Duveen, she couldn't breeze away the echo of Jerome's desolate tears or the haunting, hope-numb challenge she'd seen in Eva's eyes in Kessler's office.

"Why send only a few pages at a time?" she asked.

"Don't know, don't care. Just so long as it keeps coming."

"Why not send pages in order? The first dozen, then the next, and so on?"

He shrugged, not bothering to repeat his ambivalence. The conversation and her visit were over. He crossed the room to the door, forcing Julia to follow. As she tugged on her gloves to face the cool, drizzly afternoon, his humor returned.

"Even if nothing comes of this whole maggoty mess, at least those pages won't go to waste. Eva's novel may fizzle, but they're a gold mine for me." He grinned. "It's the best research I could dream of. So good news either way."

Julia dipped her chin. Her hat brim would shadow her eyes as her mouth assumed a polite smile. She could not bear to witness his selfish happiness. More likely the day's only good news was her escape from the apartment without a tattooed dachshund.

CHAPTER 27

It wouldn't do. Julia shook her head at Philip and let him explain to the estate agent. It was the third apartment they'd looked at since noon, and each was impossible. She might explode with frustration if she opened her mouth to speak, and the poor man deserved better courtesy.

Another day had passed since her discovery in Duveen's library, a day that had brought no inkling of fresh information about Eva or her manuscript. Philip could report only that Kessler was firming up plans for his major crackdown on Sunday. Unless something turned up before then, Eva's disappearance had sealed her guilty fate.

Philip's only genuine news made Julia's anxiety worse. A letter had arrived from his housekeeper, Mrs. Cheadle. Her train would arrive from Florida late next week. Julia and Christophine were welcome to stay on with him, he said, but Mrs. Cheadle's return meant a difficult arrangement, crowded and awkward. Christophine was as restless as Julia to unpack her things, their things, the familiars of their own household. It was imperative that Julia find them a new home—but thus far she'd seen nothing suitable for, and that would tolerate the peculiar needs of, a printing studio.

She needed a space for her Albion, the beautiful little handpress on which she'd printed each of her Capriole productions. Along with a large oak type cabinet, holding her growing collection of fonts; a proofing table and composing stone (a slab of marble set into a sturdy oak table); paper cabinets; and assorted other supplies and furnishings of a printing studio, it required a spacious room, sturdily built and with ample natural light. That and the usual needs of a reasonably comfortable residence meant her requirements were particular, and her options were—none. This ugly, dark, and serpentine flat on East Twenty-Sixth Street was their last appointment of the day.

She dreaded even forming the thought. On top of her growing despair about Eva, she felt an inchoate new fear: Would she have to abandon Capriole?

Philip wisely suggested they recover over tea. She was in a foul mood. Just a month ago she'd felt so hopeful and exultant that her move to New York would launch her into an exciting new life, with new friends, a new lover, and especially new horizons for her Capriole Press. Nothing had turned out as she'd envisioned it. At the moment it all seemed perilously close to crumbling to dust. Had she made a terrible, terrible mistake? Would she have been better off remaining in London? Should she have married David after all?

Julia shuddered, not because it was a loathsome thought but because it wasn't. Maybe she had blithely overestimated her ability to make her own way in life, independent of any man's help or approval. Everything she had thought would unfold gloriously before her had not. Was she a colossal fool? No more self-reliant than the naive and helpless females she scorned?

Philip turned the handle of the teapot toward himself (arranged, as always, toward the woman) and poured out two steaming cups. "You might as well tell me," he said. His gaze was open but not avid. He was inviting, not insisting.

As usual, he was right. He'd been true to his word, yielding up every morsel he knew about Kessler's investigation. She'd listened more than she'd shared in return, and now that discrepancy seemed not only arrogant but foolish. Philip had been a shrewd listener last fall when

Julia had struggled to understand Naomi Rankin's apparent suicide. Even though he'd stood (ostensibly) to gain should one theory prevail over another, he hadn't manipulated her reasoning. To the contrary, he'd opened her eyes to new possibilities. He might be as helpful now. And she'd promised to share what she knew.

She told him about the pages she'd discovered in Duveen's library, wondering what to make of them.

"It rather dashes any theory that the missing manuscript was only incidental to the murder," Philip said. "If Timson were shot for some other reason, why keep the manuscript?"

"You mean if he was killed for the jewelry or something else in the safe? A smart thief would assume anything locked away like that was valuable. It wouldn't take much to learn about Goldsmith's big stake in it. Maybe he's testing the market, seeing if they'll pay to get it back."

"It's conceivable," Philip said, "but why in dribbled batches?"

"To whet the publisher's appetite? Tease him with what he's lost but could recover—for a price?"

"Without any mention of said price? No, a blackmailer would get straight to business. And remember, the fellow's also a murderer. Unless that book's worth a minor fortune, blackmail isn't worth the risk." He lifted his cup. "Regardless, whoever has that manuscript is still likely to be Timson's killer. Kessler will certainly think so."

As Julia feared. "Pablo assumes it's Eva. He doesn't care much, so long as there's a book to publish, no doubt with more fanfare than ever."

"I'm afraid Miss Pruitt is the odds-on favorite. It doesn't look good for your friend."

"What if Timson simply gave Eva her manuscript? That was her plan, to sweet-talk him into returning it. What if she succeeded, and someone else came along later and shot him, by sheer, awful coincidence?"

It was a stretch, but wasn't it *possible*?

"Why hide then?" he said. "Her disappearance is the strongest strike against her."

Bernice. The betrayed nanny. Julia nearly said it aloud: Innocence was a white person's luxury. No Negro in Eva's circumstances could dare trust such a claim to protect her.

Philip reconsidered in the wake of Julia's silence. "Perhaps she knows who killed him. Perhaps she witnessed the murder."

"And is hiding from the murderer." Julia's voice rose. "But who?"

She'd exhausted every possibility, over and over. She'd even wondered if Austen could have crept away early that morning. Her current favorite candidate was Bobby Hobart, Carlotta's manager, perhaps because she'd never met the man. He'd surely known of the secret passage connecting his office with Timson's apartment. Maybe he'd wanted more power or chafed under Timson's authority. But Kessler had scrutinized Hobart's alibi and found it solid. He and all of the armed staff at Carlotta's were accounted for that night and morning. Kessler insisted none of them had had the opportunity to murder their boss.

She reconsidered Wallace. Much as she was attracted to the man, he carried a gun. He was ambitious. For a bookkeeper's son, he'd acquired remarkable wealth and power. Was there a ruthlessness beneath the steady nerve and clear head? Not that she'd seen, but he too had had no opportunity to kill Timson. Kessler believed his account of that night—and so did Julia. She could imagine him killing a man, but not in stealth or without extreme, just cause.

She ticked off her reasoning to Philip. Not Austen, not Hobart, not Wallace.

"Duveen?" Philip mused. "He could have typed and mailed those pages himself to throw further suspicion onto Eva."

Duveen and the Clarks had been drinking heavily when they'd left Carlotta's. In the blur of more cocktails, crowds, and eye-popping distractions, he might have slipped away from them. "Yes," she said, warming to the idea. "He's eccentric but also much sharper than he seems."

"Would he know about that secret stair? Unless he could levitate or otherwise slip unnoticed by the guards, it seems the only way in and out of that room."

"Maybe. He frequents the place regularly. He'd been in Timson's rooms before. Or Eva might have mentioned the passage. Or Jerome Crockett. Anyone who worked backstage might know about it and have told him. Pablo chats up everyone—and he's gathering material for a Harlem novel of his own."

Philip met this with a skeptical scowl. "He's also rather bulky. Most secret stairs are tight squeezes. Kessler said his man could barely fit. Duveen's hardly built for skulking."

"He could have telephoned to Goldsmith, who's quite slim and lied about his alibi. He's a proud, calculating man, Philip, and he told police he was at home when his wife told me he stormed out of the house again at three." Separately or together, both men had motive to reclaim property they considered stolen. Julia tried to picture Goldsmith demanding the manuscript's return. His righteous anger had been real enough. But would either he or Duveen be able to wrestle Timson's gun from him and pull the trigger? It was hard to imagine, physically or psychologically.

That left Jerome Crockett, who, like Eva, was a fugitive without an alibi. Julia pictured him in his sweltering cave in the bowels of the Half-Shell, writing poems across discarded newspapers. Her heart balked, but she had to face it: Jerome was the likeliest suspect, after Eva.

Julia and Philip finished their tea in that dreary stalemate. Neither spoke until the taxicab pulled to the curb in front of Philip's home. Lucky man, Julia thought. His flat suited him perfectly, and he seemed prepared to live out his days there. As they mounted the steps, she said as much.

"I was fortunate. It belongs to my friend Mrs. Macready. She owns most of the block." He stopped, halfway up the broad stone steps. "And I'm a dolt. A mile thick today. I forgot until this moment that she mentioned a vacancy last week."

"Nearby?" Julia scanned the block but saw no sign of anyone moving in or out.

"Around the corner. It fronts onto Lexington. Should we inquire?"

Ten minutes later they were waiting on the steps of a beautiful redbrick building adorned with the prosperous flourishes of the previous century. Boxes of red geraniums lined every window. Someone from the manager's office had promised to arrive shortly and show them the apartment.

So Mrs. Macready was Philip's landlady. Extraordinary. Julia recalled the woman's warm greeting last week in Chez Mareille, as well as her cool one to Wallace. Who was she, other than a wealthy widow? Julia was in no mood for yet another mystery. It might be rude to ask, but surely a nominal half sister merited some allowances. "She's more than your landlady, Philip. How do you know her?"

It *was* rude. Philip coughed.

"I ask because I met her the other evening, when I was out with Wallace. She snubbed him something royal, after he'd greeted her with perfect cordiality. He said it stemmed from some minor slight years ago, something he couldn't even recall but that she held against him as a grudge. I'm frightfully curious. She seemed quite pleasant to me, and obviously you like her . . ." Julia dipped her head to leave the rest unspoken.

"If she was cool to him, she must have a good reason," Philip said.

"What kind of reason?"

"It's not for me to say." He dropped his cigarette to the pavement and crushed it beneath his shoe. His jaw tightened with the exertion.

This was as close to angry she'd ever seen Philip. Why? "I gather you've known her a long time."

Julia waited, watching squirrels circling the trunk of an elm tree across the street. "We're friends," he finally said. "We met years ago, when I was, oh, not more than twenty."

Julia hoped her eyes reflected the same open patience—not greedy curiosity—that Philip's had shown an hour ago. If he chose to confide in her, she'd welcome it as the honor it was.

"We were quite close once." He looked away. "It was torrid, of course, and utterly mad, without any chance of anything. We're like an old couple now, long since gone separate ways but still good friends. Young love, though." He shook his head wistfully. "It can eat a man alive."

It wasn't so hard, this siblingesque candor, Julia thought. In fact it was quite wonderful. They should confide in each other more often. She imagined someday pushing his wheelchair out into the sunshine, tucking a blanket over his knees, as any fond and devoted younger sister might. It was an oddly cheering picture.

Julia realized he was watching for her reaction. Her thoughts had gone to Gerald, her own impossible early love. Yet while Philip's affair with Leah Macready had run its course and settled into an intimate friendship, hers with Gerald had been doomed from the start. He'd been just back from the war, alive yet broken, each hour of the carnage ringing unstoppably in his ears. Julia could only watch as the man he might have become had suffered and sickened, until he'd ended his agony with a rope slung over a beam in his parents' country house. Now she understood they had shared more urgent tenderness than lovers' passion. That kind of love ought to open into joy and delight, but with Gerald all joy had been smothered beneath the pain.

As Julia spoke of this, in low and fitful starts of sentences, she wondered at her recklessness. Not even Christophine had heard as much. She looked up when Philip touched his finger to her cheek. He dabbed away a spot of moistness and signaled the agent's approach.

Julia regrouped and swiped both cheeks, embarrassed but grateful, as the agent arrived with a fistful of keys. The empty flat was at the top, he reported between chugs of breath as they climbed. "Best," murmured Philip. He too lived in the top flat. As they viewed one room after another—a large living room with French doors onto a narrow balcony overlooking the same courtyard treetops as Philip's library, a formal dining room, a bright modernized kitchen and adjacent maid's quarters, two small guest rooms, and a larger master bedroom—Julia fought a growing excitement. Christophine could turn one of the small bedrooms into an atelier. The apartment might work, depending on the final room at the back, a semiattic space that the agent called the nursery. It proved to be a large square space four steps up, with a basin and cupboards in one corner. Best of all, a huge skylight flooded the room with light from a north-facing wall.

Philip strode toward the far wall and rapped the plaster. "I believe my flat's on the other side. If you take it, we can devise a code of sibling thumps."

Julia's mind was buzzing too loudly to answer. She asked about the weighty burden of her equipment and any objections to the work she would do there. The agent said the building was solidly constructed and could bear a great deal of weight, but he'd have to ask the owner about concerns regarding her activities.

"I'll speak with her," Philip offered. "I may have some influence there."

Julia could barely contain her thoughts. It would work. It would work well, spectacularly well. Despite the oddness—and potential pitfalls—of living so close to Philip, the apartment was better suited for her purposes than the one she'd originally leased.

A flurry of business talk followed. Yes, the agent could stay another half an hour. Julia nearly ran to go fetch Christophine. She couldn't remember when she'd last felt so buoyant. Unless Christophine had serious objections—which seemed unlikely—Julia had at last taken her first step toward establishing their new life in New York.

CHAPTER 28

"Have I missed anything? Any excitement while I was gone?"

It would be wrong to say Austen bounded into Philip's library, but only by degree. He swept into the room in a flurry of chatter and hugs. It was early Saturday evening. Nearly three weeks had passed since he'd scrambled out of this very room to pack for his trip abroad.

Unable to sit still, he paced the room as the excited recap poured out of him: a mixed-up cabin assignment that had found him sharing a suite with a Brooklyn obstetrician; gin-fueled pranks among the sons and daughters of English aristocrats even sillier (the offspring) than their American counterparts; a dawn splash in the Thames with friends made some hours earlier at the Slug and Lettuce in Chelsea; a whole afternoon dogging the footsteps of Francis Meynell at his Nonesuch Press; a spree along the Charing Cross market stalls snatching up early editions of Trollope and Hardy.

His hands bounced and leaped as he talked. A dervish of excitement, twice he dropped what might charitably be called kisses onto Julia's cheek, but which were better termed smacks. "I know I'm impossible, but it was such a knockout trip. You should have heard Meynell talking about his new Blake."

"I'd love to see what they do with—" Julia began.

"And they're doing a new Burton's *Anatomy* with Kauffer illustrations. I saw proofs. It's a howling blue beauty!"

His enthusiasm was infectious. Julia remembered his excitement about fine books a month ago in Duveen's apartment, that night of their first conversation. She knew that particular thrill and shared it now, glad for his runaway happiness.

When he saw the plate of fresh shortbread and a bottle of champagne, he swung the bottle toward Julia—*Should I open it?* She wanted to gesture, *Absolutely*, but couldn't rouse her hand. At last his eyes dimmed. "What? What's happened?"

Julia had imagined this moment several times in the past few weeks, but when the chance arrived, her thoughts scattered like unstrung pearls. How to describe the strange and troubling turns of events? The last Austen knew, they'd just learned of Timson's death and Eva's disappearance. "I'm thrilled you had a good trip, I really am," she said, "but I've been caught up in Eva Pruitt's nightmare. Have you heard?"

"Only Billie's snootful. When I stopped by the office this afternoon, she said Eva's hiding and the police are going to arrest her. Is that true?"

Streamlining the details, Julia described Eva's silence, Kessler's suspicions, Wallace's involvement, Jerome's grief and confusion, Logan's resentment, Goldsmith's deceit, and now Duveen's optimism about the pages that had arrived in his mail. But the police were no closer to finding another suspect, and soon attention would return full bore to Eva. Kessler's patience expired tomorrow.

"Sounds bad. Anything we can do?"

Julia drove her fingers into her hair and gave her skull a rattle. Empty. Or rather it was bursting with thoughts, all of them useless.

Setting aside the champagne, Austen bit into one of Christophine's shortbreads, spraying crumbs onto his jacket. "Pablo says those pages are from Eva's manuscript? That she just sent them to him, without a note?"

Julia nodded. "But they were a short excerpt, and not even from the beginning of a chapter or section. They seemed to be about a young Negro man who goes dancing with his girlfriend. He can't find a job, and they argue because he flirts with a glamorous older woman. He's dazzled, the girlfriend's jealous, and the jezebel's satisfied—nothing very original."

"So why send it?" He held the plate under his chin in lieu of a napkin as he ate three more pastries.

"That's the question."

Austen rubbed his jaw. "I wonder."

"Wonder what?"

Julia had to repeat the question before he answered. "Sorry. I was thinking. I went through my office mail today to see if a contract I'd been waiting for had come in. It hadn't, but there was something else I didn't know what to make of. Just pages, no letter. It was odd."

"From Eva's book?"

"I don't know. It was a plain envelope with no return address and four or five typescript pages inside. Came in yesterday's mail. I only glanced at it, thinking an author had sent substitute pages and not bothered to explain. They sometimes think theirs is your only project and you'll know what to do with them. But it was about some woman named Marie. Nothing I'm working on, which is strange."

"Did this Marie live in Harlem? Did she have a boyfriend named Byron?"

"Not sure. I didn't look at it that closely."

"Did you by any chance bring those pages with you?"

"No. I figured I'd sort them out next week. Why? Is it important?"

Julia set his empty plate aside. "It might be. Can we run over for a look?"

"Right now?" He glanced out the French windows. The evening was lapsing into murky twilight. "I thought we might go get dinner."

"Right now."

Crosstown traffic was light. Twenty minutes later Austen dug out keys and let them into the reception vestibule of Liveright's dark offices. "Horace doesn't like us here after midafternoon on Saturdays," he whispered, although the place seemed deserted. "We figure he holds private parties upstairs. More than once the first person here on Monday has met a chorus girl washing up in the lavatory. The poor thing goes screaming down the hall in her skivvies. It's too funny."

He knew his way well, guiding them up the wide front stairs by the glow of passing motorcar headlamps. On the second floor they entered a dark corridor and waited as their eyes adjusted. "No lights," he said. "That's the unwritten rule—people do sometimes spend the night here, when they're too drunk to get home or just have to work on something all night, but we pretend we're not here. Without lights Horace thinks we're obeying him." He listened, but they heard only street sounds. "Probably no one's around, but just in case."

He edged forward, one hand against the wall, Julia close behind. They turned a corner to the right and stopped at a door on the left. He unlocked it and switched on a small desk lamp. Julia closed the door behind them.

An untidy assortment of papers and books covered his desk, including what must be the heap of mail he'd rustled through earlier. He found a large envelope, identical to the one Duveen had fished from his wastebasket, and shook its contents out onto the desk.

Julia took the pages and lowered herself into an armchair beside the desk. She twisted away and slipped on the eyeglasses she'd furtively tucked into her handbag. At first glance the pages matched what she'd found under Duveen's typewriter.

This batch included only four pages, starting with page 114. She began to read and quickly recognized the characters. Byron and Marie were in her apartment. He fumed that Marie had no sympathy for his difficulty finding work he could tolerate. He stormed out to wander aimlessly through Harlem, frustrated and self-absorbed. The narrative ended in midsentence at the bottom of the third page, because the fourth page was numbered 192.

The transition was abrupt in more than syntax. Julia reread the first two lines twice before realizing that, for one thing, the new passage was written from Marie's point of view. Halfway down she knew exactly what this was: a page from the scene that had so angered Timson. Her chest tightened as she read the brutal account of a man named Coburn raping Marie with his gun. "Oh, Austen," Julia said faintly, laying the sheet on the desk.

He looked up from reading the earlier pages she'd passed to him. His mouth lifted at one corner. "Nice cheaters."

She pulled off her eyeglasses. "This last page is from the rape scene Timson was so angry about."

"Just one page?"

She nodded.

"Why? Why that scene? Why just one page?"

"I don't know." Julia watched as he held it under the lamp and began to read. There was something odd about the page itself, some pattern pressed into the paper. Not translucent like a watermark but something written or drawn on it without ink.

"Wait." She rose and gripped the sheet as she bent over it. "Look." She angled it beneath the light. "There. Do you see?"

Austen gazed hard at the paper. "What am I looking for?"

Julia flipped the page over and angled its blank verso under the pool of light. This time Austen's lips opened with a little pop of surprise. He saw it, a large zigzag pattern of dots and connecting lines scratched into the paper. On the verso it was more visible, but when Julia turned the sheet text-side up, it became legible too. With a squeak she recognized it: a large capital *E*, in Eva's distinctive spiky handwriting. Her initial.

Austen let out a low whistle. "What is it?"

"An *E*, for Eva."

One cheek puckered in skepticism. "Not necessarily. It could be anything, made by anyone."

"I've seen her handwriting." Julia sat back, spectacles in her hand, forgotten. Eva's large script was jutting and linear as an architect's, all angles. She'd signed her note to Jerome with a spiking *E* identical to this one. "I'm certain it's Eva's. She must have scratched it into the paper, maybe with a fingernail."

Austen whistled again. "Why would she do that?"

"I don't know."

As Julia stared at the figure, she recognized it a second time. It was the same odd pattern of scarring on Eva's hip—those dots formed the points of her own initial, like some crude homemade tattoo. Children liked to scratch their initials into wood or paint. Perhaps that was what Eva had done, in the same way children cut open their fingers to make a blood oath, declaring the power of will and courage over pain. She and her sister, Ella, shared the initial; maybe they had marked each other to seal a kind of private eternal bond. Such things were youthful rites of passage. No wonder Eva kept hers well hidden.

Julia tucked her eyeglasses into her handbag. "Maybe she wants to reassure friends she's all right. That she and the manuscript are safe."

It was exactly the kind of thing Eva would do. Julia checked the other pages for similar marks. Nothing. She hadn't noticed any marking on the pages Duveen had received, though without a strong crosslight and careful examination, it might not be perceptible. She'd have to return tomorrow to check those pages again, even if the privilege cost her the printing of a small edition of *Pookins*.

She covered her mouth with her hand as another thought dawned. She'd been so eager to finally discover something new that she hadn't registered the implications. Now she wished she hadn't noticed the damn initial. "But if Eva is the sender, it means she has the manuscript. Kessler would see this as evidence that she was involved in Timson's death."

Julia remembered her relief when Wallace had said the safe had been empty and its contents gone when he'd found Eva with Timson's body. But Eva could have already moved the manuscript to the bedroom, and she could have taken it with her when she'd fled down the hidden stairway. Dread sank in Julia's stomach. But why, then, would she beg Jerome to return it? Had that been some kind of perverse ruse, or had she somehow come across the manuscript later, after sending those notes? These pages had been sent only a few days ago.

"If she was involved," Austen said slowly, "why send anything? And why put her initial on it? Doesn't this just point the finger at herself?"

Julia silently urged her brain to persevere, to find some other explanation. Every bone in her body believed Eva—gentle, beautiful Eva—was not the killer, despite this graphic suggestion she was. "Maybe it has to do with the particular pages. Maybe there's a clue to what happened in this part of the story."

"These are mostly about the Byron character. You said Pablo's pages were too. That means she's focusing on the boyfriend. Is she casting suspicion on Jerome?"

Julia considered miserably. "Maybe. But when I talked with him that night, I believed him. I honestly think he knows no more than we do, possibly much less. And I'm certain Eva loves him. Why would she point a finger at him?" She rubbed out the creases in her forehead.

Austen's chair scraped as he pulled it closer. "You're the one with the brain. If your bean is stumped, I'm no help."

Julia again smoothed her forehead. But her bean, as he put it, remained stumped.

A full minute of silence elapsed. Austen began to tap a thumbnail against his front teeth. He took a breath and hesitated. After several more seconds he said, "There's something else odd here. I can't shake the feeling I've read this before. Are you sure it's from Eva's manuscript?"

Her elbows scooted closer. "Pablo said it was."

"Well, maybe it's just some big coincidence. But I *know* I've read something very like it, if not this exactly."

"Where?"

"Here. It must have come in over the transom. For the first six months that's all I did—read unsolicited manuscripts. I'm sure we never published it." He drummed a loose fist on his desk. "I wish I could remember more."

"Is it still here?" Her glance flew around the cluttered room. "Do you keep manuscripts you don't want to publish?"

"Most publishers don't, but this place is so careless we can't even manage the stuff we reject. It's probably around here somewhere, waiting for someone to write a letter to the author. It could be on anybody's desk, or—"

His eyebrows rose. "There's a big pile of them on a table in Horace's office. He tries to spin through everything so he can at least recognize it if some nervous author buttonholes him at a party. He can do that—ten minutes, and he can size it up. We do the grunt work, actually read a good chunk to be sure, but Horace wants them to think he did too. Anyway, odds are good it's there."

"Let's go look."

"Right now?"

Julia jumped to her feet. "Right now."

CHAPTER 29

They retraced their steps along the dark corridor and up to the top floor of the silent building. Straight ahead, Julia saw through the murk the large room that a few weeks ago had been full of partying editors and authors. To the left yawned another black hallway and the lavatory where she and Eva had retreated for repairs. Austen turned to the right. "He's forever losing his keys," he whispered, "so there's a spare over here." He felt along the molding above the door to the party room and returned with a key. He unlocked the door to Liveright's office and swung it open. Reaching across Julia, Austen switched on the light.

A loud wail nearly buckled her knees. A woman's tousled platinum head dangled upside down over the side of a divan, her arms waving uselessly in the air above her. Her dress was twisted into disarray beneath her chin. The woman squealed again in a shrill expletive, wriggling her knees in an effort to pull herself upright.

With a crude curse Liveright's contorted face rose into view. "What the hell—!" he roared, squinting in the sudden light.

Austen punched off the light switch, shoved Julia back into the hall, and leaped out after her. The slamming door sliced Liveright's furious epithet in half.

"God almighty!" Austen gasped. "I'm cooked!"

Julia pulled him recklessly down the dark corridor and onto the stairs. In a miracle of gravity, their feet stayed beneath them in the freefall descent. They spun around the corner one flight below and plunged into the black hallway, Julia hanging on to the waist of Austen's trousers by the wrenched length of her arm as he groped for a doorknob that was not locked. He found one, Julia careened into his back, and a storm of blasphemies came thundering down the stairs behind them.

They dived into the room and pushed the door shut with agonizing care, registering only a soft click. The corridor flooded with light. They leaned against the door, Austen gripping the knob for want of a lock. The curses came toward them, a cyclone of rattling doorknobs and pounding on wood.

"I'll find you, you little shit," Liveright yelled, his voice nearing.

Julia could hear his hoarse pants and garbled curses as he reached their door. The knob tensed beneath Austen's hands. Liveright caught his breath. In the abrupt silence Austen clutched the knob in both hands, bracing himself for a wrenching twist. Liveright gave it a hard but unwitting jiggle.

"Damn!" The knob went slack. Liveright pounded the wall as he moved on. "Damn damn *damn.*"

Liveright's progress along the rest of the corridor was less distinct, drowned by the roar of blood in Julia's ears. The commotion turned and approached again. Still grumbling, curses and expletives somewhat less loud, Liveright returned as he had come. After he had passed, Austen cracked open the door. They heard his furious climb back to the top floor and the distant slam of his office door, and Julia imagined the emphatic click of its lock.

Some moments elapsed, the darkness filled with their thudding breaths. Julia pressed her palm against Austen's ribs to calm his rocketing heartbeat.

"What a smash of things I almost made up there," he said when he was able. "Christ almighty. My job flashed before my eyes."

"He may not remember this on Monday," she whispered. "I don't think he actually saw us, not enough to recognize. He wasn't focusing. On us, I mean."

Austen began to laugh. "Some sheik I turn out to be," he sputtered. "Are you all right?"

"Breathing helps. Where are we?"

"In a room between the lavs we dignify by calling the SHH, the Secretary's Hidden Helper. It's where we stash all the work that will never get done, mostly filing and correspondence. Any decent secretary would take care of this stuff, but Horace is such a bear to work for we can't keep the good ones. Terrible way to run a business, but Horace scrapes along."

He turned to grope ahead, Julia following, her hand on his back. He found the light cord, and a feeble yellow light revealed they were in a small anteroom. Between the two lavatory entrances was a door opening into another narrow space. Thick black pipes flanked it, disappearing like snakes into the shadows overhead.

"Would that manuscript be in here?" Julia asked, stepping in to pull another light cord.

The SHH was well named, about six feet wide and some twelve or fourteen feet deep. Each long wall was lined with shelves crowded with boxes, bundled papers, and precarious mounds of loose pages. Against the back wall was wedged an ancient sofa, possibly kin to the one upstairs in the ladies' lavatory. Overhead loomed a web of more black pipes, glistening in the glare of the suspended light bulb.

"Maybe." Austen pulled down a large box and sank with it onto the sofa's splotched concave cushions. It groaned in a cloud of stale dust. "It's our best bet, after Horace's office."

It was their only bet. Julia would turn over every piece of paper in here if she had to. She pulled down the box next to where his had been.

"It could be anywhere," he said, "but I'm guessing it's somewhere on this side." He waved to his right. "The other stuff was here before I came."

He set the box at his feet, between his knees, and began pulling out bundles of pages, most tied with string. He considered each, sometimes peering under a curled-back corner to read bits on inside pages. He sorted them into two groups: some he set aside on the floor, and others he piled on the sofa beside him. When he had reviewed all ten or twelve bundles, he returned those on the floor to the box and shoved it aside. Picking up one of the remaining manuscripts, he looked at Julia. "It's not any of those," he said with a nod toward the half-full box, "so let's start reading." He patted the cushion next to him, then looked at his hand with distaste. He took off his jacket and laid it over the stain.

Julia lugged her box over and sat. Her shoulder knocked his as the springs pitched them together. He laughed. "This is the last thing I'd dreamed of for tonight."

She already had the string off one of the bundles.

"Okay," he said. "I'm pretty sure the characters' names were different, so we're just looking for a similar prose style and the same basic situation, more focused on the boyfriend. I seem to recall it was written mostly from a man's point of view, probably third person, but I can't swear to it. Definitely set in New York, a young man having trouble getting settled—that sort of thing." He settled down to read.

Julia fetched her spectacles and did the same.

The first six manuscripts were easy to dispatch. Julia got faster as her impatience grew, pressing Austen to hurry too. Over and over he rose and sorted through more large boxes, but none yielded anything hopeful. He then tackled the unboxed bundles stacked haphazardly on the shelves, dividing them into two high piles on the floor. After hoisting the not-possibles back onto the shelves, he dragged the remainder over to the couch. They didn't speak as they dived again into the herculean task.

Julia awoke with a start. She lay across the sofa, her feet in Austen's lap, wrapped in the untucked hem of his shirt. "No," she exclaimed. How could she have fallen asleep?

He jiggled her foot again. "Morning, bean."

A weak light shone in under the door. Papers and bundles were strewed across the floor. Her hat and shoes were off, and her spectacles had been tucked into the toe of one shoe. "Any luck?"

He patted a thick stack of pages on his knee. "Just now. The names are different, but it's the passage we read last night. Almost word for word."

He held up a page, and Julia recognized it at once. The sentences were identical. She threw her arms around him. "Brilliant man!"

A hundred thoughts stampeded through her mind. What did this mean? Eva had been more sly than anyone knew. But Julia understood how desperate authors could feel, fearing that their years of hard work might languish unappreciated and even unread on publishers' desks, awaiting their brief chance to garner attention. She knew of authors who changed their titles to snag another chance. Some even changed their names. Perhaps Eva had spent the past year creating mystery and drama for her "secret" and "new" novel as a way to incite fresh eagerness when she submitted the old manuscript again. It was a bold strategy, and it had worked—too well.

"What do you think?" she asked Austen. "This must mean she tried to publish it earlier and Liveright rejected it. Maybe she tried again this spring with a new title."

Austen teased her with the grin of a boy prankster. "Better than that."

He turned over the stack in his lap. The top sheet was blank except for the title and author's name. He held it close for Julia to read: *Till Human Voices Wake Us*. By Jerome Sanford Crockett.

Jerome. *Jerome!*

"A shock, huh?" Austen said. "Opened my eyes too."

"Jerome? What does this mean?"

"Not sure. All I do know is something's crawling under my shirt."

Julia jumped up. She shivered inside her wrinkled dress and rubbed her arms and stockinged legs, whisking away unseen insects.

He collected his jacket and the manuscript as she gathered up her hat and shoes.

"My guess is he stole Eva's work," Austen said as they hurried back to his office. "Maybe this is an early version of *Harlem Angel* he tried to pass off as his own. It explains why he's so jumpy around editors and why he won't come to Horace's parties."

Austen locked the door and whisked off his shirt. He flapped it like laundry, shaking out any fleas and the worst wrinkles. "It's possible he killed Timson to get the manuscript before Eva could give it to Goldsmith. After all, he probably submitted *Voices* to Arthur too. He couldn't risk him recognizing it and exposing his fraud."

He clapped his hands, palms a pair of jubilant cymbals. "That's got to be it. It means Jerome killed Timson. And you know where the cops can find him. By lunchtime Eva can breathe easy and come out from hiding. You're the brilliant one, bean."

He reached for the telephone. But Julia pried it from his hand and returned it to its cradle. "Hold on a tick. We need to be sure."

One more minute wouldn't matter if they were right. It was important to be sure. Julia had witnessed how Eva was treated in police custody—and she was a woman not even under arrest. Jerome would fare far worse.

"Everything you say makes sense," Julia said slowly. "But I would swear he was telling the truth when he said he didn't have the manuscript or know where it was."

Could she have been fooled? Maybe she was more gullible than she thought. She was proving to be wrong about many things she'd thought she understood about herself.

"Maybe he panicked and gave it to her to make her look guilty," Austen said.

Julia's nostrils flared in distaste. Could Jerome do something so despicable?

Her heart heaved with the answer. If he was a murderer, then yes, of course he could. Had she been duped so easily? Did she believe poets inhabited a higher order, above the fray of powerful emotions like ambition, jealousy, and hate? In fact a poet could burrow into deep feelings better than anyone. Jerome had every reason to hate Timson, and witnessing his cruelty to Eva could easily have been the final straw. Julia may have been blinded by Jerome's suffering in the dark recesses of the Half-Shell, but now she could see a larger reason for his agony. If Austen's theory was right, it suggested Jerome was what he'd seemed from the start—a cold and selfish man, a schemer, even a killer.

"That would explain why Eva's hiding," Austen went on, warming to his notion. "If she thinks she can't trust anyone to believe her, she would send out passages focused on the boyfriend character, who sounds a lot like Jerome. She wants us to see that he's the killer, not her."

He poked his arms into his crumpled shirtsleeves and fastened the buttons. He loosened his trousers and began shoving in shirttails.

"Maybe," Julia murmured, her mind still struggling as she fastened the strap of her shoe. Could she be sure? Alerting the police meant putting a noose around Jerome's neck.

"You don't think so? Makes perfect sense to me."

Rationally, he was right. It did make sense. Julia could see it laid out neatly, all the things that pointed to Jerome as the murderer. So why did her brain not feel exultant, the past weeks' cobwebs swept clean with fresh light? It only felt shrouded in a darkness more ominous than ever.

She heard herself whimper. "I can't help feeling something's not right. A week ago I would have leaped into your arms, deliriously happy we'd discovered this and figured out everything. Now I have trouble imagining the Jerome I saw last week could either murder a man or shift suspicion onto Eva. I know he's proud and unpleasant, but I'm convinced they love each other. He's terrified for her, not for himself. I believed him, Austen. I still do."

"If he's desperate, if his life depends on it, he'd believe his own lies. Then you'd believe them too." He buttoned his trousers, then his cuffs.

"Maybe." Julia straightened as a new thought began to glow, then blaze. "But there's another reason I don't think he stole her work. I saw a note she'd written. And something he said—he called her style clean and easy."

She slapped at the desk. "I'm a bloody fool. I should have seen it right away. You read those pages. Would you call this prose clean and easy? No. Nowhere near. It's elaborate, dramatic, even melodramatic. Eva didn't write this."

Austen sat down. He stared at Julia. "It's the other way around? Eva stole Jerome's manuscript?"

He rubbed his chin. His shadowy beard made a faint rasp under his palm. "That would mean we were right in the first place. If she stole Jerome's novel, she has every reason to want us to think he killed Timson. But what a grim way to hide a secret. Getting a book published isn't worth sending a fellow to the chair over."

Julia stared at the floor, barely listening to him. Then she laughed. Tears started to her eyes as light finally dispelled the morass in her brain. "No, no. She didn't steal it. She's not trying to pin the murder on him. They planned this together."

"What the—?"

"Jerome wrote the book, but Eva is pretending to be the author."

Julia hobbled peg-leg around the office, pacing with only one shoe fastened. "It makes sense, the most perfect sense. Publishers don't want what he prefers to write, and Eva's a ready-made icon for the kind of Harlem Pablo's wild to promote. I'm guessing they decided to give him the author and book he wants, one with big sales possibilities, and use the money to get away and start a new life together. I knew that's what she wanted, but I never realized she wasn't working alone.

"Come on. We have to talk to Jerome." She scrambled to find her other shoe. "Eva's been passing all along—as a writer."

CHAPTER 30

They hurried down the six steps to the Half-Shell's entrance. Eva's secret didn't explain why she would send out cryptic batches of manuscript, but Jerome might be able to.

The door was locked. Julia peered through its round porthole window into the shadowy club. An old man in baggy trousers stood about ten feet inside, leaning on a broom handle and lighting the mangled stub of a cigarette. She gave the doorknob a vigorous shake.

The old man started and shook his head. When she persisted, he sidled to the door. "Closed," he said, or something like it, through a gargle of phlegm.

Julia pressed her face to the window and smiled with every sparkle she could manage on a gray, humid morning. "Please," she mouthed, reaching into her handbag.

The old man shuffled closer. "Closed."

"Our maid's desperately ill, and her brother works inside," Julia said into the grimy glass.

He fumbled at the lock and cracked open the door. "Can't come in, miss. Closed."

Julia leaned so close her nose would be mangled if the door shut. "Jervis Carter? We must talk to him. We'll be quiet as lambs, I promise." She held a folded bill below her chin.

"Carter?" the old man croaked, the grooves in his face deepening with suspicion.

"It's a terrible emergency." The bill danced.

Julia hadn't seen what denomination she'd pulled from her bag. Perhaps it was sizable. The old man studied it and opened the door just wide enough for them to slip inside. Nodding at his toothless "Make it quick, miss," she pressed the money into his hand.

They threaded their way through the narrow aisles, chairs atop the bare tables. Swept-up piles of litter lay about the floor, waiting for the man to follow with the dustpan. Stale smoke deepened the gloom.

Julia retraced her steps of the other evening, pausing only to get her bearings before plunging into the backstage maze. Fortunately, the space was deserted and silent, and high clerestory windows offered some dim light. She picked a course in the general direction of the back hallway that led to Jerome.

She hesitated outside the door to his cell. The door was again propped open with the rusty iron. Nothing stirred. A drab light from the window in the alcove revealed the drifting lint and desiccated brick walls she remembered. Crumpled and smoothed newspapers lay stacked on the scarred table. Julia took a deep breath. "Jerome?"

Nothing. Then a scrabbling and the creak of bedsprings. More shuffling and the sound of shallow panting. A shadow fell across the table. Jerome moved warily into view, gripping his trousers at the waist. "Miss Kydd?" His voice was thick and hoarse.

"We've come to talk with you. It's important." She edged forward, brushing Austen's hand to warn him of the heat and stench.

Jerome watched them approach, eyes not yet focused. His cracked lips gaped open. He didn't move, except for the rippling of sinews in his bare feet as he fought a slight sway.

"Something strange has happened, and I think you can help us make sense of it." Julia stopped about five feet from him. "We think Eva is sending out sections of her manuscript, to Pablo and now to Austen."

Jerome dragged his tongue over his lips. He fumbled to roll his trousers waistband for lack of a belt, and he pulled back his shoulders in search of his once-perfect posture. "What do you mean? How?" His mouth worked stiffly, lips, tongue, and teeth in clumsy collision. When had he last spoken to anyone?

Julia felt Austen slip away behind her. "We don't know how. Or even why. But please look at this." She took a thin envelope from under her arm and laid its four pages on the table.

Jerome held the top page close to his face with both hands. He read the first several lines in the dim light and dropped his arms with a thud. He nodded.

"You recognize it?" Julia tapped the manuscript.

"Of course. It's from Eva's novel."

"Funny thing is," Austen said, "I've read it before. In a manuscript sent to Boni & Liveright sometime in the past couple of years. A novel called *Till Human Voices Wake Us*."

Jerome's fingers curled and uncurled a corner of the top page. "Funny, all right."

They waited.

When he looked up, it was with relief. "That's all it was meant to be. Our little joke. Putting one over on all you editors who decided I couldn't write anything you'd ever publish."

"You wrote *Harlem Angel*, and Eva claimed to be the author." Julia spoke it as a fact but held her breath, waiting for Jerome to admit or deny her conjecture.

He nodded.

"It's mostly her story," Julia went on, "plus some parts from your first book, the one you couldn't sell."

He accepted this with a sigh. "After the writing, being an author is mostly just selling anyway." He lowered his eyes and stroked his dense new beard. When he glanced up, a glimmer of his old pride returned. "We knew Eva would be a dream author—pretty, glamorous, star purveyor of Harlem strut and shine. Pablo loved it from the start, and we kept adding the things he liked. The things that make him, you know, squeal."

Julia nodded. She knew the exact sound. "Wasn't it risky?"

She remembered Eva's hesitations during their first conversation, asking if Julia had written Wilde's *Salome*. Those tentative comments must have been among her first spoken as an impostor writer. Perhaps this was why Eva had talked so much about passing after Billie Fischer had accused her of being a fraud, to divert attention from this other deception. And no wonder Eva had looked at Jerome with such alarm, even terror, when Timson had refused to return the manuscript.

"We were going to drop the charade once Duveen delivered the contract and payment," Jerome said. "But Eva discovered she fancied the ruse. She loved being taken seriously as a writer, and she thought all the attention would mean more money in the end. She wanted to wait until after we were safely in Paris before coming clean about the hoax. I thought that was asking for trouble. We argued about it. The more attention she got, the more I worried something would go wrong."

He stopped fidgeting. "I'm glad someone knows. Has Duveen figured it out?"

"I doubt it," Julia said.

"Hold on. This doesn't make sense." Jerome leaned against the filthy bricks. "How could Eva send these? She doesn't have the manuscript. She wrote to me begging for it."

He was right. Julia's mind had narrowed too quickly to the mystery of authorship, forgetting the problem of the missing manuscript. She answered slowly, formulating a new theory. "Maybe we're wrong to assume Eva is sending the pages. But if not her, then who?"

"Whoever stole it from Timson's safe."

Fear jumped in Jerome's eyes. "His killer?"

Julia could only nod. She was back to her one certainty: the killer had to be someone desperate to get that manuscript. Who? Her thoughts spun yet again to consider Duveen and Goldsmith, arriving as always at the strong though not absolute likelihood of their innocence. Wallace? For the hundredth time she reviewed his account of that night and morning. She had only his word for any of it—which was not the reassurance she'd once considered it. But she did (more or less) trust him now, and besides, Kessler had confirmed he'd been elsewhere when Timson had been killed.

Then who? Billie Fischer? It was a refreshing new thought. Billie was a jealous writer who labored to produce a single short story. She was poisonous toward both Eva and Timson. Julia even glanced at Austen. Could he have slipped away while she'd been sleeping? Absurd. Billie, though . . .

Julia's brief hopes collapsed. "But there's Eva's initial." She pulled out the bottom sheet to show Jerome. "Scratched on this page. You can see it if you hold it up to the light."

He angled it over his head. Even in the weak light from the alley, the sharply pointed *E* was clear. "That's her writing," he said.

A queasy pressure tingled under Julia's jaw. "It's also the pattern on her hip," she said. "Those five dots."

Jerome nodded glumly. "I never thought of that as her initial."

"Did she ever talk about it?"

"Not really. I think some drunk bastard did it. She only said he never bothered her again, so I figured he was long out of the picture. Monster."

Julia recoiled. No wonder Eva would cover it up. *Monster* was right. She laid down her handbag, grasped the table edge, and breathed through her mouth, afraid she might gag. Confirmation of her scratched initial meant Eva did have the manuscript. Julia couldn't bear to say it aloud or to repeat the implication.

"Eva did not kill that bastard Timson." Jerome rejected the unspoken fear through gritted teeth. "I'd swear my life on it. She would not. She could not. No."

"Then someone gave her the manuscript." It was the only remaining possibility.

"Who? And how? Wallace is the only person who knows where she is."

A conspiracy? The killer had taken the manuscript and then persuaded Wallace to pass it along to Eva. That led into thickets so absurd and mind tangling that Julia couldn't begin to consider it.

The roll of her thoughts and the room's terrible smell were almost too much for her. She couldn't be sick. She had to think.

Beneath Jerome's questions was a plea. She saw in his eyes the same look she'd seen so briefly in Eva's eyes. Hopeless yet hopeful. Damned and innocent.

She locked her knees and gulped small breaths. *Think, Julia.*

A tiny light began to blink in her mind's murk.

She waved away Austen's effort to steer her toward the cot. If she kept her head down, breathed through her mouth . . .

The blink steadied to a light, a pinprick but a light. What if she was looking at things backward? Maybe a premise or two needed to be reversed. Would that make a difference, shed enough light to navigate by?

She began with the question of why Eva—or whoever—was sending the pages. "This can't be about getting the manuscript out to be published," she said, between pants of steadying air. "If it were, she'd send the whole thing, and straight to Goldsmith. Or at least sections, in order and from the beginning."

Both men merely nodded, as if any sound might frighten away the fragile speculation.

"So there must be significance in the selections." She gestured for Austen to repeat for Jerome her description of the excerpt Duveen had received.

"That's from my first novel too," Jerome said. "Byron's more or less based on me."

Clarity dawned like a puff of cool air on Julia's throat. "But this last page is different," she said. "The one where she scratched her initial. It's from the rape scene that made Timson so angry. So we need to ask. Did that really happen? Did Timson actually rape her?"

Jerome's bony chest swelled, and his shoulders arched back. For a moment Julia feared he was angry, but it was merely a great sigh. "God," he breathed. "I wish I knew."

"If it's true, it might justify his murder," Austen said.

Jerome's expression flickered. "No such thing as self-defense, not when they think a Negro's killed a white man."

"But it must be significant if she marked this page," Julia said, cautiously raising her head. The worst of the nausea had subsided.

"She'd only say the story was from long ago," Jerome said. "I don't even know if it's true, much less if it happened to Eva. It could easily be some backstage legend. She didn't like to talk about it—who would?— but Pablo begged her to include it, so we did."

He lifted the page. "Maybe she marked this sheet to say it did happen, and to her. Maybe this was her way of signing it, of signing this whole nightmare." His voice cracked at the bleak thought. "Dear God. Like a confession."

Holding it high, toward the light, he turned it front to back, side to side, as if coaxing the shadowy initial to speak.

It did.

Its message surged through Julia. It sparked from her heels to her scalp, spooking every hair along the way. She nearly lunged for the page. Her hands trembled as she positioned it for the men—sideways.

"This is Eva's writing, but it's not her initial. Look." Julia traced her finger along the now-horizontal figure. "It could just as easily be a *W*."

"Good God." "Christ almighty." Both men registered the significance.

"Wallace," Julia said. A second realization dawned as she stared at the pattern. "The scars on her hip could form a *W*, not an *E*." She remembered Wallace's penchant for monograms on his beautiful possessions: his cuff links, his crystal, his ranks of leather document cases. One knee buckled as her mind caught up with the implications. Wallace. His voice in her ear, his warm hand confidently riding her hip, his droll amusement beneath half-lowered eyes: in so many ways he had stirred her heart, her desires. She felt sick again, as if the charming, considerate Wallace she knew had morphed before her eyes into something malign.

"Wallace," Jerome repeated, outpacing her horrified deductions. "If he gave her that scar, maybe he's the rapist she wrote about. A club owner, years ago—"

"And he's the only one who knows where she is." Julia forced herself to put aside the flailing of her heart. She spun toward the door so quickly she swayed and had to grab the edge of the table. "We need to find her."

"I'm coming with you. I know where to look."

Her mind was already scrambling back through the Half-Shell to the street. But then where to? Her thumbnail traced the groove between her front teeth, a habit both her mother and Christophine had tried to scold away. He was right. She couldn't do this without him. More importantly, this was his fight more than hers. Eva was his *wife*. "Do you have clothes? Shoes?"

Jerome groped in the shadows by his cot, emerging with a limp shirt over his vest. He crouched to tie his shoelaces and swayed when he stood. He had no socks. Into his sagging waistband he tucked the chamois bag with the revolver from under his mattress. Julia recoiled. Then she remembered Wallace's reminder that guns made people stop, forced them to consider the consequences of whatever came next. A gun could hold someone at bay, long enough to make them listen.

They moved quickly through the club's empty cavern. They heard only a distant clatter of dishes until they reached the lobby, where the old janitor sat on a chair by the door, a litter of cigarette stubs no longer than his fingertips sprinkling the floor around him. His sly smile turned to alarm when he saw Jerome.

Julia quieted him with a generous palm. "Thank you, sir. Jervis's sister will be so grateful to see him again. Don't worry."

Jerome stumbled as they hurried up the steps to the street. He blinked and shaded his eyes but kept moving, following their heels as Austen and Julia headed to the corner. They'd have better luck finding a taxi on Seventh Avenue. Julia got out another bill to persuade the driver to accept a colored passenger.

Within five minutes, miraculously, they were on their way to an address on West 137th Street. But as soon as the taxi turned into the block, they realized they could not stop. Two police motorcars were parked in front of the building Jerome had named.

Damn. *Damn.* Of course. It was Sunday morning. The police crackdown had begun. Three cops stood talking to a crowd of neighbors. Jerome melted to the floor when two of the cops eyed the slow-passing taxi. Julia returned their stare with the idle ambivalence of impervious wealth, and they stepped back to let them pass unchallenged.

No sign of Eva.

They continued to a second address Jerome supplied. Julia recognized it as the building on 141st where Wallace had said he'd sent Eva after his housekeeper had complained. This time they saw the police cars a full two blocks away. Julia signaled for Austen to cover Jerome with his jacket. She asked the driver to slow as they approached. Lowering the window halfway, she called out to one of the policemen in a girlish drawl, "What's happened here, Officer?"

He motioned her to turn around and head south. "Go home, miss. This ain't no neighborhood for you."

He turned to the driver. "Get her out of here," he shouted, slapping the fender like a horse's flank.

"Wait." Julia tried to recall the name of the building where Wallace kept an apartment for his friends' dalliances. "Take us to the—Lester. On 146th, I believe."

It was only a few blocks away, but two police motorcars idled there as well. "Hey, what's goin' on here?" the taxi driver growled uneasily.

"Drive past please, slowly." After another exchange of curious, wary stares with the policemen at the curb, Julia sat back. She had to *think*.

"Where do you live, lady?" the driver asked, resolutely turning south.

He repeated the question, more loudly.

"East Side," she said. "Just head down Fifth."

She motioned Jerome to get up and leaned closer. "I have an idea. Here's my plan."

CHAPTER 31

Julia stood on the tree-lined street. No one passed, on foot or by motor. In this neighborhood it was a serene Sunday morning. She counted to one hundred, wishing she could slow her heartbeat so easily. At eighty she leaned on the taxicab's front fender and bent to remove one shoe, remembering the London day last summer she had bought the pair. Not bearing to watch, she gripped the instep and rapped it sharply against the curb. Again, harder. The heel fell to the pavement with a clatter. She refastened the broken shoe onto her foot.

The driver watched her with open amazement, his motor idling as instructed. His eyes bulged when she gave her right sleeve a tug and the seam tore. Even Christophine could not have revived the poor frock after the misfortunes of the previous evening, Julia consoled herself. She glared at the driver, reminding him of his well-paid pledge of silence, and caught a fold of her lower lip between her teeth. Eyes shut, fingers squeezing her bag for courage, she bit down hard. Her mouth yawned wide in pain, but she tasted the satisfying metallic tang of blood.

Ninety-six. Ninety-seven. She took a deep breath, raised her left arm, and eyed the driver. *Ready?*

One hundred. She dropped her arm, and the taxi roared off in a scream of rubber. Julia threw herself onto the pavement, just past the corner of the building, into view of the rear entrance. She cried out in genuine pain, eased somewhat by the sight of blood trickling down her ruined stocking from a gash below her knee, and the sweet sound of Wallace's door guard shouting in alarm.

She spit blood onto her chin and smeared it with a gritty hand before rolling clumsily to face him. She cried for help, rising up on one hip, legs twisted beneath her.

The doorman rushed down the walk. Whimpering, she saw Austen and Jerome round the corner from the other direction and slip into the unwatched entrance. She sniffled helpless gratitude as the guard crouched beside her. "Ernie, is it?" She grasped his wrist.

"Miss Kydd?" He supported her shoulders as she tried to sit up. "What on earth?"

"It was all so—" She made little crying noises, too nervous to produce real tears. "A man—into my taxi." She turned away in distress. "He, oh!"

Ernie's fists clenched nicely. "Did he hurt you, miss?"

She shook her head, leaning heavily against him. "I tried to fight. He grabbed my—" More wailing as she peered into her violated handbag. "We flew around a corner, and he—he threw me out."

She held on to his sleeve and gazed into his face with every forlorn guile she could summon. "Thank God for you. You're my guardian angel."

"Mr. Wallace isn't at home, miss," Ernie said. "If he were, I'm sure he'd insist you come up, but I can't allow it without his permission."

Julia knew Wallace was out of town—it was key to her plan— but Ernie's loyal refusal to let her in was an unforeseen problem. She clutched the gash on her leg and came away with a bloody palm, exclaiming at it.

Ernie bit his lower lip. "Can you walk, miss?"

"Maybe. If you help." Ernie lifted her to her feet with solicitous care. She sagged against him, staggering with each effort to bear her own weight. Austen's face appeared briefly from the entry: *Get a move on!*

The pathos in her voice grew to a groan. "I think I may be sick." She glanced about fearfully, as if for twitching curtains or curious passersby. She tucked her forehead into his sleeve. "This is awful."

"Right," Ernie said, succumbing to his good heart. "You come with me, miss." He held her waist and half dragged, half carried her toward the apartment's private entrance. "We'll get you patched up inside. Mr. Wallace will understand."

He guided her into the small lobby, his concern growing with each moan. He didn't notice the ungated elevator or Jerome and Austen creeping out from its shadows.

Julia stumbled and gasped, bringing Ernie's worried face close to hers. It crumpled under the sickening thwack of Jerome's revolver handle on his skull. His sudden weight knocked her down, twisting her knee in fresh pain.

"Not so hard," Julia hissed.

Jerome stared at the gun in his hand, surprised by his own force. "Sorry," he whispered. Julia echoed the sentiment, apologizing into the poor man's senseless ear. They dragged Ernie into the elevator and climbed in around him. Julia crouched to cradle his head.

"How do we operate this thing?" Austen wondered. Jerome closed the gate and assessed the controls. He eased the machine up.

The men bound Ernie's wrists with his necktie, and Jerome loosely knotted Ernie's shoelaces together. Austen rolled his handkerchief into a makeshift gag. Julia watched their progress in some surprise, as if both men were characters in a boy's adventure story. They decided to leave the woozy Ernie in the elevator, his head cushioned by Austen's rolled-up jacket. With luck they could find Eva and get her away before the poor man regained his wits. Julia couldn't bear to see the betrayal on his face.

Mozart. *Figaro.* The first thing they heard when they stepped into the marble foyer was a tenor proclaiming his love. Someone was listening to opera in Wallace's grand living room.

The second thing was the hearty voice of a woman ordering vegetables. Julia's heart sank, capsized by the immense folly of her plan. Mrs. Hoskins was at home, likely bustling about in her kitchen. From there she might easily see them creeping by to check the vacant servants' bedrooms—Julia's guess for where Eva might be hiding. Hopes of a devout churchgoing housekeeper had blinded her to this possibility.

Worse, the music suggested Wallace himself might be at home. She'd been told he was called away to Albany, not returning until this evening. She cursed Ernie for loyally repeating this ruse, perfectly aware that the man's offense was nothing compared to her own.

Austen and Jerome stared anxiously, waiting for her lead. Julia's knee throbbed. She stood stupidly, as if she'd had a good head coshing herself. Could they storm the service wing and escape with Eva (please, God) before Mrs. Hoskins and her rolling pin, or worse, could intervene?

Ha ha ha ha! A third sound coursed through the apartment.

Eva's marvelous deep, rich laugh.

Before Julia could stop him, Jerome dashed toward the electrifying sound. Julia and Austen leaped after him.

They froze at the portal to the living room. Across the room, in two green damask chairs by the windows overlooking the park, sat Eva and Wallace. Eva's bruises had healed. She looked healthy, well fed, well tended. Newspapers lay about the floor and across her knees. A white Belleek china teapot and two cups and saucers rested beside a vase of pink roses on the table between them. Relief swept through Julia at this surreal tableau. Eva was not only safe but secure. At least Wallace had not lied about that.

Until that moment Eva had probably looked content as well. But now her face swam with shock. Shock and horror. She stared at Jerome, at his cracked lips and veined eyes, his bony neck and rolled waistband. The assault upon their rose-tinged air was no less vivid.

But mostly she stared at the gun quaking in his hands, pointed vaguely in their direction.

"Jerome." Her breath wobbled on the long vowel, freighted with fear, regret, reproof, shame, sorrow. She stood, and the newsprint fluttered to her feet.

Slowly Wallace stood as well. He edged toward Eva and moved in front of her. "Put your weapon down, son."

Julia felt as if time had folded and returned them to that moment in Timson's office when all attention had converged on the barrel of a pointed gun. Now too her vision shrank to Eva's stricken face. And once again it was Wallace's voice, calm and measured, that rose to ease the crisis.

The gun jerked in Jerome's hands. "Get away from her, you bastard."

Wallace curved one arm back to shield Eva. He held out his other palm, open and empty. "Look at her. She's safe. I've kept my promise. If you calm down and do as we planned, I can still get you both out of this mess."

He was speaking to Jerome. They had made a plan? There was a promise?

His eyes darted toward Julia. "Julia, you blessed little fool." Was it surprise in his voice or only dismay? "You're bleeding, my dear."

Julia glanced down. Blood trailed into the remains of her broken shoe. She swiped carelessly at the gash, smearing her stocking. She wiped her hand on her ruined dress, annoyed with the distraction.

"You little fool," he repeated. "Why couldn't you believe me? If you'd just been patient, trusted me for another few days, she could have been safe forever. Now you've brought a madman into my home." The rebuke fell like lead on her shoulders, crumpling her resolve.

It was an unbearable thought: Had she made a spectacular botch of things? Was Jerome a madman? Maybe he'd fed her nothing but lies, using her to penetrate Wallace's stronghold. If so, she'd played into his hand, led him straight to Eva. Had Julia done what she most wanted to prevent: put Eva's life in danger?

But no, she'd swear Jerome's urgent wish to come along sprang from love, not revenge. And Eva's scratched initial seemed meant to drive attention to that long-ago rape, as if it were the key to her present dilemma. Jerome had had no part in the Harlem cabaret scene until a few months ago. Wallace, on the other hand, had known Eva from her earliest days in the city.

His gaze settled on Jerome. He said again, "Put down your gun."

Eva craned her neck to see over Wallace's shoulder. The tendons in her neck bulged with the strain. Her face rose close beside his. Emotions and understanding seemed to slide from one to the other as if the membrane separating their fates were porous or disintegrating. "I know you're scared, sweetie. You think I betrayed you. But I swear I haven't. I never said a word."

"A word about what?" Jerome's voice cracked. "What are you talking about?"

Julia felt her own muscles tighten in the effort to silently beg him to lower his arm. Didn't he see that the gun ruined everything? He'd achieved his aim. They were paying attention, ready to listen to whatever he had to say. The only thing that gun could accomplish now was needless bloodshed. She wanted to be the wise and fearless one to step forward and break the murderous anger that gripped Jerome, but she couldn't. Even if she could be that wise and unafraid person, she was locked on the periphery of this struggle. This was a fight, a story, that stretched beyond her understanding. She could feel the currents, swirling and treacherous, but could only guess at their depths.

"Oh, sweetie," Eva began to whimper, but Wallace cut her off.

"You're meddling with things you don't understand, Crockett. Put down your gun, and we can explain everything."

"Put it down, Jerome. Please put it down," Julia urged, soft as a lullaby. Possibly it was only in her head.

"He hasn't hurt her," Austen said. "That's what matters. Let's hear what they have to say."

Jerome widened his stance. The gun stayed pointed at Wallace's chest. "Get away from her."

On a soaring high note, the Mozart recording ended. It began to thump.

"Sweetie, he hasn't hurt me. He's helping me—us both." Eva's eyes gleamed with tears. "You just have to trust him a little longer. Like with the manuscript—and now, soon, he's going to help us get away. *Please*, sugar."

"Eva, baby! I never had that manuscript. Why don't you believe me? Last I saw, Timson slammed it inside that safe. How the hell would I have it?"

The rhythmic scratch of the record seemed to count out the progress of his thoughts. "Christ. You don't think *I* killed him?"

At his plaintive, almost incredulous words, the muscles in Eva's cheeks sagged. Julia saw confusion there, sliding into doubt. Eva *did* think Jerome was the killer—or she had until that moment. It made sense. It had always made sense. He had every reason to despise Timson, and every reason to want to retrieve that manuscript at any cost. So why had her certainty just wavered?

"Don't give us that crap. She knows, Crockett," Wallace said sharply. "I'll do what I can to get you kids out of this mess, because Timson was a snake and he deserved that bullet, but I won't keep lying for you. I told her what I saw. I told her about the loot I saw in that satchel—"

"But I only saw—" Julia blurted out, remembering that blessed letter from Eliot. Her words shriveled to ash when Wallace shot her a venomous look. Shock flared in her brain.

"In that sorry satchel of yours," Wallace continued. "The stuff you took from the safe."

Jerome swallowed. "What the hell are you talking about?"

"I saw it, son."

"Don't call me son! And get your hands off her."

"Do what he says, sweetie," Eva begged, a new fear edging into her voice. "It'll all be jake. Please don't hurt me."

Jerome's shoulders heaved. "I don't want to hurt *you*," he said. "God, no. I want to get you out of here. It's him I want to hurt." The gun rolled and then righted again.

"Put your gun away, Crockett," Wallace said softly.

Julia saw nothing but Eva's mobile, eloquent face. It cowered at Jerome's next words.

"It's not *my* gun! Stop saying that. You don't think—? Eva! You know I've never even held a gun before, not until your pal there gave me this one."

Eva's eyes slid to the gun now wobbling in Jerome's hands. He shifted it like a hot coal from right to left and back again. She followed its jerky path as if she could fling it aside with the sheer power of her gaze, and then her beautiful face melted into pure and utter grief. Her eyes rose, enormous pools of it.

What had she seen? What did she know? Julia struggled to understand.

With a cry Eva seized Wallace's elbow. Their arms and feet tangled in a brief dance of strength and will. One moment they faced Jerome together, and the next they struggled against each other. Before Julia could register this sudden realignment of fear and trust, Eva was caught tight, pinioned against Wallace's chest. She gripped his wrist, but it did not move. Nor did the black revolver in his hand, pointed directly at Jerome.

"My God," Julia breathed. For an instant the revolver jumped toward her. Wallace quickly retrained it on Jerome, but in that split second Julia understood. Not everything but enough. Or rather her muscles understood—her blood, her stomach, her heart. Her mind would find the words and the sense of it later. *My God.*

"I don't want anyone to get hurt," Wallace said calmly. "Eva least of all. But if you refuse to see reason and common sense, perhaps you'll understand this."

Without moving his eyes, he said, "Julia, please step back. You and your friend."

Julia couldn't move. She was afraid to breathe, afraid a feather would jar Jerome's trembling finger. Now he was the one in danger. They all were. They had been from the start, from the moment a bullet had entered Leonard Timson's brain. She tried to speak, to muster a squeak of bravado, but her throat had closed.

Wallace shrugged. No doubt his aim was perfect. And with Eva now shielding him, he held the advantage. Jerome would never fire, never risk hurting Eva. Wallace was using that certainty to ensure Jerome's death. The Wallace Julia had known was shrewd and unflappable, the consummate business and political leader, but here was a cornered animal, fighting to survive.

"Lay down your gun and give yourself up, Crockett," Wallace said. "Think about it. You'd never get away. We have two impeccable witnesses who'll verify everything, and my staff will confirm that you broke into my home. You might get away with one murder, but never two."

"Murder?" Jerome repeated. The word broke in his throat.

Eva sobbed, the howl of a trapped and wounded animal.

A howl sounded inside Julia too. Something momentous had just leaped into the room, but before she could grasp its contours, Wallace spoke again.

"I will ask you one more time." His eyes bored into Jerome's face. "Drop the gun. Bend your knees slowly, and lay it on the floor. If you make any other move, any other movement at all, I will take it as an attack. I must warn you I'm a very fine shot. Especially in self-defense when threatened in my home by an armed fugitive."

Julia agonized, willing obedience into Jerome's listing arm. The plea seeped from her pores: *Just bend your knees. Put it down. Let it go, Jerome. Let it go. It's your only chance.*

Her agony, though, came in knowing he had no chance. Proud, righteous Jerome was doomed. Even if Wallace let him live, he'd be torn to pieces by the law. The only small victory Jerome might claim now was in shaping the story of what Wallace would call his crime.

Wallace was already rehearsing his version of events, justifying the bullet before he fired it. By yielding peacefully, Jerome could at least die with a modicum of honor. Julia would testify to that—if the shooting stopped before the rest of them were dead too.

Time swelled. It was probably only one or two seconds, but the harrowing moment pressed air from her lungs, bled light from her vision. It seemed to last forever, that unblinking stare between two guns not ten feet apart, one trembling and the other steady.

A noise. Shouts. Clattering voices. Then running feet, what sounded like a thudding herd from the entry hall behind them. Eva's eyes lifted in terror.

Jerome's head swung to see.

"Drop it, boy!"

Eva jerked, her entire body twisting to get free, but Wallace reclutched, cinching his forearm like a rope across her ribs. With a powerful heave she seized his hand, pulling it and the gun into her stomach. She gave a terrible shriek.

A blur of motion. The shatter of a gunshot. A starburst of blood.

Eva and Wallace jackknifed together. They doubled over, Eva folded inside his crumpling body. They fell as one to the carpet.

CHAPTER 32

Fury struck Julia, knocking her sideways. She stumbled hard against the corner of the living room portal and fell. Austen disappeared into the hallway, his head cracking against the wainscoting. Three cops swarmed past her, sticks already raised. One hit Jerome's jaw, bouncing his head back in a spray of blood and sweat. The gun skipped away across the carpet as Jerome collapsed beneath the frenzy of blows. Grunting with exertion, one of the cops drove his boot into his belly. His mouth yawned wide—pink and wet and silent.

"Stop!" Julia had never heard herself scream. Her ears rang with the terrible sound. "Stop!"

She tried to crawl toward the melee, but a cop shoved her away. She clawed at his arm. She'd have bitten it if she could. "Stop!"

Another gripped her shoulders, pulling her back. "Calm down, lady! You're safe now."

She tried to twist free. "No! Stop!"

Austen's voice from somewhere echoed her, before he was violently sick.

The pounding gradually stopped. She squirmed free of the cop's grasp.

Time shimmered like light on a hot horizon. Two minutes? Ten? An hour? Julia pulled herself upright onto hands and knees. She saw only carpet. Every breath brought the hot reek of blood. Voices hummed and spiked. She remained on all fours, head down, waiting for her throat and her stomach to unclench.

She lifted her head and sat back on her heels. Austen was upright, barely, his face in his hands. He staggered into the hall.

A few feet away, Jerome was propped against the other side of the portal. His eyes were tightly shut. Chin lolling above his chest, he was groaning. His shirt was splattered with blood, and a stream of pink saliva oozed from his mouth. His wrists were shackled behind his back.

"It wasn't him." Julia's words were hoarse and muzzy.

"Let us figure out what happened here, Miss Kydd." The voice was familiar. Her head flopped to the right. Sergeant Hannity.

"He never fired."

"We'll get your statements in a minute," Hannity said. "I can't wait to hear what the hell you two were doing here." He jabbed a thumb toward Jerome. "Meanwhile, this johnny stays put."

Julia tried to protest again, but Hannity cut her off. "Save it for Mr. Kessler, miss." He hurried forward to meet the assistant commissioner.

Kessler's voice approached from the foyer, speaking in a rapid-fire command. The room stirred as men Julia hadn't noticed turned at his entrance.

"Good Lord."

She recognized Philip's voice. He squatted beside her. "Are you hurt?"

She shook her head. His hand on her forehead helped quell the dizzy tumult.

Kessler spoke sharply. "I'd hoped the sergeant was mistaken when he said you were here, Miss Kydd. You'd better have a very good explanation."

"Christ," Philip said. "Give her a minute."

Kessler ignored him and followed Hannity into the living room, where several uniformed policemen milled about, their banter low and matter of fact. "So, Sergeant, what do we have here?"

"Can you stand?" Philip asked quietly.

She nodded, with only a little queasiness. She heard more than she understood. Too much still rang in her ears—the shot, and especially Eva's scream. She rested on her knees for several seconds. Then Philip helped her up.

"Why are you here?" she mumbled. Her face felt numb, her mouth stiff with tension. Her shoulder pitched against his ribs.

"Hannity had a man watching this place," Philip said into her ear. "He notified Kessler when you and Crockett went inside. He telephoned me, and we hustled over here. This is serious, Julia. Wallace's death will cause a terrible stir when word gets out."

Julia forced herself to look at the lifeless couple. Eva lay curled face-down, the lower half of her dress crimson. Her arms and a gun would be buried somewhere beneath her, in the remnants of her lap. The police had turned Wallace over, or maybe with her last strength Eva had heaved him off. He lay sprawled on his back, a glistening cavern where his groin had been. Only arteries could have gushed so much blood.

Julia began to shake. After being unable to see beyond their two faces, now she couldn't look at either one. This was a scene, a tableau, seared in memory and meaning. Maybe with time she could pull them back into the living souls they had been, souls she'd cared about deeply in different ways. Now she could only shake, like a machine laboring to function.

Philip steadied her shoulders and turned them away. He nudged her with something in his hand. Her broken heel lay in his palm. "There's a chap with a bad headache in the kitchen, muttering about a lady in distress," he said under his breath. "He mentioned someone sounding eerily like you." He slipped it into his pocket.

A coughing moan pulled her eyes back to Jerome. His head hung down, mouth working to spit out blood. But when Julia moved toward him, a policeman blocked her. "Stay back, miss. Sarge?"

Hannity looked over.

"What about them two?" The guard gestured toward Julia and Austen, who had sheepishly reappeared under the portal's arch. "Where you want them?"

"There must be a bedroom or something. Have Pensky get their statements. Separate rooms. I want to talk to them too."

Hannity's broad face wrinkled in distaste as Jerome snuffled, unable to wipe the bloody mucus running from his nose. "That boy's going downtown."

Julia slapped the guard's hand from Jerome's shoulder. "No!"

Hannity stared in surprise.

"You can't arrest him." Julia realized she was shouting and lowered her voice. "He never fired."

Silence. Kessler turned.

"Why do you say that, Miss Kydd?" he asked from across the room with schooled quiet.

"I saw everything. Wallace had hold of Eva. She turned his gun and fired it into them both. Jerome didn't shoot anyone."

The hum of voices down the hall stilled.

Kessler excused himself from the conversation by the windows and came closer. "The men on the scene swore they saw Crockett shoot," he said in a low voice. "We'll be taking your statement shortly. Until then, please keep your voice down. You're distracting my men."

Julia protested. "You're making a terrible mistake. You must believe me."

"You've abused my confidence before, Miss Kydd. Why should I listen now to your ravings?"

The words stung. "Because I know what happened. I can tell you who killed them"—she waved feebly at the bodies, not ready to speak either Eva's or Wallace's name—"and who killed Leonard Timson too." In that instant she realized it was true. She did know.

Kessler bridled in disbelief, but Philip stirred. "Let her speak."

"If you'll give me time to settle my thoughts, I can explain everything. Please. Tonight?"

Kessler was about to repeat his scorn when Philip produced a small cough. "You're making an ass of yourself, old man," he murmured. "She knows a far sight more than you think."

Julia did not allow her gaze to stray from Kessler's face. He fixed her with his hard gray eyes.

Philip sighed at Kessler's resistance. "*Quel enfant terrible,*" he said. "What can one do?"

"So where do you want him?" asked Jerome's guard as another officer handed Kessler a note.

He read it and looked up. "Downtown."

"No!" Julia didn't care how shrill she sounded. "I told you! Check his gun."

Kessler grimaced, but he allowed a nearby fellow in white gloves to examine the gun that still lay on the rug where it had flown from Jerome's hand. After a minute the man shrugged. He wrapped the weapon in a handkerchief and handed it to Kessler. "She's right, sir. No one's fired this baby in some time. Couldn't have. It's not loaded."

Not loaded? Wallace had given Jerome a gun without bullets? If the police had found his hiding place and he'd so much as lifted that weapon, he'd have been riddled with lead. Another, more sickening realization dawned on her. That entire scene she'd just witnessed, every moment of heart-stopping fear, had been a sham. Wallace had known that gun was empty. He'd let everyone believe Jerome posed the threat, that a peaceful resolution lay only in Jerome's hands, when he himself had held the only killing instrument. He had goaded Jerome, wanting just one flinch to justify shooting him. Julia felt the bile rising again in her throat. It was all too monstrous to comprehend.

"Book him, murder charges," Kessler said.

It felt like another blow. Impossible! Before Julia could subdue her treacherous stomach and exclaim again, he said, "No, you listen to me,

Miss Kydd. Wallace gave us several addresses to search this morning. One of them was a club on Seventh Avenue. My men just found what looks like Crockett's hiding place. They also found Pruitt's jewelry at the bottom of an old bluing tub."

Kessler held up his index finger to silence her. "For the past three weeks we've been looking everywhere for that," he said, unwrapping Jerome's gun and lifting it to reveal a small insignia of silver and turquoise inlaid into the base of the handgrip. "It matches exactly the description of Leonard Timson's missing weapon."

CHAPTER 33

Julia slid deeper into her bath, driving the sting of heat over her chin and jaw. She'd drained and refilled the tub twice, sponging away blood, grime, bile. Her clothes had already disappeared, the unspeakably torn and filthy garments she'd begun sloughing off as soon as she'd come through the front door. Christophine had helped peel away every last stitch, and then she'd sunk down beside Julia on the bathroom floor until the shaking had stopped.

Still she felt filmed with filth. Still she smelled blood. She curled a shoulder and rolled into the scalding pool. Slowly her body righted itself, and her thoughts began to knit straight.

⁓

At eight that evening Julia pushed open the doors to the library. Austen jumped to his feet. He was well scrubbed and shaved, dressed in freshly laundered and pressed clothes. He squeezed her shoulders. "That's more like it, bean," he said.

She'd dressed with care to bolster her spirits: her best lingerie, a new Nicole Groult frock of blush-pink crepe, tinted stockings to mask the plasters and bruises on her left leg. Her lower lip bulged where she'd bitten it, but a deeper shade than usual of lipstick disguised it well enough.

Philip stood. "The world's back on its axis," he agreed.

She smiled faintly. She needed all possible reinforcements tonight.

A commotion in the hallway meant the other guests had arrived. Julia shot a grateful glance at Philip, who did not see it as he went to greet the men. In the chaotic taxi ride home from Wallace's apartment, she'd been distraught. For over an hour she'd repeated her account of events to various policemen. By the time they let her leave, she was quaking, teeth chattering and vision blurred by the sights and smells and sounds she couldn't force from her brain. Philip wrapped her in his coat and held her so tightly only her head could move, swaying and jerking. As they sped home, she begged him, over and over, to do one thing. *Make them listen,* she insisted. *Give me time to think, and I can explain everything.* He had shushed her, but he'd exerted his mysterious powers, and now both Kessler and Hannity had come to hear her account of the past month's events.

Christophine poured several brandies and set the glasses on a tray. Without speaking, she led Julia to the sofa and sat in the chair pulled up beside her. There was no need for discussion. They had traveled every inch of this terrible business together and would now see it through to its end. Julia was certain Christophine cared no more than she did that their guests might wonder at her presence. A moment later Pestilence was circling Fee's lap as Julia flexed her fingers. The men found both women waiting, somber and composed, when Philip led them into the room.

He did not blink. He introduced Christophine and Austen to Kessler, waited as the men chose seats, and circled with the brandies. He followed with his cigarette case. For Sergeant Hannity he produced a cigar from his breast pocket.

Philip settled into his fireside chair. "Ready and fortified, *ma petit soeur*. We await your tale."

Julia set her glass aside. She wasn't fully ready, and nothing more could fortify her, but she had to do this one last thing. She had failed spectacularly in her effort to save her friend from a violent end. This at least she must see through as best she could.

She plunged in. "You've arrested an innocent man, Mr. Kessler. Jerome Crockett hasn't killed anyone."

Kessler sighed. "I appreciate your flair for the dramatic, Miss Kydd—it's apparently a family trait—but that's wildly premature."

"Your own man told you. Jerome never fired that gun."

"Yes, yes. We've accepted your account of this morning. But a great deal of evidence implicates him in the murder of Leonard Timson."

"The evidence points to Jerome because it was meant to," Julia said. "You were meant to arrest him."

A spark crossed Philip's face. Austen clicked his tongue in surprise. Both Hannity and Kessler glowered with doubt. None of it came close to the horror and shame she felt at what she now believed to be the truth.

She paused for a swallow of brandy. "As we all suspected, Timson was murdered for the manuscript of Eva Pruitt's novel. But only nine people knew it was locked in his safe. Five of us had no reason to steal it. Austen Hurd and I certainly didn't, and neither did the couple visiting from California. Martin Wallace didn't even know it existed before that night. Plus we were all elsewhere when Timson was shot.

"Two of the remaining four, Paul Duveen and Arthur Goldsmith, had strong interests in the manuscript but had alibis. And the last two possibilities, Eva Pruitt and Jerome Crockett, made such obvious suspects that the police were content to focus on them." She nursed her wounded lip. "After all, no prosecutor would allow close scrutiny of wealthy white people, not with two suspicious Negroes involved."

For a long moment the room was silent. A few muscles jumped in Christophine's face, but she did not drop her chin or squirm beneath the intense attention suddenly focused on her. She kept her eyes squarely on Julia, refusing to cower under the others' awkward gazes. Julia envied her composure, so swiftly mustered. She silently cheered that others might see the Christophine she knew and loved.

"Hey, now," Hannity objected in a strident burst. "We did everything on the square."

"You focused on finding evidence of Eva's guilt." Julia raised her voice over Hannity's. "But even that was a sham. You knew a Negro woman would be easy to convict for the murder of her white boss. That gave you time to let Wallace calm jittery nerves among Timson's friends. Meanwhile, Eva was doomed unless something pointed to a better suspect. I couldn't let her suffer that unjust fate. I wanted to talk to her but didn't know where she was. My only breakthrough was to find Jerome. He told me Wallace was hiding Eva."

Kessler frowned. "Wallace? He told me she gave him the slip."

Julia nodded. "He deceived us both. He planned to hide her until you gave up looking or found another suspect. It would have worked, had circumstances not changed."

"Circumstances?" Kessler repeated. "Nothing changed in this case until this morning, when one death turned into three, thanks to your interference."

Christophine stirred with indignation at his tone, and Julia retorted, "A great deal changed, but there wasn't time to inform you."

Before Kessler could heap more blame on her, Philip stood. "More brandy?" He was treading lightly too. He hadn't been entirely forthcoming either.

Kessler covered his glass, scowling away the offer. He still viewed her involvement as marginally culpable, and his patience was thinning. She'd have to move quickly, streamlining the narrative. All that mattered was getting to the truth as she now understood it.

"I realized I'd been looking at this from the wrong angle," she said. "We all assumed Timson was killed so Eva's book could be published.

What if he was killed to keep it *un*published? Suddenly Eva and Jerome had least motive, not most."

"Who'd want to prevent its publication?" Kessler asked sourly.

"Timson, obviously. That's why he locked the novel in his safe. But what provoked him was a particularly gruesome scene in which a Harlem club owner rapes the heroine. Timson feared readers would think it was true and about him."

"Maybe it was."

"Eva denied it. She said only that it was a story from before her time at Carlotta's. Then I remembered Wallace knew Eva in her earliest days in New York. As an owner of the first club she worked in, he helped launch her career." Julia paused. What came next was both the most critical sentence and the most painful. She had wrestled with it all afternoon, forcing herself to confront the worst wound of all. "I believe that years ago a much younger and rougher Wallace raped a much younger and more vulnerable Eva. I imagine that afterward he was contrite, making it up to her with years of help."

Wallace and Eva. The two people she'd come to care about so deeply in the past weeks, in completely separate ways, were bound by that act of unspeakable cruelty and its shame.

Philip's gaze sharpened. Kessler sat back warily. "You'd better have compelling grounds for an accusation like that, Miss Kydd."

She chose her next words carefully. "I do, though you may resist, as I did at first. But it fits. Eva had a strange pattern of scars on her hip, which she said she received from an abusive lover long ago. It was a pattern of dots that, if connected, form the points of a *W*. Wallace was proud of his monogram. And he was adamant that a man should not force attentions upon a woman." Julia studied the carpet, avoiding Philip's eye as she added, "He made a point of insisting any intimacies he enjoyed were freely given."

"That's hardly—" Hannity began.

"Imagine his horror," she said, cutting him off, "on hearing that Eva has not only written of that long-ago rape but is about to publish her account in a widely touted book. No wonder she was so distraught about her quarrel with Timson. Afterward she fretted that he'd witnessed the scene, that he'd feel betrayed after all he'd done for her. At first I guessed she meant Timson. Then I assumed *he* meant Jerome, since she looked at him fearfully when Timson objected to the rape scene. Now I think that anxious look was for Wallace, who was standing in front of Jerome. *He* referred to Wallace."

The room fell quiet except for Pestilence's steady purr.

"Wallace had a powerful motive to steal the manuscript. Everything—his business empire, his political ambitions—would be in jeopardy if that rape came to light."

Hannity snorted. "Now you're just shooting steam, miss. You said it yourself. Mr. Wallace is as fine a gentleman as they come."

"My sergeant's right, Miss Kydd," Kessler said, sitting forward. "And before you go haring off down that slanderous path, remember Wallace couldn't have shot Timson. Senator James swore they were together in Wallace's club until the next morning, after Timson was found."

Julia was prepared for this. "Wallace kept an empty flat for the senator to use for discreet entertaining, if you understand. Whether Wallace pressured him for an alibi or a grateful James offered, I don't know. You could ask him, Mr. Kessler. He might squawk."

Before Kessler or Hannity could take umbrage at the term, she spooled out the narrative she'd painfully constructed that afternoon. "I believe Wallace returned for the manuscript and, whether in an argument or because there was no other way, shot Timson. He was back at his own club before Hobart telephoned. Taking charge like the responsible man he'd worked hard to become, he rushed over and went up to Timson's office a second time. Only this time he found Eva there, kneeling beside the body."

Kessler slapped the arm of his chair. "So she was there—"

"No, let me finish. He told her to run and hide."

"Nonsense. It was *Crockett* who had Timson's gun and the missing jewelry," Kessler said. "Fact, not speculation. Everything points to the pair of them, not Wallace."

"Wallace urged you to abandon the investigation," Julia said. "When you didn't, he had to have a better suspect than Eva for you to find. That was to be Jerome. He told Eva that Jerome had the manuscript because he'd murdered Timson. No wonder she was shocked and wary to see us this morning. While I can't—"

"Enough," Kessler said, uncrossing his legs. "This whole account is nothing but fanciful theory, Miss Kydd. If that's all you have to offer, I'm afraid you're wasting our time."

"Manners, old man," warned Philip. "Let her finish."

Kessler hesitated, but Julia could see Philip's admonishments wouldn't hold him in the room much longer. He wanted tangible proof. She had no choice but to plunge directly into her last huge gambit.

"You accept that Timson was likely murdered for the manuscript," Julia said. "Would finding it convince you of the killer's identity?"

"It would be real *evidence*, which is more useful than the tale you've spun so far."

Julia turned to Hannity. "Is someone stationed at Wallace's apartment, Sergeant?"

"We got a man at the entrance. Why?"

"If you'll ask him to go upstairs, I can direct him to where I believe Wallace hid the stolen manuscript."

Hannity looked for permission to Kessler, who raised both palms in surrender.

"Have him ask Mrs. Hoskins to unlock the doors to the library. Along the bottom bookshelves are leather-bound boxes of papers and records. Tell him to look in the boxes where the dust on the shelf has been disturbed." It was a guess, a calculated hunch. If she was wrong, nothing would persuade Kessler to drop the murder charge against Jerome. Julia gulped another swallow of brandy to brace herself against yet another great failure.

Hannity wrapped his mouth around the cigar and disappeared into the hallway.

"If you'll bear with me in the meantime," Julia continued over Hannity's too-loud conversation, "that brings us to the fateful encounter this morning. When Jerome swore to Eva that he never had the manuscript, I could see she believed him. She began to see Wallace's treachery.

"The gun convinced her. She probably recognized it right away as Timson's special gun, which is why she was so alarmed. At first it suggested Wallace was right, that Jerome was the killer. But when Jerome said Wallace gave the gun to him, she understood two things in one awful moment. Wallace was the real killer. And he'd set up Jerome to take the blame. I saw her face, Mr. Kessler. I've never seen such despair and grief.

"That's when your men came storming in. The black man holding a gun was the only criminal they would ever see in that room. It was hopeless. Eva did the one thing she could to save him."

Julia realized there were no eyes she cared to meet. She swallowed more brandy. For a few moments no one spoke, as each listener fit the last fatal piece into the puzzle.

"Why take such drastic measures?" Kessler asked. "Why not just divert Wallace's shot?"

"He was going to kill Jerome. He'd already reminded us that Austen and I were witnesses who could testify Jerome threatened him and he responded in self-defense."

The telephone bell rang. In the hall, Hannity's voice boomed.

"But why kill him?" Kessler persisted. "Especially at the cost of her own life?"

"Wallace could truthfully say he'd found her with Timson's body. Her life and her future depended on his good graces. At any moment he could turn on her as he had on Jerome, exposing her to certain conviction. I think she wanted to save the man she loved from the same fate." Her *husband*, Julia thought. It was too painful to breathe aloud.

In that moment an elusive piece of the puzzle slid into place for Julia too. This explained why Eva had slipped her marked page into the envelope. It was her only way to hint at the truth, if things went badly and Wallace turned against her. Julia could only imagine Eva's confusion when she'd discovered he had the manuscript; no doubt he'd told her Jerome had returned it, as she'd begged him to.

Kessler released a lungful of smoke and pinched his forehead. "Let me add this up. You're telling us Wallace shot Timson. Then Pruitt killed Wallace and herself." He sighed. "Your story's thorough, I'll say that much."

"Two murders, one suicide. All villains dispatched. Not much left for you to do, old man," Philip said. "Dashed considerate of her."

Hannity reentered the room, scratching the bristly ridge of his head. "You must be clairvoyant or something, Miss Kydd. Our boy did like you said, and quick as a flash he pulls out a box full of typed pages. Something called *Harlem Angel*. That what we're looking for?"

A knot ballooned in Julia's throat. Just a month ago she'd heard that title for the first time, amid joyous celebration. Kessler coughed in surprise, and Philip shot him a triumphant smirk.

"All right. I've heard enough." Kessler ground out his cigarette and stood. "If that is the missing manuscript, you've given me a great deal to consider, Miss Kydd. I'll have to run over all of this again tomorrow more carefully. Don't go anywhere. I may need to talk with you." To Hannity he added, "In the meantime, Crockett stays in custody."

Julia remained seated as Kessler and Hannity exchanged brisk new instructions. Philip joined the discussion as the men moved absently toward the door. Kessler thanked her—grudgingly, she thought—but she didn't reply. She felt only exhaustion, relief washed away by yet more horror at the day's tally of betrayals and loss.

Austen crouched in front of her and sandwiched her limp hand between his. In a husky voice he asked if she wanted him to stay. He was so young and so charming, his face so kind and fresh. He was good to the world and it to him.

His smile was warm, but she shook her head. *No. Thank you, but just no.*

CHAPTER 34

"Care for a sibling powwow?" Philip asked Julia as he closed the door on the departing guests.

She had already insisted Christophine retire for the evening and not even consider clearing the dirty glasses. The two women embraced, saying nothing and communicating everything, and Christophine disappeared down the shadowed hall to her quarters. Though she'd known beforehand of Eva Pruitt's misfortune, she looked shaken to hear again its relentless course toward grief.

Julia and Philip returned to the library. She accepted a cigarette but waved off more brandy. He settled in his chair and smoked nearly his entire cigarette before speaking.

"Too bad your young swain couldn't stay. Maybe next time he'll undress."

Julia coughed on a startled draw of her cigarette.

"A wise old eye can always tell, you know." He tapped at the corner of his. "The difference between clothes thrown off in haste and those merely slept in. Better luck next time."

She wanted to resent his teasing, but he was right. It had been a ridiculous ruse, that Sunday morning when Hannity's visit had roused her out of bed. She'd wanted to appear worldly with a lover in tow, but the pretense had been comical. She had to smile. One could only laugh at oneself, in the end. "I was mortified," she admitted. "He slept on the divan. He preferred to safeguard my virtue."

Philip smiled too.

"At any rate, about this morning, brava," he murmured. "Though it must have pained you to sacrifice that rather fetching little shoe. No doubt your dress was maimed by the same steely hand? Well, I suppose they had to be sacrificed, under the circumstances."

Philip stretched out his legs and loosened his tie and collar. "Nice work tonight, first to last. Things might well have happened as you described, though I suppose you know the tale's full of holes. Any good lawyer could send marching bands parading through it."

"That doesn't mean it's not the truth. We may never know with absolute certainty, but my version makes sense. I believe it's true to the spirit of what happened, if not the exact letter. Nothing refutes any of it."

"Hence its beauty, yes. That business with the initial was positively spine tingling. Do you think the lady had the foggiest notion it read both ways?"

Julia had described the mystery of the scratched initial in her ramblings as they'd returned home that morning. She shrugged.

"Willard Wright could use it in one of his shillin' shockers." Philip cooled his amusement with a swallow of brandy. "Yet I'm afraid your lovely work tonight will evaporate in the harsh light of tomorrow's scrutiny." His voice lilted softly. "You know that, don't you?"

Julia rose and poured herself more brandy after all. She wouldn't sleep tonight—a headache later was a fair price for immediate solace. She returned to her chair and rested her head against the smooth leather wing so that she could look out into the black night.

"Kessler's a good fellow, but consider his position," Philip mused. "Timson may be unmourned and unmissed, but Wallace? The morning editions will hemorrhage ink over his death. Politicos across the state will don black armbands. They'll dance to dirges at every debutante ball. Charities will keen for their handsome benefactor. It will be damp and noisy—all that clamoring for justice. And smack in the center, bearing the brunt of their woe, will sit Kessler." Philip issued a lazy procession of smoke rings into the room. "What will he do? He'll sit down at that imposing desk of his and tot it all up in his usual thorough manner."

Philip went to the trolley. Returning with the decanter, he poured another finger's depth into Julia's glass and refreshed his own. "And what will he have? Two murders and one suicide. One murder clear and undisputed, the other still in some question."

Julia took a fresh swallow of brandy. She couldn't prove the identity of Timson's murderer, not yet, but there was plenty to dispute about Wallace's death. Even to call it murder was a travesty. Wallace had brought death upon himself by refusing to let Eva go. Had he acted one last time as the calm and reasonable man he'd aspired to be, she and Jerome might be on their way to Paris by now. Julia despised the Wallace revealed to her that morning, but she pitied him too: brought down, as so many ambitious men were, by his own pride.

Philip took a deep breath. "How do you think poor Kessler will answer that lachrymal chorus of *why*s? Will he bow to your compelling deductions and proclaim the truth about Mr. Wallace? Will he tell the world that the charming friend of orphans, bankers, hostesses, and senators was a murdering rapist felled by his avenging victim?"

Julia closed her eyes. Wallace had been charming. He'd been a friend to orphans and all. Those facts about him would always be true, no less than the violence he'd once turned on Eva. If Julia could barely hold both Wallaces in her mind, she despaired that anyone else could ever do so.

They both knew the answer to his question, but only Philip had the courage, or the cynicism, to speak it aloud. "I fear not," Philip said. "How much tidier and more plausible simply to add one more crime to the résumé of the late Miss Pruitt. She *is* a murderer, after all. Why not twice over? Can it make any difference?"

Julia took another quantity of brandy into her mouth and let it burn her tongue, inscribing itself into her palate, before sliding down her throat.

"Two dead murderers were carried out of that apartment this morning," Philip continued, his voice as smooth as the liquor was vivid, "both guilty, both already punished. Does it even matter how we choose to understand? Would Kessler's losing his job—as he well might, should he announce your version of things—make the slightest difference to anyone concerned? He's a pragmatist, you know. Be content that what you understand allows you to sleep at night. He'll simply choose the same prerogative for himself, and for those suffering hordes at his door."

Julia accepted another cigarette, and they smoked for some time in silence, both absorbed in the starless night sky beyond the French doors. Sleep at night? Would she ever again sleep in quite the same peace?

At last she spoke. "You might call Eva a murderer, but her action was the single jot of justice in this whole appalling affair."

"Agreed," Philip said amiably.

"She chose her death, you know. She wanted Jerome to live."

"And now you've helped her succeed."

Julia traced an aching groove along the bridge of her nose. "I was a fool, Philip. A monstrous fool. I was taken in. I believed him. I fell for his charm. No, that's not right. I fell for his refusal to ply me with charm. I thought that made him honest and direct. Trustworthy. And attractive." Her cheeks stung to remember her desire. "I thought I knew him. I mocked your warnings, but I *was* careful. I chose to go with him that night. I wanted to go with him."

She looked away, aghast at what she was telling Philip. She didn't even speak to Christophine about such things. Was she drunk? Or simply so shaken that every normal signpost in her life had toppled over? She was finding her way through a landscape she'd thought she knew but didn't. She couldn't bring herself to say it: she'd been seduced.

"Yes," he said, a sound as pensive as his rising smoke ring.

"But we were interrupted," she went on, "and I had to leave. I wanted to stay, Philip. Is that shameful? I mean, that I gave myself to him, not seeing any hint of the man he truly was? Yet even at the time, some small part of me was glad to go. Maybe that bit, that tiny bit, saw his treachery, though I didn't know it at the time."

"Shameful?" Philip mused. "Hardly. But maybe old Kessler did one thing right by you in this whole wretched business, eh?"

It took a long moment for Julia to process. Kessler? How did Philip know it was Kessler who had telephoned at that ungodly hour that night? She sat up. "How on earth . . . ?"

"Surely one has a few prerogatives."

"You? You asked him to telephone? To call Wallace away?" She could barely speak for rising outrage. Her suspicions that night had been justified.

He lifted his palm, both accepting and halting the barrage.

"Not even a brother—which you are *not*—should ever interfere like that." Her voice dropped at the secret, though no one could hear it.

"I'm sure you're right, under most circumstances."

"Under any circumstances."

He sat back, face suddenly dark. "No, you're wrong there. I stand by what I did, however heinous in the faux-sibling department. You need to hear a story. Or I need to tell it. Either way, you must swear never to repeat it. Do you swear?"

She did, cautiously.

"Yes, I've pestered you about Wallace from the start, and it has nothing to do with your virtue or our little lark of passing as siblings. This isn't my confidence to share but Leah Macready's, and today she gave me permission to tell you." He gripped his knee.

"Wallace raped her when she was nineteen." Julia's head swerved to dodge yet more excruciating news. "Yes. And it's worse than that. She was poor then, very poor. Working the streets. She was a prostitute,

Julia. She was beautiful, charming, smart—every bit the woman she is today—but she was a prostitute. Wallace took a fancy to her, and not in the debonair ways you so extravagantly experienced."

Julia listened with closed eyes. She felt blindfolded, condemned to hear what had once been (and still at times remained) unimaginable. Certainly unfathomable. How a man she'd found caring and considerate could once have been so vile. She held her breath, bracing for Philip to go on. Every muscle feared what he would say next.

"He was ruthless, violent. He tracked her down, repeatedly. He damaged her inside. That's why she never had children. He scarred her. She has several small burns, from cigarettes, on her left hip. He called it his brand. He treated her like an animal."

Philip tapped a column of ash into the overloaded dish at his side as Julia absorbed the word. *Brand.* She saw again the constellation of small scars on Eva's hip. Was it over now? The worst of what she would have to live with for the rest of her life?

"So when I learned you'd gone with him, I understood what would happen. Oh, I never doubted he'd treat you with every gentlemanly care—you're nothing like a prostitute or chorine, of course—but I simply couldn't let him take his pleasure. Not from you. Preferably not from anyone, but especially not the one woman in this world for whom I can claim some right—however misguided, however fraudulent—to intervene."

Julia had never seen Philip like this. His low voice might punch through tin. In a moment his wry mask would return, but in that instant his dark eyes loomed bottomless.

Words clotted in her throat. She remembered the white bearskin, its teeth and claws. Wallace's attraction had been beguiling, almost a drug. "I seem," she said, "to have vastly overestimated my powers of discernment."

A smile quirked Philip's cheek. "You're a dervish of discernment, my dear. With one or two lapses."

The levity helped but faded. "I once thought I'd fare rather well in the men department, you know," she said. Since they might never again share such a frank conversation, it seemed safe to sustain it a moment longer. "I'd hoped to find someone in New York, you know. Not a boyfriend, not a husband. Just someone. You understand?"

He nodded, wry again. Of course he understood.

"And now my two prospects have both gone awry. One turns out to be a killer, and the other, well, more of a brother."

They smiled. In truth Austen had never really been a prospect. She liked him and enjoyed his company, but while Wallace had ample allure, Austen had none. He was, for Julia, too . . . happy. "I seem to have gone from having no brothers to having two, neither of them the slightest relation to me."

It was a lament, however lightly made. Julia's hand returned to her forehead. The evening was beginning to etch itself into her skull. Philip stood and helped her to her feet. She lifted her chin, eyes closed, and received two kisses, one on each cheek. "You've a few last conversations, I imagine," he said, hands warm on her shoulders. "But you'll triumph. We Kydds live well with our ghosts. Even if I'm only a nominal member of the tribe."

The night was still heavy with heat, and the house was silent. Christophine had long since gone to bed. Julia's own bed awaited, sheet turned down, nightdress laid across the pillows. A vase of yellow roses stood beside the packet of Luminal and glass of water. In the heat the flowers' fragrance swelled.

Julia undressed, laying her frock, stockings, and chemise across the back of the chair at her dressing table. She drew on her sheerest orchid pyjamas. She tied the drawstring across the hollow of her belly.

When had she last eaten? Days ago? No, she remembered strawberries. Swallows of cheese, a croissant.

This was not right. She pulled the pyjama bodice over her head. She wanted to feel something, not that teasing cloud of weightlessness. She dug into drawers until she found what she wanted: a thin boy's cotton undervest that she wore when she wanted to erase all but the faintest swells of her figure. Normally she needed no bandeau to achieve the flat, swift line of fashion, but for acute occasions, she used this little vest. She struggled to pull it on, wiggling into it as a lean sausage into a casing. That was it, the squeeze to numb the ache.

Her effaced form in the mirror pleased her. She padded back through the dark apartment and out onto the library balcony. A few stars punctured the low sky but offered no light. The chaise's white cushions guided her forward. Wood decking licked the heat from her feet.

The cushions gasped at her weight, disturbed by this meaningless vigil, this determination to witness every hour of this day of death. That was what one did with life. One held tight and rattled it; one gave it no respite, demanding more when it offered less.

Julia twisted, stretching backward on the chaise like an acrobat in midtumble. Her back sloped down where her calves should rest, her legs poking up into the night from sagging silk trousers. Her hands splayed across her abdomen, collapsed into its bony bowl. The Mozart aria from *Figaro* throbbed in tempo to the pain in her head.

One ghost haunted her body; the other haunted her heart. Fused in death, Wallace and Eva clung to Julia together, their weight oppressive. The heat was ferocious. Bound into a child's underthing, face flushed, skin slick—she couldn't breathe. There was no conversation with these ghosts, only a wringing, a weeping of skin and sex. Eva and Wallace were dead. Ghosts of her making.

Julia twisted to right herself and sat up. She jumped to her feet. With a wrench she jerked apart the side seam of her vest, pulled it over her head, and tossed it away. The cool air felt glorious on her damp skin.

She went back into the apartment and, for the first time, walked past the dark kitchen and Christophine's quarters, down the short hall to Philip's rooms. No light shone from below the door. She tried the knob. It turned, and she went in.

He sat sideways in a deep window seat, his profile silhouetted by a distant streetlamp. He was smoking, a saucer for ashes balanced on his raised knees. They were dressed alike, he in black pajama trousers, she in orchid silk ones.

For a long moment they looked across the room at each other.

He ground out his cigarette and set aside the saucer.

"Lock the door, love."

EPILOGUE

Several weeks later, Julia stood at the typecase with her stick in hand, composing a thirty-pica line of Garamont italic. Packing crates remained scattered about the studio, contents waiting to be sorted and organized. They could wait. She was eager to print invitations to her first party, a press warming three weeks hence. Jack had promised a small wood engraving that would also serve as a new pressmark, a fresh interpretation of her namesake gamboling kid. Although ephemeral, the invitations would mark Capriole's baptism with American ink.

"Where else would we find her?"

Philip's voice spun her around. He stood in the doorway, beside Christophine. He was back.

He'd been due to return last night after a long trip to visit friends in Cairo, Istanbul, and Athens. Slouched against the doorframe, he was lean as ever and dark as a Bedouin. He carried a parcel wrapped in brown paper wedged under his arm. "Silks!" Christophine exclaimed, lifting an armload of Mediterranean colors: lime, citron, azure, pomegranate.

"Clever man. Welcome home." Julia set down her composing stick and extended both hands. He took them, kissing her lightly on both cheeks.

"I brought you something too," he said. "Though it's only from the bottom of my accumulated mail."

Christophine made a clicking sound on the roof of her mouth—
After so long away? Nothing better for his very sister?—and carried the
colorful bounty to her new atelier in the second bedroom.

Julia kept hold of Philip's left hand, revisiting its weight and warmth,
those long, lithe fingers resting between her palms. "Good trip?"

He quirked his familiar smile. There would be tales to share, she
understood, but later, deep in the lovely night ahead. He gave her the
lumpish parcel from under his elbow.

Julia recognized Jerome Crockett's writing before she read the
return address.

"What do you hear of him?" Philip asked.

Jerome had moved to Chicago. The police had dropped all charges
once their firearms expert had concluded that Timson had been shot
by a gun found at the back of Wallace's locked desk drawer. Jerome's
name was never mentioned in the tumultuous newspaper coverage
of Wallace's death at the hand of what everyone was soon calling the
Harlem Hit Girl. One rag called Eva the Harlem Angel of Death. Nor
did they mention that Wallace's body was claimed after two days by his
father, Pavel Walachevsky, who'd been located in a Queens boarding-
house for the aged infirm.

"He's started another novel, nothing to do with Harlem." In a softer
voice she added, "He was never jolly, but I'm told he gets up every day.
I think he'll be fine, with time."

"What's become of Eva's book?"

Through a series of legal negotiations Julia could only imagine, the
jewelry recovered from the Half-Shell's backstage had been awarded to
Goldsmith's publishing firm to resolve their claims against Eva. After
liquidating the collection and deducting their expenses, Goldsmith had
allowed the rest of the money to go to Jerome, along with the remaining
fragments of manuscript recovered from Wallace's library. He'd accepted
the money but wanted nothing to do with the manuscript. Duveen had
snatched it up.

"Pablo took it for research," Julia said. "He's writing his own Negro novel. He jabbers about it constantly, so I suppose Arthur Goldsmith will publish it and Pablo will scamper off to the bank yet again. He's become quite famous lately—*Vanity Fair* teases him about his heavy tan. If anything he's whiter than ever. I doubt he leaves his apartment before sundown."

Julia picked at the knotted string. The package was light and soft. She couldn't imagine what was inside. She didn't want to open it, but she knew her reluctance was childish. Thoughts of Eva were still raw, but she needed to remember her friend more, not less, in all the ways she'd been rare and wonderful.

The knot yielded, and the paper fell away. Roughly folded into a thick square was the shawl Eva had borrowed the night she'd dined at the Plaza. Julia fingered the fine wool. As she lifted it to shake out the creases, a smaller envelope dropped to the floor.

Philip retrieved it. Julia took it but hesitated, tapping one corner lightly with a fingertip.

"Go on," he said. "If he could write it, you can read it."

Julia eased open the seal.

Her Waterman pen was wedged diagonally inside the envelope. She closed her eyes against the memory of his need of it in that wretched hour, then laid it on the composing stone and pulled out a folded rectangle of paper. Wrapped around it was a sheet of stationery. She had to puzzle out Jerome's handwriting, small and angular as sparrow tracks.

She read the message aloud:

> *Miss Kydd, I have learned to say least when I feel most. Haste cheapens honesty. So I simply send you this poem, which you saw naked at its birth, the squall before the song. Eva and I would be honored by whatever typographic raiment you might choose to bestow upon it. With sincere gratitude, Jerome Crockett.*

Julia unfolded a sheet of newsprint, already velvet along the creases, striped with the crabbed palimpsest poem she'd seen in his hiding place at the Half-Shell. With it was the typescript. He'd given it the title of his ill-fated first novel, taken from the concluding line to Eliot's "Prufrock": "Till Human Voices Wake Us."

Beneath the title, Jerome had added a dedication: *For my wife—my lost, best life.*

Julia's fingers curled around the sheet. It was too much. Before he'd left town, she'd been shy to ask if she might print one of his poems, but now that he'd obliged, she couldn't bring herself to read it. She couldn't speak. She couldn't lift her gaze.

Philip took the papers and laid them aside. He unbent her fingers, one by one, as if each was a just-born poem, still ink smudged and uncertain, but later—soon, tonight—a song.

"Will you teach me?" he said, after some time, looking about her half-assembled studio. "To set type? To squawk in double-pica Baskerville?"

She eased her hand free and considered. More than a sentence or two of twenty-four-point lead type would test his wrist strength and deplete her font.

"If you teach me to blow smoke rings."

AFTERWORD

The 1920s was a watershed era in American literary history. This novel explores the tangled intersection of two of the decade's most dynamic developments: the coming-of-age of the modern American publishing industry and the important cultural movement known as the Harlem Renaissance.

While Europe's storied traditions lay broken or exhausted after the Great War, American writers and artists represented youth and vitality: fresh voices, subjects, and styles. As a new generation of editors and publishers sought to champion this bold energy and declare the nation's literary preeminence, a new generation of African American writers and intellectuals asserted their place on that stage.

This novel is my attempt to shine some light on the interplay between those two great ambitions: how each served the other's ends, embracing their kindred aspirations, and also how their interests often worked to cross-purposes. Like any story about such aspirations, it is ultimately about power. I hope readers, with Julia, may gain some insight into the power dynamics among the players—what was achieved, and at what costs.

Several real people inspired characters in this novel, though I've privileged fictional freedom over strict biographical accuracy. Notable among them is Carl Van Vechten, a flamboyant white novelist, literary scout, and self-described tour guide and promoter of all things Harlem.

In 1924 he became "addicted to Negroes," as he put it, and quickly grew famous for lavish parties featuring leading black intellectuals, musicians, writers, and artists, including Paul Robeson, Langston Hughes, Countee Cullen, Zora Neale Hurston, and others. In 1926 Knopf published Van Vechten's controversial novel *Nigger Heaven*, whose title alone ignited a polarized reaction in Harlem and beyond.

Chief among other players in the era's lively literary community who inspired characters is Bennett Cerf, a high-spirited twenty-seven-year-old vice president at Boni & Liveright who a few years later would launch his own publishing company: Random House, initially specializing in fine and limited editions. Others include Alfred and Blanche Knopf, American publishing's first power couple, and Countee Cullen, an award-winning twenty-one-year-old Harlem poet who refused Van Vechten's help in finding a publisher.

While this is a novel, not a historical study, I hope it might provoke readers' interest in the era and issues portrayed here. The following books offer a good range of further information and insight, and each leads to deeper questions and other excellent resources:

Bernard, Emily. *Carl Van Vechten and the Harlem Renaissance: A Portrait in Black and White*. New Haven: Yale University Press, 2012.

Claridge, Laura. *The Lady with the Borzoi: Blanche Knopf, Literary Tastemaker Extraordinaire*. New York: Farrar, Straus & Giroux, 2016.

Douglas, Ann. *Terrible Honesty: Mongrel Manhattan in the 1920s*. New York: Farrar, Straus & Giroux, 1995.

Gates, Henry Louis, Jr. *Stony the Road: Reconstruction, White Supremacy, and the Rise of Jim Crow*. New York: Penguin, 2019.

Kaplan, Carla. *Miss Anne in Harlem: The White Women of the Black Renaissance*. New York: HarperCollins, 2013.

Larsen, Nella. *Passing*. New York: Knopf, 1929.

Lewis, David Levering. *When Harlem Was in Vogue*. 2nd ed. New York: Penguin, 1997.

Loughery, John. *Alias S. S. Van Dine*. New York: Scribner's, 1992.

Molesworth, Charles. *And Bid Him Sing: A Biography of Countée Cullen*. Chicago: University of Chicago Press, 2012.

Stewart, Jeffrey C. *The New Negro: The Life of Alain Locke*. New York: Oxford University Press, 2018.

Van Vechten, Carl. *Nigger Heaven*. New York: Knopf, 1926.

Van Vechten, Carl. *The Splendid Drunken Twenties: Selections from the Daybooks, 1922–1930*. Edited by Bruce Kellner. Champaign: University of Illinois Press, 2003.

Watson, Steven. *The Harlem Renaissance: Hub of African-American Culture, 1920–1930*. New York: Pantheon, 1995.

White, Edward. *The Tastemaker: Carl Van Vechten and the Birth of Modern America*. New York: Farrar, Straus & Giroux, 2014.

ACKNOWLEDGMENTS

I declared this book finished more than a decade ago. Then, like so many first novels, it languished as other writing projects intervened, including the prequel companion novel that became *Relative Fortunes*. Its publication brought Julia Kydd into the world, and now this book plunges her into the lively cultural vortex that was New York in the 1920s.

I'm grateful to encouraging early readers, especially Emily Chamberlain, Kathleen Thorne, and my sister, Laura Bjornson. More recently, I'm deeply grateful to Joyce Simons, who helped me breathe new life into this story, and to Susie Rennels, for her always-perceptive comments.

Many thanks also to my agent, Amanda Jain, and the terrific team at Lake Union—particularly my editor, Chris Werner; Tiffany Yates Martin; Riam Griswold; and Stephanie Chou—whose insights and expertise helped make this a much better book. And I'm grateful to my husband, Paul, as always, as ever.

DISCUSSION GUIDE

I hope this novel stirs many questions in readers' minds. Here are a few to start the discussion:

1. Julia cares deeply about Christophine, yet they are neither family nor friends in the conventional sense. Why is their relationship complicated, and how does it evolve?

2. Pablo Duveen proclaims himself a champion of black people, eagerly promoting Harlem's lively nightclub culture and emerging writers. How do Eva, Logan, and Jerome feel about his patronage, and why? How does it help them, and how does it hinder them?

3. Scholars talk about "the gaze" and the power relationship between those who are looked at and those who look. What undercurrents—psychological and historical—did you sense on the several occasions when black characters perform for white audiences?

4. What does Julia mean when she remarks that everyone passes in some way? Do you agree? Why does racial passing in particular often provoke volatile reactions?

5. Julia observes that American society renders black people largely invisible to whites. What made this possible in the 1920s? In what ways have things changed, or not?

6. What motivates Julia to find the truth of Timson's murder? How does race complicate her decision as well as her undertaking?

7. Logan Lanier resents being labeled a black poet. Similarly, Julia chafes at the term *lady printer*. What are the merits—and hazards—of highlighting race, gender, and other aspects of identity?

8. Consider the various kinds of power and will exercised in the final confrontation involving Eva, Jerome, and Wallace. How does race affect their respective options and choices?

9. Julia declares confidence in her ability to judge men's characters. In her dealings with Philip, Wallace, Jerome, and Logan, how accurate does her assertion prove to be?

10. Throughout the novel Julia becomes aware, sometimes painfully, of her cultural blind spots. What does she come to learn about herself?

ABOUT THE AUTHOR

Born near Boston, Marlowe Benn grew up in an Illinois college town along the Mississippi River. She holds a master's degree in the book arts from the University of Alabama and a doctorate in the history of books from the University of California, Berkeley. A former editor, college teacher, and letterpress printer, Benn lives with her husband on an island near Seattle. *Passing Fancies* is the second novel in the Julia Kydd series.